'. . . one of the more inventive and gifted writers of horror and dark fantasy to emerge in the past decade.'

Tim Pratt, *Locus*

'. . . depraved and elegantly ambivalent stories . . . Williams writes with a poetic brutality that definitely makes him a dark voice to note.'

Publishers Weekly (starred review) on *Use Once Then Destroy.*

'. . . a genuine, deeply macabre spellbinder.'

Ray Olson, *Booklist* on *London Revenant*

'A gritty, phantasmagoric tour de force.'

Locus on *London Revenant*

'Powerful and tragic. Five out of five stars.'

Horror-Web on *London Revenant*

'Pacy, hard-edged, and almost feverish in the intensity with which it moves towards its blood-soaked and righteous climax.'

The Alien Online on *Game*

'Conrad Williams possesses a ruthless imagination and the sensibility of a poet.'

William P Simmons, *Infinity Plus* on *Game*

'A ferocious adventure. It is amazing.'

Cemetery Dance on *Game*

'Like Hieronymus Bosch or M John Harrison, he is a painter of infernos, his torments always briskly inventive, his grotesquerie always delineated with flair; pure visionary acid. *Nearly People* is cruelly brilliant, a dagger in the vitals.'

Nick Gevers, *Infinity Plus*

'Conrad Williams delivers a tour de force experience with *Nearly People*. This is a tremendous piece of writing, destined for great things.'

David Howe, *Shivers*

ABOUT THE AUTHOR

Conrad Williams is the author of two previous novels, *Head Injuries* and *London Revenant*, as well as the novellas *Nearly People*, *Game*, *The Scalding Rooms* and *Rain*, and a collection of his short fiction, *Use Once, Then Destroy*.

Born in 1969, he sold his first short story at the age of eighteen and has gone on to sell over 80 more to a variety of small presses, professional magazines and critically acclaimed anthologies.

In 1993 he won the British Fantasy Award for Best Newcomer. His work has since been shortlisted for awards by the British Fantasy Society and the International Horror Guild, the latter proclaiming *The Unblemished* as Best Novel.

He is married to the writer Rhonda Carrier and they live with their three sons and a monster Maine Coon cat in Manchester, where Conrad teaches creative writing at a local university.

around the broken image of her baby. She was crying because she couldn't remember what Claire's face looked like.

When she revived, it was dark again. It was as if daylight had forsaken her. She heard movement towards the back of the house. Outside, in the tiny scruffy garden, a cardboard box, no bigger than the type used to store shoes, made a stark shape amid the surrounding frost. The creatures were hunched on the back fence, regarding her with basilisk eyes. They didn't speak. Maybe they couldn't.

One of them leaped down and landed by the box, nudged it forwards with her hand, as a deer might coax a newborn to its feet.

Sarah felt another burst of unconditional love and security fill the gap between them. Then they were gone, moving fast; they were more limber, more muscular than the others she had seen. Sarah took the box into the living room with her and waited. Hours passed; she felt herself become more and more peaceful. As dawn began to brush away the soot from the sky, Sarah leaned over and touched the lid. She wanted so much to open it and say a few words, but she couldn't bring herself to do it.

In the end, she didn't need to. Whatever shifted inside the box managed to do it for her. Here it was, a pathetic comma of skin and bone, barely formed, barely functional at the point of what ought to have been its death. Its head was smashed in, its fishbone-thin ribs threatening a collapse under the speed of its heart, the labour of its lungs. The tiny belly was translucent; Sarah could see the thousands of eggs that it would release over its lifetime.

There was so much blood on the thing's mouth that it took Sarah a long time to realise it was smiling at her. And much longer than that to find the strength to return that smile, and to reach out her hand.

THE UNBLEMISHED

CONRAD WILLIAMS

First published in paperback in Great Britain in 2008 by
Virgin Books Ltd
Thames Wharf Studios
Rainville Rd
London W6 9HA

First published in the US in hardback by Earthling

A catalogue record for this book is available from the
British Library.

ISBN 978 0 7535 1351 4

The Random House Group Limited supports The Forest
Stewardship Council [FSC], the leading international forest
certification organisation. All our titles that are printed on
Greenpeace approved FSC certified paper carry the FSC logo.
Our paper procurement policy can be found at
www.rbooks.co.uk/environment

Typeset by Phoenix Photosetting, Chatham, Kent
Printed in the UK by CPI Bookmarque, Croydon, CR0 4TD

1 3 5 7 9 10 8 6 4 2

ACKNOWLEDGMENTS

I couldn't have written this without the love and support of my selfless wife and our beautiful sons Ethan, Ripley and Zachary.

Thanks also to Jeff VanderMeer, Jim Frenkel, Joel Lane, Paul Miller, Robert Kirby and Adam Nevill.

The title of Chapter Twenty Two is a line of dialogue from the film *Blade Runner* (1982), written by Hampton Fancher and David Peoples, directed by Ridley Scott.

For Ripley
I love you, squawker

CONTENTS

PROLOGUE

Horror and reverence are declensions of the same bewilderment – the bewilderment of being fully alive. When one is fully alive, the entire world is alive. The observed observes. The forest becomes a congeries of eyes.

Robert Pogue Harrison, *Forests: The Shadow of Civilisation*

What scared Claire more than the encroaching trees and the worsening state of the road was that the immutable faith she had in her map had proved misplaced. According to the atlas, the B4525 ought still to be carrying on merrily squirming like a tapeworm through the guts of Northamptonshire. She was a good map reader, but something had gone wrong within the last hour and she couldn't figure out what it was. Her boyfriend, Oliver, had run the gamut from mild irritation to apoplexy, via sarcasm and exasperation. Now he was hunched over the wheel, trying to peer through the imbroglio, his throat clicking whenever he swallowed. Darkness was coming on, and the possibility that they might have to spend the night in the car was growing firmer by the minute.

She wondered again why they had decided to do this. Oliver had pointed out their lack of funds when she suggested a holiday, even though her idea – a week in a tent on the French coast near Arcachon – had been modest and well within their means. She guessed he had been waiting for her to offer her plan, just so he could trump it with his own. The fact that he gave what seemed almost a presentation on the benefits of remaining in the UK – all that was missing was a

PowerPoint display and photocopied handouts – exposed his extensive preparations. He bullied her into agreeing. *How much of our own country do you really know?* he'd asked her. *How much of it have you actually visited?*

Her rejoinder, that Skegness in the wet would have the same attraction as the Lakes in the wet, or Dartmoor in the wet, was dismissed. And after all, it was his car they would be using had she won the vacation argument; his tent too. She felt she had to go along with him. She supposed she could refuse. But where would that leave them? Further down the road to the end of their relationship. And she didn't want that. Not since she discovered she was pregnant. This holiday was meant to provide a peaceful, neutral arena where she could feel comfortable enough to tell him he was to be a father. She didn't know him well enough yet to gauge how he might take the news. He was a difficult winkle to prize from the shell. But she felt she ought to share the news with him first before letting her mother know. God, there was a happy moment awaiting her. It had been tough enough trying to get her to agree to this little break. Her mum was sweating panic so hard over her debt and the wanker that was chasing them for it that Claire was convinced she could see it leaving acid tracks in her skin. She wanted to wrestle her down to the sofa, give her some hot tea, tell her to slow down, to breathe. That way, at least, Claire supposed, she would be getting some practice in at being mother.

She looked at Oliver and thought about reaching out a conciliatory hand. But then he glanced at her with that disgusted, dismissive expression that he always seemed to wear in her company. She felt a stitch of dread, certain that it was on his tongue, this talk of finishing it, of moving on. He was tasting the flavour of it, that was sure. She wanted to tell him that he gave her a jolt whenever she saw him, as if he was someone she were seeing for the first time. She never seemed to recognise him. She wondered if this in itself was a good thing. She wondered why she couldn't open her mouth to try to help seal some cracks. There was a big one in their age difference, one that she hadn't even considered until it became clear there was something of him growing inside her. Eighteen and twenty-five. Suddenly she felt as if she were being driven around by an uncle.

The long, white beaches of western France seemed further away than ever now. Rain began to fall, inviting the squeaking, metronomic rhythm of the wipers that irritated her, but at least they cut into the terrible silence building between them. Thunder was a distant godly footprint, that of something determined to track them down. *All we need now,* she thought, *is a flat tyre.*

'When was it that you lost the plot?' Oliver asked suddenly. Claire felt it was a cruel question, full of the kind of ambiguity that he seemed to enjoy. He liked playing with people, tying them in knots.

'We haven't turned off the B road,' she replied, refusing to fall for the bait. Arguing wasn't going to magic them back on track. 'So the map must be wrong.'

'Yeah, right,' he said. 'How does that saying go, the one about craftsmen and tools?' His voice wasn't right, though. He wouldn't look at her. He uttered his insults flatly, without any of the chiding, bitter humour, the come-ons that she sometimes found bizarrely attractive. His eyes flashed at the rear-view mirror more often than seemed prudent. Something in his actions reminded her of a bird. It was a nervous, jerky routine.

Claire checked the publication date of the atlas, in case it was out of date, but it was the latest edition. 'Maybe we should just turn around,' she said. 'I vaguely remember seeing a pub before things started going wrong. About half an hour ago. We might find we know where we are if we get back there. And if not, we can always stop for a drink. Ask for directions.'

Oliver wasn't answering, and she looked at him. She almost instantly turned her attention back to the road, convinced that the person she had got into the car with, all those miles and hours ago, was no longer the same. His face was utterly alien to her. The light from the dashboard had picked out punctures and hollows that shouldn't have been there, and perhaps hadn't, before the tension of their situation had started to dig in. She wondered if she appeared the same way to him.

'Turn around,' she whispered. She didn't like the way the road ahead was failing beneath the weather, as if it was being erased. She wanted to be with her mother. She wanted that controllable sense of hysteria. Domestic madness.

Sweat crept out from beneath her fingertips where she clutched the edges of the atlas. She was pressing half-moons into the paper. The blackness beyond the windows was so complete that she was no longer certain they were on any kind of road at all, and suffered an awful, vertiginous pang that lit upon the nerves in her legs as she imagined the car falling through space. She flipped down the vanity mirror in the sunshield above her head. Now she saw what it was that Oliver was so intent on, what had robbed him of his ability to speak to her. Now she saw why they could not retreat. In the occasional red wash from the brakelights she saw hundreds of figures squirming in their wake on to the rubble-strewn road, many of them limbless, eyes reflecting as pale discs of silver. She yelled involuntarily, a nonsense sound that caused Oliver to flinch. 'What are they doing?' she shouted. 'Why are they chasing us?' Her hand went to the door handle and jerked it open. Oliver screamed at her to shut it.

'What do they want?' she asked. She could not recognise her own voice above the grind of the engine, the slam of her own heart.

'I don't know,' Oliver said. 'But what are we going to do? Reason with them? Look at them. I mean, *fucking look at them.*'

There were so many of them wriggling over the embankment it seemed that at some point they would be engulfed. The car jounced as it crunched over bodies that slithered beneath the wheels. Claire screamed. And then she heard Oliver swear and ram his foot on the brakes. A fallen tree, twenty feet ahead, blocking their path. Oliver reached out and squeezed her hand. Sweat cellophaned him. He was all tendons and cords and failing intent. He opened the door and the howling wind and rain swirled into the car. He did not look back at her. He said: 'Run.'

Immediately Claire lost him in the squall. She guessed he must have moved in a straight line as soon as his foot hit the soil, hoping that, once over it, the tree would act as a barrier to the crawling hordes behind them. She didn't for one second consider his behaviour, his abandonment of her. Neither did she consider the identity of the creatures hunting them down. All she thought about was catching up with him, not wanting to be out here on her own while whatever it was slid and slithered at her heels through the mud.

'Oli?' It was her first and last cry to him. The storm turned her words into confetti that fell around her ears. She decided to save her breath and follow the route she guessed he must have taken. She lost a shoe to the mud. Her leg rippled with fire where a stinger danced along it. She felt the rain almost instantly permeate her clothes and set about her skin. Finding Oliver was her task, her be-all and end-all. Sanctuary was now as fantastical an idea to her as heaven. Her determination to track him down before succumbing to whatever was closing in around her helped her to keep going. Dying out here seemed a given, all of a sudden, a fate instantly assimilated. What she must rage against was doing so without making some effort to reconnect with the person she loved. The fear of being alone at the end outweighed the terror of death to a point that she found almost amusing.

The headlights of the car helped her to see where to put her feet as she scrambled over the tree, although a protrusion of some kind tore a hole in her blouse and scored a breast with pain. Beyond it the light was less helpful, and she had to rely on the flashes of lightning to give her moments in which to reorient herself. Within one, she believed she saw Oliver pinwheeling through a clump of trees to her right, so she altered her course and gave chase.

The lightning was coming more frequently, scattering across different parts of the sky in sheets, as if searching for a seamstress to stitch them all together. Thunder filled in the gaps, shockingly close, at one point seeming to vibrate within her. The adrenaline, the storm, the hunt, all of it was conspiring to excite her. For the first time in her life, she felt alive. She screamed and laughed. Terror purged her of any logic. Instinct reduced her to the basest animal. She sprinted, a forgotten joy, and no longer felt any nettle or knock. She was suddenly insane, and loving every second.

She reached the trees where she thought she'd spotted Oliver. There was no point in trying to search for his tracks. The rain had already turned the ground to nonsense. She heard something breathing hard and wet not too far behind her and pushed on, knowing that to stop was to die and she mustn't allow that until she knew what had become of her man. The synapses of the sky flared with another packet of energy. She saw the land fall away rapidly. At the bottom of the hill light glanced off what could only be a barbed wire fence. She must get through that and hinder their progress some more. She needed time.

She started a gingerly descent, but knew how she would reach the bottom. It didn't take long before she lost her footing. Part of her wished that she might clout her head against a rock to inure her against whatever they were planning for her. But the fall was muddy and nothing else. Back on her feet she found a sagging portion of barbed wire and picked a way through it: she entered a zone protected from the worst of the storm by a thick canopy overhead.

The deluge had failed to find a way through and the sudden lack of rain was as shocking as it was welcome. Even the thunder and lightning seemed subdued. The rich smells of damp bark and fungus hung thickly in the air. Broad, waxy leaves, Mesozoic in their size, sweated pungent sap that stuck like syrup to Claire's skin. There was the breath of something old in the forest, a stale atmosphere filtered through centuries of shadow and heat. The air seemed to have been recycled to the point where there was no oxygen left. Claire sucked the stink and fumes into lungs that were working so hard, so shallowly, that it didn't really matter what was in the air. The silence was not compromised by any rustles of animals in the undergrowth. There were none of the kind of caws or cackles she thought she might hear on any ordinary tramp through the woods. That concerned her more than she expected.

Her mind was fixed hard on Oliver, trying to put up a barricade against the dark, which was deepening, and putting pressure on her flimsy defences. Terror, she was learning, was like gorging yourself at the dining table: it filled you up and threatened to move outside of you, as if it could affect your surroundings too. It became more than what you were.

She had always loved the forest and cherished the memories she had of playing there with her father when she was a child. But she pushed through the undergrowth now, panicked and confused by this old friend of hers, this betrayer. Her fear was so great that she was oblivious to the thorns and stingers that stood in her way. Her legs became striped with welts; a spine on a creeper scratched her eyelid. Blinking furiously, tears ruining half of her vision, she misjudged the space around her and careened into a tree, knocking herself off balance. She went down hard and winded herself against a fist of rock in the slippery earth. Her left leg caught beneath her and she was forced on to her front. The torrent had loosened a thin scree of rubble and mud; she travelled with it, her mouth filling with grit. Bottoming out, she was able to steady herself and get upright. Pain flew up her right side; her shin was bathed in blood.

Queasily she felt around for a bone protruding through the flesh, but it was only a deep cut. She could walk. She became aware, as she angrily swiped at the tears and grime on her face, that the rain had stopped, replaced by an enormous heat; it was similar to the time she had stepped from a jet on to a Bahrain runway. The smells of vegetable mould were uppercuts punching through the heat. The canopy curved over her head, complete and unbroken, as if the trees were ganging up on her. They blotted out the black anvils of cloud to the extent that she questioned whether it had rained at all. A hissing sound, so low as to be almost subsonic, rose around her. It reminded her dimly of sprinkler hoses in her grandmother's garden.

It was while she was thinking about that garden, with its buddleia, magnolia and lemon thyme, that she stepped on what remained of her boyfriend's face.

Reality drained away from her. It was as if she were suddenly watching a film, or reading a book. Her detachment was so acute, so utter, that she imagined she heard her sanity uncoupling, like a giant bolt sliding back in its chamber. A couple of feet away she saw Oliver's clothes, discarded as they had been on the first night they slept together. He had come hopping after her, trying to get his socks off, while she scooted back on her arse towards the bedroom, blowing him kisses, chanting, *Come on then, Oli, come on then . . .*

Part of Oliver's leg was protruding from his jeans. Something in the shadows was trying to pull it into privacy, perhaps to finish its meal. Her breath was gone, she wasn't going to argue with it, or try to defend her lover when there was nothing left to defend. She just wanted to get away. She retreated, keeping her eyes locked on what was left of Oliver, feeling slighted that they had discarded some of his organs. This had been her man. She loved him completely. It was an insult to think that he was not entirely palatable.

Mad laughter shot out of her.

The rain started again, or was it just that what had landed on the uppermost parts of the canopy had percolated through? Heavy drops, pattering on the forest floor. She didn't feel any wetness on her skin. Shadows loped and reared and tumbled but there was no light to generate them.

Claire was screaming and shouting but she couldn't understand what. She just wanted to make some kind of noise to confirm her place in a rapidly deteriorating world, to combat the weight of sensations trying to shut her down. She turned and saw shapes rising from where they had dropped from the branches. They were vaguely human, but they all seemed malformed, unfinished. Some of them wore grotesque make-up, the rouge that had been splashed from Oliver's violated body. They smelled of meat: old meat, fresh meat.

They were naked and she could clearly see their ribs shading thin flesh like stripes on a white tiger. They dragged themselves through the mulch towards her, the nubs of what existed of their legs scoring painfully into the ground. They didn't seem to notice. Hunger, she recognised, would do that to you. Their faces were human, but all humanity was absent.

'Don't eat me,' she whispered.

There were dozens. They kept coming, dropping from the trees. She wondered, crazily, how there could be enough of her to go round. They fell on her. Her screams were muffled, her attempts at batting their arms away futile. But they weren't biting her, or shredding her flesh with their long nails, the way they had done with Oliver. They tore only at her clothes and when she was naked they moved aside to let something through that resembled the others but was larger and more ponderous. Like her, it was naked, and Claire shuddered at the sight of the thing that swung between its vestigial legs. This creature was blind but it needed no help in seeking her out. What it did to her when it finally found her took her mind away to a remote spot from which it would never fully return.

Part I

RESURGAM

Then I look about me at my fellow-men. And I go in fear. I see faces keen and bright, others dull or dangerous, others unsteady, insincere; none that have the calm authority of a reasonable soul.

HG Wells, *The Island of Dr Moreau*

1. THE HOUSE OF FLIES

The man appeared from nowhere, his skin the colour of rum. 'Buy me a drink, come on, I'm asking you all nice, like,' he said, although the cut of his clothes suggested he was flush enough to supply his own, and many more. 'Buy me a drink and there's secrets in it for you.'

He'd been away, he said (though Bo hadn't asked), he'd been away for years, but now it was time to come back. A matter of unfinished business, apparently. Bo had been sipping from his pint of lager in front of the log fire, wishing he'd worn something a little less wintry than the cable-knit sweater and suede jacket, heavy denims and big black boots, though he'd be grateful for them later, much later, caught in the teeth of this December night. Sweat peppered his face – the area Keiko, a slave to cosmetic products, referred to as his T-zone – forehead, nose and chin. He hadn't wanted to come out, he hated these congested Friday nights in the city centre, but a colleague was leaving work and it would have appeared churlish to cry off. Now he wished even more that he'd stayed in with a few cans of Guinness and a DVD. Fish and chips with Keiko. A game of chess. A game of Scrabble. Bed, maybe.

'Buy me a drink, like. Buy me a drink.'

The Princess Louise was typically rammed. The Friday night of a week during which he had hardly put down his camera. At the newspaper offices there were yellow flimsies signifying new jobs piled up on his desk like limp birthday decorations. A week filled with cheque presentations, shivering football teams lining up before meaningless matches, overfed mayors and their cartoonishly coiffured wives standing outside town halls. *Smile please. Names please. How do you spell that? Should be in next week's paper, all being well.*

The only photograph he had taken over the past seven days that quickened his blood was of a car crash on the A40(M) – the Westway – just as it became elevated from the Marylebone Road: an S-Type Jaguar had torn into the back of a Vauxhall Nova, catapulting it over the edge of the expressway on to the Edgware Road twenty feet below. Six out of seven occupants in both cars dead. The seventh had slammed through the Jag's windshield and was found crushed into the boot of the Nova. It took the emergency services six hours to release him. He would be in a wheelchair for the rest of his life, if he made it out of Intensive Care. Bo couldn't tell if the slick around the mashed vehicles was oil or blood. It was dark, and the pictures were in mono anyway. It was a mystery he was glad not to ponder. The traffic police unit to which he was seconded for the job weren't too bothered either way.

'The clothes help to keep you together,' one fireman had said over double espressos Bo had procured for them both from the nearby Coffee Republic. 'If it weren't for the clothes, you'd get the doors open and they'd pour all over the street like jelly. The clothes . . . *contain* them.'

For a short time in that crazed zone of blood and lights and sirens he understood what it must be like to be one of the great war photographers. Don McCullin, say, or James Nachtwey. The frisson. The risk. He had been pulled out of himself, become a stillpoint. Taking photographs he did not remember shooting, his heart had belted around his chest, yet he had never felt so calm, so focused. He kept the unpublishable prints in a black folder at home. One of the driver whose jaw had been sheared off and lay in the well beneath the handbrake. His tongue had reached down to his belly. The passenger seat was a froth of blood and hair, a face at the centre of it all reshaped by the window and the dashboard.

That one reminded him of another job he had been on, early in his career, when it seemed he might forge a great career as an edgy, unconventional news photographer. There had been a minor traffic incident at the roundabout at Highbury Corner. A dark-green Peugeot 306 had tonked a Mini Cooper. A rear indicator light had been broken on the Mini, a cracked bumper on the Peugeot. Nothing to burst into tears about. But the driver of the Mini had decided that he didn't like Peugeot man's attitude, and had hit him on the side of the head with a tyre spanner. He fell down spurting blood at an alarming rate, too alarming for Mr Mini, who decided to get back in his car and drive off. He drove straight under the front wheels of an articulated lorry swinging into Canonbury Road. Killed instantly. The guy who had been spannered was now in a wheelchair, paralysed from the neck down and making nil progress whatsoever. Bo had arrived ten minutes later, when the emergency services were working with their defib-kits and car-cutting tools. It had been so cold that the blood on the ground shed steam.

A couple of jobs out of what? Two or three hundred? It was getting him down. The shoots that energised him were few and far between and more often than not involved the police. His camera was capturing the type of pictures a novice could achieve, not someone who had the art in his blood, who had gone to college, gravitated towards photographers that strongly attracted him, who spoke directly to him, almost as if they were waiting for him to come along, to deepen their footprints or maybe even veer off on some new track of his own: Alfred Eisenstaedt, Jacob Riis, André Gelpke. Part of him wished, as he relented and bought the stranger his whiskey, that he could escape the freelance life and move on to a more exciting part of town, or foreign parts, somewhere where he didn't have to bring the art down to a level that became all about the mechanical recovery of money. He needed to be taking pictures for nothing but the love of it. Photography as a marketable skill was crushing him. He needed a project to stretch him, a project that carried a little risk with it. Taking pictures of a school sports day didn't have anything to do with risk; it was treading water. Taking pictures of cats stuck up trees wasn't pushing any envelopes; it was drowning in your sleep.

'They won't, like . . . *give up*,' said the stranger.

'Who won't?' Bo asked, irritated, still thinking of corpulent mayors, of freezing rain pelting on to soccer pitches. They were standing at the bar, having miraculously found a gap in the human traffic. However, they were standing so close together that Bo felt awkward facing him, and chose instead to observe his companion in the mirror behind the bar.

The man seemed to come to his senses. He laughed, short and sharp, embarrassed almost, and took a large gulp of his whiskey. The spirit seemed to chase off his twitches. He sighed deeply and pressed his lips together, looked down into his glass.

'My name is Rohan, like,' the man said. 'Rohan Vero.'

Bo nodded, impressed. 'Nice name. Sounds like a writer's name. What are you? A writer?'

'I'm wanted,' he said.

'By the police?' Bo asked.

Vero looked up at him with sad, watery eyes. 'If only,' he said. And then: 'Ancestrally, I come from very weak stock. I'm paying for crimes perpetrated by people long dead. Can you believe that, like? Can you believe how unjust that is?'

Starved of the remarkable for such a long time, Bo was happy to go along with any madness Vero uttered. The evening seemed to be picking up.

'What do you mean?' Bo asked. 'This come out of a search for your family tree?'

'Family tree,' Vero said, neutrally, neither agreeing with nor scoffing at the words. 'I have no family tree. Any link to the past, like, whether through bone dust or ashes, all of it has been destroyed. They are slowly *erasing* me.'

'Who?'

Vero turned to Bo and smiled, and now he saw how the other man was crying.

'You don't, like, want to know,' Vero said.

'I, *like*, do,' Bo countered, setting his glass down harder than he had intended. How could anybody but himself know what was best for him? All through his childhood he had railed against people giving him orders. It set one up well for the freelance life, he supposed, although it didn't win him many friends. Everyone had to be told what to do sometimes. Bo could just never swallow it.

Vero appraised him with dark humour in his eyes, and perhaps a little admiration, but he did not convey anything more for a while.

More lager for Bo; more whiskey for Vero. The noise and the heat intensified. English pubs. No ventilation. No air conditioning. Maybe the breweries wanted it this way: when you were hot, you drank more.

Finally, into this sultry clamour, Vero said, 'I have seen the house of flies.'

'Really,' Bo said, his initial enthusiasm on the wane. The guy was a nut. Or rather, Bo was, for furnishing him with booze. 'Where's that then?'

'It's on the map.'

'What map?'

'You have to ask me for it. You have to want it. Really want it, like. It's the only way I can get . . . it's the only way I can pass it on.'

'Okay,' Bo said. 'Give me the fucking map. Let's have a look.'

Vero's expression changed. The lines in his face seemed to soften and sink back into his skin, as if they were being rubbed out by an invisible eraser. He licked his lips. His tongue was such a deep red it might have been a corner of liver he was sucking on. 'You want it? Do you mean that? Do you need it?'

Bo felt fresh tingles of unease. The man was clearly insane, or off his rocker on some kind of drug, but his intensity, the passion for what he was spinning, seemed genuine enough. What if there was a map that led to a house of flies, whatever the hell that was? What about it? What harm could come of it? It might mean a decent photograph, at least. It might give him the chance to slip his bounds and gather together the mess of his career. At the very least it would confirm that Vero was certifiable, and Bo no longer saw that as a pity.

Now it was his turn to lick his lips. 'Look at us,' he said, his voice trembling despite his scepticism. 'A couple of lizards.'

Vero didn't smile, didn't say anything. All he did was stare, like an obedient dog waiting to be let off its lead.

'I want it,' Bo said, in a voice that didn't sound anything like his own.

Vero seemed to slump against the bar. '*Omne vivium ex ovo,*' he said.

'*What?*'

Vero looked up. There was sadness in his eyes, as if he had been suddenly bereaved. 'Every animal is carnivorous, in its first beginnings.'

Bo was shaking his head, frowning, trying to grasp the running water of Vero's nonsense.

'The map . . . it's yours,' Vero said, reaching for his glass, closing his eyes. He seemed simultaneously disgusted and relieved. 'It's been dry so long, like, that map. It's been dry for centuries, thank God, but recently. Christ, recently . . .' He looked down at his hand, as if seeing it for the first time. He rubbed at it gingerly with his fingertips, then clenched and unclenched it. The sigh that followed this strange little act was something one heard on the lips of a man who has escaped death by millimetres.

Vero's hands were empty.

Had he actually said anything worth listening to? Or was he just full of uncanny sound bites, stuff that sounded interesting at first, but then proved as insubstantial as the food they sold behind the bar? He was grandstanding, he was the joke at the audition who barely begins his scene before the crook appears to drag him off stage. He was little more than a crackpot with a cute turn of phrase. Rohan Vero. Good name, bad storyteller. If he was a writer, he was stuffed. Bo felt his irritation come back, with interest.

'You've swallowed about eight pounds of my hard-earned, and for what? A couple of cryptic crossword clues? What about these secrets? What about something worth one of those doubles you've been sinking?'

Despite his indignation, Bo felt unable to turn and confront the other man. He kept his eyes on Vero in the mirror behind the bar. And then, a change. The sound reduced, as if someone had turned down a volume switch, or someone famous had entered the room. The heat dropped too; Bo felt the sweat on his brow turn cold. The reflected drinkers carried on chatting, laughing, pouring ale down their throats. They hadn't noticed any such wobble in the status quo.

But Bo was suddenly, acutely aware that things weren't right. And that he was deeply, almost religiously, afraid. Vero was standing, as Bo was, watching Bo in the mirror. His face was etched with concern as he told his story, yet loosening every second, as if finding peace at finally being able to disburden itself of the facts. And yet. The person standing next to Bo, the figure he saw in his peripheral vision, was not gazing into the mirror. It was turned towards him, eyes filling its head, and its mouth was widening as torrents of hot expletives fell from it. He could smell violence, inches away. The face in the mirror was like something trapped from earlier in the evening. It was benign, becalmed. Innocuous words fell from its lips: '. . . you can get flights to as far away as Sydney these days for next to nothing . . .' But beneath this, he heard another message, delivered as if the man had two tongues and the speech that slipped off it possessed stealth, insinuation: *You have to go. Please leave. Please. I don't know. What might happen to you. If you stay.* He smelled raw blood, as if Vero had badly bitten his tongue and was breathing its coppery fumes all over him.

And then a sense of time leaving him, or being taken away from him. The drink and the heat and the insanity threatening to knock him senseless. He felt Vero's hand drop on his own, like some thin, leathery claw, felt his rotten breath rape his nostrils. Vomit rose slowly in his chest. He barged his way outside and sucked in the freezing air. His nausea abated. When he turned back to the pub, it was dead, lights doused, as quiet as sculpture. Through the cracks in the door Bo could make out what seemed like acres of emptiness, after the impossible crush he had been a part of. Ambient light drizzled along chrome and brass. A sour reek of spilled beer and nicotine squeezed through to him. He checked his pockets again, but apart from some spare change, everything – his keys, his wallet – was gone. The bastard was just some pickpocket, a cheap thief with a cheap trick. Maybe he'd spiked Bo's drinks, given him this weird headache, this numb feeling in his stomach. And there was something wrong with his hand. Bo studied the skin on his left palm. A series of weals, red and broken, like Morse code, studded the flesh.

Frustrated by the locked door of the pub, Bo turned to make his way along High Holborn towards Centre Point where he would be able to flag a cab to take him home. In the turning of his body through one hundred and eighty degrees, he lost sense of himself, and what he was doing. The only glimmer of a clue as to what had happened in the black hole between Vero's warning and his standing cow-eyed in the cold was a scrap of speech: Vero's voice, trembling and low, bordering on beseechment:

. . . *him, him, not me, he's your gateway, him, him* . . .

For a moment it felt as if, as his body turned, his head had remained where it was, pressed against the door of the Princess Louise, in the act of trying to rescue his reality from a night that was now rapidly passing him by.

*   *   *

High Holborn was dead. The lights were out on the street and in the office buildings crowding him. Even the traffic lights were playing blind. The road itself looked too unstable to have ever carried vehicles. West, the convergence of Charing Cross Road, Oxford Street, and Tottenham Court Road seemed unformed, as if the architect's designs were mathematically awry. Or maybe it was just the drink that suggested to Bo that the roads didn't quite meet properly. Everything seemed out of kilter, soft, not right. It had the flawed authenticity of a film set.

Bo's shoes on the pavement made the only sound. No late buses, no mini cabs, no squabbles outside fast-food outlets. 'Fuck,' he said. 'Wrong. Wrong. Wrong. Three out of ten. See me. Detention.'

He had dreamed of a London like this, fantasised about it, even. A city sprawled, spread open, for him alone. But not quite like this. Not a city of shadows and lies, a place that seemed to possess secrets jealously guarded from him. Not a city where danger lifted off the concrete like steam. The emptiness of the street, the sheer expanse of it, confused him. He stopped, unsure how to proceed. There was something else not right about this. Something so huge that it was beyond his recognition. His fear, like the city around him, was woolly, imprecise. He had nothing upon which to hang it.

He slipped down Sutton Row and found Soho Square dead, the parking spaces that ringed it deserted, the winter trees empty-handed.

What ought to have been Frith Street was yet another dark avenue without a name. He had walked along here many times, preferring it to the overcrowded thoroughfares choked by tourists who didn't know about the rat runs existing off the beaten track, but now any familiarity had bled away, leaving a street that might as well exist in any other town or city. It meant nothing to him. Again he paused, wondering if he was trapped in a nightmare, wondering if there was some way of jolting himself out of it. It felt too real, too intense.

You have to want it. Really want it. It's the only way I can get . . .

Get what? What was it Vero had meant to say? *Get rid of it?*

He turned back, determined to find the older man and have it out with him, persuade him with fists to explain his nonsense. But he knew that Vero was gone. He could scour the streets from Bloomsbury to Broadgate and he'd do well to clap eyes on another soul, let alone Vero. Terror plucked at his insides. Without anyone around, his sense of time was ruined; it didn't matter what his watch said. What did the time matter if you were mad? Nothing appeared real. He sucked in breath to call out for help, but stayed his voice, in case it sounded nothing like his own.

Home would have to do; he prayed that it was still there. He could go on the hunt in the morning, if madness's stain persisted, when daylight and a hangover might focus him.

Head down, he tramped vaguely northwest, knowing that he would not luck into a night bus, or a taxi, and that the miles to Shepherd's Bush would have to be ticked off under his own steam. Not for the first time after a drunken binge in the city centre – when he didn't have enough cash left over for a cab, or the queues for the buses were too off-putting – did he wish that Keiko's flat was nearby, instead of in Kilburn, much further away than his own base. She would be there now, propped up in bed, maybe, with a bowl of hot chocolate, Garbage or PJ Harvey or Sneaker Pimps in her earphones, as she leafed through one of her magazines, or a Graham Greene novel, or one of the biology textbooks from her UCL course, or washed her hair clean of the chlorine from her part-time shifts at a Kensington spa.

It cheered him, thinking of Keiko, while the faceless streets passed by on either side of him and the cold connived a way through his clothes. With a jolt he realised that it had been a year ago, and he had met her in a pub, just like Vero – only the outcome had been far more pleasing. She had been with a group of her student friends, sitting around a table slowly accumulating more empty glasses, more bowls of chips and mayonnaise, more cigarette butts in the ashtray.

He had spotted her early on in the evening and had casually glanced her way on a number of occasions as the night progressed, liking the way she didn't seem to possess any of the self-consciousness, the outspokenness, the air of superiority that her colleagues were guilty of. They all wore hooded tops and voluminous jeans, except her: happy in a skirt and loose blouse, looking almost gypsy-like, a rustic simplicity engendered by the long, straight black hair, the lack of make-up, the pints of cider. He wondered what her name was, and spent much of the evening ignoring his workmates, guessing silently to himself: Maisy, Daisy, Cherry, Millie . . . At the end of the evening, she had approached him as he prepared to leave and he froze, his jacket halfway across his back, as she said, 'What, you spend all night staring at me and you're not even going to ask me out?'

She liked Kubrick and told him there was a showing of *Eyes Wide Shut* on at the Prince Charles the following night that she'd like to go to, but not by herself.

'So I'll meet you outside at seven,' she had said.

'Right then,' he had replied, stupidly.

She was twenty, ten years younger than him. 'Keiko,' she said, when he asked her name. It felt strange on his tongue, and he wasn't sure he liked it, but at her flat after the film she brought them syrupy vodka from the freezer in bullet glasses while he sat on the end of her bed, riffling through her paperbacks. She kissed him, her eyes, the colour of treacle, open throughout. She smelled so good, the great shield of hair falling across his face as she sucked his tongue gently between her small, white teeth, and he thought: *Keiko . . . what a fucking great name.*

He rubbed his face, which had grown inflexible under the rip of the wind, like something semi-defrosted, and thought of Keiko's fingers as they stroked the same places, that first night. They hadn't made love, just caressed each other through their clothes, listening to Ella Fitzgerald singing *Lover Man* on the stereo, watching the light lose its softness against the white walls of her room.

He checked his mobile phone again, but the signal was still flatlining. The public phone he found once he'd drifted back on to the howling wilderness of Oxford Street was similarly unhelpful. 'Wrong. Three out of ten. Three out of fucking ten. Deee-tention. You bastard.'

To combat his frustration at not being able to contact Keiko, he pulled out the battered Ixus camera from his back pocket and fired off a few shots of the desertion. The flash exploded into the creases and wrinkles of this near-total dark, serving only to give some definition, before the flash died and the dark came piling back in around him.

He was reminded of the controlled panic he had once felt during a game of hide-and-seek played at some birthday or other in his infancy. He had climbed into his father's wardrobe, squeezing in among the heavy twill and tweed jackets on their wooden hangers, stepping carefully over the old biscuit tins in which Dad kept his stash of pens, coins and worthless trinkets collected over the years.

There were cricket balls in there. A Stetson. Bottles of unopened whisky from the 1960s, stuff that he had never seen before. But the smell of his father's clothing was familiar to him, as was the shape and solidity of the wardrobe, the feel of its grain under his fingertips, and the room beyond its closed doors. But the dark was different to anything he had known before. Nothing like the soft, granular dark that sifted through his window on summer evenings, or the exciting, eminently controllable dark under his bedclothes the moment before he switched on his torch to read his comics. It seemed so ubiquitous, so complete, that it put him in mind of bitter cough medicine forced between his teeth. This dark felt as though it might easily fill him up, an oily meniscus rising to, and then beyond, the Plimsoll line of his fear. He felt as if he were gagging on it, drowning in darkness.

But here he couldn't simply lean against the doors and stumble out into fresh air and beloved light. Here he had to swallow against its ceaseless tide, push on, hope that he, or daylight, outstripped it before panic pulled him down. He needed coffee, or water, something to combat the sludgy mess of his head, the mess caused by too many pints of lager and Rohan Vero's senseless yammering.

Marble Arch loomed on his left, trying its best to lend some kind of ghostly pallor to the night. Wind channelling through the arch sounded like the aspiration of a dying man. Beyond it, at the fork where the Edgware Road and Bayswater Road separated, he saw a house. At the same time, he felt fluid slide across his palm, as if he had unwittingly rested it against a slick of juice on a café table. He lifted his hand and saw that the weals in his skin had become more pronounced and were weeping lymph and blood. He wiped it off against his jeans, but the flow was becoming more free with every step. He couldn't remember how he had wounded himself, but it must have been during his blackout. One more item tonight on a growing list of things to piss him off. Pausing to wind his handkerchief around the puzzling injury, he returned his attention to the house, and wondered why he had been distracted by it.

The house resembled any other in the area. A spruce Edwardian semi, approached by a short drive flanked with yew trees. Its windows contained a grainy blackness, as if the glass was speckled with dust. Bo took a picture, and the light from the flash jagged across the surface of the uneven windows. But there was something out of the ordinary about it. Of all the houses within his field of vision, this one seemed lived in. Having walked London's freshly abandoned streets for a good couple of hours now, he was suddenly, acutely tuned to this isolated spot of . . . well, what? It wasn't warmth. Or light. It went more subtly than that. It was the kind of attenuation the sky knows just before a snowstorm. An immanence. Without understanding why, Bo knew that this house had that kind of suggestive occupancy, in spades.

As if in a dream, he approached the front door, knowing that he would not need to ring any bell, aware that the door would open for him, as if he were a key slid into its lock: his teeth a perfect match for its tumblers. On the stoop, slightly sunken and burnished from a century of approaching or departing feet, he pressed his damaged hand against the gloss of the painted wood and the door swung away from him.

He stared at the black riot that swarmed within its frame. A silent writhing; it mesmerised him: an ecstasy of chitin.

'The house of flies,' he whispered, and he barely had the words out before a flotilla of insects lazily detached themselves from the greater mass and swarmed against his face. Paralysed by fear, he felt the flies skid greasily across his skin and pour in between his lips with the kind of excited buzzing that suggested they had waited for nothing but this moment all their lives.

He came to on a bench in St James's Park, his body so cold that it was as if he no longer occupied it. Mist unfurled across the lake, turning the swans and moorhens within it into strange, meandering stains. Big Ben rang for a quarter to the hour, although which one, Bo couldn't imagine. It must be close on six, or maybe seven, judging by the roseate smears trying to penetrate the mist to the east.

Buzzing remained in his ears, although when he had struggled to his feet and walked to the perimeter of the park, where The Mall was a ruler placed hard against its edge, he learned that the buzzing was traffic. He had never felt so happy to see the usual parade of coughing buses and farting cars. He pulled the stench of their exhausts deep into his lungs as he crossed the road and angled up Queen's Walk, further encouraged by the sight of joggers in Green Park, and early-morning shop workers walking to their shifts, sleep still in attendance, softening their faces. *Where were you all last night?* he wanted to scream at them.

At the tube station, he paused in his purchase of a single ticket to Shepherd's Bush and, reluctantly, bought a ticket to Bond Street instead, one stop away, but more than he could bear to walk. It was warm down on the Jubilee Line platform, the smells of scorched diesel deepening his sense of security. He endured the short trip to his destination alone in a carriage where the lights were too bright, and the patterns on the seats too complex to settle on for more than a few seconds without causing his head to pound. He struggled with the nausea that comes from too much alcohol and no food, and ascended to an Oxford Street that, already at this hour – ten past seven according to the station clocks – was alarmingly busy with people.

Again he walked west, following the same road as he had a mere couple of hours ago, and yet not. This was nothing like the same road. It held life like a flame in the crucible: it was incontrovertibly there in the cut-price fashion in the windows of the clothes shops and the stultified queues for buses and the fruit vendors on their stalls fighting their losing battle against the coffee shops for freezing customers.

Some night, he thought. *Some hangover.*

At the foot of Oxford Street, the Marble Arch gleaming pale white in the morning sunshine, he breathed in deeply and said: 'Okay. Okay.'

There was no house. A deep, brittle part of him had known this would be the case all along, yet it still came as a shock to find that motorbike couriers, black cabs, white vans and endless cars were now racing over the spot where the house had stood the night before. He looked down at the sodden, scarlet handkerchief. He remembered the sound of his boots as they moved across the short gravel driveway and the feel of the door beneath his fingers. He remembered the sound of the door swinging open, a well-oiled sigh.

He remembered –

The frantically motile sheet of black insects like a million dead eyes sucking in his image on the doorstep, a blackness that is absolute, intimidating. A disarming blackness. He takes a picture. Greased light reflects off a billion compound lenses, a million commas of chitin. Fractals of metallic green and blue and black glint and dance, prettier than they ought to be. The flies sweeping like a curtain of beads against his face, rushing into his mouth. Impossibly, driven by the crazed impulses of a dream, he steps inside, the flies shifting to accommodate him and, without being able to see more than a millimetre in front of him, he knows that every room in the house is crammed with insects. He smells their mealiness. The drone fills his head so completely he believes it might never release him when finally he leaves, or is allowed to leave. This thought propels him to turn and flee, but he can no longer see the way out. The crawling all over his scalp. The tickle of chitin against his skin as insects find a way into his clothing. Fat, slow flies, close to death, flying in erratic trajectories, bursting against his face. He can't open his mouth to scream for fear of allowing more of the filthy things to invade him. When he believes that madness or death are his only releases, and he feels himself sinking to the floor, suffocated by the massing of the insects, they part and he falls through them into a space. No floorboards coming up to meet him. Just the withered, naked body of a man – is that you, Rohan? – who is peppered with punctures, his flesh drained to the point that it resembles the colour of lard. The soft tissue of his face so wasted that his teeth seem to have grown through the puckered hole of his mouth, giving him a smile that couldn't possibly have been there at the moment of his death. He lands on the corpse and it disappears in a great plume of dust around him at the same moment that he hears, like an echo gradually amplified, the sound of chewing. And then there are words caught up, couched in the chewing, a skilful rolling of meat around a tongue spilling myth and meaning, but he can't work out what is being said.

He remembers –

Nothing more.

His eyes scoured the area, as if determined to find some remnant of the house to prove to him that it was something more than a hideous dream fuelled by a night of excess. Or Vero might have slipped him a Mickey Finn. Nothing would surprise him now.

All that happened was that the traffic grew in volume and became snarled at the corner, and the pedestrians tutted and swore at him as they found him blocking their path.

He turned to leave and felt something with his tongue, tucked between his teeth. He worked at it on his way back to the tube, some stray shred of meat from the previous day's dinner, perhaps, and the thought made him hungry for breakfast. At the mouth of the tube station, he dislodged the morsel and picked it off the tip of his tongue with his finger.

A fly. Mashed and mangled, its head gone.

The world went away from him again, but in an infinitely more manageable way. Bo put out his hand to stop himself from falling and jarred it against the wall. He leaned over and vomited copiously, so hard that he saw black spots dancing behind his eyes. But once the straining and the retching were over and he was aware of the sounds of disgusted pedestrians avoiding him, he saw that the black spots were more fly corpses studding the brown gruel of his own waste. He staggered away down a side street and breathed hard until he thought he had a grip on reality once more. He craved Keiko's warmth, her cat eyes, the softness of her lips on his neck: *There, there*, he could almost hear her whisper. *There, there.*

He bought a bottle of water and drained it before returning to the tube and buying a ticket to Kilburn. He sent Keiko a text before he sank to the platform: *brkfst, hny? my trt. xx*

The train wasn't long in coming, but it was busy, and he had to stand all the way. His thoughts were a pendulum between Keiko and the house and by the time he had reached his stop, he was determined that he would never get as drunk as that again. To lose control was to risk everything, and he had too much to live for. But in thinking this, he knew that booze could not have had such a profound effect on him. He felt he should be tested for narcotics, but it was an empty impulse. Something inside him had opened itself to this moment. Something inside him understood what was going on, and welcomed it.

Now that his involvement with the house was over, the world rushed in to fill the vacuum. He felt better as he reached Kilburn High Street, but suddenly realised, as he passed through the ticket barriers, that despite the fact that nobody else had got off at his stop and the platform was empty, he was being followed.

2. OUTFANGTHIEF

Sarah Hickman was trying to find a radio station that might carry some news of her crime. She had been driving for hours, risking the M6 all the way from Preston. Though she had seen a number of police vehicles, the traffic had been sufficiently busy to allow her to blend in and anyway, Manser would hardly have guessed she would steal a car.

But Manser was not stupid. It would not be long before he latched on to her deceit.

She had a cigarette going, and the window was open slightly despite the cold, so that the smoke would stream out. Claire was asleep in the back, or dozing at least – she never seemed to sleep deeply much these days, if at all – and she didn't want her daughter breathing in her second-hand fumes. She'd determined to quit, but this intention was one of a great many things that had somehow become irrelevant in her life now. Few things mattered, and they were of such crucial importance that focusing on them made everything else seem pallid and shallow at this ungodly hour, as she fled Preston. Crucial things that, along with the cigarette she wasn't enjoying, were helping to keep her awake as the odometer slowly rolled off the miles.

Get some money (steal it? or risk stopping at an ATM and exposing our location?).
Dump this car and get something else soon?
Claire. What the fuck is wrong *with her?*
Where the hell are we going?
Who is Gyorsi Salavaria?

Gyorsi Salavaria. The name – she had heard her daughter murmur it in her sleep – meant something to her but she couldn't understand what, or why. A name like that oughtn't be too difficult to check up on, but she was afraid to do so. She was uneasy around computers and suspected that feeding the name into one would again alert others to her whereabouts. Her paranoia was such that she had taken to using her own plastic cutlery with which to eat meals, which she then destroyed, to prevent her DNA from being readily available. She slept with a hat on, to stop hairs from transferring to the pillows. She did not look anybody in the eye. She had read somewhere that this reduced a potential recognition by up to eighty per cent.

Claire's response to all this was uniform: she bore the glazed expression of the drunk, of the junky, of the terminally ill. It was the bored expression of a teenager taken to extremes. When Sarah attempted to talk to her, she played hermit crabs and wouldn't return until she was hungry, or darkness had fallen. She became something new at night. Sarah had watched her change one evening, unfolding from her prone position on an upturned milk crate in the disused factory they had been camping in, slowly filling with animation like colour introduced to a pencil sketch. She was no more responsive to her mother than she was during the day, but something clearly found her 'on' switch once the light began to fade. Sarah had wanted to ask her about drugs, but she was obviously clean; they were in each other's pockets twenty-four hours a day and Sarah would notice if there was any snorting or smoking or needlework taking place. Trying to talk to Claire only caused her to withdraw. Especially when she asked her about Oliver, her boyfriend. Something had happened on their little jaunt. An argument, a fight, something more. She flinched when Sarah mentioned his name. Sarah wondered if it was over; certainly Oliver had not attempted to get in touch, although he had had the chance before they took to the road. She supposed it was enough that Claire hadn't attempted to run away. And it was not as if there weren't things that she should be turning inwards to escape from.

Claire had suffered greatly over the past months. Her routine had been torn from her; a cosy cycle of family and work and Oliver and swimming and half-heartedly learning to play the guitar. Her father was dead now, and the only constant in her life was her mother. It wounded Sarah when she saw in her daughter the frank expression that this was not enough.

As the traffic thinned, and night closed in on the motorway, Sarah's panic grew. She was convinced that their disappearance had been reported and she would be brought to book. When a police Range Rover tailed her from Walsall to the M42 turn-off, she almost sent her own car into the crash barriers at the centre of the road.

Desperate for cover, she followed the signs for the A14. Perhaps she could make the 130 miles to Felixstowe tonight and sell the car, try to find passage on a boat, lose herself and her daughter on the continent.

'Are you all right back there, Claire?'

In the rear-view mirror, her daughter might well have been a mannequin. Her features were glacial; her sunglasses formed tiny screens of animation as the sodium lights fizzed off them. A slight flattening of the lips was the only indication that all was well. Sarah bore down on her frustration. Did she understand what she had been rescued from? Sarah tried to remember what things had been like for herself as a child, but reasoned that her own relationship with her mother had not been fraught with the same problems.

'It's all okay, Claire. We'll not have any more worries in this family. I promise you.'

The motorway unravelled beneath the wheels. The car was temporary comfort, she knew that, and it would need to be ditched before too long. For now she could enjoy it. Yet through the warmth and the snug feel of the leather upholstery, her mind sought the reason for their upheaval. Malcolm Manser. She hadn't wanted to think about him, but he was relentless, even when not there in person. She had been trying to recall her relationship with Claire's father, an innocent time, yet he invaded it like a stain. He filled all of her horizons, an albino's dreaded sun.

She had met Andrew in 1989 in the Preston library they both frequented. A relationship had started, more or less, on their hands bumping each other while reaching for the same book. They had married a year later and Sarah gave birth to Claire not long after.

Both of them had steady, if unspectacular, work. Andrew was a security guard and she cleaned at the local school and for a few favoured neighbours. They eventually took out a mortgage on their council house on the right-to-buy scheme and bought a car, a washing machine and a television on the never-never. Then they both lost their jobs within weeks of each other. They owed £17,000. When the law centre they depended on heavily for advice lost its funding and closed down, Sarah had to go to hospital when she began laughing so hysterically, she could not catch her breath. It was as Andrew drove her back from the hospital that they met Malcolm Manser for the first time.

His back to them, Manser stepped out in front of their car at a set of traffic lights and did not move when they changed in Andrew's favour. When Andrew sounded the horn, Manser turned around. He was wearing a knee-length, nubuck trenchcoat, black Levi's, black boots, and a black T-shirt without an inch of give in it. His head was hairless save for a sculpted black beard. His Ray-Ban Randolphs allowed the merest glimpse of his eyes, hooded but alert, like something reptilian. From the trenchcoat he pulled a car jack and proceeded to smash every piece of glass and dent every panel on the car. It took about twenty seconds.

'Mind if I talk to you for a sec?' he asked, genially, leaning against the crumbled remains of the driver's-side window. Andrew was too shocked to say anything. His mouth was very wet. Tiny cubes of glass glittered in his hair. Sarah was whimpering, trying to open her door, which was sealed shut by the warp of metal.

Manser went on: 'You have 206 pieces of bone in your body, fine sir. If my client, Mr Anders, does not receive seventeen grand by the end of the week, plus interest at three per cent a day – which is pretty bloody generous if you ask me – I will guarantee that after half an hour with me, your bone tally will be double that. And that yummy piece of bitch you've got ripening back home. Claire? I'll have her. You test me. I dare you.'

He walked away, magicking the car jack into the jacket and giving them an insouciant wave.

Shortly after that, Sarah discovered that her husband was injecting himself with temazepam, using needles shared with friends from the pub where he spent most evenings. She forced him to quit and took him to be tested for HIV. When they received the results Andrew set himself on fire in the car that he had locked inside the garage. By the time the fire services got to him, he was a black, twisted shape in the back seat. *Set himself on fire*; Sarah refused to believe that. She was sure that Manser had murdered him. Despite their onerous circumstances, Andrew was not the suicidal type. Claire was everything to him; he'd not leave this world without securing a little piece of it for her.

Now she spotted the flashing blue and red lights of three police vehicles blocking her progress east. She turned left on to another A road bound for Leicester. There must have been an accident; they wouldn't go to the lengths of forming a roadblock for her, would they? The road sucked her deep into darkness; on either side wild hedgerows and vast oily swells of countryside huddled up to them. Headlamps on full beam, she could pick nothing out beyond the winding road apart from the ghostly dusting of insects attracted by the light. But Sarah felt anything but alone. She could see, in the corner of her eye, something blurred by speed, keeping pace with the car as it fled the police cordon. She took occasional glances to her right, but could not define their fellow traveller for the dense tangle of vegetation that bordered the road.

'Can you see that, Claire?' she asked. 'What is it?'

It could have been a trick of the light, or something silver reflecting the shape of their car. Maybe it was the police. The needle on the speedometer edged up to 80. They would have to dump the car somewhere soon, if the police were closing in on them.

'Keep a look out for a B&B, okay?' She checked in the mirror; Claire's hand was splayed against the window, spreading mist from the star her fingers made. She was watching her hand intently. Or she was watching something else. Sarah swallowed against the thin spike of steely cold fear that moved through her skin, raising it. It suddenly seemed as though Claire was waving.

On the long, serpentine road that leads into Southwold off the A12, Sarah twice saw shapes that weren't actually there, at one point actually taking the Alfa Romeo on to a high-sided verge.

Exhausted by the long drive, she parked in front of a butcher's shop in the small square at the heart of the village and wound down the window. A broad wedge of glaring sodium from the lighthouse slid across the roofs and fled to sea. Her heart still seemed to be beating at twice its normal rate after dodging roadblocks back in Leicestershire.

Claire's eyes were large and glassy in the rear-view mirror. The only clue to her consciousness was in the faint glimmer of the silver chain around her throat, which picked up the beat of her heart.

The soft hiss of the tide came to Sarah over distance like breath. She had no idea how far from the beach they were, or what time it was: the dashboard clock was on the fritz, only ever reading 7:04 or 7:05 depending on the whim of some gremlin in the circuitry. What now? At least she felt safe: this place was so charming it might actually wither away and die should Manser come anywhere near it.

She wondered if the hotel just a little way back on the left was still open for business and might give them a room for the night. She cleared her throat gently and watched Claire for any reaction.

'Chick,' Sarah said, 'we'll go and get a room, yeah? Have a good night's sleep in a nice bed for a change. Okay?'

Claire licked her lips again. She said, 'Blood.'

'Come on, Claire. Come on.' Sarah delicately shooed her daughter out of the car and put her arm around her as they took the few steps to the hotel entrance. She tried not to recoil at the thinness of her shoulders or the hot, shivery feel of her skin, too soft it seemed beneath her light V-neck pullover.

She cupped her hands and peered through the window of the hotel. Save for one weak bulb spinning a yellow band across the bar, the lights were off. A member of staff was standing, arms folded, talking to a man sitting on a stool, his back to the door, both hands slowly turning a large white cup on the counter.

She knocked gently on the glass and both men looked up at her. The man on the stool drew a finger across his throat and she swallowed hard against the blasé way he mimed so violent a charade. Perhaps something in the way she looked attracted the barman to the doors. She could see the other man pulling a face, imploring him to ignore her.

'We're closed,' the barman said, looking up and down the street, then at Claire, before returning his attention to Sarah. He had an Australian accent. 'It's late.'

'How late? What time is it?'

The barest shape of a frown ghosted across his face. She guessed it was a strange question. Everyone knew what time it was. Everyone had access to it. 'It's after one,' he said.

She said, slowly, 'I really need a room.'

The barman, whose name was Nick, could only offer her part use of his own room, which was given to him off season for a huge discount.

'If it's off season, then surely the hotel can't be full.'

'That's right,' Nick said, with a hint of irritation.

'Then why can't we have a room to ourselves?'

'You'll have to pay premium rate.'

'I can do that.' She could see where this was going. Some other time, some other place, she might have let herself be persuaded to spend the night with him. He was young and attractive and Lord knew she could do with a little affection, a little fun. But Claire needed looking after and, although she never got enough of it, sleep was the most important thing to her now.

'Maybe more than premium rate. We don't have the staff to make your breakfast or clean your room. You know, the manager didn't want me to open the door to you. But I have a charitable heart.'

Yeah, I bet you do. 'Just sort it for us, would you? It would mean a lot to me. As you say, it's late, it's cold. We have nowhere else to go. You wouldn't have us sleeping in the car, would you?'

Sarah put Claire in the lounge by the fire while she went to collect their bags from the car. When she got back Nick gave her a key to a room on the top floor but didn't offer to help carry their luggage. With a stiff 'Sleep well,' he went back to the bar and started wiping down a counter that was already gleaming.

Sarah ushered her daughter up to the room and set about making the bed while Claire sat by the window staring in the direction of the sea. When the sheets were on, Sarah felt fatigue wanting to pull her down, but she fought it and made them both cups of tea. She sat down on the arm of Claire's chair and stroked her daughter's shoulder. She could see Claire's expression: slack, vapid, reflected in the black glass. She was blinking so slowly it was as if there were invisible weights on her eyelids.

It was difficult to remember a time before this, when she was a happy, normal girl. When had she last laughed? Sarah placed a hand on her shoulder, trying to infuse her with some of her own energy, however much it was flagging. She thought back to before Manser, when Andrew was alive. She supposed they had been happy then, if not deliriously so. It was hard to be truly happy when you were struggling with debt. At least life had been simpler. You knew what you were up against. Sarah regretted the days lost to spreadsheets and solicitors and advice centres; she couldn't remember what she had said to Claire to get her out of her hair at those times. Go and see your friends. Go and watch TV. She couldn't remember how her daughter had changed from a small girl into a young woman with her own opinions, standards, expectations. They had rowed, but only because Sarah had been so tired all the time, not because of any teenage stand-off. She vowed that once this whole mess was cleared up, she would make time for her daughter, if Claire wanted it.

Claire refused, as she always did, the food – bananas, energy bars, chocolate – Sarah proffered from her bag. She shook herself free when Sarah attempted to help her undress; locked the door of the bathroom to attend to her ablutions in private. She was compliant when Sarah pulled back the covers on the double bed and pressed her gently into it.

Sarah waited for Claire to go to sleep, but her daughter merely lay there, staring up at the ceiling. She didn't like watching Claire sleep. Even before this, she had never kept her eyes properly shut. It was too much like keeping guard over a body. In Preston Sarah had taken her to the family GP, who gave her a full physical examination and took a sample of blood to be sent away for tests. There was nothing wrong with her. In fact, ventured Dr Parks, she was in excellent condition. Sarah had to hold herself back from grabbing his lapels and screaming into his smug little face: *Are you blind? Does she look as though she's in excellent condition?*

'It's just a phase she's going through,' he'd said as they were getting ready to go. 'She's a teenager. She finds everything boring at the moment. That's about the shape of it.'

It didn't help that Claire seemed to be going off the rails at the time of their crisis. Also, her inability, or reluctance to talk of her father's death worried Sarah almost as much as the evidence of boys entering her life. At each of the safe houses, it seemed there was a trap in the shape of a young misfit, eager to drag someone into trouble with him or her. Claire gave herself to them all, as if glad of a mate to hasten her downward spiral. There had been one boy in particular, Edgar – a difficult name to forget – whose influence had been particularly invidious. They had been holed up in a Toxteth bedsit. Sarah had been listening to City FM, a talkshow full of languid, catarrhal Liverpool accents that was making her drowsy. The sound of a window smashing had dragged her from slumber. She caught the boy trying to coax her daughter through the glass. She had shrieked at him and hauled him into the room. He could have been no older than ten or eleven. His eyes were rifle green and would not stay still. They darted around like steel bearings in a bagatelle game. Sarah had drilled him, asking him if he had been sent by Manser. Panicked, she had also been firing off instructions to Claire, that they must pack immediately and be ready to go within the hour. It was no longer safe. And then:

Claire, crawling across the floor, holding on to Edgar's leg, pulling herself up, her eyes fogged with what could only be desire. Burying her face in Edgar's crotch. Sarah had shrunk from her daughter, horrified. She watched as Claire's free hand travelled beneath her skirt and began to massage the gusset of her knickers while animal sounds came from her throat. Edgar had grinned at her, showing off a range of tiny, brilliant white teeth. Then he had bent low, whispered something in Claire's ear and charged out of the window with a speed that Sarah thought could only end in tragedy. But when she rushed to the opening, she couldn't see him anywhere.

It had been the Devil's own job trying to get her ready to flee Liverpool. She had grown wan and weak and couldn't keep her eyes off the window. After being dragged on to a dawn coach from Mount Pleasant Claire had been unable to stop crying and, as the day wore on, complained of terrible thirst and unbearable pain behind her eyes. She vomited twice and the driver threatened to throw them off the coach unless Claire calmed down. Somehow, Sarah was able to pacify her. She found that shading her from the sunlight helped. A little later, slumped under the seat, Claire fell asleep.

Sarah had begun to question ever leaving Preston in the first place. At least there she had the strength that comes with knowing your environment. Manser had been a problem in Preston but the trouble was that he remained so. At least back there, it was just him that she needed to be wary of. Now it seemed Claire was going to cause her more grief than she believed could be possible. But at the back of her mind, Sarah knew she could never have stayed in her home town. What Manser had proposed, sidling up to her at Andrew's funeral, was that she allow Claire to work for him, whoring. He guaranteed an excellent price for such a perfectly toned, tight bit of girl.

'Men go for that,' he'd whispered, as she tossed a fistful of soil on to her husband's coffin. 'She's got cracking tits. High. Firm. Nipples up top. Quids in, I promise you. You could have your debt sorted out in a couple of years. And I'll break her in for you, if she hasn't been done already. Just so's you know it won't be some stranger nicking her cherry.'

That night, they were out of their house, a suitcase full of clothes between them.

Leaving the bathroom door open so she could keep an eye on the bed, Sarah switched on the radio and drew a hot bath. It had been such a long time since she allowed herself a pleasure such as this. She felt almost guilty about it. Andy would never have a bath again; why should she? But this was the way she had been feeling ever since his death. She had not been allowed the time to grieve. All of these mad thoughts, she knew, were the result of insecurities and stress poisoning her in their need to be ejected. She was getting there, but Christ, it was hard.

As she peeled away her clothing, she had to close her eyes. She stepped into the bath and allowed herself to become totally immersed. When her heartbeat was translated into violent spasms on the surface, she emerged.

Reached for the razor blades tucked safely into their fold of paper inside her washbag. Traced a finger over the recent scars that ran along her arm like chevrons on a warning sign.

Her veins had grown plump in the heat. They throbbed, bluish, in time to the piano music's pulse. She pressed the edge of a blade against her wrist and scored lightly till a red bead bubbled there. Now the other wrist. Now the sensitive flesh around her nipples. She imagined Malcolm Manser's hungry mouth positioned above a hot jet of blood from her carved forearms. She jabbed the razor into her belly three, four, five times, just nicking the skin.

Breathless, she flung the blade away before her compulsion for deeper wounding went too far. She bathed her cuts, weeping over the lack of control she exerted, and the fear that one day she might find some. Her past welled within her. The memory of men spilling a different fluid over the pulse points of her body, no less vital, made her feel sick. She told herself then that she was taking their money for her family's betterment; that this was how survival among the dregs was secured. You had to eke it out. You had to earn the right to do it.

Sarah remembered the empty nights sitting in the corner of a squat hoping that the last candle wouldn't die out before morning.

Claire had not hesitated to leave her alone and Sarah had not asked her to stay in those grim months after Andrew's death. It was better, she believed, that Claire be out with friends, doing the kind of things that young teenagers did, even if the risks were slightly increased with Manser on the prowl. If he wanted to take her, she reasoned, he'd do it whether she was sipping cider outside the local Spar or reading magazines in her bedroom. She had done her best to instill the kind of values she believed any child should possess. Compassion for others, courtesy, a little steel in order to help her stand up for herself against boors and bullies. She was determined that, the further away from convention her family strayed during this nightmare period, the tighter their bond would become. Andrew had been the focus, the ostensible barrier between Manser and his desire. Andrew never stood a chance. He was a dead man, really, long before the flames took him.

Sarah dried herself, her eyes following the diminishing smears of mist on the mirror. Before long, the steam had retreated to a tiny disc that eclipsed her reflected centre. It ceased to dwindle.

She checked the windows were all locked and brewed more tea. She sat in the dark by the window, watching the people pottering about in the buildings opposite. They too seemed slothful, dislocated, as if trundling from room to room might expose the purpose that was missing from their lives and provide a diversion.

A storm worried the horizon. As she watched, its thickness blotted out the furthest part of the street. Lightning forked silently, far out to sea, making white cracks in the night. Its enthusiasm failed to muster anything so energetic from her; rather, it only served to make her feel even more exhausted, as if it were sucking the life from her.

She made it to the bed as a clap of thunder caromed overhead. Jesus. What a day. Switching off the radio, she reached for Claire's hand. It was still, thin, cold. Sarah squeezed; Claire did not reciprocate. Sometimes Sarah felt as though she were trying to mourn two people. Sometimes the word 'family' was as alien to her as a phrase of Russian.

She slept fitfully and dreamed of a swarm of lazy, bloated flies invading her room. Some settled nervously on her wounds and fed there. She imagined something larger flitting outside the window. The flies, fattened, lifted like a black-beaded curtain and droned away. She saw them coalesce beyond the window where her dream figure hovered. He turned and favoured her with a shocking smile and she saw it was a man made from shifting photographs cut from a newspaper.

'Our time has come.' He enunciated each word with relish. Although they were separated by glass, she heard every word. 'I return,' he said. 'I return.'

Thin sexual warmth spread through her groin and she rose through layers of sleep till the room swayed unpleasantly before her sticky eyes. She padded to the bathroom and splashed water in her face, confused and upset by the directionless need of her sex. The cuts itched furiously. As she wrapped one of the hotel bathrobes around her, Sarah caught sight of her body in the full-length mirror attached to the back of the bathroom door. She loosened the sash of her bathrobe and appraised herself for a moment, tried to see what it was that Nick had been attracted to. Tried to ignore the swollen red slashes that overwrote her figure. Her breasts were still good, heavy and round and with a pleasing jiggle when she lifted her arms to check out her profile. Her bum was firm, her legs shapely. Her face was beginning to display its little collection of lines and shadows, but her brown eyes were still clear, her short, sandy blonde hair free of grey, her mouth full, with its little upturns at the corners of her lips. Andy had said that made her always seem happy, even when she was crying.

Back in the bedroom, she watched the clean village high street glisten after the storm. The country seemed fresh, almost alien to her. Newly scrubbed, laid bare for the gradual soiling its inhabitants would be party to. The roads were veins to be furred by traffic and smog. She scratched her wrists and, when the sun came up, she was too horrified by its colour to notice that she'd made herself bleed.

She must have drifted off to sleep again, because suddenly the daylight was harsher, pressing bright fingers across her eyelids. She sat up, panicked, her head filled with twisting shadows that bore splintered, unreadable faces. Claire was sitting naked alongside her, gazing out at the village. Sarah was shocked by her daughter's burgeoning sexuality. Her breasts were already almost as big as her mother's, her hips broadening, the flush of womanhood surging through her like heat. She was beautiful and, Sarah could see, she had that ingredient, that seasoning that would have men stumbling over their own tongues for her. Sarah herself never had that power over men, but it was in Claire's eyes. A spark, a dangerous gleam of knowledge. The leap between holding her baby in her arms, moments old, to this seemed all at once too short. Her child was grown up. That time of innocence, trust and reliance was shrivelling away like petals in a fire. The pain of that loss, despite her daughter sitting with her in the room, was staggering, overwhelming.

Claire continued her vigil, rubbing at a sore, red area of skin beneath her armpit.

'What's that?' Sarah asked. 'Rash? You having a reaction to the bedsheets or something?'

A shake of the head.

'Want me to get you some ointment?'

Another shake.

'Okay,' Sarah relented. 'So. Breakfast? Boiled eggy? Soldiers?'

Claire turned to her and – more pain – she smiled, one right out of her infancy. Sometimes she seemed to be rallying. Sometimes Sarah felt they could almost see an end to the running and rebuild the crumbled foundations of their relationship. It was bad enough that her family had been ruined; she had resigned herself to an uncertain future. But she could do without Claire's distance. She needed her daughter as an ally, even though the pain of what had happened must be worse for her. She hoped that her condition, whatever it was, was a temporary symptom of the damage of all this upheaval, not a permanent result of it.

She dressed, taking care that Claire could not see her, wincing as the fabric drew across the tender incisions she had made. Her breasts sang with pain where she'd criss-crossed them with the blade; her belly looked as if it had been shot with pellets.

Downstairs there was no sign of Nick or his manager so Sarah left a note thanking them for their kindness but could they stay longer, and might there be a chance of some work? She often found that written pleas like this were successful. It gave someone time to think *no*, and then, *I can't do that to someone*, and then, *well, maybe* and *yes, all right*. If you asked them straight out and they said no, you might be fifty miles along the motorway before their heart had a chance to soften.

She and Claire walked a short distance to a little tea shop located on a small side street not far from where the car was parked. They had hot buttered toast, bacon and eggs, and sugary tea. The simple meal lifted Sarah, and Claire seemed to come out of herself a little, commenting on the fresh, lemon-coloured decoration, and the little sign on the door which read *Credit is given, but only if customers are accompanied by both great-great-grandparents.*

They could have been any normal mother and daughter, enjoying a day out together at the coast. The threat of Manser was as fleeting as a message in the sand. They walked slowly along the beach towards the pier, picking through the pebbles for shells or warm, golden stones that might or might not be amber washed up from the Baltic Sea. Claire stood with her hands in her long, curly blonde hair, looking out at the horizon, and again Sarah was winded by how mature she was. She was tall and limber. Her daughter. *Her daughter.* She felt a surge of love and pride move through her and she went and stood next to her and put her arm around her shoulders.

'I love you,' she said.

Claire leaned her head against her mother's arm. 'I love you, too.'

They shared a large mug of hot chocolate on the pier, and bought each other cheap novelties from the coin-operated dispensers.

'The sky seems too big,' Claire said.

Beyond the distant shape of Sizewell to the south, great mushrooms of black cloud were rising. To the north, sunlight painted a series of obliques above the sea. The sky was filled with weather. The wind was cold, fresh and good. The future suddenly seemed as clean and unbroken as the horizon.

They walked back to the hotel where a note had been pinned to the door. *Room, yes. Job, no. But come and talk to me. Nick*

She left Claire and went hunting for the barman. He was in his own room, a small attic space barely big enough for a folding bed and a small table. On the walls were some framed album covers – *Grace, To Bring You My Love, The Soul Cages, OK Computer* – and pictures of models in bikinis torn from glossy magazines. Embarrassed, he explained that he was studying fashion design. It touched her that he was moved to defend himself, as if he were trying not to besmirch himself in her eyes. She liked the attention. She had not played the game for a long time.

He told her he had a friend, Ray, who ran a junk shop off the main road, just before it pushed on alone out of the village. Ray was getting on a bit and could do with some help. He wouldn't be able to pay much, but it would cover the room, which, the manager had decided, she could have for less if she was to stay longer. The village didn't exactly close down over winter, but the difference was striking. Nick said there might be other odd jobs going – bar work, cleaning – but that she'd be lucky to find anything. Most of the pubs during the winter employed a single member of staff behind the bar serving, at peak periods, one customer and a dog.

In the time it took Sarah to have this conversation, and to gently rebuff his offer of a drink, Claire had shut down again. The bruises of the coming evening mirrored the darkness settling into the skin around her eyes. Her lips were ruddy; everything else was turning to porcelain.

'Claire?' she said. Her daughter didn't reply, but pushed softly past her and lay on the bed.

'Claire? Can you hear me?'

Her daughter pressed her hands against her breasts, traced a journey down to the tops of her thighs and stroked herself there, in small circular movements.

Sarah swallowed, looked away. 'Claire,' she said.

Claire licked her lips. She said, 'You know how small a foetus is at three weeks old?'

Sarah couldn't speak. She shook her head, both in reply to the question and in utter confusion.

'It's no bigger than a grain of rice. I felt it being ingested. I felt my baby being sucked clean away, by . . . by . . .'

Sarah put out a hand. Claire's eyes were closed. There was a smile on her face. She continued to stroke at herself.

She licked her lips again. She said, 'He comes for me.'

3. THE DEVOTEE

He scrubbed and lathered his skin and hair, the suds still pink. He would find traces in the creases of his skin for days after; that was blood for you. Steam filled the wet room completely, like being in fog. He loved his showers as ragingly hot as he could stand them. It was all or nothing for him. He used to fantasise about what his nickname might be were he to be something special in a field where nicknames were *de rigueur*: boxing perhaps, or mass murder. Malcolm 'The Ton' Manser was his favourite. Whatever he was interested in, he gave a hundred per cent. His website's address was www.mcm.com. He had a large 'C' tattooed on his left biceps.

The gorgeous bitch currently losing consciousness in his fuck pad knew how full chisel he was, how dedicated. A man who could bench-press 450 pounds, do 600 press-ups, 400 crunches and piss a five-mile run in half an hour before breakfast was of a particular, if not peculiar, focus. He could not remember his mother and father and took this as a blessing. It meant he had nothing to live up to, no standards to meet save his own. It was as if he were the first in a new strain of human beings. He was Adam, in his own way. And he was strong.

He switched off the scalding water and stood under an ice-cold jet for a full minute, just like James Bond. He towelled off in front of a full-length mirror in the anteroom adjoining his bedroom. He shaved his head and touched up the trimmed black beard, making sure the tops of his sideburns were militarily squared off level with the top of his ears. He applied Shu Uemura massage refiner and Clinique Moisture Surge to his skin and dressed quickly, pulling from his walk-in wardrobe a red John Smedley rollneck sweater, a pair of black Hussein Chalayan trousers and a Donna Karan raincoat. Kenzo shoes. Rolex Oyster. The Randolphs. He closed the bedroom door and padded over to the locked room where he had left her. Cocked his head against the jamb, listened for a few seconds. Still breathing. Shallow, irregular. Near the end.

Downstairs, he read the newspaper, circling with a Mont Blanc fountain pen a few horses for the afternoon races at Towcester, Lingfield, and Market Rasen. He placed thousand-pound bets with his bookies. He chose horses whose names chimed with him, regardless of the odds: Musclebullet, The Pioneer, King of Roads. He made five more phone calls: Jez Knowlden, his driver, to drop by in the Audi in twenty minutes; Pamela, his wife, to say that he would be away for the weekend; Jade, his mistress, to ask her if she'd meet him in London. Doc Losh to get him to come and clean up his mess and find him a number four. And then Chandos, his police mole, to see if that cunt Sarah Hickman had been found yet.

Manser always watches while Doctor Losh does what he gets paid handsomely to do. He does not look away. He has to be there to step in quick before the amputee's life pulses out of her stumps. And anyway, it would be a bit rich to come over all queasy.

The procedure for amputating a limb is dependent upon the area where the scalpel and the Gigly saw are to go in. Manser is a strictly 'above knee amputation' devotee. He doesn't get off on the fingerless, the handless, the armless; it's got to be the legs, both of them, about halfway up the femur. Losh is quick and discreet, if not the consummate professional. Hygiene is more likely to be something he'd say in greeting to a woman than a prerequisite to surgery.

The textbook amputation calls for a large, circumferential incision to be made into the skin around the thigh, shaped like a fish's mouth to facilitate the neat closure of the wound after limb removal.

The musculature and other soft tissue must then be divided around the thighbone. Veins, arteries, and nerves are transected and the femur separated with an oscillating saw. The end must be bevelled and smoothed to prevent any pain from the stump later, when introduced to a prosthetic limb. The skin flaps are folded over the stump and sutured.

Dr Losh does not own a scalpel or a Gigly saw. He has an amputation knife from the 1790s made by Laundy of St Thomas Street, bought on eBay for thirty-five notes, and a hacksaw purchased from the local B&Q. He does not operate by the book. He is fast, efficient, dirty.

A Marlboro red in the corner of his mouth, his apron cracked with the patterns of dried blood from his previous patient, Losh assesses the girl, who is gagged and restrained on the bench with half a dozen nylon ties. He's spilling ash on her thigh as he unwraps the curved amputation knife from a fishmonger's flimsy carrier bag and drops to his knees. Losh curls his arm under the leg so that the sharp, inner curve is resting on the top of the flesh, the tip a mere few centimetres from his own nose. He executes the *coup de maître* swiftly, cutting deep, sweeping the blade around the leg, bringing the hilt of the knife sharply back to him, and standing up in the same motion. Meat parts; bone is the wet tooth glistening up through a bloody grin. Her body arcs in shock and pain; two of the nylon ties sink through her skin. He quickly saws through the femur and repeats the operation on the other leg.

Manser is as hard as a brick by now. There's no time, no point in suturing the hot, spurting wounds. Losh is transferring the three grand into a money belt around his waist while Manser is losing himself to the feel of her, slick and denuded, flapping around his hips.

'You want these leftovers, or what?' Losh asks.

He encloses his hands around her stumps as he comes. If she's at all conscious, he doesn't see, can't see. Losh is long gone by the time he returns to the world. So is the girl, usually. Sometimes they cling on for a while, as if something inside them was inspiring hope.

He wants the Hickman bitch for his number four.

Salavaria, he thought.

Manser parked his S-Type at the leading edge of the deep forest. If he listened hard he could hear the faint shush of traffic on the M1, a mile or two south. He reached inside the car for a plastic lunch box and a black leather document wallet. He put these in a rucksack and slung it over his shoulders. He had collected the sandwiches from Losh that morning, as he always did, once a week, on the day of his visit to Fetter Woods. Six days' worth of photographs in the wallet had all been printed directly from a memory stick the previous evening. He set off into the trees.

Salavaria.

He was still impressed by his feats, achieved in a different decade, a different century. Manser's murders were almost a by-product of his intent, an unavoidable side effect of his need. Death was not the goal for him, and it had been a surprise to discover that Gyorsi Salavaria's crimes, in this way, were similar to his own.

The monster's lair announces itself about two miles into a part of the woods where the canopy is so dense there is permanent twilight. The first indication is a single, lichen-covered block of stone in a clearing that is really nothing of the sort. There are no well-established trees here, just a swarming pile of shrubbery that looks as though it has been dumped rather than rooted. Foundations are visible through the moss. More stones. Move deeper and the stones find some kind of form. They climb to a point where they create impressive shadows in the dappled sunlight. They are enough to warrant a window frame, albeit naked. Spiders' webs so thick they create the illusion of frosted glass stretch across the gaps. A shattered doorway stands at the head of a flight of steps turned green with lichen and time. Manser strides up them, recognising his footprints from his previous visit, one week before. The rucksack is hot now against his back despite the time of year; he is aware of sweat ringing his neck, the waistband of his black trousers.

It is still a strange feeling for him, as used to this place as he is, to walk a corridor that has no ceiling. It feels faintly ridiculous, and not for the first time he has the peculiar sense that he has never before been here, that there is nothing to see, that the ruins will turn back to rubble as he proceeds, that the trees will take over once more, that there will eventually be a road leading away.

Insects cling to the walls like strange decoration, the dead carapaces providing the only sounds as he strides forwards, crunching underfoot.

Out of the confusion of stone and creeping vegetation, he sees faces where there are none, surging from the shadows like something exuded. The walls develop greater height, and now parts of a ceiling appear. Rooms suddenly stitch themselves out of the fabric of green and black. Things skitter within them, either too blind and damaged to reach the open doorways, or more preferring of the thick gloom. He thinks he hears singing, but it is over almost before he can identify it as such.

At the end of the corridor, a windowless room with its door hanging off the hinges. Out of the dark, one hand reaches to curl around the splintered, rotting jamb. It grips so hard that the knuckles whiten in an instant.

Gyorsi Salavaria says, 'I like what you bring me, Malcolm.'

He thought back to their first meeting, arranged after Salavaria had written to him, specifically to him, expressing his admiration for his crimes and wishing to meet him face to face.

'Why?' he had mouthed, unable to summon a squeak of sound when he stood before the great man for the first time.

'Do you know what it is like to float in a bath of blood?' Salavaria had whispered in reply. 'To sleep in a bed with corpses that cannot close their eyes? Do you know the feeling, when you take something as incontrovertibly positive as life and turn it, with your own hands, against everything that is outlined in its code, to oppose what nature intended?'

Ostensibly this was no longer the man who had torn an unborn child from the womb of Emily Tasker and partially devoured its face while the mother haemorrhaged to death. His withdrawal from the game had apparently ruined him, left a husk that was so fragile it would be blown away by the breeze. But Manser never bought that. He saw Salavaria's strength. The body might seem to have dwindled, but there was sinew there, and force, and the brains and blood that powered it were stronger than ever.

Today though, he could see that something was seriously wrong. Salavaria was sitting in a steel chair fastened to the floor with rusting bolts. His chin rested against his chest, his grey hair tumbling forwards. He appeared exhausted. He seemed to have shrunk inside his clothes. Manser wondered if there was an illness he had not been told about. He wondered if guilt had come charging into this vulnerable body, after all this time, and had finally broken him. He couldn't believe that.

Manser waited. He had cleared his throat, said hello, the first time he had visited and had not been acknowledged for another five minutes. Salavaria knew he was here. And Manser, after all, was no stranger to waiting.

Thirty years on, still, with some frequency, the bones of his crimes were picked over by the carrion eaters who published the red tops every morning. There was a regular froth over the fact that he had escaped arrest for so long, usually when a new editor was appointed. Or the flames of fear were fanned with an article on the most dangerous men in the UK still at large. Salavaria – or rather, because they did not know his real name, *The Picnic Man* – featured prominently in those. Some ventured that he must have died; it was the only answer for the sudden end to the sequence of killing. Some said that if he was still at large, then he must be a harmless old man now, whose reputation was being stoked by lurid journalists.

But a new generation was unmoved by his crimes, despite the tabloids' sanctimonious outrage. Salavaria was old school. He was slowly being forgotten.

'I smell lunch,' Salavaria said. His voice had never lost its Romanian accent, the slashed vowels, the unusual intonation, the unexpected pauses and stresses. Perhaps because nobody ever spoke to him. He had chosen this life of voluntary solitary confinement; it made for a dull existence if you liked to converse. Salavaria did not seem to mind. He had books, a radio, and these had kept him sane. If, Manser reasoned, you could call someone sane who carried slices of thymus around in peach paper on the off chance he grew peckish. But then, who was Manser to cast judgement on sanity? He chuckled lightly to himself; Salavaria raised his head. His eyes were the palest green, like the iridescent flash of mould on a shaving of ham. When they favoured you, it felt like you were slowly being reamed out. Thick white eyebrows beetled at the slightest change of expression. His face appeared sucked in, as if something had deflated him, but the skeletal appearance was offset by the shining beauty of his skin. It was elastic, uncreased, as smooth and colourful as that of someone half his age.

'You find something funny?'

'Not really,' Manser replied. 'Just my twisted mind.'

'Your twisted mind is what I rely upon,' Salavaria said. 'Don't ever attempt to straighten it out.' Salavaria winked at Manser, who again felt a surge of pride that he had been chosen above all others. He felt affection, maybe even love, for the man and slid the greaseproof packet across the table.

'I'll try my best,' Manser said.

'I'm famished,' Salavaria said. His hands shook as they lifted one white triangle with its insert of pinkish meat. As he bit into it, his eyes rolled back into his head.

Just like a shark, Manser thought.

He could not watch him finish the sandwich. Not because of the animal way he devoured it, although that was shocking enough, but because it disturbed even him to see slices of a woman he'd slept with the previous night being consumed. This was Jacqueline Kay, or at least a part of her, a student he had picked up in a pub on the Finchley Road six days earlier.

You need to fast them, Dr Losh had advised him at the start. *Forty-eight hours is best but you can get away with half that. Just give them a little water, that's all.* It was part of his thrill, his fetish, he supposed, that he must wait for them to be physically prepared for the traumas their bodies had to be subjected to. Salavaria was an extremely demanding person but he didn't care how the meat was treated after his delicacies were harvested. Manser might have been able to dispense with Dr Losh had Salavaria been happy to eat cold cuts from a cadaver, but he was adamant that his slices of buttock and breast be carved from a warm donor.

Manser's prick stirred as he recalled the way he had slid, unhindered, into Ms Kay that morning, the expression on her face of dulled shock that her body was still being ravaged, that she was still having to endure this. *When does it give up?* she seemed to be asking. *When is enough too much?*

Now he heard the balling of the greaseproof paper and a clearing of the throat. Manser returned his attention to the other man in time to see him dabbing crumbs from the tabletop with the tip of a finger. A comma of grease on his chin provided the welcome break to a terrible sentence.

Salavaria's eyes were glazed. His voice was content, sated, a little sleepy when he said: 'Thank you, Malcolm.' And then: 'Do you have the next menu ready for me?'

As Manser fiddled with the straps and buckles on the old leather wallet, he totted up their atrocious total so far. Five years, nine victims. Salavaria was insistent he feed once every six months. He had not yet fully divulged the reasons for his proxy return to murder and Manser was grateful for that. He did not much care to know. It was enough that they were in league. He was pleasing a legend and being allowed to pick through the leftovers for as long as was hygienic. Dr Losh was a competent if slapdash surgeon and a great help when it came to disposing of bodies, and body parts. It was a brilliant system; he just had to make sure he remained careful, and travelled widely in order to choose potential victims. *Don't defecate where you masticate*, Salavaria had warned him, early on.

This philosophy informed the latest batch of 'applicants', as Salavaria referred to them. From the wallet Manser extracted two dozen black-and-white images, all taken in landscape mode, all 6″ × 4″. None of the targeted subjects was aware of being photographed and all of them were of a graininess to suggest they had been taken at long range. Four from the tennis courts of a sixth-form college in Sunderland; eight from a café in central Bristol; two on the beach at Cardiff; three at a funfair outside Leicester; five on the ferry across the Mersey; and two at a service station on the M6.

Salavaria placed one of this last pair to the side. He held its mate with trembling hands. 'This one,' he said, falteringly. 'This one . . . how . . . who . . .'

Manser thought he was trying to establish how someone at a service station could be tracked. All of his applicants would have been followed to determine an address, should they need to be acquired at a later date. He thought of explaining this to him, but Salavaria finally spat out a complete question. 'Who is she?'

'She's the daughter of some cunt I nailed once,' Manser said, and immediately apologised for his language. But Salavaria did not seem to be aware of his indelicacy. 'I know where she lives,' he went on, quickly. 'Her mother, that's her in the other picture, she's on tick up to her tits and I've been giving her some heavy about it. Well, I was until she upped sticks.'

'You mean you don't know where she is?'

'I've got my contacts. It won't be long. What? You want her on toast?'

'Not her. I want the girl.'

Manser shifted uncomfortably. He was hoping Claire could be his little bonus once the latest victim was selected. It wasn't even an infocus shot of her: Sarah had been the option he had authorised. It bothered him too that Salavaria's mask was slipping. He had never displayed any signs of weakness before, but here he was with tears in his eyes. His fingers trembled as they held the edges of the print. Manser wanted to say something, but he felt he didn't have the words Salavaria needed to hear, the depth of feeling. Now he seemed to be muttering to himself. Within seconds he had turned from everybody's bogeyman into wittering bag lady; granite to sandstone.

'Her,' Salavaria said. 'I want her.'

'Consider it done,' Manser said, battling to keep the irritation from his voice. He tried to look at the good that might come of it. He could at least finish his business with Sarah Hickman, teach her some manners, some lessons. Maybe even introduce her to Dr Losh, and his mattress, with its protective plastic sheeting. He could let her watch while he had Claire stumped, and –

'But I don't want her . . . spoiled in any way.'

'Gyorsi. We have a deal.'

'The deal is now changed,' the old man said, looking up at him fully for the first time.

'But I don't understand,' Manser persisted. 'What good is she to you in here? What good is she to you at all? You can't risk coming back to normal life. You wouldn't last a second.'

Salavaria's eyes were those of a man half his age. He said, 'I am coming back. But in order to do so I must *change*.'

Salavaria spoke at length, in great detail and without pause for breath, almost as if this were a speech he had prepared and learned over many years.

He told Manser what he needed and what Manser would do. By the end of it, Manser was in tears.

4. MISTER PICNIC

Two young off-duty police officers, glory-seeking constables so eager for a trophy collar they hadn't called for reinforcements, got lucky. They were suspicious of this wiry man in his jeans and pullover, his iron-grey ponytail tied neatly off at the back of his head. They didn't like the way he hung around the sixth-form college, or tried to chat to female students as they waited at the bus stop.

They lost him for a while, then one of them thought they saw movement by the wooden fence surrounding a field. Locals tramped across it in order to collect chestnuts in Thinways forest each November. They followed the figure through deep snow to a crumbling stone platform in an abandoned North Yorkshire train station where they found him trying to swallow the heart of ten-year-old Jemima Cartledge. The rest of her body lay in the snow nearby, ringed with an ugly spattered circle of blood and faeces. He'd attempted to set fire to her corpse but her clothes were too damp. Her singed hair sent an unbroken line of thin smoke into the cold blue sky.

'Kill me,' he'd begged them. They hadn't, so he had dispatched the two of them, informing them of his retirement as they breathed their last red gasps into the snow.

November 18, 1976. The Picnic Man. Gyorsi Salavaria. The final bow.

He thought of that moment of his ending every day. He should not have allowed it to happen. He had been weak. He'd had no faith. He should have kept going, knowing that he would need to remain at the peak of his fitness, both physically and mentally. This was not the kind of thing you just tossed off, like a hobby. It took an enormous amount of psychological steel to turn a living creature into a dead thing. And now it was time to return to it. His enforced hibernation was at an end. They expected him to turn it on, go back to being the monster, the phantom, the slippery Picnic Man.

Everything that had occurred since then – the TV coverage, the stupefaction that his reign of terror was suddenly over, this long period of hiding, the self-doubt, the late-night radio phone-ins where lonely women had asked for his hand in marriage – all of it seemed to have come from a time before his retreat. Only that moment seemed to exist within his memory with clarity. Everything else was lustreless, befogged. He supposed that time in the snow, with a throat full of warm blood, was the last time he had felt alive. Thirty years withdrawn. Happy fucking birthday.

He could and should have gone on. He had endured a moment of stupid weakness and it had deposited him in a self-imposed exile, a hell.

Once upon a time he had pranced clear of anybody with his scent in their nostrils: young, intelligent, hungry, he was a man whose senses had become super attenuated. A fly seeing the approaching swipe almost before it has been launched. The police had been moving through syrup. But he had allowed himself to be found cheaply, for a momentary lack of confidence. He thought *his people* had abandoned him, were unimpressed with his work; *they* had simply read the situation much better than him, with the coldness and logic that he had yet to learn. His exposure might lead to his capture, which in turn could lead to their being discovered. And so they had created some distance. Shedding the emotive side of himself, the human part, had shielded him from understanding the situation. He understood that now. Any warmth or sympathy that existed within him before his self-imposed exile had shrivelled and was as useless as a vestigial organ or limb.

They had needed to aestivate that long-ago summer, they told him; they could sense it would be a hot one. Despite his offerings, there seemed to be no change in the Queen's condition and they decided they must preserve their energies until the inevitable occurred. He was to go into hiding for as long as it took. It had been hard for him to comprehend. He had struck out in this direction, driven by an instinct planted within him since birth, since *before* birth. He had killed nine children on a spree that lasted three years. The media storm that surrounded his activity did not impress him, nor his reputation as Britain's most feared serial killer. He derived no pride from eluding the police, no consternation that the newspapers wrongly accused him of eating his prey. All that mattered to him was the means to an end.

Thirty years on, that end was here, but not in the way he had envisioned it.

He knew he must leave soon, because although She was dead, Her replacement would need to be found. A return to strength was not out of the question, but it could not happen while he was decaying in a collapsed, forgotten barn. What was important was the quality of his flesh, the commitment, the speed and efficiency of the kill. What really mattered was how they read his dedication, his passion. He must return.

He rose from the uncomfortable metal camp-bed with its thin mattress and death-grey blanket. He walked the three paces to the shattered door that separated him from the corridor.

He ran his hands through his hair, felt the soft stubble on his chin. Long hair now, turning silver – he could see it if he pulled it in front of his face. He would not cut it, although he shaved regularly, religiously. He had not seen himself in a mirror for so long he had begun to doubt that they had ever existed. Mirrors seemed too fantastic to him to be true, like the technology they used to show on *Tomorrow's World*. He had forgotten what his own face looked like, even as he traced the blunt blade of his straight-edge razor over its planes and curves and runnels. Even if he could remember, it would have changed beyond recognition now. Thirty years without being able to stare into his own eyes, question himself about what he had done with his life, demand some answers, some confirmation that he was on the right track, no matter what. It was difficult to keep focused when there was nothing to focus on any more.

What did he miss from normal life? Really, there wasn't that much. A pint and a paper, the odd football match, a blow-job, a curry, and the feel of a cricket ball in his hands. Once he had been a fair cricket player, a bowler, able to swing the ball in or out depending on the state of the wicket, the state of the ball, the moisture in the air. Once he had been in love. Once he had thought about fathering children, rather than eating them. Destiny ruined your choices, ruined the notion that you ever really had any choices in the first place.

The only thing that hurt him was wondering about his mother, dead a long time now, but not so long that she didn't know her son was a beast. Now and then it pinched him to imagine her holding him as a newborn, kissing his forehead, wondering at the size of his fingers, the softness of his skin. He would have been faultless in her eyes. His laughter would have brought her to the edge of tears, his simple look of need and love from his cot in the morning when he wakened would have given her belief in God.

When did you become disappointed in your offspring? Was there ever a time? When they grew obnoxious with teenage hormones, defaced by acne? Or were you always in thrall to them despite the way the dice fell? You sent them letters and cards professing love even while their irritation with your parochial life threatened to choke them. No detail, no matter how boring to them, was anything less than fascinating to you.

Time, studied in this way, was of immense interest to him. There was a poignancy in seeing the thrum of his heartbeat in the soft skin of his wrist and remembering a moment when a girlfriend from his teens pressed her tongue against the same spot after they had made love. Looking at that pulse in his skin made him feel that no time had passed between then and now. You grew older, but your memories kept you young. You could always be a virgin if you wanted it.

He touched his fingers to his eyes; he felt the tender flesh, the minuscule network of wrinkles and the way his tears filled it. He thought of death and love and the way the two were so intertwined that it was difficult to untangle them in his thoughts. He had killed but he had loved, too. Did that make him a bad man?

Death. It was both an end and a beginning. Tears were just his way of showing some respect.

He moved, as best his tired limbs would allow, to the part of the corridor where the wall gave itself up to the sprawling forest. He remembered a news programme he had listened to on the radio, not long after going into hiding. One of the ten-a-penny psychologists was talking about what Salavaria was really like, how a fiend like that functioned, how he had slipped the widening net persistently over the years. That he would never make eye contact because he must have the kind of penetrative eyes that people remembered.

The psychologist said he must be a very lonely man. But Salavaria had never felt that way. He felt separate. Intended. Chosen. Different. He was a link between the past and the future.

Nonsense from these psychologists – a breed of repellent, indecorous creatures who were regularly called upon to spout forth over wars and TV reality shows – did not impinge on him. When these so-called experts opened their mouths to speak, Salavaria sent his mind elsewhere. He imagined the purse and slither of other mouths as they talked their rot, and remembered the flavour of Rhiannon Tate's freshly harvested kidneys, poached by the heat of her fear. He remembered the softness of Lisa Kerwin's throat under his fingers and the yield of her trachea, like a Styrofoam cup. He remembered the almost supernatural sweetness of Debra Finnegan's blood. He drank so much of it that his piss turned to treacle for days after.

The forest both stretched out around him and muscled in on his space. It was a paradox he loved. In many ways, he saw himself as the forest. He was patience and frustration; ancient and modern; strength and fragility. He had been here so long he had become a part of the forest. And somewhere beyond it, things were in motion; there was a way back, if he wanted it. He realised he did, very much.

The taste of hot meat. It would soon be back in his mouth, filling his nostrils with copper. The special flavour and texture. For the first time in three decades, he became impatient about having to wait.

5. NICE WORK

'I'm just going out for a few minutes. Then we'll have dinner, okay?'

Claire regarded her with incomprehension, as if her mother had asked her to do something immoral or had spoken in a foreign language. Sarah brushed her fingers against her forehead and left the room, hesitating a moment at the threshold before turning the key in the lock. As she walked along the road leading out of the village, guiltily enjoying this moment of freedom, she felt bad about shutting her daughter in. What if there was a fire? What if Claire wanted to nip down for a glass of milk and found herself imprisoned? She might freak out, throw herself through a window. Sarah angrily shook away these thoughts, annoyed that her daughter's behaviour was turning her into such a drama queen. She had once never had nightmares, or black thoughts about depression, disease, or death, but now the moments before sleep seemed to be filling up with misery. She would see herself toppling off the roofs of tall buildings, or falling in front of express trains as they passed through stations. She watched herself be eaten by thin, rabid dogs. She observed a madman in a scarlet mask gutting her with a bowie knife. It seemed to be a price she must pay for relaxation, no matter how feeble.

She found the junk shop on a lane so small it didn't have a name. A porch was filled with dusty paperbacks for ten pence each. Inside was all dust motes and worn floorboards. More bookcases were lined along flaked, peeling walls but were so obscured by old furniture that she couldn't read the spines. A bowl of cat food was positioned by the door. Clutches of tarnished silver cutlery were held together with elastic bands for £5 a pop. Chipped saucers cradled mismatched nuts, bolts, screws and nails, or defunct currency, or marbles, thimbles, buttons, matchbooks. There was no great care given to any of the artefacts, no sense of order, yet Sarah got the impression there was a lot of affection for what was being sold, and guessed that the owner knew where everything was to the last inch. The smell was that ancient, musty aroma of steady, incremental deterioration.

She loved the place. In the far corner, a counter separated a small office from the rest of the floorspace. On it were positioned a vintage cash register and a tiny brass bell, for customers to ring. It was getting near six and she guessed the junk shop would close soon. True enough, as she reached out for the bell, a tidy man with a small goatee beard, maybe just this side of sixty, ducked out of the office, his hands holding two lever-arch files, a bunch of keys dangling from his mouth. He was wearing a grey cable-knit sweater, a pair of black jeans and a stone-coloured woollen beanie. His eyes crinkled a little when he saw her; he held up a forefinger. He placed the files on the counter and retrieved the keys.

'Yes, miss?' he said. She decided she liked him instantly, and not just because he might have a job for her. His face reminded her of her father's, lined but pleasantly open, still retaining a childish quality.

'You must be Ray.'

'I must be.'

'My name's Sarah. I'm, uh, a friend of Nick Skeaping. He said you might have a job for me.'

Within five minutes they'd shaken on her appointment. She was to begin the next day. 'This means I get to go fishing with my boy without feeling guilty about shutting up shop,' he said. She was only sorry that he wouldn't be around to chat with during the workday.

On the way back to the hotel she bought a bottle of Cava to celebrate. Work, a roof over their heads, a young man flexing his muscles for her, the sea. It had taken a day for her to swing between the scales of no hope and promise. She wanted to get drunk and dance with Claire. Hug her until she popped. Emboldened by her good fortune, she was adamant that she would get the girl right again. Claire could help in the junk shop, creating a proper inventory. Together they would breeze through the place and freshen it up, give it some youth, some vibrancy. Hard work might be just the panacea Claire needed.

A dozen steps short of the hotel she felt her chest leap into the back of her throat. A police Rover was parked next to the Alfa Romeo. A police officer was inspecting the car, leaning in close to the passenger window to have a look inside.

She could come clean, have it out with Manser through the courts, perhaps escape without punitive measures being taken against her. But she knew she was stupid to hope. She had no evidence against Manser. If they both walked free, he would kill her, maybe even on the steps of the court buildings, and then Claire was his to ruin how he liked. It didn't matter that she would lose the car. It had done its job for them. It was just another thing from her past that she had to turn her back on – something she was getting used to, but she hoped it would be the last thing she was forced to abandon.

6. FAST FOOD

As if in some awful act of sympathy, the sky had turned out in similar colours to those erupted from the grave of Leonard Wright. Precious little, in a body two weeks dead, contains any vibrant hue; the mush spread around the disinterred corpse bore the monotone consistency of wet newspaper. Despite that, the bite marks were still visible.

This was how Bo envisaged it, as he took refuge in Sammy Dyer's Volvo, not for the first time wishing he owned a car of his own, rather than the motorbike. From where Bo was sitting he could see Sammy, occasionally leaning over the porridge of the body. His camera flash went off intermittently, moments of bright excitement to lift what was otherwise a terribly grey kind of crime.

His own fingers itched to be holding a camera out there with his friend although he wasn't sure how equal to the task his stomach might be. Sammy was the unshockable type. He had once brought to a party a sheaf of pictures he had taken at the home of a suicide. The victim had shot off the top of his own head, somehow preserving the face beneath it; the brain was photographed where it had landed, ten feet away on a bookcase, like some unusual grey knick-knack.

The young man's expression was what stayed with Bo. He looked as if he had just been told a joke he couldn't quite understand.

Bo wound down the driver's window. He could hear the sound of the shutter release even from here, such was the respectful quiet, and it carried a strangely queasy note that he had never noticed before.

The camera captured its undignified rectangles of atrocity, which would have to be experienced again, later, in the darkroom as they surged out of the developing chemicals. Well, they would if Bo was doing the work. Not for the first time did he rue the many opportunities he had had to switch to digital equipment, as Sammy had done. Bo's argument that prints from film contained better detail was wearing thin, especially with the new breed of cameras that were being introduced. And the downloading of bits on a computer screen would be a lot less personal, a lot less in your face. He wouldn't have to get his fingers wet. But then, his way meant that you were always holding something incontrovertible. Computers were unreliable things. *Data loss* was a phrase he had heard more often than he felt comfortable with. And he loved all the paraphernalia that the geeks didn't get to play with: the little plastic tubs that contained the film, the glassine bags, the stop baths, the stirring rods and lint-free cotton gloves, the stainless steel tanks, the offcuts of cardboard he used for dodging and burning; but most of all he loved the hands-on element of it all, the excitement of manipulating an image, watching it ghost out of the developer.

Thinking of Keiko while he watched Sammy tiptoe around the grave and its dispersed resident was no help. He imagined that what was being photographed was her, under that maddeningly soft, warm skin. Eventually, she was this. But minus the bite marks, he hoped.

Sammy spent another twenty minutes documenting the attack, while black clouds built up behind him. When he'd taken more pictures than seemed necessary, he stowed the camera in his bag and left the forensics team to their painful deconstruction of the crime scene. Laurier and the other police officers were drinking tea from paper cups. The Detective Inspector poured Sammy one from a Bob the Builder flask, which was gladly accepted. Bo got out of the car and ambled over. No tea was offered. There were a few perfunctory introductions but nobody was really paying attention. It was a nasty morning and even these hardened coppers were cheesed off with how low people could get.

Bo looked back over his shoulder at the white figures bent over the spoilt body. Beyond them, like targets lined up on the wall, the head and shoulders of a dozen rubberneckers. They were hunched, almost fearful beneath the slate-coloured scudding.

'Any ideas?' he asked. 'What about the bite radius?'

Laurier's cup froze on its journey to his mouth. '*Bite* radius? What the fuck are *you*? Richard Dreyfuss?'

'I was just –'

'– being a knobend. That's what you were just,' Laurier said.

'I was just showing an interest. Trying to help.'

Laurier's face screwed up as Bo talked. Bo realised he'd be better off not saying anything. This was a man who would take the piss out of his own mother. 'You're a photographer. You take pictures. That is help enough. Try not to have a brain while you do that. Your opinions are as much use as a eunuch's cumbucket.'

Bo reached out and poured himself some tea from the flask. Nobody objected. Possibly because it tasted like piss anyway. He turned his back on Laurier and strolled away, trying to look as though Laurier's lack of generosity had nothing to do with it.

Bo finished his tea in Sammy's car, watching the brutal tableau become softer with the steam as it clouded the window. Just before it was obliterated completely, Bo reached out and swiped clear a path with his sleeve. He had noticed something, despite only vaguely observing what was happening in front of him, as his mind still fretted over Vero and the constant pains in his hand. He had noticed a figure, off to the left of the ghouls trying to find something to spice up their table talk that evening. Tall, with glasses that caught the light and turned his eyes to silver coins. A beaten corduroy jacket and a brown leather document holder clasped primly between both hands. Something about him seemed familiar, but not in any way that was comforting. There was threat and reverence lifting off that figure. Even at a distance where he couldn't be sure, Bo thought the other man was keeping an eye on him.

He swallowed the rest of his tea and got out of the car. He reached for his Nikon and fired off a couple of shots. Immediately the figure turned and walked away. By the time Bo reached the spot where the figure had been standing, he was gone.

Feeling strangely embarrassed and cheated, and somehow prickly with proximity, as if the man were still there in some unexplained way, he returned to the Volvo, where Sammy was stowing his equipment, and said his good-byes. He got on his motorbike and started the engine. He drove back to his flat automatically, and would have been incapable of relating any of the mundane incidents that occurred between Kensal Green and Shepherd's Bush had he been asked.

He had not disclosed to Keiko any of what had happened, and certainly nothing of his suspicion that he was being followed. He didn't want to alarm her, believing there to be shadowy figures capering in the streets outside her window. He wondered if he was going insane. He rubbed the raw, purpuric weals on his hands and decided no. Keiko had not discerned any difference in his behaviour, and she knew him better than anyone.

His front door closed behind him, Bo made his way immediately to the rear of his apartment where his dark room was positioned. It was a cramped area, little more than a reclaimed nook beneath the stairs, but he had sealed it off well and rerouted a couple of pipes to give him access to cold running water.

He set up his developing trays and switched on the safelight. Unloading his camera, he thought of the way the man at the wall had seemed imprinted over the scene, an all too obvious addition. He appeared too glossy, super-real. Bo scrutinised the negative for the frames he needed and fastened it into the holder. Once he had exposed the negs to light, he began the process of developing prints. He moved quickly and easily in the hot, cramped space, his mastery of the tools he used so complete that he worked almost on autopilot. Once he had a batch of half a dozen prints ready, he switched off the safelight and ducked out of the chamber. He poured a glass of milk and seated himself at the kitchen table, then scrutinised the prints for some hard evidence of the strangeness he had experienced. He didn't have to look too hard.

The area where the man had stood was smudged, as if he had fingered the surface emulsion of a Polaroid before it had fully dried. He couldn't understand. The shutter speed had been 1/250, fast enough to freeze action. Weirdly, the teeth and eyes were discernible, almost violently so, pin-sharp and acid white. What made Bo's skin contract, a shudder work its way up from his guts, was the way they appeared separate to the skull in which they were housed: the teeth a clenched bar, the eyes shockingly round.

The mark of a fine picture, he thought. *If I move around the room those eyes will follow me.* He snorted laughter, but it didn't last long. He forced his chair back and it scraped on the lino; milk sloshed over the lip of his glass.

He didn't begin to feel better until he'd substituted the milk for a hefty measure of vodka from the freezer and secreted the prints in an envelope that he shut away in a desk drawer. He submerged himself in a hot bath, slid *Hunky Dory* into the CD player. He tried Keiko's number and couldn't get through. A wall of static. Ditto the mobile. He thought about going round there anyway, but it was getting late, and it was foul outside. She could call him for a change. She could come here.

He went to bed, having had to abort his viewing of the late film, something starring a woman who looked familiar but whose name meant nothing to him. He couldn't concentrate. The colour of the night was too strong outside the windows, even after he had turned on all the lights and shut the blind. He felt the bald glare of those eyes through the thickness of the manilla envelope and the woodchip of his Ikea desk, the yards and walls that separated them from him lying here under blankets that would not get warm.

He thought about getting up for toast, or more vodka, or to switch the heating back on, but he knew that to do that was to be sidetracked further. He might not get back to bed for another hour or so. Often he found himself pottering about the flat at a ridiculous time when all he had meant to do was double-check the door was properly bolted. There were newspaper articles to distract him, or he'd idly switch on the radio and find himself absorbed by some music, or a news bulletin, or a book about Paul Strand or Emmet Gowin.

These thoughts, and others – Keiko nude, pulling him down on to a beach towel furnished only with a bottle of sun lotion and a packet of condoms; the kitchen from his childhood with the shadow of his mother falling on a shaft of sunlit floor; sitting on a rock eating sandwiches with his dad, neither of them talking, but sitting close, smiling at each other now and again as they shared the view over Ullswater, knowing they were in the middle of a Good Time – amalgamated in his mind as he turned inward, towards sleep, and then his mobile phone purred into his ear from the side of the bed and he was snapped awake, trying to recognise the unfamiliar number displayed on the screen.

'Hello?'

'It's you.'

Bo couldn't explain the sudden loss of moisture from his mouth, or why his tongue seemed to now fill every available space within it.

'Who is this?'

'You thought it was a dream. *We* thought it was a dream too. We could never have believed there would be a door made available to us, so soon after the last one shut.'

'Who the – what are you talking about? Who *is* this?'

'One of many. Come to the window.'

He stood before the blinds for an age while the voice on the phone exhorted him breathlessly, *wetly*, as though through a mouth heavy with saliva, to *do it, do it, do it, do it* . . . He saw a hand rise up in front of him – surely not his own – and draw back the fabric.

The man was standing in the flowerbeds beneath the window. There was no phone in his hand, no Bluetooth earpiece. When he spoke, his lips did not move but a viscid curtain of spit fell from them constantly, like a roll of unravelling cellophane. A sigh lifted from him as Bo appeared. Some compulsion forced Bo to place his right hand flat against the glass.

The man on the ground nodded and said: *Come over to us quickly.* Bo waited for him to go, unable to make his voice work, though he didn't know what it was he wanted to utter, and the man shaped to leave but did not depart. Not in any conventional way at least. He became dismantled, piecemeal, like something made of salt, or sand, blown away by the wind. When only a thin cast remained, he opened that reluctant mouth of his and showed Bo what was crammed within.

He could see what Keiko was trying to do, and he wished he could respond to it, but what he had seen over the previous twenty-four hours had turned him inwards. He was trying to burrow into himself, to read his body's secrets, worrying if maybe this strange dislocation he was feeling was cancer, and the oddities he had witnessed were how it introduced itself to his brain. He had not yet told Keiko of his fear because he knew she would usher him to the doctor and he was not yet ready to know, either way.

He thought that seeking refuge in Keiko's arms would help him shrug off all these threatening feelings. Already he had forgotten about his stand, his determination that she should contact him. His flat had been too small and too large all at once. He hankered after some company, and hers was the best kind he knew.

They hardly spoke at all, at first, when he arrived. She bathed him, played him music, rubbed oil into his shoulders and back. But her closeness put him in mind of the shadow that had been following him and a lonely walk through a city he no longer recognised or understood.

'Stop it, please,' he said now, as Keiko ran her fingers down his spine. Her breathing had grown ever more ragged, and she was intentionally brushing her breasts and thighs against him as she worked his flesh. He knew she wanted to fuck, but it wasn't in him. Desire had been tied up into a knot that refused to come undone. Usually her ministrations would be enough to help him relax, but now he saw he would have to hurt her in order to find the solitude he craved. He should never have come here. And, as if she read this in him:

'Why did you come here, if you're going to be so stiff with me?'

'Good question,' he said, although he was wounded by the implication that his visits to her were solely about sex. It was still early in their relationship, and the physical side of things was enormously compelling, animalistic, desperate even, but he needed more from her now. He needed to know he could just be with her, gain strength and comfort from her without any fluid exchange. Again he wondered about her age. He oughtn't put too many demands on her that she could not fulfil. But it was becoming an issue. Perhaps the novelty was wearing off. Perhaps he should end it, before things became too painful. And then he realised selfishly that he couldn't. He needed her.

He lay on her bed as she undressed, grateful that she had not pursued the conversation into darker territory, and took in the pictures on her wall. Her taste wasn't exactly in tune with his own, but that was a good thing, he thought. Her pictures were interesting to him nonetheless and, though it was taking it a bit too far to say he liked them, he certainly didn't dislike them. They were her, which was good enough for him. There was nothing expensive, just a few prints by Colin Slee, Nel Whatmore, a couple of photographs by Andy Warhol and Eve Arnold. It was a relaxing montage, and not for the first time he found it triggering the question of him, *What is it you want to do?* He felt as though time was passing him by and he had yet to find his voice – or more accurately, his eye – with the camera. It prickled him a little that Keiko did not have any of his photographs on her walls, but why should she? What had he contributed to that rich tradition? His work was a mess. Yasushi Nagao had been 31 when he won the World Press Photo Award. Stanislav Tereba had been 20. His own enthusiasm could not be called into question, but maybe he should be feeling more hungry, more driven.

'Relax, Bobo,' Keiko said now. 'I know you don't want me, but was all my hard work in vain?'

'Sorry,' he said. 'Just had a shitty day. I can't let go of stuff.'

'So I see.' She climbed on to the bed with him. She was wearing a white cotton thong and a tight white vest. Her breasts were clearly visible beneath it. It helped a little. She was very easy on the eye. Her long, professionally cut hair was so black it seemed almost purple in this subdued light. Her playful features always seemed to be mocking him. He liked the thin spray of freckles across the bridge of her nose, the constellation of five beauty spots in the gulley between her breasts. He reached up for her and she held him. He breathed in the fresh smell of her hair. Sirens dopplered along Christchurch Road. He suddenly felt sick and lurched to the bathroom. She was at his shoulder immediately, and he could feel her watching him as he retched fruitlessly into the toilet. Her hands on his shoulders again felt too invasive; he shrugged her off and could tell just by the shift of air in the room that she had left him alone. He sensed the light intensify; the music died. The impersonal chunter of TV sound replaced it.

He washed his face and brushed his teeth. Although he hadn't physically been sick, he felt a little better.

The mood she had tried to create was shattered for good. She had changed while he was composing himself; she wore pyjamas and a towelling bathrobe knotted at the waist. Her arms were crossed on top of it. He resisted the urge to offer to get her a padlock, just to make sure. She steadfastly refused to acknowledge that he had returned to the bedroom.

Newsnight had just started. He cursed his rudeness; now he saw that he must put up with the whole Leonard Wright affair again. It was the lead story. He perched on the edge of the bed and felt the heat drain from his face as it became clear that the desecration of Wright's grave was no ugly one-off. Seven more cemeteries across the capital had been filched of fresh cadavers. As in Wright's case, the bodies had been mauled, partially consumed, and discarded for some poor sod to stumble upon as they brought flowers for their relatives' graves. 'Oh God,' he said. 'Oh God.'

There was no need for him to apologise to Keiko; her hand came again to his shoulder. He realised he couldn't watch any more of the news report, not because it was too harsh to stomach, but because he was crying so hard he could no longer see it. Her voice was ragged with shock.

'I'm sorry,' she said. 'I didn't realise how awful . . .'

He couldn't say anything. He drew her close to him and cried until his stomach hurt. By the time he had purged himself, she was asleep and the news programme was over. He watched what had replaced it blankly for half an hour without any attempt to follow its thread. He switched off the set and lay in the dark, trying to combat the rush of fear that swept in with the shadows. He knew what he would see if he went to the curtains and looked down to the main road. Every time he closed his eyes to escape the play of night he was granted a peek inside that foetid mouth that had yawned for him earlier in the evening. The contents had been chewed with gusto, and their shape was not so easy to discern, but there was no doubt in his mind that what he had been staring at was a jumble of fingers from Leonard Wright's hands.

He left early the next morning before Keiko wakened, wanting to avoid any awkwardness with her. They had been involved long enough to be able to sit comfortably in the nude with each other – Keiko had no compunction about peeing with the bathroom door open – but emotional nakedness was another thing. Bo went straight back to his flat and collected his camera and however many rolls of film he could carry in his pockets. He scanned the BBC website to find out which cemeteries had been desecrated, then set off for the nearest.

He powered his Kawasaki through the somnolent streets of Maida Vale, wishing, as he did occasionally – but more often than not when he wasn't riding the bike – that he had used the cash to buy a couple of luxury holidays. He had not enjoyed a decent vacation for over five years. He had bought the bike in a moment of insanity, believing that to be able to chicane through London's traffic to a job would give him precious advantages over any car-bound competition. It was pure look-at-the-size-of-my-bollocks testosterone ... and a skilled salesman who had nudged him into buying the ZX9R Ninja, a superbike that was more at home on racing tracks than inner city congestion zones. Opening the throttle on the M1 at dawn or on some of the winding hilly roads in Derbyshire, he felt utterly vindicated in his choice of transportation, but mainly he was faintly disgusted with himself. A cheaper, less thirsty model would have proved just as useful, and left him with change to keep his bank account ticking over, or cheer him up with the odd treat.

Abney Park cemetery he'd visited just once before, around ten years previously, when he first arrived in London and was living with a woman who had a thing about headstones. They'd gone looking for blue-chip graves but the only name Bo had recognised belonged to the founder of the Salvation Army. But it had been early days with that new girlfriend. He hadn't spent a lot of time paying much attention to the scenery.

He chained the motorbike up on Church Street. Apart from one unmanned police car parked on double yellow lines there was nothing to suggest anything was amiss here. He bought a newspaper and a takeaway coffee and nervously perused the headlines, keeping half an eye on the entrance. The camera hanging on his shoulder burned into his flesh. Why was the entrance not cordoned off?

The newspapers were all over the story, but Abney Park was not mentioned in the article, which gave him pause. For the first time he suspected he'd got things wrong, but he was convinced that Kirsty Wark had named this cemetery in her report on television the previous night. He called Keiko to confirm this but either her phone was switched off or, more likely, she was ignoring his calls.

Bo folded the newspaper and stuck it in his back pocket. He approached the steps up to the entrance and at the top scanned the street behind him, while absently rubbing at the palm of his left hand. He had crazy ideas of police snipers on rooftops, a helicopter buzzing in low to observe his actions, but there was nothing, just a few bleary-eyed people making their way to work.

Inside, no forensic tents, no constables forming a human blockade. He opened his camera bag and took out his Nikon, loaded it with a roll of Kodak Professional.

The graveyard retained that same controlled wildness he remembered from before. Much of the planting was from Victorian times and the pathways had just the right amount of greenery threatening them without making headway uncomfortable. The trees exuded a gravitas that didn't exist in the parks; they were broad, sombre. Pretty soon it became easy to forget that one of the busiest main roads in north London – Stoke Newington High Street – was just a couple of hundred yards to the east.

Abney Park had been specified, he tried to persuade himself. It had. It *had*. But no, it hadn't. Not on this evidence: the cemetery was empty. He was relieved and disappointed in equal measure, but not so hung up on his various psychoses that he couldn't smile a little at the contradiction of an 'empty' graveyard. And anyway, there didn't appear to be any new plots. This must be a cemetery that had reached its limit, which was refusing new members as they queued at the gates.

He began to relax, taking photographs of the partially concealed stone sarcophagi. Bronze angels half consumed with verdigris rose out of the shadows in frozen appeals. Headstones planted square-on had, with time and the unsettled stomachs of the earth, been rendered askew. The trees breathed on him, a hissing rhythm that nagged because it had been still on the main road. The leaves shivered, flashing their pale underbellies at him. The black branches at their hearts criss-crossed against the blue sky like banning signs. He was composing a photograph involving a weathered statue that somehow still retained its poise and elegance when he became aware of movement in the corner of the eye jammed to the viewfinder.

He looked up in time to see something thin move stumpily into the trees up ahead and off to the right, as if it had been walking on bare feet across flints. Its clothing was ragged, like the flayed clothing he had seen still attached to blast victims in photographs from the war. The blades of shadow cast by the crosses and obelisks had interfered with the figure and made its head seem deformed. It might be a tramp or someone visiting the cemetery to get a break from the constant headache of traffic. But he couldn't get the thought from his mind that it might instead be some famished thing with dirt under its nails and a need that could not be conventionally assuaged.

Bo attached the 200mm lens with shaking hands and trained it on the area of foliage that had swallowed the figure. He cursed himself for not bringing his tripod: his heart was beating so hard that it was difficult to keep the camera steady. What he thought was movement might only be the sway of shrubbery, or his own trembling. It was pointless. The only way he would make sure of what he'd seen was to follow it.

He had to wrap his handkerchief around his hand as he was rehousing the lens in the camera bag. His sudden fear was blinding him to the blood and lymph creeping out of his palm; the welts there resembled strokes from a cane. He couldn't read the injury's significance. Finally he had to curtail his scrutiny of the trees in order to pack the camera bag properly and clip it shut. He was crouching, his breath tearing in and out of him, stripping his mouth of moisture. Why couldn't some other fucker come through here walking his dog or carrying a bunch of lilies?

He felt compelled to investigate, despite the urging from his back brain to get the hell out. More movement. He thought he saw another shape descending quickly, spastically, through the trees, with so much foolhardy intent in its limbs Bo thought it must fall. He angled towards the disturbance, moving off the path so that his feet could not crunch on the gravel, his finger tapping gently, nervously, against the shutter release as if it was the trigger of something that could defend him. He reached a border of grass that fringed the top of his thighs. Brambles and convolvulus lay beyond like mantraps. He picked his way through it all, aware of the branches leaning down as if to shield his eyes from something he must not see. He heard violent sound now: splitting, cracking. He heard the squabbling of things that didn't own voices.

It was enough. He could not proceed. He was turning to leave, no longer keen to have his curiosity assuaged, when he saw three shadows stagger across the path he intended to retreat along. He looked up and saw movement, then heard something whisper although he couldn't be sure if it was grass or tongues. He was put in mind of scarecrows come to life.

He resumed his forward movement, more urgently now, as it seemed more attractive to approach something that in all likeliness was unaware of him than something that appeared to be hunting him down. He broke through into a clearing and had to drop to his knees, not so much to keep himself concealed but to prevent himself from seeing more of what he had glimpsed. A glimpse was enough. It would remain in his thoughts for ever, as if he had taken a photograph and framed it on a wall he walked past every day.

He found himself weeping as something stumbled through the grasses trying to find him. He almost didn't care if it did. Perhaps it would help him, in some unspeakable way, to forget the sight of denuded creatures ransacking the bones of a small skeleton.

Time passed. The shadows grew longer, but they were attached to nothing more aggressive than trees. He rose and walked ploddingly and nothing and nobody provided an obstacle. He did not look up. He unlocked his bike and sat astride it for a long time, staring at the indicator on his camera that showed how many exposures were left. What had he captured? He rode back home without realising it. He put the camera in a drawer and went to bed. He slept solidly for fifteen hours. When he wakened he stared at his hand as if it was not his own. Sleep had teased him with the wound's logic but consciousness had snatched it away again.

He stepped out of his bed and on to a floor that was littered with mouldering hearts.

7. SUBTLE INVASION

They entered the city on the 18th November 2008. They filtered in like refugees, wide-eyed, dazzled, uncertain. Hungry. They came by various modes of transport. Some were so brazen as to hitch-hike, though to have presented themselves before a human being at any time before would have been unthinkable. The drivers who picked them up thought them a little odd, a little shy, and so beautiful as to be unnerving. They would not have been able to put their finger on the reasons why, but it nagged them long after their rides had departed.

They came in by the river, barnacles clinging to the barges and motorboats that cruised up and down a waterway that was as known to the genes in their blood as the impulse to breathe. They came in by the sewers and the tube, trudging miles through tunnels like tired blood returning to the heart. They came in on foot, marching across countryside that gave way to ugly urban conurbations. Some were physically sick when they had reached the busy centre of this new world, a thousand miles and years from what they had been used to, or had expected. They bent double and vomited into the gutters beneath the city's skyscrapers. The icons that had drawn them were the very things that inspired vertigo and dislocation. Their heartbeats were out of time with the thrum of the city. Panic hit. If they could not feel at home here, then where?

But slowly, they dispersed and found more modest shadows. You might have spied them from a night bus somewhere in the city. A couple standing in a doorway on Knox Street, so still as to be unrecognisable from the stone that framed them. A man swaddled in scarves to the point that his face was almost eclipsed waiting halfway down the steps at Bethnal Green tube station, underlit by blue light. Thin figures crouching by bus shelters near an estate on Seven Sisters Road, rubbing their chins, their heads, trying to reconcile themselves with a city that turned its back on them half a millennium before.

And how to assuage this hunger, this burn within stomachs that seemed to have lasted as long as they themselves? There were easy targets. Bins, skips outside restaurants; waste disposal depots on the outskirts of the city. Instinct intervened where physical weakness and mental unpreparedness had undermined them over the centuries. Hospitals were treasure troves, especially if they lucked into a garbage chute, or an unsecured door to a chilled room where harvested organs were stored.

Abattoir sluices. Pet cemeteries. Warm graves.

They knew the city, and sometimes, at an hour so late, so temporary, that London itself seemed to be asleep, the city relaxed and unlocked itself to them. They found niches within it in which to hide. They learned the shape of the new shadows it cast. Slow, frail and frightened, they nevertheless began to absorb the city's rules and laws.

Times were different, more sophisticated and yet somehow less elegant. Hunger meant they had to learn quickly or die. After centuries cowering in damp corners of unknowable buildings, it was difficult to slough off the timidity that had settled into them. It was like somebody who has never seen snow being asked to clear a driveway of the stuff. Fear hung around them at all times, a caution and an incentive. Fear was nothing new to them; they had learned that fear could put you under and that it ought to be respected, but met head-on, too.

It was time for others to know fear. It was time for them to instil it.

Some were more savvy than others. They caught on quickly, assimilating the patois of the street, understanding the impression that clothes and haircuts made, recognising the aloofness, the forced diffi-dence, the faux ennui of its inhabitants as a part of identity. You lived *in* the city, you did not live *for* the city. It got to you in the same way that it got inside you. You loved it at the same time that it vexed you. It was a city thrumming with life at the same time as it was stifling, smothering, struggling to keep its head above water. Shit filled its veins. Its breath was that of an asthmatic. Night was an excuse for it to slob out, *sans* make-up, allow its true face to be seen.

The weakest fell away, took to scraping by on the banks of the river, dodging the police patrols, feeding off scraps rejected by the affluent crowd who came to skim the South Bank every evening like roosting birds. They might infrequently be rewarded for the patience with a dead dog, bloated and ripe, floating along the edges of the current, a feast that would last a day or two. There were other bodies too, on rare occasions, washed up on the shingle, long dead from a bullet or a blade; a suicide leap or an overdose. They ate anything that couldn't fight back and relished anew a flavour lost to time and banishment, remembered only through instinct or race memory.

Some people were aware of the invasion, albeit subconsciously, tangentially. They noticed a difference in the atmosphere, maybe, or the slow unfolding of hairs at the nape for no apparent reason. It was the kind of uncanny prickle that you get when you enter a room that has just been vacated, as if the air still contains a little of what goes to make a presence.

They felt uncomfortable in the park eating their lunch, when the only other person was sitting in a hooded coat, knees drawn up, on a bench a hundred feet away. They felt the sudden pressure of threat as they passed a bus stop, but there was only a young woman sitting on the plastic seats, resolutely staring ahead. Or there was the sudden drop in temperature as they sat at their favourite stool at the bar, but nobody had walked through the door, there was just the barman and the guy in the corner chewing his nails with more gusto than made you want to watch for too long.

They might get home and drink a little more than usual, or make love to their partners with a touch, almost, of desperation. There was the nebulous sense of danger thwarted, violence dodged. But it was nothing unusual for someone living in the city. Living in London, you understood death's timetable intuitively. They knew what could happen and how nasty it could be. There was always the feeling that death was on another tube or bus or waiting in a park in the shadows. You got up each morning and kissed your loved ones good-bye and then you went out and gambled with death. Death was somewhere in the city, wearing one of its billion costumes. The game was avoiding death by going about your life as if nothing was going to happen. You got home and it was good to be alive.

The first wave was frail. It was overwhelmed by the lights and sounds and pollution. It was shocked by the brashness of its foe, the way they drank and swore and fought and fucked and worked with a fervour that was like unfettered flame. The first dribs and drabs were like turtles just hatched, making an insane charge for the sanctity of the sea. There was too much here to pick them off. They succumbed easily to the capital's night breeds; its muggers and vandals, its sex offenders and violators. The dead were consumed by their own: easy pickings.

But despite the woundings and the ugly surprises, they understood what it meant to hide. They knew how to bide their time and recognised that their time had come again. Half a millennium was not long to wait, really; a couple more weeks in the dark was nothing to them. So they waited, and watched, and learned, and grew stronger. They, more than most, understood that the city was up for grabs. Nobody truly owns the city. Nobody belongs. Everyone is in one kind of transit or another. Know that and you have the upper hand on your enemy.

8. DEVELOPMENT

He was asleep, but he was aware. At the same time he was questioning himself: how can I be asleep if my eyes are open? The moon was up, full and clean, and he might once have thought about getting his camera and taking a long-exposure shot of it. Now all he thought was how the moon, along with everything else in his life, seemed to be eclipsing him.

Bo dressed shakily, unable to remember the last meal he had eaten. He did not feel hungry but his body was clearly telling him it needed something to boost his sugar levels. In the kitchen he made a bowl of hot chocolate and raided the cupboard. He ate a Kellogg's Nutrigrain bar and a couple of preserved apricots. He drank the chocolate sitting by the window, looking out at the roofs. Five minutes later, despite trying to keep it down, he vomited his breakfast into the toilet.

He snatched up his keys, helmet and camera and got on his bike. He phoned Lewis at the offices of *The Urbanite* and asked him if there was anything that needed doing. A cheque presentation – there was a surprise – at the library in Victoria.

He set an alarm on his phone for the three o'clock shoot and decided he had to keep busy or the dream would pile in, filling too many spaces opening up inside him. He thought about unfinished projects, people who had asked him for photographs but who he had rebuffed because he either did not like them or the reasons they gave for the commission. There had been a self-published writer, not very good, who wanted an author photo for a new book that nobody would read; a woman touching her forties who wanted some shots of herself naked before her body went to seed; a bunch of teens who wanted some publicity material to promote their band; a couple who wanted him to take pictures at swingers' parties.

He tried the band first but the lead guitarist told him they'd split up a couple of months earlier. He called the writer but he was out of town, at some convention or other. He didn't want to call the wife-swapper so he tried Emma, who was probably forty now, and had overcome her sad urge to trap a part of herself in the past.

'Hello?'

'Emma Lerner?' There was something in her voice that was not how he remembered it. Something awkward, cracked. 'Is this Emma Lerner?'

'Hello?'

The line went dead. Bo checked his Filofax. Emma Lerner lived in a flat on Liverpool Road, Islington. He could be there in twenty minutes, get the shoot done how she wanted it, and bomb on over to Victoria. The day would be filled with things to do; he would be distracted by appointments, lighting, organising poses, Emma Lerner's body, even. With luck he would not have time to brood on what was happening to him.

He bought half a dozen rolls of fresh film and drove out to N1. He rang the bell to Emma's flat and she buzzed him in without asking who it was. He climbed the narrow staircase to the top floor, where her flat was a small, split-level affair with a door positioned a couple of risers down the staircase. It was open. A bad smell was filtering down from the flat and Bo paused at the final landing, looking up at the gap between the door and its frame. He couldn't pinpoint the smell, that was the problem. It wasn't a dead smell, he knew that, thanks to his work with the police. It was the smell of his grand-parents' house, but worse. It was the smell of an attic in a boarded-up shop he and his old mate Ian Ford had broken into having bunked off school one day during a punishingly hot summer. They had found a dozen birds dead among the old boxes of till receipts and ledgers, rotten shelving, ancient cash registers, discarded signs and posters, newspapers from a different generation. The birds had all died, apparently, while airborne: their wings were frozen in an attitude of flight. The feathers from the carcasses were gone, the tiny bodies dried out. When Ian poked one with a finger, it disintegrated into dust. He had been unable to get the powdery, ancient smell out of his clothes or nostrils. It seemed to hang around him for days, permeating everything. He felt he understood a little about death that day that wasn't in life's users' manual, something he could never have learned from any number of deaths in his extended family, or passages read in books.

Bo licked his lips and called out. There was no reply, but he felt a change in the movement of air, as if someone had carefully relocated from one room to another, creating a little eddying gust in their wake.

I don't need this shit, Bo thought, and turned to go. But thoughts of Emma in trouble tied his feet up. That hello she'd offered, it had been more than a little awkward. It had been pained, strangled. And was it even hello at that? Couldn't it have been *don't go*? He reached in his pocket for his keys and held them in his fist, allowing the jagged ends to poke free of his clenched knuckles. He swept up to the door and nudged it wider. He saw a body sitting at the head of the staircase. It was sitting with its knees drawn into itself, its arms bowed over the top, its head resting in the hollow between. It was naked, and as white as chalk. He could see enough to confirm that the body was male.

'Emma?'

He heard something coming from deeper within the flat. It sounded like someone knitting.

'Emma? I'm calling the police. Can you hear me?'

He pulled out his Motorola and flipped it open. He dialled 999. Dead line.

Okay.

He squeezed the keys tighter between his fingers and pushed the door wide open. Anyone coming within striking distance was going to get a mouthful of Yales. He stepped around the body, gritting his teeth as his jeans brushed against its tinder-dry hide. He moved deeper into the flat, questioning his sanity, wondering how long it would take for his bladder, his bowels and his mind to give up to the fear climbing his chest. Emma's flat was in a bad state. How long since she had first approached him? He thought back to that time, in a tapas bar in Farringdon Road, six, seven months ago? when he had been talking to a magazine editor and showing her his portfolio. At the bar, Emma had introduced herself, apologised for spying on him, and explained, tipsily, her ambition. He'd taken her card and a kiss on the cheek, never intending to follow it up. But here he was. And he hoped she was too.

Bo told himself that everything was okay. The body on the stairs was a joke from a trick shop. The dark stains on the walls were splashes from a glass of wine. The knitting sound . . . just that. 'Hi,' she'd say as he rounded this corner into her living room. 'I turned forty. So I started knitting. Want a cardigan?'

'Emma?' he tried again, his voice as dry as the aged spider silk festooning the rooms' crevices. The sounds were coming from what he guessed was the living room; the kitchen and bathroom were straight on and to his left respectively, their doors open. Plates and pans were stacked in the sink, along with what looked like a matted hank of hair. The shower curtain was drawn in the bathroom; as far as he was concerned, that's the way it would stay.

He moved through to the living room and saw Emma on a sofa strewn with pieces of human flesh. She was naked, squatting, trying to draw the body of a large man high enough from the floor for her to be able to bite into it. He saw that the clicking sound was coming from another man, sitting apart from the others. He too was naked. His teeth couldn't stop chattering. His lips were blue. His eyes seemed tired and wide at the same time. Shock. He was bound with some kind of clear twine; his hands and feet were blackening. Blood threaded the kink of his inner arm, the creases where his neck lifted from his shoulders.

Above the sofa were six commemorative plates. It looked as though they were meant to spell out the word CHRISTMAS but either the payments hadn't been completed or Emma had grown bored of them. It was an apt reaction to the tableau he was looking at. The carpet was a Jackson Pollock of urine, blood, and shit. There was a hole in the wall to the left of the sofa. It looked as though someone had been chiselling at it rather than it being the result of any structural failing.

Bo took a picture.

Emma did not look up. The chattering man did not look up. The dead man was fractionally consumed.

Bo left. He noticed that the man at the head of the stairs was not kneeling, but was suspended on a thread that was attached to the ceiling. He moved in the draught created by Bo's desperation, like a paper figure on a baby's mobile. He took another picture. Smile, you cunt.

He fell down the final flight of stairs, his legs were shaking so much. He took off a layer of cells from his cheek against the wall, and staggered out to his bike wiping lymph from his face, although he thought it might be sweat, or tears.

He managed to keep himself from being sick, and sat astride the Ninja for a few minutes, looking up at Emma's window, which from here looked frosted. He thought of the hole in her wall. Two teenage boys walked past him bouncing a basketball and talking about breasts. An ice-cream van played saccharine melodies as it turned on to Liverpool Road from Offord Road. Bo thought crazily of ice creams he had liked as a kid, running out to the van as it parked outside his parents' house. They always had a choc ice, because that was sophisticated. He had all kinds of rubbish, pumped so full of E numbers they might have glowed in the dark. Some of them might still be in his gut, undigested, indigestible after all these years. Zoom. Screwball. Tangle Twister.

And then he *was* sick, copiously, and the dead flies in his vomit reminded him of his mother's rock-cake mixture before it was put in the oven.

'What's happening to me?' he whispered. 'I don't know who I am.'

He looked back up to the frosted window and saw a face in the moment of its retreat. His eyes shifted to the next window. That too was frosted, although it might have been the reflection of the morning sunlight, or net curtains in need of a wash. He kicked the bike into action and moved away, thinking of honeycombs, of networks, of death worming through the terraces of north London.

'Okay, and now just one of the councillor and Pete. Pete, if you could lift the cheque a little higher. Level with your head. And bring it in a bit so that your cheek is touching it. Councillor, if you could get close enough so your cheek is touching the other side. I know, I know, but space is limited and we might only be able to fit that shot in. Nice. That's good. And that'll about do it, I think. Thank you for your time.'

* * *

He sat at a table on his own in the Albert, the little old pub on Victoria Street that seemed out of place among all the glass office blocks muscling in around it. He drank a lot of strong lager. He ran his finger over the camera, tripping it against the wind-on lever as if it were the rosary. He tried Keiko on his mobile but she wasn't answering. That meant she was probably at the British Library where mobile-phone use was prohibited, boning up on entomology, or sending rude emails to her friends. He desperately wanted to be with her. He wanted to hold her so tightly that she left an imprint on him.

He finished his pint and walked across the road to the antique jewellers on Artillery Row. There he found a silver brooch in the shape of a bee. He bought it and wrapped it in gift paper, placed it in a bubblewrap envelope, and wrote a short note:

You've always been strong for me. But I don't know if that's enough any more. I don't want you to end up as my crutch. Have you noticed things changing? Can you see what I see? Am I going mad? Does it mean I'm going mad if I have to ask the question? Do you see a difference in me?

He thought about it, then crumpled the note in his fist. He posted her the bee on its own.

There was a man standing on the corner of Albemarle Street and Stafford Street eating a baby's arm.

He didn't understand how he got back home without causing an accident. He had drunk too much, driven far too fast, leaning into corners like a superbike racer, his leathered knee sometimes kissing the tarmac. His head was full of clicking noises: teeth, shutter release, his propeller pencil as he fed fresh lead for names for his notebook.

Councillor Tom Leyland. That's L-E-Y-L . . .

He parked and locked the bike, covered it with green tarp, went inside and took a shower. On the way home, as fast as he had travelled, what fucking things had he seen?

He had seen a couple of tramps sitting on the road as he throttled down through the lights at Notting Hill Gate. They had been kissing, hoods up, holding on to each other too violently for passion yet too controlled for drugs or booze. That's what caught his attention. He saw his mouth so deep inside her face it was as if he were trying to hide.

Figures as white as candles swaying in windows.

A small child, so gaunt as to suggest translucency, gnawing at her own fingers, staring up accusingly at him, flattening lips dripping with blood.

He poured a long measure from a bottle of vodka he kept in the freezer. Tiredness had settled against his skin like cold bathwater. He sat on his bed and went for another sip to find he had already drained the glass without tasting it. He picked up the phone and tried Keiko at home. No answer. He left a message that he despised for its wheedling tone. *Come over. I need you. I don't want to be on my own.*

I. I. I. Me. Me. Me.

He reached for his biker jacket and fished out Detective Inspector Laurier's number. He'd barely dialled the number before it was picked up.

'Joseph Laurier.'

'It's Mulvey,' Bo said.

'Mulvey. I don't know any Mulvey. Expound or remove yourself from my phone line.'

'I'm a friend of Sammy Dyer's. I'm a freelance photographer. I was at Leonard Wright's grave the other –'

'Richard Dreyfuss. Yes, I remember. What do you want? You want to show me some big shark you caught?'

'I just wanted to ask if you'd had any luck finding the grave-robber.'

'Graverobber. Jesus. What are you? Can't you talk in any terms of reality? Do you live in some film world, some fantasy world? This is London, Dreyfuss. Two thousand and eight.'

'Well, what do *you* call him?'

He heard the line grow muffled. He thought he heard Laurier say something like, *I'll be with you in a minute, just got to get rid of some wanker.* 'I call him the perpetrator. We haven't got a name for him yet. We haven't been introduced. Maybe you know him. Do *you* know him?'

Oh Jesus God, friend, I think so. 'Is the person digging these people up the same person taking chunks out of them?'

There was a long pause. Laurier's voice, when it returned, was more careful, more sedulous, more seductive. Bo could suddenly see how Laurier was a good policeman. He would hate to be in an interrogation room with him. He was slick. He was a serpent.

'Who said the bites we discovered were from a human mouth?'

Bo struggled to answer but could only convey an insinuating silence. Laurier penetrated it.

'Do you know something we don't?'

'I just guessed. They looked human.'

'Yeah,' Laurier said, suddenly sounding weary. 'That bite radius shit.'

'And I've seen . . . things.'

'Talk to me, Dreyfuss. Speak slowly. Speak some sense.'

Bo considered putting down the phone. He didn't know what he wanted to say. He had called Laurier on an impulse and now things seemed to be sliding away from him. He could see Laurier jotting his name in a notebook. Maybe getting someone to run a check on him. He was in his thoughts now, whereas five minutes previously he hadn't been.

'Just . . . suspicious figures. Loners on the street. I think they might be violent. They had a look about them. They . . . I was just wondering if you'd seen anything? Or had any reports?'

'We get reports every day, son. We live in fucking London. "Loondon" they call it in here. We're busy, all right? We're trying to find out what's going on with the disinterments. We don't need your paranoid witterings to bog us down. If you know something, then squawk. If you don't, then fuck off and stop mithering.'

'I'm sorry,' Bo said. 'I just —' The line went dead.

Bo tossed his handset on to the sofa. Brilliant. They had him down either as a potential suspect or a time-waster, a nut.

He stormed to his darkroom and switched on the safelight. He sat on the floor and rubbed his eyes until they were sore, trying to push some ideas into view. But all he could think about was how he had been unable to stomach any food for the last two days.

In the red glow of the safelight, his hands seemed too smooth and soft to belong to him. The half-moons of his fingernails were jet black, ragged. He wondered if the previous night's dream had been a dream after all.

The process chemicals are at the right temperature. There are two rolls of film to be developed.

Like a Marine reassembling his rifle after cleaning, you could do this in your sleep. You wish you did. It might distract you from what occurs when you are in that alien country you enter every time you switch out the light.

You remove the film in total darkness. You always shut your eyes when you do this, as if keeping them open brings greater risk of the film's exposure to light. You cut the tapered leader square, carefully load the film on to a spiral, and place it in the stainless steel developing tank. Pour in the developer quickly; development begins the second the chemical makes contact with the emulsion on the film. You tap the tank against the work surface a few times to get rid of any bubbles. For ten seconds of every minute the film is being developed, you must tip and shake the tank to ensure a uniform flow of fresh solution. Start the timer.

Gone midnight, where do you travel? And why? You peel yourself away from the soft, warm curves of your woman or your dreams and dress quickly. You pad downstairs and stand on the doorstep. Why do you sniff the air? Why is your face upturned to the night, as if bathing it in the light of the moon?

The chemicals react until the second all is drained from the developing tank, so you also have to do this quickly. Now pour in the stopper until it overflows the neck of the tank. Agitate to neutralise any remaining developer. Pour away the stopper and add fixer. This stage can take up to ten minutes. Again you must shake the tank regularly. Wash the film thoroughly for thirty minutes with cool, filtered water.

You walk away from people, yet towards them. From light to shade. From noise to silence. You walk barefoot through dew-soaked grass. The moonlight is sometimes so intense that it blinds you. Everything is painted by its strange pallor. You tread through this talcum wasteland expecting to see footprints following you when you check behind. In the urban quiet, you can sometimes hear a heartbeat. You can't tell if it is your own, or that of someone pursuing you, or of the city itself. It can't possibly belong to the person you are going to see.

You hang the long strip of film and remove excess water with a sponge. You lightly blow a cool hairdryer over it. When it's ready, you cut the negative into strips and place them, one at a time, on a lightbox. You pull out the Schneider loupe that goes with you everywhere and find your hand shaking as you try to identify the shots you need to enlarge. Here's the one taken at the graveyard in Stoke

Newington. And here, on the other film, are the shots of the events in Liverpool Road. None of the pictures contain any immediacy for you. It's almost as if you never took them. You make the enlargements, your hands falling to tasks they know almost better than themselves. The test strip, the cleaning of the negative and the enlarger; the familiarity is a balm that anaesthetises you from the fresh shock of the images stolen from recent days as they loom out of the ghost-white printing paper. A picture at the cemetery of a face you don't recognise, snapped in an attempt to break into the horror of that day. Close-up, blurred, the features loosened by shock, the skin white. The eyes filled with a crazed look, of hunger, of lust. Fear.

The shots at Emma's flat on Liverpool Road: plenty of handshake, crazy angles, images taken from an aspect of retreat. You slip the shots into a glassine bag and tuck it into your sweatshirt.

You switch off the safelight and emerge into a room that seems to have been infected by the artificial dark of the past few hours. The digital camera is in your hand though you never remembered pausing to pick it up. You lock the SLR in a suitcase and stow it in the back of the wardrobe. No development, no darkroom from now on. You feel as though you've been living your life more fully on the photo paper than in reality. The Ixus will go everywhere with you now. It will be the only way to keep hold of reality, a shield to protect you; a charm to ward off the changes you feel inside.

There are three messages on your mobile phone, all of them from Keiko. You delete them without listening. You must not see her again. She'll be safer that way. And then the phone is ringing again and her name is in the display and your thumb hovers over the touchpad. But to let her in is to kill her.

You hurl the Motorola at the wall and watch it turn to plastic rain.

Darkness is coming and you can feel every cell of your body reaching out to meet it. You pack a rucksack. You check your wallet for cards and cash. You check the phone book. No *Vero, R.* No disappointment because it's no surprise. So it's to be done the hard way.

You go out. You're hungry and you're beginning to intuit what it is you're hungry for. You pull off the tarp, climb astride the Ninja, and kick it to life. The dark fills your nostrils and settles against the back of your throat. It jags around your brain like an inhaled narcotic.

North or south. East or west. It doesn't really matter. All roads lead to the same dark little bolthole. The taste of insects on your tongue. The spectral glitter of chitin.

Darkness has fallen and there are mouths to feed. You open the throttle and let fly.

That face from Abney Park cemetery. That was you, wasn't it?

That was *you*.

9. CARBON

Five days after his final visit to the prison, on a late afternoon in early December, Malcolm Manser got his driver Jez Knowlden to pull in at the Esso garage on Edgware Road and fill a gallon container with 4-star. They then drove to a pub in Notting Hill where Manser disappeared into the cellar with the manager and a member of the door staff. Twenty minutes later he returned to the S-type with a bin bag wrapped tightly with gaffer tape. He placed this on the back seat and instructed Knowlden to follow him up the main road while he did a little shopping.

He bought three disposable Bic lighters, a garden spade, and two large green plastic sacks for garden waste. He bought a black Maglite torch. He bought two steak-and-cheese subs from Sub City and gave one to Knowlden. They ate them while parked illegally on the main road, laughing at the people who went into the retro clothes shop to buy overpriced rags.

A call came through from Tim Chandos at New Scotland Yard. Sarah Hickman's car had been found in Southwold. It wouldn't be long before they picked her up.

'Don't pick her up,' Manser said. 'We'll sort it. We'll take it from here.'

* * *

Jez Knowlden was known as 'Knocker' to his friends because of a dirty fighting habit. He invariably got the first punch in, although it was more like a rap, as if he were knocking on a door. The blow would come from up high, directed down on to the bridge of the nose, which bled easily if hit right. Once a man was bleeding, the fight was over: they often had no stomach to continue. If you saw Knowlden eyeing the space between your eyes, step back and walk away because big pain was coming.

He had served in the first Iraq war as a driver for the Army. When he came back to the UK his ability behind the wheel brought him to the attention of the Secret Service, for whom he spent five years shuttling ambassadors, diplomats, ministers, and other VIPs through late-night London streets. He was the prime minister's driver for his last six months of office. Driving was his life.

He was dishonourably discharged from MI6 for drug offences: off duty he was signing out cars with false papers to make overnight cocaine runs up to Edinburgh and Glasgow. He received a five-year suspended sentence, escaping prison thanks to the intervention of a number of high-ranking military and government staff. Nevertheless, he gravitated towards the criminal fraternity and used the cover of his new job – driving HGVs for a brewery – to continue trafficking between Scotland and the major cities south of the border. He ended up as a chauffeur again when he was being stopped by motorway police more times than he felt comfortable with, but this time it was for Big I Am villains trying to be something they weren't: drug dealers, pimps, and gun sellers. He drove second-hand souped-up BMWs, Bentleys and Mercs, almost always in black or white. He was wiping down seats covered in come, coke, and Krug. The deals being negotiated in the badlands of south London were for three- and four-figure amounts. Skulls were being cracked for £150. He was taking orders from teenagers who wanted 50 Cent pumping on the car stereo all day and who thought class was an off-the-peg suit matched with Nike trainers and plenty of bling. The gold was so soft, it bent if you looked at it.

He almost crashed a car one night when his boss for the evening told him his shoes had cost more than Knowlden earned in a month. The guy went home with a bloody nose, and Knowlden was finished in the underworld.

In May 2003, Knowlden was back in HGVs, working for a removals firm specialising in trans-continental relocations. He and his mate, a fey student called Colin with a beard that looked like an accumulation of dust, had spent three hours hefting boxes filled with books and more crockery than could ever be used by a young couple, newly married or no, into a dilapidated pile of Charentaise stone situated in a blink-and-you-miss-it village fifteen miles north of Cognac. The job finished, they repaired to the town eager to quench their thirst with some of the famous spirit manufactured there and maybe bring a couple of bottles back for the gimps at HQ who were on less glamorous duties.

They hit the bars full steam, knowing they weren't expected back before the following evening and could sleep off their inevitable shitstorm headaches in the wagon's cabin on one of the open parking lots up in the industrial area of Chateaubernard before the long haul back up to Le Havre.

'What's this half-pint shit?' Colin said, when they asked for their first beers. 'I've been working like a bastard. My throat's drier than a nun's cunt.'

'You have to specify that you want a large beer.' The voice came to them from their left. They both turned: a guy wearing immaculate clothes, sunglasses. He had a bald head and a neatly trimmed full beard. He was looking down at the bar, at his glass of Ricard and jug of water. 'The French . . . they're a civilised lot over here. They think you want a beer, it's something to wet your throat with while you chat about Camus or Sartre or Zidane. *Une grande bière, s'il vous plaît.*'

'Grande bier, hey?' Colin said, rubbing his pathetically coated chin. He made his order and a pretty waitress came back with a litre of Pelforth. It had been poured into something that resembled a glass bucket. The boy was overjoyed.

The stranger, Knowlden thought, really was wearing some beautifully cut gear – an Armani jacket, some kind of subtle designer T-shirt, moleskin trousers that were a kind of dark grey but were probably referred to as anthracite by the manufacturers, and leather boots that screamed pound signs. Next to him on a stool was a carefully folded nubuck leather jacket and a snazzy Merrell briefcase. Knowlden knew instinctively that he wanted to work for him. He was dedicated to him, a hundred per cent loyal, and they hadn't even shared a conversation yet.

They stayed on at that one bar all night and drank litre vases of Affligem as well as pastis and Meukaw cognac. It was a good bar, and the waitress flirted, and they could order *entrecôte* and *frites* and *salade verte* after nine, which was unheard of in any London boozer they knew. The stranger introduced himself but never once took off his sunglasses. It didn't look pretentious on him, somehow, Knowlden decided. And there was something else he noticed. No matter how much they drank, the stranger remained in control, like Knowlden himself. He liked that. It was reassuring. This was not a man to go off half-cocked. He would not render himself vulnerable by getting into a rage.

Colin, on the other hand, was bladdered. He was leaning over the bar, his jeans slowly travelling south while he attempted to ask the barmaid to marry him. Knowlden and Manser talked. Manser was impressed by Knowlden's career. Knowlden liked how Manser didn't brag about his position in the world. He had a few fingers in a few pies and he was making headway; that was all he said, although Knowlden knew it was more than that, and he knew that Manser knew he knew that.

By the end of the night, with Colin slumped against the bar and the barmaid singing to him, Knowlden and Manser were finishing each other's sentences.

'I could do with . . .' Manser began.

'. . . a driver like me,' Knowlden completed.

'Actually, I was going to say "a piss".'

They got on. There was chemistry. Drinks finished, as Knowlden carried Colin off to the wagon, there had been a handshake, a swapping of email addresses and mobile numbers, a nod, a look, an understanding. Two months later, Knowlden had again handed in his notice on the long vehicles and accepted Manser's offer of work. Chauffeur, bodyguard, right-hand man.

'I need someone I can trust,' Manser had told him. 'Someone who isn't squeamish. Who accepts that different people have different needs and doesn't make judgements.'

'You could be diddling your grandmother with *merguez* sausages and I wouldn't double take,' Knowlden said. But he did, when Manser told him what he was into.

A long pause. The sense of a line being crossed.

'I'd take a bullet for you,' Knowlden said.

'How about a *merguez* sausage?'

He didn't want to expose Knowlden to this kind of nasty shit so soon, but he needed some help. Gyorsi, when explaining his plan, was adamant that he would not fight what must come to him, the disfig-urement that was necessary if he was to return to his public, but Manser knew what the body was capable of when it was taken into realms it ought never to experience. Instinct took over.

In the end, though, Knowlden was unfazed. They had spoken about his experiences in Iraq in 1991, specifically about the friendly-fire deaths he had witnessed when an A-10 accidentally dropped its payload on a pair of light armoured vehicles fifty miles south of the burning Burqan oil fields in southern Kuwait, a day after the commencement of Desert Storm. Three of the four crew members were obliterated, six smoking boots the only indicator of how many grunts had been travelling. The other crew member had survived, somehow protected from the fireflash that liquified his colleagues, but he had been mortally wounded by shrapnel. A burning piece of metal had carved through his stomach, cauterising the wound as it went. He was sitting on the desert floor looking through the massive hole in his torso, his stomach burning in the sand a few feet away like something fallen off a barbecue, when Knowlden got to him.

'He watched me pull out my pistol and he was asking me, in this calm voice, not to do it. He could see that he was going to die, he wasn't going to see the sun set or place his head on a pillow, or a woman's breast, ever again. I just sat with him and waited for the shock to hit him, and then he didn't even know who I was or where we were or what had happened to him. He watched me shoot him between the eyes and by then I don't think he even knew what the gun was.'

Twilight was approaching when they turned the S-Type on to the gravel lay-by edging the forest. In this flagging light, the evergreens of the forest – the moss coating the bark, the creepers, the ferns – appeared to be staining the sky immediately above. They walked without conversing, as if the discussion they had just had in the car had exhausted all topics for a time, made them redundant. They moved swiftly, following Manser's compass and his acquaintance with the trees. Darkness moved into the gaps around them like something being absorbed. Apart from their boots in the mulch of dead leaves and rotten sticks on the forest floor, the sounds of their breathing, the occasional clatter of wings in the heights and the chitter of insects coming to life under shadow, there was little noise. Until, fifteen minutes deep into the forest, they heard tinny music coming from a cheap radio.

The crumbled edifice of the old building announced itself; candles were dotted around the small clearing, yellowing the sterile layout and making it seem almost welcoming. Gyorsi Salavaria was kneeling, naked, in front of a broken shard of mirror, shaving, his old radio sitting next to him in the grass. The Chordettes singing 'Mr Sandman'.

'Are you ready for this, Gyorsi?' Manser called. He placed the rucksack on the floor and removed the plastic can of petrol, began unscrewing the cap.

'Yes, Malcolm . . . are *you*?'

Knowlden stepped forwards and held Manser down.

Manser struggled, but Jez's arms were like branches from an oak tree. 'What is this?' he whined. 'Gyorsi? Jez?'

When the fire was lit, the roar of it was grand enough to drown out any screaming.

Part II

BLOOD MEALS

All sorts are here that all the Earth yields,
Variety without end.

John Milton, Paradise Lost

I'm an insect who dreamt he was a man and loved it. But now the
dream is over . . . and the insect is awake.

Seth Brundle (Jeff Goldblum), The Fly (1986)

10. HIDE

Sammy Dyer lived in what he liked to call his eyrie, the attic room of a top-floor flat shared with three other people in a grand old house in well-to-do Belsize Park. It was the only way he could afford to live in the area, a place he liked for its independent cinema, restaurants, and delicatessen. The England was visible from his room, a good pub with wooden floors and a basement area packed out every Saturday night for stand-up comedy acts. Sammy's room was a health and safety hazard. Because of the narrow, steep staircase providing access to his room (he doubted there had ever been an official application to the Planning Department) he could get no sizeable furniture up there. It was, as a result, a riot of soft furnishings: a couple of large overpriced bean bags in blue and red from Camden Market, cushions, throws, blankets. A MacBook and an iPod dock sat on top of an old detachable wooden desk salvaged from an office sale which Sammy had plastered with hundreds of discarded images from his photographic past, all varnished fast. So many books and magazines were piled precariously against the walls that the futon mattress would appear to be more comfortable to shelter beneath than sleep on.

Bo Mulvey ascended the punishing staircase at the rear of the building, five flights of *Jesus* and *Shit*, wondering if this had been the right choice to make. He felt ill, probably looked less than well too; his skin felt hot and thin to the touch, his fingertips coming away wet where they had trawled his greasy forehead. He felt shaky from hunger, that hollow friable feeling that comes when blood sugar levels have taken a plunge, but the thought of food made his stomach convulse.

Sammy was at the entrance to the flat, waiting for him.

'Yo, Blood,' he said, in his best Samuel L Jackson, offering his knuckles, which Bo ignored. 'God. You look like the proverbial sack of. What happened? You find out what your real mother was?'

Bo smiled, a tight, toothy grimace. 'I could do with a drink,' he said.

'Kettle drink? Or something harder?'

'Tea,' Bo said. 'Sweet. Very sweet.'

He waited in Sammy's room, studying the spines of books stacked almost floor to ceiling without taking in any of the titles. Music was coming from the MacBook, which was hooked up to futuristic speakers and a sub-woofer. But it was so subdued Bo couldn't identify it. The screen was black. That was the thing about computers these days: they went to sleep when they weren't being used, they didn't need screensavers any more. Bo missed the old operating systems that ran mind-bending savers. There were the visuals that came with iTunes, but who wanted to watch attractive swirls when PJ Harvey or The Smiths or Kristin Hersh was playing?

He heard the sound of a spoon in a mug, its clatter as it was discarded in the sink. Bo sat down, then stood up and went over to the window. The view south took in the BT Tower and the net enclosing the birds at London Zoo. He could see St Pancras from here.

He had to make Sammy see that he was normal, not as strung out or as panicky as he felt. He had nowhere else left to turn. Keiko was too smothering in her concern for him. It was too much like being mothered; he needed space now, and time to think about what was happening to him and around him.

'You working?' Sammy asked, his head rising into view from the sheer staircase.

'The usual rounds of handshakes and hellos. I could do this in my sleep. In fact, I think I do, sometimes.'

He took his tea, failing to prevent his hand from shaking. Sammy steadied the mug with his other hand before letting go. Bo could feel the heat of his friend's scrutiny but was unable to meet it. Instead, he said, 'It's not drugs, if that's what you're thinking.'

'I wasn't thinking anything,' Sammy said, levelly.

'What about you?' Bo asked, returning his attention to the window. The sky was filled with a rain that would not come. Bo felt the weight of all that pressure behind his eyes. The city seemed to have been drained of its colour and light, as if someone had stolen through it, painting every building gunmetal grey.

'I've been busy, visiting cemeteries,' Sammy said. 'I feel guilty. My grandparents have been dead twenty years and I've been to their graves, what, maybe half a dozen times? And here I am, in two weeks, taking photographs of headstones, more than double that amount.'

'More disinterred?'

'What do you think?'

'More bite marks?'

'Oh yes. Laurier's doing his nut. Forensics have come back with – get this – *seventeen* different bite patterns.'

'Seventeen? I thought they were pinning their hopes on one mad bastard.'

Sammy was nodding. 'They haven't finished collating evidence yet. Expect that number to be revised. Upwards.'

'What's the rumour? A cult?'

'I don't know. There haven't been any theories. None that I've been in on at least. One thing, though. Funniest thing. Every single set of teeth marks on the bodies produced a completely perfect dental cast.'

'I don't follow.'

'No cavities. No occlusions. Nothing missing. Nothing bent or twisted.'

'Jesus. Who are they? Americans?'

Sammy laughed. 'That, or an army of denture-wearers.'

Bo looked up. Sammy was still studying him, his expression that of someone trying to place a name to a face, or recall a word that has gone missing from the tip of the tongue.

'You deflected yourself, you know that?'

'I know,' Bo said. His tea was too hot, too sweet. He knew he would find fault with anything he tried to put in his belly at the moment. He forced himself to drink it. What could be more normal than drinking tea? 'I'm okay,' he continued. 'I just, well, I'm not with Keiko any more and I'm feeling a little down.'

He detected a shift in the atmosphere. Sammy slumped a little, retreated, as if to say *That's it?* and maybe *He's got me to listen to this sob story?* too. Or maybe even, *I'm not swallowing that, but if you aren't prepared to tell me the truth, why should I care?*

'So what can I do for you? Go home. Eat chocolate. Drink wine. Watch old movies. Buy a box of tissues.'

'I can't go home.'

'Are you in trouble, Bo? It's not just about Keiko, this, is it?'

'I need a place to crash, Sammy. Just for a few days. I need to get my head in the right place.'

'Removing it from your arse, you mean?'

'Maybe. Maybe that's it.'

Framed black-and-white photographs hung on the walls in the spaces the books had yet to invade. Photography – any kind of photography – suddenly seemed a totally pointless activity. It was too stylised, too intrusive, too arbitrary. Sammy Dyer's work – portraits, landscapes, explosive moments from sport – were both naive and hubristic, at the same time the worst shots Bo had ever seen, and yet so brave, so good as to make him feel talentless. The flat closed around him, but he realised that anywhere would feel claustrophobic to him now. It was inside him that the space was filling up most alarmingly. He felt like a sponge that was being squeezed but not releasing its cargo. He felt too small for what was contained within.

'I have to go to Portugal the day after tomorrow,' Sammy said, his voice bereft of its usual bearing. Everything about him was saying no: his posture, his tone, his eyes . . . but the word wouldn't come. Bo felt awful for him, and wished he could help him out, take away that responsibility by walking away, but he was too weak and afraid.

'You can stay until then.'

For a while, as Sammy was turning to leave the room, the collar of his shirt shifted and, as if in slow motion, revealed a patch of his neck shadowed into a vague Y. He saw the minute dimples and diamonds that formed his skin, the silvery hairs, minuscule, lifting or flattening in response to micro-changes in the room's temperature. He saw, in a thrilling, guilty moment, how Sammy Dyer's blood moved through its thin, red prison, coursing in fluid bursts in tandem with the rhythm of his heart. Beyond that, as if his friend had been flayed, he saw the dazzling beauty of his entire circulatory system, as if he had been frozen at the point of some cataclysmic explosion, the capillaries, veins and arteries suspended, a strange coral, a model in a biology lab.

The illusion withdrew. The moment died. Bo found he was holding his breath. He slowly exhaled as Sammy sank from view.

The pangs in his gut had vanished. For a short time, he felt normal, even hungry, again.

The longer he remained in the room, the less claustrophobic it became. He lay on the floor, looking up at the unshaded bulb of the ceiling light, and waited for his body to offer some clue as to what it was becoming. It became easier, now that he was no longer moving – or clenched by panic – to isolate the problem, but he couldn't offer a definitive diagnosis. The overriding feeling was of a tightening in the skin, as if someone standing behind him was taking all of his slack into one giant fist and squeezing. His eyesight also seemed to be affected: colours were improved to the point where his vision was saturated. It was as if the whole world had been trapped on a roll of Fuji Velvia. It was deep and detailed and gorgeous.

If he opened his mouth, his ability to hear increased by such an extent that he could pick out occasional words uttered by two men conversing on the pavement in Eton Avenue, a good hundred metres away. His body screamed with possibilities.

He sat up and almost immediately something bothered him. Nothing in the room had been altered – he had been its sole occupant in the half hour since Sammy left for work – nevertheless, he felt very strongly that something had changed.

Needled by the imprecision of his thoughts, he moved to the other window, which looked down on to England's Lane, and at once saw a woman in the window of one of the flats opposite, staring directly at him. She was naked, immobile, and as soon as she saw she was being watched she beamed at him, a smile so broad he almost felt heat from it, despite the distance between them. He smiled too, uncertainly, and moved away from the window. He wanted something ordinary to come out of the day and surprise him, to reaffirm him and where he was.

A bit heavy on the old numinous, he remembered a teacher at school saying, whenever anybody handed in a story during writing exercises that was even minutely fantastical.

A bit heavy on the old numinous. Too fucking right.

He wanted a little banality to counter all that old numinous.

Bo felt the room changing as the light left it. The air seemed to thicken, to become less ready to leap in and out of his lungs. The books against the wall sucked the darkness into their pages, making them bloat, become more than what they had been. He watched lights emerge from the skin of London as it fell away from him to the south. Menace materialised, became something almost tangible, like the air he was breathing. The threat sat heavily in the room.

Bo sat on the floor, wishing for some company. He needed to talk this all out. He was finding it hard to control the feeling that this person who was a guest of Sammy Dyer was anybody but himself. He was struggling to prevent the visions that kept tripping through his mind, flashes of wet redness, of white teeth, the deep, splitting sounds of bones broken in violence. He was convinced that the sounds were already happening, perhaps even within his own body, and he didn't know how to react, or even if he wanted to.

He was checking himself in mirrors at every opportunity and he looked no different to the Bo Mulvey that had looked back at him at any moment over the past few weeks. There was no obvious deviation, nothing that stuck out like a blister or a pimple or a scar to mark him as separate to others. He felt hunger without being able to open his mouth; his thirst was unquenchable because water only nauseated him. He saw through people as if he were wearing magical eye glasses, the X-ray specs you could buy from old Spider-Man comics along with Sea Monkeys and offers to turn yourself from a seven-stone weakling into some man-mountain. People seemed to shine, to project an aura into the immediate space around them, like the body's electro-magnetic fields trapped in a piece of Kirlian photography. But he found himself questioning these subtle turnings in his body's combination, which suggested that he still retained some say in how things might turn out. He was not too far gone. *Is it thirst if I can't drink? Is it hunger if I can't eat?* Only terrible possibilities remained, but he felt, beyond the panic and the fear, as physically sound as he had since his teenage years. He wondered if, at the end of whatever was happening to him, he would be in danger, or he would prove a danger to others.

Something moved behind the wall. It sounded too big to be a bird, although it skittered as if it were one trapped in a flue. Bo turned his head slowly towards the door. The darkness and his being alone might have alarmed him, if there were any capacity for alarm to begin with. It had been burned away, quickly, perhaps on that visit to the cemetery, perhaps on his waking to a sea of rotten hearts. His ability to be surprised, let alone shocked or scared, had been removed from him like a diseased organ. At the same time, there *was* a state of terror to deal with, a steady, almost steadying pulse of dread that he could do nothing about. It was there and it was either keeping him going or showing him what quality of life he might come to expect if he gave up.

After a while, when the sound had not replicated itself, Bo rose and moved to the wall. There was a door, but it was locked. He put his fingers to the covered join between the door and the jamb, traced it around, feeling for any breeze that might suggest a crack in the paint. He felt the keyhole and the doorknob too. A slight gasp of air came through from the other side. He wondered if Sammy Dyer had a key for the door. If he did that might suggest he had painted the seal. But if he was renting this property, wouldn't he want as much space as he could get? Was he hiding something? It didn't make sense. No, the landlord must have created the divide. Presumably the sealed annex beyond that door was undeveloped and therefore uninhabitable. Or the landlord was using it as storage for his own things.

Bo placed the side of his head against the door and listened for a while. He could not hear the skittering sound any more, but there was something going on in there. A slow, rhythmic tread; a measured breath. He could hear something else, an odd sound, and all he could think of when he heard it was a dry tongue licking an even drier pair of lips.

He stepped back from the door and stared at the keyhole. The dark was so profound now as to render it as something that was waiting to be lost. Staring at it seemed to have this effect: it blurred, it dissolved into the general grain of night. Sammy's room had long vanished; it was as if Bo were standing in a void, somehow being prevented from falling away to eternity by dint of the magnetism attaching his gaze to this tiny metal tunnel of tumblers.

He quickly switched on the light and ducked to the keyhole. He had hardly pressed his eye against it before another swam out of that room's darkness to meet his, so swiftly as to suggest there was a mirror placed flush against the lock. But if that were so, it would mean that Bo's eye was somehow too small for the eye socket that cradled it, for there was a large black gap all around this, and a sense of strain, of trying to keep the eye where it was, and that if the strain were given up, the eye would fall in, or tip out altogether.

He moved away from the door, the stillness in the flat seeming to echo a new quietness at the centre of his chest. Death might only be a step away, something that waited on the other side of a threshold. Its proximity shocked him into greyness; he felt it creep into his lips, his hair. A look in a mirror would show a whitened, famished figure, a creature that existed at the margins of things, peeking into windows showing a warmth and humanity that it struggled to remember. He only realised he was still moving when he backed into Sammy Dyer's futon mattress and stumbled over. He sat there waiting for impossibilities. He knew the door could not be opened, but he was tensed for its swing anyway. He wanted to call to that mystery inhabitant but keeping quiet helped him in some way to cling to the possibility that what he had seen was an illusion; the room was empty, he was not going mad. But he had glimpsed what it was he might become. Terrified, too scared even to reach out and switch on a lamp, he sat on the mattress and watched the door. There were no other sounds from behind it, and by the time Sammy entered the room, he was asleep.

He woke up to red. A tea light burned low in a scarlet container, its shiver magnified across the whole room. Sammy was sleeping beside him in a paint-stained Nike T-shirt riddled with holes, and a pair of knee-length jogging shorts. A little cairn of spit bubbled up between his lips. Bo fought the urge to wipe it away. He inched his way upright until he was sitting with his back against the wall, facing the room. He wanted to turn on the TV or the radio, anything to scour his ears of Sammy's wet breathing, or the unstable memory of something dry and thin moving too rapidly in the small room next to this.

He should get dressed, get going. Coming here had been a mistake. He had hoped that in Sammy, his colleague, his drinking buddy, he might find someone who could also be a confidant. But Sammy was not right for this; nobody was. He was in up to his neck and he was alone. If he didn't grasp what was happening, how was he to explain it to someone on the outside?

He was decided and determined, about to tease back the sheet and rise, when the tea light died. He smelled its acrid last breath at the same time that the sealed door cracked and juddered open. Bo pissed his pants. His eyes were so wide, sucking at the paucity of light in the room, that he thought he might tear them. Fear seemed too puny a word for his condition.

Now he saw the shape of a hand reach around the edge of the door, its fingers shockingly long. Each of them came to rest against the wood, nails tapping lightly as though it were still incarcerated, knocking politely to be let out. Its smell reached Bo before anything else did: old things left undisturbed for too long; wet rags that had not been allowed to dry properly, desiccated newspapers, woodworm and rust. It shifted like someone whose joints had recently been operated upon, or someone coming back from a traumatic accident, at the start of a physiotherapy programme. Bo resisted the insane drive to offer assistance. He heard a terrible, dry clicking sound and, though he didn't want to know what was producing it, found his mind throwing up any number of horrid possibilities. What disturbed him was the knowledge that the truth would be far worse.

Bo stood up and felt the coldness of the room focus itself on the hot patch of dampness settling against both thighs. He couldn't leave Sammy here. He nudged him with his foot but his friend merely burbled some rebuke and rolled on to his side. The figure stopped and shifted its head, like a dog that has heard a noise it finds interesting.

It came forwards, a shadow without a host.

'Don't,' Bo begged it, unable to shape the rest of the sentence, unable to put into words an act that was unspeakable.

It was trying to say something. Bo could just make out the tortured shift of a mouth that was little more than a painful dark hole. As it reached the end of the bed, it folded, as if exhausted, or let down by its weak limbs. It dropped to its knees and breathed hard, the dry, clicking sound coming rhythmically, like some weird, skeletal heart.

Bo dithered, the fear puddling out of him as it appeared the other had no intention of violence. He too dropped and they regarded each other like boxers with no fight left. Bo inched nearer and was able to pick out individual features. This was a very, very old man. He seemed to wear a shroud, but closer scrutiny proved it to be a rotting grey shirt and long pants made of linen, with a cloth stirrup under each foot. His hair was scraped back from his forehead and plastered to his scalp with oil or sweat or grease. His strange, detached eyes floated in their orbits, perpetually affronted, or scared. The flesh of his face had pulled away from his chin, nose and forehead, making those central dividing characteristics seem more prominent than they might have been. The face was like a blade, or a shark's fin. The remaining teeth in his mouth were pebbles of dark glass set in a concrete pediment. As his face became discernible, so Bo's must have become to him. A smile cracked into it like a collapse in unstable land as a type of recognition dawned. Blood escaped from tensions apparently unknown for many years.

'Who are you?' Bo asked, and the voice was someone else's, someone detached by fright and shock and exhaustion.

'My name is Charles Bolton,' the man breathed, a sound spoiled by that persistent click, a sound like words being punched out of a dulled typewriter.

Bo didn't know what else to ask. The situation perplexed him. This was Sammy's flat. This ought to be his conversation, his little pile of dust to sweep up and hide under the rug. He was about to suggest calling for an ambulance when Bolton began singing, huskily, tunelessly, as though through a mouth filled with hammers falling on dry chambers in a gun too old to use.

You are my sunshine, my only sunshine.
You make me happy, when clouds are grey . . .

'What?' Bo asked, hoping the desperation in his voice might force a resolution. '*What?*'

Bolton pressed a finger to his lips and indicated Sammy Dyer's slumbering body.

Bo's shoulders slumped. He felt close to tears. He felt like the character in that old episode of *The Twilight Zone* who wakes one day to find everyone speaking English differently, every word he thought he knew suddenly meaning something else.

'I was born here,' Bolton said. 'I lived here all my life.'

Bo could only sit and shake his head, waiting for whatever was to happen to play itself out.

'I was warehoused by the eaters, the rogues you know, there are always a few running around, no matter that most were chased away during the fire. They thought I was promising nourishment. I was for nectaring. Felt proud, I did. They kissed me all over, filled me up, left me sleepy. I would have liked to say night to my Kate, but what's the point of wishing now that time's knocked on, hey?'

A bit heavy on the old numinous. Bo could barely stand the stench of the man's breath, but he found himself leaning closer to him, trying to unpick the knots from his confusing yarn.

'And here we are,' Bolton said. 'Thank you, I say. Thank you for waking me up. Thank you for letting me go.' He smiled again, and it was horrible. *Click-click-click.* Bo was sure the man's face would come sliding off him if he kept taxing it like that. Behind him he could hear Sammy stirring. Bo no longer wanted him awake to see any of this, despite it being his little pile of dust. He didn't think there were any rugs big enough to put this under and forget.

'Who are you?' Bo asked again, but really he wanted to ask *why are you*? The man was regarding him with an expression like love with those loose, liquid eyes. Behind that was yet another question, too entwined with his psychosis for him to contemplate, but Bolton was not too ravaged to pick up on it.

'Who are *you*?' Bolton said gently. 'Who are *you*? That's what you're really after. And all I can say to you is that we don't care. You are the light through the window. You are the alarum.'

'The light? The alarum?'

'I would have liked to say night to my Kate. I would have liked to see the sea.'

His eyes were fogging. The click in his throat was becoming more pronounced.

'Would you like some water?' Bo asked.

Sammy Dyer sat up behind him and said, 'Who the fuck is *that*?'

Things began to slip away from Bo, then. There was enough ambient light in the room to see that Bolton was dying, or dead already. Sammy flipped a light switch and suddenly Bo wished he had not been leaning in so closely to their uninvited guest. As Bo took in the heavily runnelled skin, the bones pushing eagerly through the denuded flesh of his arms like black branches covered with frost, he wondered who, actually, was the guest. How long had this man been lying in state in the sealed room waiting for his *alarum*? Ten years? Twenty? By the state of him, Bo would not have been surprised to find it had been a century or two. Maybe even longer. It was warm in the room, but Bo felt his scrotum convulse as Bolton began to squirm on the floor. The clicks were louder now.

'He's dead?' Sammy asked. His face was a shock of shadows and lines. 'He's still fucking breathing? Who is he? What are you fucking playing at, Bo?'

Charles Bolton began to unravel.

Sammy had seen too much by the time he tried to stumble out of bed and get away. His foot caught in the sheets, spilling him heavily into the corner of the surround that housed the stairwell. A loud smack managed to prise Bo's attention from Bolton's corpse. He saw Sammy drowsily turn on to his back and blink up at the light while blood pumped from a wound just above his left eye.

'Shit,' Bo said. He went to his friend and wrapped him in the blanket from the bed. There were noises from deeper within the flat. He heard a door open and someone call, 'Sammy?'

Shit. Shit.

'It's all right,' he called down. 'Just dropped a stack of books. Sorry.'

By the way, if I were you, I'd jump out of any fucking window that's available.

Some of the larvae trickling from Bolton's seams were still blind, but others could see, and turned their eyes on Bo, as if for direction. He had to struggle against the urgent desire to scream the place down. Human eyes. They had human fucking eyes.

He raised his foot in order to trample them as they spewed on to Sammy's carpet. There were so many now that it was hard to discern Bolton's body beneath them. Many of them were trying desperately to return to this convenient source of food but the numbers were so great that there wasn't enough space for all of them to gain purchase.

Bo could not bring himself to kill them. Something was stopping him.

Sammy's groans became less of a distraction. He would live. For now he had to do something about this flood of grubs.

He got down on his hands and knees and tore open Charles Bolton's garments. With his hands he scooped up as many of the infants as he could and trickled them into the creases of the dead man's body that were still soft, or moist. He heard a voice and turned to look, but Sammy was in some kind of catatonia, staring down at the patterns in his rug while his forehead swelled and darkened.

A little while later Bo became aware that it was his own voice, cooing over the feeding brood, gently inciting them to tuck in, to enjoy, to eat it all up.

'And then you'll grow big and strong.'

11. SEEK

A few hours before dawn.

A light frost on the pavements, knubbly slush on the roads where the gritters had already travelled. Nobody but fools and the determined out on the streets at this hour. Labourers on their way to building sites, security guards clocking on or clocking off a shift. And Bo, on the Ninja, prowling down New Oxford Street, searching for Rohan Vero, the man who had promised he was going to lose himself as soon as he could.

Spot the fool.

But he had no other choice to make. Nowhere else to go. Getting out of London wasn't an option, not when there were changes going on in his body that he needed to check if he were to have any hope of leading a normal life again.

The Princess Louise was an object lesson in closed. Desperation forced his hand; he rapped hard on the windows with his keys. Nobody came to help him, not even a face at an upstairs window telling him to fuck off. He briefly considered breaking in, but for what purpose? Rohan Vero was patently not here, enjoying a lock-in at 6 a.m.

He stood in the road not knowing what to do. He'd burned some bridges last night. Work and home were off limits; Keiko could find him there. He didn't want her help. He didn't want her near him. Not when he could wink out of consciousness like that, and do God knows what without even realising it.

Burned bridges. Opened doors. Entered rooms. A house whose address he did not know, a place where he never wanted to be.

Keiko was at the end of a line, worried for him, ready to receive him. All he had to do was call her, say sorry, allow her to draw him near, hold her until time stopped.

He wiped his lips with the back of his hand and hugged himself in the morning chill. Sammy Dyer sat on the back of the Ninja like a crash test dummy in a helmet waiting for another pummelling. More people coming outside now. Light creeping into the deep blue of a night Bo wanted rid of. He tried to persuade himself that the pedestrians walking past him were staring at him because he was static, something Londoners were not prone to be. But there was something in their scrutiny of him that wormed inside him and fed the slow panic he had been nurturing since the night he had met that bastard, Vero. He felt like some sort of totem, something that was being regarded as much for its curiosity value as its potential as a giver of knowledge, reassurance, understanding. He sensed heads turning wherever he walked, wherever he drove. His rear-view mirrors were awash with small, pale ovals following his progress. He swerved and sprinted to St Bart's. He dropped Sammy off outside the entrance to Accident and Emergency. He cared enough to do that, but not to take him inside. He didn't like enclosed places much these days.

'I have to be alone,' he told Sammy. 'I have to do this on my own. It's safer for you this way. I can't, I will not endanger you.'

There was nowhere to go. He just had to keep moving. He pushed the bike up to sixty along Gray's Inn Road, trying to blur the faces as they leered after him and generate some cold air to slap him awake. On Bernard Street, opposite the entrance to the Brunswick Centre, he found an old second-hand bookshop that had been boarded up. The state of the wood that shuttered the windows suggested that it had been closed for a long time. Once-white lettering, SIMON BLONDELL: BOOKSELLER, was fading into the awning above the shop as a cadaverous grey. The shop was little more than a tattered façade of ripped green canvas and buckled, rusting metalwork. On the doorstep, a kind of offering almost: a dead rat was lying on its back, its stomach torn apart like an envelope from a new lover. It was empty, gaping. Neatly eaten. Bo stared at it for a long time.

He cruised around to the alleyway behind the main road and stopped by the back gate. It was padlocked; razorwire made an ugly spiral across the coping stones that topped the wall. He leaned the bike against the gate and leaped up on to the saddle. The back yard was a mass of collapsed cardboard boxes, receipt rolls, and bloated paperbacks. Spare shelving formed a warped lean-to against the back door, perhaps serving as a last-gasp attempt to keep people out. Bo hopped down and examined the padlock. It was strong but the gate it was protecting was not. A few stiff kicks took it off its hinges.

He wheeled the Ninja in and locked it, then repositioned the gate as best he could, using the shelves to wedge it in the frame. The shop's back door was open. Inside, a narrow corridor floored with black-and-white diagonal tiling led through a flimsy plastic curtain to the front of the shop. It was dark and stale here, with notes of damp and rot. Light through cracks in the window boards picked out four rows of bookshelves and a chair, so that punters could sit and flick through potential purchases. It spooked him a bit, that empty chair, with its sunken faux-leather seat and high back, so he turned it around to face the wall. He tried the light switch and was mildly amazed to find that it worked, although the forty-watt bulb served only to somehow make the room seem even gloomier.

The cream paint on the walls was blistering. Spiders had created weird shelving of their own in the high corners where redundant webs were stacked, made visible with dust. He sat down on a table that contained a pale square to indicate where the cash register had once stood. On the wall behind him were fliers for book fairs, literary festivals, and readings, the most recent being five years in the past. Unopened post was still being forced through the letterbox: a tongue that reached almost to the counter. Circulars and bills made a mosaic of white and beige on the floor. What was that all about? Stupidity or dedication on the part of the postal service? That he could entertain a silly thought like this heartened him; he had not fooled around with his imagination for too long. He suddenly felt safe, anonymous again, if not entirely at home. He decided to get to know his new space. There was a staircase leading up to two small bedrooms, a kitchenette and a bathroom. There was a free-standing gas cooker but the good fortune with the electricity had not stretched to butane. On the wall in the bathroom he found a montage of postcards from Lanzarote, all finished with 1970s fonts and poor photographs of camels, badly designed hotels with lethal swimming pools and black, volcanic beaches. The bedrooms were empty.

Back down in the shop he browsed the shelves, astonished that none of the stock had been removed when the shop closed down. There must have been a couple of thousand pounds' worth of paperbacks here. He found tight, unmarked copies of early JG Ballard novels, John Wyndham Penguins, Puffins he remembered from his childhood: Leon Garfield, Iain Serraillier, David Line; a first paperback printing of Ian Fleming's second Bond outing, *Live and Let Die*, a proof of Alex Garland's *The Beach*. He only realised that a big chunk of time had passed when he began to feel faint from hunger. He had been owling the spines for three hours.

He went out on the bike to buy bread, milk, bacon and eggs, a Baby Belling from a branch of Robert Dyas, and a sleeping bag from the outdoor pursuits shop a few doors down. On the way back to Bernard Street, a woman threw herself in front of him as he changed up to third gear. He braked hard and swung the bike to his left, ramping it on to the pavement for a few seconds before dragging it back on to the road and coming to a halt. She was on the ground, looking after him with a mix of desire, hatred and fear on her face. In her belt a knife with a long thin blade was stowed. She peeled her lips back and, Jesus Christ, she *growled* at him.

He stalled the bike in his haste to be away and she was almost upon him at the moment the engine fired and he squealed up Southampton Row, car horns blaring as he and the woman spilled out in front of the usual parade of aggressive London drivers.

Adrenaline and the bike's spiked accelerator took him too quickly into the corner of Guilford Street and he almost drove into the side of a Royal Mail van. He forced himself to stop and check his breathing. Sweat created a thin scarf around his neck, despite the bitter cold. He retched, imagining himself newly dug from a grave topped with fresh black soil, his flesh barely cold. Mouths all over him . . .

Just a London nut. Just a mad woman. Wrong place, wrong time.

But he was offering these words as a balm too often for them to be of comfort any more.

'Are you all right, mate?' A face swinging out of the sky, concern written all over it. But it was the concern of a man trying too hard. An actor. A bad actor. Someone who has been reading *Expressions for Beginners*.

'I'm fine,' Bo said, falteringly.

'You don't look fine,' the man said. His skin was like something pressed from a plastic mould. His nostrils seemed too symmetrical. They looked *painted* on to his face.

'You've seen worse, I'm sure,' Bo said, readjusting his position on the bike, feeling panic rise again.

'I can help you,' the man said. 'We can all help you. You just have to accept what's happening. Sooner or later, you'll have no choice.'

Bo kicked down hard on the starter and shoved the man away with the heel of his hand. The man stepped back, smiling, spreading his hands. He looked like an unbearably smug clergyman. His eyes were like peeled grapes. His mouth was an oscillator awaiting a signal. He said something else. Bo throttled up and stuck a hand to his ear, shook his head. Another serene smile. The man knew he had been heard.

Don't fight it.

Yeah, right, Bo thought. *Fucking watch me. All the way. All the fucking way.*

... *body of Gillian Kynaston was discovered yesterday lunchtime near a track at Clowbridge Reservoir, just south of Burnley, Lancashire, by members of a local rambling association. A police spokesman said they were keen to speak to any members of the public who might have seen Ms Kynaston in the twenty-four hours before she was found. The police were also eager to quash rumours that the murder of Ms Kynaston was in any way connected to that of Jemima Cartledge, a teenager who died almost thirty years ago to the day. That murder was the last in a string of attacks nationwide, committed by one man, according to experts, who was never apprehended and was assumed to have died some time in the late 1970s. New techniques in forensic science, notably DNA testing, have resulted in a number of possible suspects being tested posthumously, all with negative results, leading some to believe that the killer went into hiding for some reason and is still at large. The death of Ms Kynaston will only help those rumours to pick up steam, despite New Scotland Yard's insistence that, although they consider the file on The Picnic Man to still be open, they judge Ms Kynaston's death to be a completely separate incident.*

Other headlines today. The spate of graverobbing across London continues with another two bodies being unearthed last night at a cemetery in Stockwell despite a pledge by the Police Commissioner to safeguard the capital's graveyards and bring the perpetrators into custody . . .

12. SHOCK

Manser felt alternately light and heavy, as if one moment he had taken a whiff of oxygen, or done some exercise and then overeaten, or become bogged down with fever or a messy cold. He could hear Jez Knowlden's voice, but it was as if it were coming to him from the end of a very bad telephone line, or a dream. His head was thick with aches or hangovers, something that made everything slow motion, tortured. He liked Knowlden's voice; it was strong without being authoritative. He knew his place. He knew the limits of his own abilities. Knowlden always listened. His acknowledgment, when they were driving together, came in a smooth burst of acceleration, a purpose unveiled. It came in the focus he gave the damp road and the way he flexed his shoulders or tightened his grip on the steering wheel. He was gearing up. Manser felt utterly confident with Knowlden alongside him. Manser would take a tilt at Satan if Knowlden was there to back him up.

He felt a little shimmer of excitement in his gut, childish stuff, the kind of butterflies you got when you were in the alleyway with the cute girl from school, thirteen, fourteen maybe, psyching yourself for that first kiss. He always got that when there was the smell of blood in the air. He imagined Claire prepped and reduced within twelve hours, arcing her back for him on a wet leather couch, mewling around a gag made from his jockstrap and a metre of duck tape.

Something wrong. A smell of bonfires. A smell of death.

First time he saw her, when was that? Five years ago, lounging back against the bus shelter waiting for her folks, library was it? High summer. One of those evenings that contains so much light you wonder how it could ever get dark. Light so real, so close, you might grab a handful out of the air, keep it in your pocket for a special moment. Romantic evening. Love at first sight. God but she was hot. Twelve years old? Thirteen? Must be. What was she wearing? Like you have to try to remember. It's there in your mind like an inoperable tumour. A black, tight T-shirt. Naughty, naughty logo: *You have to be at least eight inches to ride this.* How did she slip that one past her cold, ramrod mother, and that streak of piss she called Dad? Maybe they didn't even get it. Maybe they were too whacked out on diazepam or Prozac, shitting it over all those red figures in their accounts to be able to register that they had a kid.

Blue jeans with spangly hems, pink lining poking free of the pockets, a Barbie belt. Plenty of midriff, taut, with that gorgeous little vertical shadow right down the centre of her tummy, the kind of thing you usually only find on girls who worked out. Scruffy, unlaced Adidas Kick shoes. White, hooded cardigan with drawstrings round the neck she liked to chew on. She was standing, irritable, clumsy, on the shadow-line, ready to take the plunge into womanhood. She was nearly there. Thirteen? Fuck. Get those pretty little teeth. Tiny, square, even. Pink gums, she shows a lot of gum when she smiles. Strawberry lip gloss. Long, naturally curly blonde hair tied off with red elastic bands cadged from the postman. What does it smell of, that hair? Maddening, that's what. Apples. Peaches. Thirteen? Fucking hell. Thirteen-year-olds like that. When did that happen?

In the leather seat in the back of the Audi, Manser closed his eyes and imagined his hands winding through that hair, plunging his face into its thickness. Her blood so young, so fresh, it would fizz as it fled her.

He bit down suddenly on his cheek when Salavaria shivered into his thoughts. His own blood flooded across his tongue. He wouldn't be able to keep his tongue away from that bite now, a bit like his thoughts and Salavaria. He always crept back. His master, his ambition. He was treading on Manser's toes now, with Claire, but what could he do? He was to Salavaria what Knowlden was to Manser. You didn't answer back. You didn't create ripples. You swallowed and nodded and said yes sir, three bags full sir, what else can I do for you today?

Something wrong though. Something out of whack.

What a pain. What a setback. She was his. She ought to be his. Could still be his. Salavaria didn't need to know. Deliver her alive. Get Loshy to stitch her up properly, do a good job. He could wear a surgical mask and wash his hands, for a change.

This year's number three had died badly. It had been a pity. He liked that one, but what do you do? You can't keep the fuckers. What are they, pets? You have to feed them, clean them, wipe their arses. He was no nurse. But Claire could be different. He could go the distance with that one. The sutures on her legs might heal in such a way as to chafe his thigh as he thrust into her. That would be a plus. Any infection and he could pour antibiotics down her throat. Loshy would see him right. They would talk about the best way to prevent gangrene. He knew what Losh's response would be: *let it heal, don't mess about with it.* But he liked his meat so very rare when he was fucking it. He liked to see a little blood. Acceptable risk. There was such a thing as acceptable risk. Salavaria would understand. I'm a weak man. I have my fetish, just like the next guy. I can't work at a hundred per cent if I'm not happy, if I don't fill my boots, wet my beak once in a while.

What did Salavaria want? Did he want The Ton? Did he want MCM? Or did he prefer someone who wasn't firing on all cylinders? This was big school. He needed top men working at full capacity. If he fucks with me, I'll fuck with him. I don't want to, but that's how it pans out. Reciprocity, sir, there's the key. Let's get some backscratching going, Master. Co-operation. Synergy. A melding of minds. Mutual masturbation. Whatever the fuck.

Something wrong. Gyorsi. What happened? What happened between me and you? Old friend. Something wrong. Something out of whack. Something burning. Something dead.

13. SAFE HARBOUR

At lunch time, Ray would leave her in charge of things and have a pint of Broadside and something to eat at the Lord Nelson. Although she had warmed to him quickly, Sarah was glad to have these few hours to herself. Claire seemed happy to sit in the deep leather armchair in the office, warming herself by the three-bar electric fire, drinking raspberry leaf tea, flicking through ancient copies of *Chat* and *Take a Break*. She found them hilarious. It cheered Sarah almost to tears to hear her daughter in another room chortling over the knitting patterns, or the letters pages *(Top Tip: Clean dusty Venetian blinds with L-shaped pieces of crusty bread)*, or the true-life stories *(Love Me, Love My Piles)*.

The work itself was really anything but. All she had to do was make sure no kids came in to shoplift the comics. Every now and then there would be a couple, obviously tourists, come in for a mooch of the paperbacks and the Wade Whimsies. They'd shell out twenty pence for a William Trevor or a John Braine or a Len Deighton, giggle over the handwritten lines on the old postcards, and that would be it.

For the first time in days she had felt able to relax. The jolt at seeing the police officer checking her car had receded. There had been no enquiries made at the hotel, no further nosing around the Alfa Romeo. Just a spot check. These things happened, she supposed. There had been no shadowy surveillance from the window opposite hers, unless you counted an old woman with a blue rinse leafing through magazines over endless cups of tea and peering into the street. It was time to kick back, take stock. She had slipped Manser. And that meant she could work on Claire, start to try to bring her back from the brink.

The jingle of the small bell at the door. Another customer. Or just someone browsing, or coming in from the cold for a while.

The man came into view through the hillocks of furniture, the tall bookcases groaning with creased, stained, water-bloated copies of Barbara Taylor Bradford, James A Michener, and Harold Robbins. She thought, immediately, *police*. Her breath shortened; a band tightened around her ribs. The ego boost she'd given herself earlier dissipated like mist beneath a noon sun.

Everything about him screamed of office, of telephones, of too much beer and pies. He wore a faded grey raincoat that looked like an extension of his skin: his face carried the pallor associated with pub snugs and fluorescent lighting. There was too much tea inside him, too many bacon sandwiches. She knew he hid a bottle of cheap-blend whiskey in his desk. She wouldn't be surprised to know that he was married but kept a mistress. His wife and his bit on the side both took turns in ironing his Y-fronts. His shared secretary at the station reminded him whose birthday was when.

Despite her freshly ignited panic, she couldn't help but laugh. She tried her best to disguise it by coughing, covering her face with a used tissue stowed up one arm of her cardigan. The man looked her way. Thinning hair, moustache, plain blue tie. All he had to do was bend himself at the knees, put his arms behind his back and say: *Hello, hello, hello.*

'Can I help you?' she asked, to deflect his scrutiny.

'Much obliged, but no,' he said, staring levelly at her. 'I'm just browsing.'

Much obliged? He didn't blink. He said *browsing*. Nobody who walked into a junk shop said they were *browsing*, even if that was exactly what they were doing.

'No problem,' she said, calmly, as he moved along the tables that contained old plates crammed with coins that could no longer be offered as legal tender; cracked porcelain drawer knobs; used stamps still framed in hinges that had lost their adhesive; heavy-metal pins and badges from the 1970s: Judas Priest, Rush, Black Sabbath.

The worst he could do was arrest her, but for what? Then maybe he wasn't police, or rather, he was ex-police. Which meant?

Manser's stink was all over him.

Sarah busied herself with the ledger that Ray kept up to date, a recording of everything that came in or went out of the shop, how much was paid, how much was received. She added up rows of figures that didn't need totalling, numbered blank pages deeper into the ledger with a black Biro. Now and again she would glance up at the man in the grey raincoat as he browsed, and failed to hide his interest in Sarah as she worked behind the counter.

His slapdash approach reached its nadir as he pretended to peruse a copy of *National Geographic* magazine, which he help upside down in his hands. Sarah might have laughed at his ineptitude had his presence not meant that she and Claire were looking at yet another upheaval. How could she have even entertained the fancy of escaping Manser's clutches? His stain was on everything. Of course he was going to have bitches who wore stripes accepting his dirty money. How could she have believed that he wouldn't, or that his sphere of influence would somehow be weaker out here on England's east coast? It was as if the UK's profile were Manser's profile. His aggressive head was Scotland's most northerly part, bent over, inspecting his Welsh navel while his Cornwall leg stretched out and his Kentish arse shat into the English Channel.

The man with the inverted copy of *National Geographic* looked up sharply when Sarah's harsh bleats of laughter echoed around the junk shop's high ceiling.

'This job does strange things to you,' he said.

What, yours or mine? she suddenly felt like asking. She didn't like the man's skin. It was too pink, and bumpy, like an orange. He had a bad scar on his jawline, livid and white, perhaps a shaving accident. She guessed with skin so uneven he sustained a lot of nicks and slashes. She also didn't like the set square parting in his hair, which was too ginger to be described as red, or strawberry blond, which was, she ventured, how he liked to see it. His eyes were too small and close-set. His teeth were uneven. His shirt had not been ironed, or ironed too well . . .

'Yes,' she said at last. 'I spend far too much time staring at old curiosities.' She wanted to laugh again. The urge was in her like that of wanting to pee.

He seemed discomfited by her apparent slur, but was either too polite or too stupid to challenge her on it. He put down the magazine he had been reading, and Sarah noticed with a pang of regret that he had been studying one of the stapled supplements, a map or graph of some kind, and that it had been inserted the wrong way up.

'What do you do for a living?' she asked, then chided herself for being so upfront. What was he going to say: *My name's DCI Doe. Would you come with me to the station, please, madam?*

He seemed mildly astonished by the question. 'I'm an insurance salesman.'

Oh yeah, sure you are.

'Is there anything I can help you with?'

'Possibly, Miss –'

But she wasn't falling for that. She simply arched her eyebrows.

'I'm interested in old watches. I collect them. Do you have –'

'We've not got any watches at the moment. You could try the antique shop, just up the lane.'

'How about clocks?'

'Not really. The stuff we stock is a little further down the antique food chain.'

'If I could leave you my card ... you could contact me if something horological came in.'

Horological. Very good. Boning up on his subject back at the station before he came over ...

She took the proffered white rectangle and gave it a quick glance: *Mick Goodhart, Salesman.*

'Could I have your name? Just as a point of contact?'

Point of contact ... police if ever she heard it.

'Ray Carver owns the shop. You'd be best speaking to him.'

'And you are?' He wouldn't give up. He was staring at her, unblinking. To evade him again was to incriminate herself.

'Martha Peake,' she said, removing the Patrick McGrath novel of the same name from the desktop. She gave him a piece of paper with the junk-shop name badly photocopied across the top and its contact details.

He made a play of inspecting an opened tin filled with brooches, but she could tell he wasn't really looking at them, and then he quietly turned away and walked out of the shop. She followed him to the door, fully expecting to see him climb into an unmarked squad car and radio in to HQ, but he was standing by the window of the furniture shop, staring at a dining table. She watched him pull a hand from his pocket and assess his loose change, then he crossed the main road and entered the fish and chip restaurant.

She wiped her hands against her blouse, as if ridding herself of his oleaginous residue; she could still smell him, a mix of stale tobacco and coffee, and something else, something acrid: shoe polish, maybe. Brasso. Wrinkling her nose, she went back to the counter.

Claire was no longer reading. She was asleep, her face laced with weak, wintry sunlight. Something chased her in her dreams; she was restive, agonised. She was mouthing words that Sarah had to stoop to get any hope of understanding. Millimetres from her daughter's face, she thought they might have been *Come to me.*

A yellow comma of slime was curled across her top lip. Sarah dabbed it away with her finger, wondering if Claire might have sneezed in her sleep. When she saw the broken spider in her left hand, moist, too moist to be alive, missing five of its legs and most of its abdomen, she recoiled.

It's okay, she thought, *it's okay to eat insects in your sleep* ... *most of us do it without knowing.*

The way she was holding it, though, like some little fondant fancy. Like some ... some fucking *praline.*

'Claire? Claire, darling?'

She stirred a little, enough to lift her hand with the remainder of her snack and try to push it between her teeth. Sarah gave a strangled sob and slapped the spider from her fingers. Her daughter came up out of sleep fast, her eyes bloodshot, a snarl wadded in a throat that sounded too wet, too animal. Her teeth were shocking. White. Deep. Like a shark's. Sarah clattered backwards, knocking over a chair and skinning her back on the hinged edge of the counter.

Claire's aggression faded as quickly as it had risen; she slumped again, sucking her fingertips, making babyish lalling noises. A few moments more and it was as if Sarah were seeing her asleep for the first time. She seemed peaceful, content. Sarah shakily got to her feet and drew the blinds. The sudden darkness made her feel giddy, spangled with fear. She retreated into the cold space of the junk shop and busied herself with tidying the magazines the so-called Mick Goodhart had disturbed. She did not go back to check on her daughter. She waited for her to wake naturally. When she heard her stirring, a little less than half an hour later, it was all she could do to stop herself from running out of the junk shop and away down the high street.

My baby. My baby. Where are you? Where did you go?

Later. Had she slept? She must have done; the darkness was somehow less dense, less invasive. Nevertheless, she did not feel refreshed. Claire's hand was no longer within her own. She reached out but the duvet had been thrown off. The dimpled area where Claire had been was now cold.

Sarah switched on the bedside light and sat up, blinking, a fist tightening inside her chest. Sometimes Claire preferred to spend the night by the window, staring out at the dark. Frequently she did this while nude, no matter how cold, her skin rising off her in a pimpled mass. But she was not sitting by the window now. The door was ajar. It was just shy of 5 a.m. At least, Sarah saw as she hurried to get dressed, her daughter had taken her clothes with her.

She closed the door behind her and put her hands to her face. Stupid. Stupid bitch. Who was that aimed at? Her. Her daughter. Both. It didn't matter. Just get on and find her.

The door across from hers opened. It was Nick, the barman. He was in a pair of shorts. Soft, trancey music followed him out on to the landing.

'You doing a runner without paying?' he asked.

'It's my daughter. She's gone.'

He held up one finger, his face suddenly serious. He ducked back into his room and she was suddenly convinced he would return with Claire, freshly deflowered as some kind of rebuke for Sarah's lack of interest in him.

He returned in seconds, wearing boots, jeans and a hooded top. He handed her a sweater. 'It's cold outside,' he said. He carried a heavy black torch with a long handle. Sarah hadn't considered that her daughter might have gone out. She thought she would be in the lounge, or sitting at the bar, but a cursory check suggested Nick was right. The wind bit her as they stepped into the street. A brindle cat moved rapidly along the row of shops opposite, belly low to the ground. There was nothing else.

The sky was tinged with green where dawn touched it but it was still too dark to see properly, especially away from the streetlamps.

'Are there any cliffs?' she asked in a small voice, seeing the worst, as she could never help but do.

'Not near here,' he said. 'Further, much further up the coast. Don't worry.'

It seemed too quiet to start calling Claire's name, but she chastised herself for being so stupid. She cried out for her as loudly as she could and was bolstered by Nick echoing her call.

She didn't know where to start. She looked to Nick for leadership and he was moving off to the left, in the direction of the sea. She followed, guessing it was the best place to begin. If she had been a wounded teenager, she'd prefer the mystery and sympathy of all that black water, although she felt bad about reducing Claire's problems to some hormonal sulk. The street forked, becoming narrower. A bookshop, a tweedy clothes shop, a fishmonger's, a charity shop, all reflected her image as they moved towards the beach. She hated the reluctant stoop of her shoulders, as if already weighed down with the awful truth of her daughter's death. Or even worse, the unforgivable wish that she was gone, because life would be so much easier.

A pub on the left, the Lord Nelson, was the last building before the world dropped away to nothing. Although she couldn't see the sea, she knew it was there; it sucked what light there was out of the sky, creating a dark band, like a huge no entry sign. She called for Claire again and Nick reached out, held her arm.

'Are you all right?' he asked. 'I mean, stupid question, I know, but . . . do you want to wait here?'

'No,' she said, and shrugged herself free, pushing past him, down the steps to the shingle.

'Claire!' The wind made a mouse of her voice. Minute, pale tiles of light showed her where the rebuilt pier reached away from the land. Behind her, strange smudges of orange hopscotched away, as far as she could see. She turned to Nick, his torch beam picking holes in the darkness.

'Night-fishing,' he said, when she asked him what it was. 'We can talk to them if you like.'

Her exhaustion and fear tossed up awful images, her brain would not stop with its terrible games. She saw herself pulling back the flaps of one of the fishermen's tents to find someone baiting a hook with slivers from her daughter's face. Downwind from Nick she called for Claire again and let the name turn into a howl of pain. She screamed it all out until she felt dizzy, sick, better. She was turning to follow Nick back towards the tents when she saw a flicker of white.

At first she thought it was litter, a page from a newspaper or a white carrier bag caught in the stones. But its movement was too controlled, she believed. She approached cautiously.

'Claire?' she called, but again the wind nipped in and shredded her voice. She turned away from the force of it and her hair bracketed her face; sensation came back to her skin. She waved to Nick, shouted his name, and the beam of his torch swung her way, picking a route through the shingle towards her. She turned again into the teeth of the weather and stopped walking. She desperately wanted to establish whether the restless shape was her daughter but the persistent play of shadows bothered her. It was like looking at an omen, of something due. Sarah didn't want to be confronted with something she didn't understand. She was worried that what was up ahead might be nothing more than the denigration of her own mind. Nick could confirm or deny that for her. Unless he too was an invention. She felt like laughing. At any moment, all of this – the beach, the sea, the village – would unravel, revealing her to be sitting in a chair wearing restraints, grinning through a haze of tranquillisers.

Nick arrived by her side, his breath steaming out of him. He smelled good, of clean sweat and too much wine. She liked the gently hollowed area beneath his cheekbones, the soft, boyish sweep of his jawbone, the cheerful curve of his chin. Bed hair that no amount of brushing could tame. She felt suddenly attracted to him, and simultaneously appalled that she should allow her carnality any headway when her daughter might be in jeopardy.

Nick was staring into the same anarchic spot on the beach as she, which was, in one way, a good sign, but only served to heighten her anxiety about Claire. She felt herself moving forward, impelled by a decision she had apparently come to in some ancient part of her that didn't listen to reason or sense or in fact anything inspired by the brain at all. This was a chapter in her life that needed animal responses. All that mattered was protecting her baby, whom she still loved to the point of distraction. It didn't matter that she liked to eat spiders. It was a trifling matter. Hadn't she herself had a habit of eating worms and soil as a child? Claire could be a mass murderer of disabled children for all Sarah cared; her love transcended anything.

Nick was saying something to her now, but all she could hear was the slow beat of the tide against the stones. The arc of the beam from the lighthouse became something too intense to look at; it slowed, as if affected by the treacly rhythms of the ultra-black ribbons winding themselves around that penetratingly still white heart. Every pulse of acid-white light illuminated the lovely ruin before her as it collapsed and reassembled itself, like wounded tissue knitting itself well again at supernatural speed.

Claire's face swam out of it, upturned, gilded, rapturous. She was rising and falling, like breath made solid. She was moving as though beneath the thrusting body of a lover.

Sarah cried out and sensations swarmed back into her. She ran to her daughter as Claire, startled from her reverie, fell back against the shingle with a sickening crunch. She was still smiling when Sarah reached her, Nick's torchlight flashing crazily across the stones, and her daughter, as he rushed to keep up.

Her lips were black, the teeth behind them stained too, as if she had been eating licorice. Sarah scooped her up in her arms, immediately aghast by the weightlessness of her, and picked her way unsteadily back to the road at the top of the beach. The noises Nick was making coalesced into sense again now that she had Claire safely back in her arms.

'We should call an ambulance, don't you think? She's in her pyjamas. She could be suffering from hypothermia.'

'No. She's fine.'

'She is not fine. She could be in shock. Shock is a killer.'

Sarah made his voice go away, simply turned down the volume and allowed her own thoughts to provide an obscuring clamour. Once she had reached the road, she sat Claire down on a bench outside the Nelson. The silence here, guarded by sleeping buildings from the asthmatic sea, was shallow and wrong. She felt threatened, as if whatever had detached itself from Claire were still in close proximity, perhaps watching them, looking for an opportunity to steal in again and whisk her away.

Claire could not sit up unsupported; she lolled her head against her breastbone and smiled drunkenly. She turned sportive eyes upon her mother, but the pupils were dilated, beyond the capability of focus. Sarah shrugged off the sweater Nick had given her and wrapped it around Claire.

'We have to get her back to the room,' she said. She hooked her arms under Claire's armpits and waited for Nick to grab her feet. He had stopped trying to argue with her.

She felt a swelling beneath her fingers; Claire hissed and writhed when she palpated it. 'What's this?' she asked, but her daughter wouldn't, or couldn't, answer. Sarah brushed away Claire's flapping hands and tugged back her nightshirt. The flesh was blue-grey under the streetlamps. The lump was a tight, neat ball of shadow rising out of her skin. It was hot to the touch. 'Claire,' Sarah said. Her voice contained no weight. 'Baby, what is the matter with you?'

They puffed and cursed as they carried the girl back to the hotel, despite her lack of weight. It was as if, in swearing, in pretending Claire was an awkward piece of furniture being shifted from one place to another, they could manage the insanity of the evening more adroitly. But the charade was forgotten when they moved into the light of the hotel lobby and colours – specifically the red smeared over Claire's mouth – came back to their world.

14. PACK MENTALITY

A dream. The strangest dream. Instead of being asleep and seeing everything as though still awake, this was the other way around. Surely it was. Bo was awake, and seeing everything from within dreamland. He had better be. Oh Christ, he had better be.

A flat tyre on the Ninja. A determination not to let the enclosed spaces, his new fear of people (what was that called, in the great dictionary of phobias?) cow him. *Push your chest out. Flex some muscle. You are as good as, if not better than, any of these fuckers.* Stalking hard these cold London streets he thought he knew so well, and yet all of the shadows and shapes seem so alien to him now. The cold is like something he could peel off the air; layers of it fasten to him, slowing him down, turning him sluggish.

At Russell Square tube station he sinks gratefully into the heat of engines, diesel and crude body warmth. The slam and clatter of ticket barriers, sliding doors; the blur of legs, the expressionless choirs of monotony. The sway of carriages as the tunnels sheathe the train. People who don't know each other, don't want to know each other, moving in concert, a sexless fuck rhythm. A coming to and sliding away from.

Where are you going? He doesn't know. He bought a ticket, he boarded a train. North or south. It doesn't matter. This is a dream. The dream will sort itself out.

Only somewhere between stations, a foot lands against his and the pain rockets him out of that cosy, seductive illusion. This is *real*. The people around him are *real*. He looks at them: the seven in his half of the carriage, sitting primly on the vomit-patterned upholstery.

Directly opposite, the man with the grey hair and the grey trimmed beard. The tanned skin. A copy of the *Financial Times* and a worn leather briefcase. Blue suit. Red tie. Speed-reading.

Next to him, the slacker chick, mid-teens, an expression of boredom or disdain never far from her features. Wide green eyes, a little nub of a nose, lips plastered with gloss. Smack of gum. Eyes fastened on the tube's route above your head. Converse sneakers. Jeans way too long for her legs, hems rotten and ragged from dragging in the dirt. The gleam of a stone in her navel. Pale-blue Babydoll T-shirt and a black woollen cardigan, sleeves stretched, clenched into her palm by ragged nails dotted with chipped black polish.

Next to her, a forty-something Chinese woman in a smart green trouser suit. A clutch bag held neatly between the fingers of both hands. White earphones. Eyes closed. Listening to what? Classical music? A Podcast? Minutes from some medical symposium? A laminated badge hanging on a chain around her neck. Her face on it, smiling. Her name, Linda Ho.

Next to her, a skinny black man in a plain white T-shirt, sifting through a handful of photographs. Big, bright smiles now and then. Clean-shaven. Blue jeans with creases ironed into them – oh dear. Black, no-name trainers.

Opposite skinny, three away from Bo: hard to tell. A glimpse of blonde hair and a sharp profile. Too much make-up. A Dan Brown novel. Her funeral.

Two from Bo. Hard to tell. Long legs in red jeans. Doc Martens. A shimmery black silk shirt. A furled Burberry umbrella.

Next to Bo. In the window you can see the reflection of a man in his late sixties, early seventies. His hair salt-and-pepper, combed neatly, perhaps trained with a little Brylcreem or Dax. A beige raincoat buttoned up to the throat where it frames a neatly knotted green woollen tie and a white shirt. Tired collars, slightly grey. Highly polished shoes nevertheless showing their age. Eyes on his shoes, perhaps thinking the very same thing. He looks Germanic.

Somewhere between stations, something odd happens.

Bo looks away, contemplating his own shoes, the deep rind of dirt in the half-moons of his nails.

And.

The prickle of self-consciousness. He knows, for a fact, without looking up to confirm it, that everyone in the carriage, every last fucking soul in the carriage, is *staring right into him.*

He looks up, trying not to appear too spooked, too shit-pant fucking terrified, and Linda Ho is still enjoying her recording, her eyes closed. Black guy is still grinning at his snaps. World-versus-me teen is stretching and winding apple-flavoured Bubblicious around her little finger, her eyes following the Piccadilly Line's rich-blue slash on the map through the belly of London . . . but there's the electric feel in the carriage of eyes having been averted at the last split second.

Bo looks away and again their eyes, as one, swing back on to him; he feels the weight of their stare, their eyes peeled back, hot on him, intent, searing. Unblinking. The scrutiny of the desperate, the ravenous. He knows it.

He looks up and maybe this time he catches grey beard at it, just for a second, the lunacy and ire packed into those insane eyes.

Somewhere between stations, the train judders to a stop and the lights go out.

Bo sits in the ticking, tutting blackness, the soft slither of panic piling up against his open mouth and the dead weight of his heart. The darkness is so utter that he can't even see the gleam in a single eyeball that is straining his way. He feels a claw grip his knee and he yelps, getting to his feet, stumbling away into the well between doors. Unsure, after all, if that was a claw, or somebody's jaws closing around his leg. He reaches down and tries to wipe away the feeling. His hand comes away wet. He backs into another body standing by the doors, but there had been nobody there a moment ago.

'Sorry,' Bo whispers.

'It's all right,' something whispers glutinously back, something whose breath is hot and heavy with decay.

The moment stretches out, like the gum the girl has been twirling around her fingers. The hostility in the carriage is as palpable as the heat. Vomit climbs in his throat. The feeling of imminent violence is so strong he's flinching, although the blows never land.

A fretful, excoriating few minutes later, the lights splutter into life, and for a split second Bo feels the heat of everyone looking at him so powerfully he believes he must be burned by it. And he blinks, and the train judders into movement, and the woman with the Burberry umbrella is picking a label off the sole of one of her new shoes, and the Germanic guy is folding his hands over each other as if he has a fan of invisible cards he doesn't want anybody else to see. Nobody is looking at Bo. It's as if he doesn't exist, such is the lack of interest in him.

He gets off at Hyde Park Corner; nobody raises their head to watch him go. But through the window as the train departs, he feels the weight of a hundred maniacal stares. He walks up to Marble Arch, where he first saw the house of flies. The same old gyre of traffic. The same old buildings. One of London's black pockets, the air thick with souls, the ground forever boggy with blood. Execution ground. A fine place for the house, a fine address for the original map reader.

Everyone he sees, whether they be jogging the perimeter of the park proper, queueing at the Odeon cinema, or swinging around the roads in taxis and buses, gives him different levels of attention. But they give him attention. For the first time, the new muscle within him flexes and a glimmer of understanding runs with it. He grasps the possibility that a map does not necessarily have to be drawn on paper. He gathers that other people's interest in him might be due to something deeper than the cut of his clothes or the style of his hair.

So then, if I am a map, what secret country do I represent?

He wakens into cold, a sour taste in his mouth, the soft, blurred images melting away. A dream after all, but so gravid with truth that it might as well have happened. He digs the heels of his hands into his eye sockets, trying to grind away the unbearable feeling that his life has been replaced by some robotic devotion to servitude. His frustration becomes amplified. Who is he in thrall to? When will they reveal themselves?

A part of him suspects, as he rises from his damp sleeping bag, his breath turning to ghosts in the cold back bedroom, that they already have.

15. GRAHAM GREENE

In any band of society there are factions. There are always dominants and submissives. Some find it easier to climb that triangle of power and sit at the pinnacle, looking down on the poor souls wondering how to even get a leg up to a level only slightly more rarefied than their own.

So it is with London's one-time saviours.

Blinking, coming back from the brink, they vibrated with awareness at each others' proximity. They knew their mass was great, but their muscle lacking. Their instincts had been dulled by many generations of sleep. They spent long, cold days trying to orient themselves within this newly huge, labyrinthine space, many times greater than how they remembered it. Their eyes sucked in drilling moments of light and pain with every blink: too much glass, too many reflections. They spent a lot of time goggling at themselves in office-block windows, pulling on clothes too big or small for them, stolen from warehouses, washing lines, the dead and the drunk.

They had forgotten how to kill.

It itched within them, this knowledge, in the way that a stump will itch in its memory of the departed limb. The compulsion was there, but it was directionless, imprecise. It manifested itself in fruitless intra-family squabbling. Hands lashed out but weren't primed for connection; shapeless cries and screeches were uttered, but more from an ecstasy of frustration at the self, rather than in genuine animosity towards fellow lost, fellow eaters. Once they had been feted as saviours of the city, thanks to their unconventional appetites. They could still, over those vast tracts of race memory, recall the peculiar flavour of spoiled meat, and hanker after it again. They were alive, awake; they were here.

A buzz of anticipation sizzled through the community, as if they were all hooked up to the same battery. One or two pieces of the puzzle were needed, that was all, before they were able to get over that first hurdle, this all-consuming blindness of hunger, sate themselves, and rebuild the broken bridges between themselves and their banished fathers. Gain understanding, rekindle the fires of envy and revenge that had gone cold for so long. They had waited four hundred years. They could afford to wait a little longer.

They had safety in numbers. They had the protection of the cathedral, if they needed it. Things, they felt, in that frisson running through the cold, damp London air, were on a knife-edge. A reckoning, of sorts, was at hand. They would wait and try to learn, try to stay alive. Try to slough off this debilitating skin of weakness.

Some, though, were not weak. The pyramid's summit-dwellers, they could flex their muscles and sniff the blood of prey that they were already laying into, albeit on a much smaller scale than their brothers were considering. This cadre comprised of few. A dozen, give or take. Freakishly large, they were nevertheless regarded as the runts of the litter and had the personalities to match. They shunned their family and its fond regard for ancient times. They dressed in modern clothes, stealing labelled garments that fitted well. They cut their hair, shaving it flush to the skull. They sought out tattooists to pattern their skin, the babyish finery of which sickened them so, and branded each other with knives held over gas rings till the metal glowed orange. They slashed and flensed the flesh, creating deep, intricate markings to emphasise their otherness and indicate a fellowship that was elsewhere. Instead of taking the first name they saw on a television set in a shop window – the usual recourse to identity the lost took – this splinter group browsed bookshops, record shops and video shops for their names, shoplifting the titles that appealed to them, jacketing the volumes and laminating the by-lines, attaching them to their clothes.

One of these bulls of men, Graham Greene, with his violet eyes and a penchant for red suits, so despised the pathetic mien of his own kind that he determined to alter his look, to opt out of their foul beauty. One freezing night, frost on the pavements, he was with his chosen sidekicks, Stanley Kubrick and Kurt Cobain, stalking Praed Street, considering how he could radicalise his look to the extent that he would not be recognisable to others even from his own sect. Talk had been of limb removal; of tweaking out organs so they hung on the body's exterior; of peeling off the outer coats of skin so that the sinews and muscles could be seen; of breaking legs to the point where the bones were rubble within the limbs and they had to get around by dragging themselves with their arms.

They huddled by the entrance to Paddington Station, watching the suits and the briefcases and the brollies, sneering at the stooped creatures as they came home or went to work, at the smell of sweat that powered out of them, at the scars and boils, the acne, the bandages and wheelchairs. The bald heads. The port-wine birthmarks like still fire on downturned faces. The hare lips. The mastectomies. The withered hands. The blind.

Greene turned away and vomited into the gutter. He pulled his raincoat more tightly around him and wiped tears from behind his blue-tinted sunglasses. He was simultaneously appalled by and attracted to their failure, their physical imperfections. He assessed his brothers, the friends he trusted with his life, and was glad to find the same blend of distaste and veneration on their faces. They had been lucky, he felt, to find themselves, once pulled from sleep, in the foundations of a forgotten corner of St Mary's Hospital.

They had had to burrow through ten feet of soil and failing concrete, floorboards, a mass of discarded boxes and folders filled with papers recording the deaths of people who must now be little more than dust. They had emerged into this dumping ground, a plaster and lath construction at the rear of the complex, and stared at the great swathe of glass buildings that adorned the Paddington Basin. Soon they discovered that the morgue was sited not far from this location, and they were able to feast without foraging for scraps. They grew strong quickly, and scorned the lesser lost as they grubbed for the bodies of dead pigeons on the banks of the canal, or fought over the bones in discarded fast-food cartons in bleak car parks on the edge of this opulence, wastelands where construction had not yet reached.

Now, as Kubrick and Cobain shuffled and stamped on the pavement, trying to drive the cold out of their aching legs, Greene thought again of the reasons for their revival. It was always chemical in nature, this resuscitation. And it meant that a Map Reader had been found, someone to make sense of this alien country, someone to open up unknown routes within this people who had been lost to time.

Greene didn't need his hand held. He wanted to explore these territories on his own terms. If they wanted a Map Reader, an explorer, a true visionary, why didn't they approach him? Instead, they had a clown, ponderous, unaware, inattentive. He could see him – they all could, if they closed their eyes – this messiah, a slight man with delicate facial bones, large hooded eyes, a downturned, fleshily attractive mouth and a sparse beard that either couldn't, or wasn't allowed to, flourish. His look was one of perpetual confusion.

We could all die of boredom before this fuckwit drops his penny.

The thought was seized upon and torn to shreds. Hundreds of dissenting voices flew back at him, howling out of the darkness.

Give him time.

Patience. There is no need to rush.

London shall be our playground once more. He is the right man to lead us into it.

The right man. Greene sucked his teeth ruminatively. He had not been chosen. He had lucked into this map. How could he shoulder the responsibility? How could they even consider allowing him to be their front line? He had no vatic quality, no obvious warrior talent. He was running away all the time. How were they to learn anything from him?

Greene's frustration reached his fists: he punched himself hard in the mouth, eager to drive away the maddeningly calm, bovine voices that pleaded with him to give the Map Reader a chance.

Give ME a chance, he raged, and hit himself again. He sensed a massive recoiling from his mind. He felt wild, dangerous. It was good. A tooth, one of his bright, white, too-perfect teeth, jumped clear of his gums and fell to the floor, like a chunk of solid ice. He spat blood. For a second he felt like any of the people heading for the trains, or fanning out of the station seeking food, or love, or warmth. He felt damaged, tired, alone.

He punched himself again. Another tooth cracked, splitting his lip. Cobain and Kubrick were regarding him with amusement.

'Come with me,' he said.

He led them across the bridge spanning the canal. They walked the North Wharf Road to a subway that led under the Marylebone Flyover. Here Greene found a half-brick that he held aloft like a trophy. He handed it to Stanley Kubrick.

'Empty my mouth,' he said.

From: chewingman@yahoo.co.uk
To: saycheese@mac.com
Sent: Thursday, November 27, 2008 15:15
Subject: progress

i wl hld yr hnd 4 u if u nd it. i cn shw u thngs. our pple nd 2 grw. thy r hngry 2 lrn. all u hve 2 do is b yrslf. thy r vry vry hngry

16. FORCE MEAT

How did this chewing bastard finger him? What was going on? He felt a twinge of regret at even opening his online email package. All he had come in here for was a chance to track down Rohan Vero, an act that had led him up so many dead ends that he doubted he'd ever be able to manoeuvre himself back out into the real world. He had sworn to himself to cut all links, which was why he had discarded his mobile phone. But he wanted to see if Keiko was trying to contact him. He had felt tartly irritated to discover she had not.

Where had this freak picked up his email address? Bo was no geek, although he had taken computer studies in his final few years at school – and failed it spectacularly – when the Sinclair ZX-81 was still making jaws drop. He'd got his parents to fork out for a Spectrum. He'd sold his dad on it by telling him that it contained more sophisticated circuitry than was used on any of NASA's Apollo missions. He'd spent three fucking hours on Christmas morning keying in a couple of hundred lines of Basic from the user's manual in order to display a Union Jack on the TV screen.

Big wank.

All he ever used it for was to play *Jet Set Willy*. Or, oh the hilarity:

```
10 WRITE 'Jacko is a spastic'
20 GO TO 10
RUN
```

He pulled the lapels of his denim jacket closer around his throat and touched the edges of the black beanie rammed on to his head. Keiko always found his wearing of woollen hats sexy, she said, because his longish, dark-brown hair would curl under them. *It works for me*, she'd explain, when he gave her a confused look. Now it worked for him because it made him feel concealed, no matter how demonstrably untrue that was.

Maybe I should just give in, he thought, suddenly. *Let them have me.* But an internal instinct kicked out at him. He could not, would not allow that to happen. This wasn't the cosy seduction of something like vampirism. You didn't get a couple of cool bite marks on the neck and a fashionably pale look. You didn't get to join the ranks of the immortal and drink salty Shiraz for the rest of your days. You died. You died horribly.

He emailed a friend, a long-suffering guy who was hot on Apple Macintosh computers and who more often than not received emails and phone calls that began: *Hi Mike, how are you – we've got to get out for a beer again soon. By the way . . . I'm having trouble with my Mac*, and asked him how his address could have become available to the public domain.

Mike replied within ten minutes:

LMAO

Which was how, spam-filtering system or not, Bo learned it was a stupid question.

He felt the occasional jab of adrenaline threaten to shred his stomach as a person walked by the window, looking in on the intent ranks of webheads, but it was not as acute a feeling as his journey on the tube. He found himself casting nervous glances around the room nevertheless, and jumping whenever somebody walked behind his chair. But it was better than venturing out at night. The people,

Christ, some of the people in this city after dark, it was as if they had been injected with a kind of intensity drug. They didn't gaze benignly around them as they pottered about their evening activities. They stared with a blatant ferocity that threatened to scorch the skin off you if it fell your way.

He pulled up Google and entered *chewingman*. There were no relevant entries, unless the figure shadowing Bo was a cunnilingus expert working on porn films out of Venice Beach, California. The Yahoo! profile for chewingman was similarly fruitless, devoid of any details. Bo rubbed his eyes and wondered if he should contact Detective Inspector Laurier and tell him of the email. Yahoo! would presumably have to divulge chewingman's whereabouts if the police came knocking, but Bo had the feeling that any given address would be bogus or, if it wasn't, then chewingman certainly wouldn't be sitting on the sofa with his feet up when the feds piled through the door.

He made fists of his hands, squeezed until the knuckles were sore, and his nails were digging into the meat of his palms, and then he replied.

From: saycheese@mac.com
To: chewingman@yahoo.co.uk
Sent: Friday, November 28, 2008 12:07
Subject: Re: progress

Who are you?

A few seconds after he sent the message, his inbox indicated a new arrival.

From: chewingman@yahoo.co.uk
To: saycheese@mac.com
Sent: Friday, November 28, 2008 12:07
Subject: Re: Re: progress

dnt mtr wh i am. jst knw this. we wl bry u in pces if u dnt flfl yr role in our rsrectn. lt th mp thru. lt yr veins b r roads. lt yr skn b th rf ovr r hds. lt ths hapn. b th mp or die

Bo slid back sharply on his chair, creating a shriek on the linoleum floor that brought hisses and shouts of rebuke from his fellow browsers.

This isn't a fucking library, he wanted to yell at them, but he was too afraid of how hysterical his voice might sound. That first sentence

dnt mtr wh i am.

It was not so obvious, once you read it a couple of times, that the *wh* meant *who*. It appalled Bo to be thinking more that perhaps it meant *what*. And *rsrectn*. What did that mean? He knew it was the skeletonised remains of *resurrection* – he had taken his NCTJ course in Teeline shorthand and, though he never used it any more, he remembered the basic idea of reducing any word mostly to its consonants – but whose resurrection? How could he have a hand in it if he didn't know what he was supposed to do?

Almost immediately, he felt a strong, molten pain run through the centre of his head. He closed his eyes and put out a hand to steady himself. His hand slid over the surface of the table, skidding off the edge, almost spilling him from his chair as his fulcrum was suddenly, severely shifted. A woman's voice said: *Oh Jesus. Oh my God.*

He snapped his eyes open and saw a long bloody smear running half the length of his desk. The woman was sitting next to him, leaning away, her face white. A man had shot out of his seat and was screaming for the management, pointing a wavering forefinger at Bo and his mess, his face etched with naked aggression suggesting that bleeding wounds, along with chewing gum and dogs, ought to be left out on the street.

Bo tried to say something, to explain it away as an accident with scissors, but by then pandemonium was close to breaking out, and his attention was being drawn away by the strange thing he had seen when he closed his eyes.

A woman was shouting *don't touch him, don't touch him, you don't know what he's got*. Two men came out of an office at the back of the cyber café, and Bo decided it was time to make himself scarce.

He had the sense to quickly sign out of his Internet account, and then he marched straight out of the café, his damaged left hand tucked into his right armpit.

The traffic on Victoria Street was a slap to the face. It roused him more effectively than any number of the coffees he'd been downing. The strange grid that had overlaid the iridescent mud of his interior vision flashed back, as if it had been trapped there, like a neon sign that remains for some time after it has disappeared from view. It resembled some poorly rendered street map, all uneven lines, grunge patterns, something created by a child with a crayon. He closed his eyes again to improve its definition, and pondered the section that was – he struggled for a word to describe it – *bruised*. It was less bright that the other sections, and some of its lines were incomplete.

Bo heard a car horn and swung his head towards the sound, his eyes still closed. The grid turned on an invisible axis. Sudden excitement leaped inside him. It *was* a map. And now he saw how to decipher its codes. The leading edge, that part at the bottom of his vision, was where he was standing. All that was missing was a large red arrow and the words YOU ARE HERE.

The spoilt part of the map was away to the right, high up. If he opened his eyes while looking at it, he would resemble somebody trying to recall an important fact, or delving for an answer to a tricky question. All he had to do to reach that section was keep his own position locked to the base and follow the lines that angled their way to it. The novelty of the task almost inured him to its bizarreness, its inherent threat. Part of him again wondered, almost disconnectedly, if this was some symptom of cancer, a tumour inoperably deep within his brain.

Before he knew it, he had carved a route deep into Pimlico, following a vaguely southeast direction. He bypassed many people and tried to keep his mind on the task so that the brilliant, fiery suggestion of their organs, embedded in the darker flesh of bodies being exposed to him, would be quelled. He tried to ignore the pangs in his belly when these little knots of tissue were made known. He swallowed the saliva that suddenly seemed too copious for his mouth. The way his teeth felt larger than normal, clenching together as if of their own accord they had developed a need to bite something, was a factor he ought not to dwell upon, for now.

Other people were unreadable, to him, as if their clothes were made from lead to defeat his X-ray capabilities. All of these, without exception, assessed him with a passion he noticed peripherally. As on the tube train, whenever he returned their gaze, their focus was elsewhere. The heat in their eyes remained disguised; he was no clearer as to whether it was born of hostility or admiration. At least in daylight, he felt able to withstand that concentration of curiosity. At night-time, the fear of it was crippling.

He turned and strode, strode and turned, moving through streets and alleyways as if on the end of a cable that was being wound in. The grid behind his eyelids shifted liquidly as he changed direction, as though on a gyroscope. That strange, bruised area drew nearer.

He faltered when he began to consider what that decayed chunk of the map might represent. It occurred to him that it might be a trap or, less grand but no less worrying, a wild goose chase, and that the object of his search would be nothing he could relate to this violated, organic reference point. He had to go on in order to prove his sanity was intact.

He opened his eyes and saw someone staring straight at him, unashamed, unaffected by the niceties the other Bo-watchers were affording him. This man locked eyes with his own in an unspoken challenge. Here it is, Bo thought, here's where things come to a head. But the man remained still, eyeing Bo as if waiting for him to make the first move. He was Bo's height, with longish hair, straggly and unwashed, plastered against his scalp like something painted on. His clothes were besmirched, hanging off his frame. When Bo opened his mouth to ask what the fuck the other guy's problem was, the other guy opened his mouth too.

'Jesus Christ,' Bo said, and the guy mouthed the same words. He stepped back and realised he was standing before his reflected image in a shop window. He couldn't get over the bug-out weirdness of his eyeballs. It was as if they were on the verge of prolapse.

It's because my vision is deteriorating . . . it's because I'm becoming like them . . .

He broke into a trot, forcing himself to close his Mussolini eyes, his Rasputin eyes, and read the map, get back to what it was he needed to do. A sinuous voice rose up, like something trapped for too long in stagnant water: *What will it mean to be like them?*

Nothing good. Nothing good.

His feet were hurting. He was mildly astonished that he had not yet bumped into another pedestrian, or a lamp post, or walked out in front of traffic, even though he was spending more than half the time with his eyes shut. The corroded part of the grid suddenly meshed with the point at which he was standing. He opened his eyes.

Battersea Dogs' Home.

Okay.

He had been expecting something more . . . dynamic, more apocalyptic. What, exactly, he didn't know, but a look to his left, where the iconic, disused power station stood, like a giant table that has been upended, gave him some measure.

He waited at the entrance, listening to the yelps and whines of the inhabitants, wondering when exactly the treasure he had been tracking would yield itself. Nervously, he licked his lips. A defining moment lay ahead, he felt. Something that would seal his involvement with the London that was dissolving around him. Either that, or abject disappointment, a return to square one.

There was nobody sitting in the reception area behind the entrance, and no signs of human life deeper into the building, as he passed through doors marked STAFF ONLY. The smell of dog food, dog shit, and *dog* was everywhere. He turned a corner and found a corridor that looked to have been partially painted with blood, before its decorator got bored, or distracted, or the thing that was providing the colour ran out of product.

More streaks meandered across the floor further along, leading to a pair of swing doors. Bo marched grimly up to them and forced them open, trying to avoid the soft impact marks where whatever it was had been unceremoniously dragged through into the next room. What greeted him seemed suddenly so commonplace as to confuse him regarding its nature. It was like walking in on a bunch of staff performing stock-taking duties; it was a scene so pathetic, so repellent, that it inspired only pity in him, rather than shock or fright.

The middle-aged man on the floor was naked from the chest up, his body spattered and slathered with blood from the six or seven dog corpses lying around him. All of their bellies had been rent apart, their ribcages gleaming jaggedly. The man was still plucking at fragments of meat poking from the torn hides, jabbing them absently between his teeth while he gazed at the far wall, in the same way a compulsive eater will burrow into a bag of chocolates or chipsticks. Bo watched the man occasionally dabble his fingers into the wounds he had created, or press a faded eyeball, his expression frozen into childish wonder at death's accommodating nature; no indignity was too great. Even when he realised Bo was in the room with him, his lassitude was too pronounced to impinge on his meal. He looked like a glutton who had reached bursting point.

Bo squatted next to him and tried to understand what it was he had to do.

'What's your name?' he asked.

The other man blinked at him, docilely, bovinely, and said: 'Shand. I think.'

'Shand. What are you doing?'

Shand surveyed the carnage around him as if it were the aftermath of a child's session with a stack of building blocks.

'I was hungry,' he said. 'I wanted to eat, but I wasn't . . . I'm not strong enough to take what I'm really hungry for.'

'How do you mean?'

'It's been so long. I forgot how. I'm weak. We're all weak. We're all grubbing. Surviving. Sleeping . . . it's made us so weak.'

Bo spread his hands. The dog nearest to him, a German Shepherd puppy that had been scooped clean as though ready for the taxidermist's magic, moved its leg suddenly, violently, and was still. Bo tried not to flinch, was in fact trying supremely not to flee the corridor, screaming, begging for help.

'Where is everyone?' he asked. 'Where are all the staff?'

Shand seemed unable to comprehend.

'What am I supposed to do?' Bo asked.

Shand blinked at him, suddenly resembling a lost little boy. His skin, those parts of it that weren't painted with canine blood, was almost lambently clean and tight, free of wrinkles. His eyes were clear, no hint of shadows or blood. When Shand talked, the glint of brilliant, even teeth drew Bo's attention to his mouth. There was something else about him that gave Bo the creeps, but he couldn't pinpoint what it was.

'What are *you* supposed to do?' Shand asked. 'What are WE supposed to do? You tell us. *YOU TELL US!*'

Bo tried to step back from the sudden tirade, flashing his hands up to ward off the flecks of dog and saliva being scattered his way. He skidded on blood, or piss, or faeces, and went down hard on his backside. He scuttled back, alarmed by Shand's electrifying change of mood, abruptly afraid that his hunger might not yet be sated and he'd take a swipe for the soft parts of his own body.

'I don't know,' Bo said, finally. 'I've not been . . . taught how to.'

As he said the words, Shand seemed to withdraw all his spikes. He studied Bo's face as if it had suddenly changed into something new, something that commanded attention and respect. He wiped away the blood bracketing his lips, and pushed away the remains of all the lost puppies who had found a warm home in his gut. He stood up, his cheap slip-on shoes struggling to gain purchase in the slick of mongrel effluvia. He nodded, though Bo was no longer saying anything. He regarded his right hand, which he clenched and relaxed a few times, as if surprised by the dexterity he could see there. And then he left, quickly, facing Bo as he backed towards the doors, bowing slightly, his eyes reverentially averted.

Bo left soon after, eager not to be discovered standing in the middle of a pack of obliterated animals, but could not see where the man had gone. A flurry of movement up ahead suggested that someone was hurrying away on the overland rail tracks, but Bo was not up for a pursuit. He didn't know what he might say if he caught up with Shand. He decided that he didn't want to know where he was going, especially if he was still hungry.

As the sun touched the rooftops, darkening to the colour of melted butter, Bo made his way back to his bolthole on foot – too wary to take any form of public transport that might have somebody else's face inches away from his – and locked himself away with the forgotten paperbacks, reading until he was distracted enough to be able to fall asleep. He had heard of books saving lives before, but never in such fraught circumstances.

In the shimmering seconds before actual sleep received him, he heard noises on the street that suggested the onset of a dream, or a nightmare. Awful, carnal, carnivorous sounds. Death in full cry. Terror's song. Out of those black notes, another map composed itself, red and unruly, just behind his eyelids. His body clenched involuntarily as it struck him that somehow he was playing a part, a crucial part, in that discordant opus.

17. SPECIAL DENTISTRY

D r Edward Houghton had watched a new brass plaque being
fixed to the wall that afternoon, in a rare break between
patients. He still referred to them as patients, though he knew other
private dentists who described them as customers or even cash cows.
His relationship with many of his patients had been eroded by their
suspicion – unfounded, though perfectly understandable – that he
was pulling them in for treatment they didn't need, or providing
fillings that contained a built-in obsolescence, to ensure they would
return. Still, he was busy and doing well.

Now the small waiting room was empty and Lorraine, his
assistant, had gone home. Houghton had spent the last hour
disposing of sharps, cleaning his equipment and updating files on his
work computer. He was looking forward to getting upstairs to a glass
of Talisker malt, a lamb curry, and an hour or two of *Grand Theft
Auto* before logging on to the discussion boards at the BDA website.
The game was a guilty pleasure of his, a habit he had developed after
stillborn experiences of trying to initiate some sort of relationship
with members of the opposite sex. He accepted that he was not the
most attractive man in the world, that his hangdog expression, his

boxer's nose, and his small piggy eyes had had their last chance of landing a mate. A balding head, expanding waistline, and wrinkles were only going to work against him. Good teeth were no aphrodisiac on their own.

He had been favoured with a few pitying stares whenever he brought up his interest in the game with Lorraine or the patients he liked enough to have a chat with before or after their check-ups. One man of around forty had barely been able to suppress a snort of derision before suggesting he read a book. And yet this very same man had met his fiancée on the Internet at a chat site. If there were levels of sadness with regard to computer activity, surely he merited a rosette, too.

Houghton didn't care. He liked the game, liked how involved he could get. He could roam the streets freely, off mission, play little sub-plot games, drive around, go to the gym, buy a new wardrobe, beat someone to a pulp, be involved in thrilling police car chases, shoot the Christ out of things. It was enormous fun.

Frantic knocking at the door gave him pause as he was about to climb up to the living quarters above his surgery. He went to the window and looked out into the street. Lauderdale Road was busy with cars, as was the case every evening at around 6 p.m. London's rush hour was more like a rush three hours. He couldn't see quite enough of the entrance to reveal who was standing there, clouting the door again and again, but the security light cast at least three shadows across the gravel driveway.

He hurried to the door and placed his ear against it. Worry was unfolding itself like the slow spiny leaves of a carnivorous plant. He couldn't understand his discomfort. He often received unheralded visitors after work, it was a source of pride to him that his was a house where friends felt they could drop in whenever they wanted, rather than have to make extensive arrangements, as most Londoners seemed to do. But something about the anger in these knocks – urgent without any vocal accompaniment – seemed utterly wrong to him.

Another barrage. He steeled himself and called through the letterbox: 'What is it? Can't you see the surgery is closed now?'

'An emergency.' A man's voice, young, hurried but smooth. *Someone putting it on.* But even as he thought this, he saw a long, looping rope of bloody saliva drop down into sight.

'Please help.' Spoken as if recited from a script.

'All right,' he said, and unlocked the door, pulling it open as far as the security chain allowed. Three men, large men, dressed extravagantly, all with hair dyed fiery red, shorn almost to the skin, crowded his doorstep as if desperate to prove they could all fit within its frame. They wore sunglasses with coloured lenses. Silk handkerchiefs frothed from top pockets. He thought they were clowns at first, and then rock stars.

One of them, the tallest, seemed to be holding his face together with blood-drenched hands.

'Bloody hell!' Houghton barked. 'Get this man to a hospital. My God. I'll call an ambulance. What were you thinking, bringing him h–'

'No,' the injured man said, stepping forward. He raised a hand and slammed it against the door, which sprang open, the chain snapping as if made of spun sugar. The other two men moved swiftly inside and led Houghton to his surgery. The leader calmly closed the front door behind him and followed.

'Anybody else in the building?' he asked, the words coming awkwardly slimed with gore, heavily slurred. Houghton could now see that there were few, if any, teeth left in the man's mouth. For someone who had been violently attacked, he seemed admirably calm about it.

'Yes,' he lied. 'My wife will be down in a moment to help me clear up.'

'Already clean,' the man said quietly, with difficulty. 'Nobody else.' It wasn't a question.

He sat in the dentist's chair and put his head back on the rest. He put his hands down by his sides and a stream of blood drizzled off them, creating two crimson pools on the brilliant white-tiled floor.

'How can I eat, if I don't have any teeth?' he said.

'What happened?' Houghton asked shakily, trying to understand his serenity. His pain must be insufferable, yet he didn't show any signs of being on the drugs that might combat it.

The man lifted his sunglasses; blood made a series of strange punctuation marks on his face. It was leaking steadily from the corner of his mouth. 'I walked into a lamp post,' he lisped.

His companions chuckled.

'Right, that's it. I'm calling the police.'

Without looking at him, one of the other men, who was wearing a laminated photograph of Stanley Kubrick on a chain around his neck, stepped across his path and closed the door. He stood in front of it, almost obscuring it, and waited with his eyes politely diverted, his large soft hands folded primly into each other, like sleeping doves.

Houghton could only stand and wait for something to happen, too frightened to realise that the others were waiting for the same thing.

'We brought you something to replace my teeth with,' the man on the chair said. A paperback of *The Human Factor* peeked from his jacket pocket; his fingers strayed to it frequently, as if it were of some comfort to him. A series of red fingerprints were arranged across the top block of pages. The other man who, Houghton noticed with horror, was holding a piece of brick that was shiny with bloody pulp, held out his other hand and opened it.

'You must be joking,' Houghton said, looking at the three of them in turn, his eyes wide with shock, burning with the intense operating lights that removed every shred of shadow from the surgery.

Graham Greene indicated his nude, seeping jaws. 'Does this *look* like a joke?'

'This is beyond me,' Houghton said. 'What you're asking. It's beyond me.'

'Breathing will be beyond you,' Greene said, 'if you don't get to work. Now.'

Houghton took off his jacket. 'It will take time,' he said. 'My first patients will be here at eight-thirty tomorrow morning. This is going to take . . .'

'Begin,' Greene said. 'And I'll have a touch of anaesthetic. I'm not much of a one for pain.'

Houghton moved in on that riot of wet reds as laughter crashed around him. For the first time in his career, he wished he'd followed his father into the waste management industry.

18. REHABILITATION

Sometimes, as Manser swam in and out of consciousness, he spoke to the dead man by his side but was disappointed to get no reply. He controlled the pain by concentrating on him, asking him what his likes were. Asking him what kind of soap he used, what toothpaste, what brand of toilet tissue. That and the sheer force of his will kept him together.

He was constantly surprised out of his fugues by the simple fact of this man's death. Manser was lying next to him in a large deserted car park. It was late, but somewhere nearby there was heavy traffic. The dead man's eyes were large dark shadows. Assessing them, he wondered how he could be dead if they were open so wide. But then another ripple of reality would work through the morphine haze and he saw how he had no eyes at all, just ragged black holes where they had been torn out. The man's heart was gone, but try as Manser might he couldn't remember eating it, or taste the richness of the organ on his tongue. He supposed he must have consumed it, but then he couldn't remember killing him, or how he had come to be here.

Manser drew a hand gingerly to his face and flinched when he felt the crisp, tender mask that it had become. The heat from the fire had caused his eyelids to melt and slide down over his eyes; he turned Jez Knowlden's body over, catching a carrion whiff from those gouged sockets, so he could reach inside his jacket. Knowlden always carried a pair of nail scissors with him; he wouldn't need them any more. Manser used them to snip the membranes from his own brow.

All Manser could smell were the carbonised parts of his body.

Gyorsi had left him for dead. His friend, his mentor, had betrayed him and as good as murdered him. His throat felt raw where the heat and smoke had scorched it. He couldn't hear too well because the shells of his ears had been burned clean away. The forefinger and middle finger of his left hand had fused together and become little more than a black claw of protruding bone and ligament.

He wondered if he would be able to come back from this and be anything like his former self. He doubted it, but here was Knowlden, and he hadn't killed himself.

In the distance, he thought he could hear sirens. London. So what? But a tremor of adrenaline drew him upright. Something didn't feel right. He almost laughed at that; a burned man in a car park at the Devil's hour, spending time with a cold, opened body, and something didn't feel right. Maybe Knowlden was wearing odd socks. Now he did laugh, a brutal, dry cackle that transformed itself into a painful cough almost immediately.

He shambled away, towards a more complete darkness, away from the hard sodium glare and open spaces of the shopping centre, the Toys R Us, the Holiday Inn's inviting lights, at the fringes of the car park, the low ceiling of the Brent Cross flyover. His instincts were right. A couple of minutes later, as he moved through shadows that reeked of stale urine, the hot grease of cheap hamburgers and his own foggy, smoggy smell (although he cringed to think that all of those smells might be emanating from his own body), the blue scatter of lights from police cars and a van tossed and turned the night this way and that. A couple of unmarked cars brought up the rear. He squinted through the trees at them and the headache they were inspiring.

They drove right up to the body and immediately half a dozen armed, heavily armoured policemen leaped out of the van and began spreading out. High-powered torches sent the night scurrying back a little more. Over this industry came the distant throb of a helicopter. He knew that he must hide soon, within the next five minutes, if he was to escape the infrared cameras on a police chopper. His body would stand out like a piece of white chocolate on a black carpet.

He hurried along, feeling alternately too hot and too cold, but knowing that if he discarded his coat he would be dead before he realised it, either from the freezing November air or a bullet in the back of the head when his trail was picked up. He heard dogs. What was this? Not some arbitrary location search. They knew what they were going to find. And, he realised with a thud in his heart, they thought they'd find him too.

He found the strength to run, although the movement caused furious reactions in his face, neck, and left arm. At the far end of the parking space – an area he guessed was too remote for shoppers, but a prime location for lovers and junkies – he clambered over a fence on to a litter-choked walkway alongside the thin thread of water that was Dollis Brook. Darkness stretched away into what seemed to be cold miles of empty space. Stars were visible here, just a few hundred feet away from the light pollution, like spilled talc. He moved through the long grass, knowing that he was done for. His pathetic, stumbling figure would be picked up by the thermal imaging cameras within a few minutes, with him barely a hundred metres along the bank. He had hoped for busy streets to lose himself in, places bustling with people. Where was London when you needed it?

He imagined the pilot coming in low, swooping over the crime scene, moving on across the brook, which was, he realised with disgust, the most obvious escape route, its cameras trained on the acres of black, on the look-out for a staggering white ghost. But he had a chance, as long as he could find something cold to hide beneath.

He followed the brook as best he could, trying not to slip in the mud, resisting the temptation to keep feeling that his face was still where it ought to be. At Staples Corner, where the M1 begins its journey out of London, he struggled over another fence, dropping into a slope of gravel and weeds that led down to the railway. He staggered south, following the moonlight as it skated along the parallel lines, until he reached Brent Sidings. The helicopter's noise had bottomed out now; he could see it suspended in the sky, a white beam poking into the urban landscape, trying to expose him. Without warning, it swooped his way. He reckoned he would have about thirty seconds before the cameras picked him up. He must be the warmest body out on the streets for miles, despite the winter crawling through his veins.

Shapes emerged from the darkness. Rolling stock. He reached the first of them and relished the bite of cold the metal gave his fingers – so cold as to almost cause his skin to fuse to it. He got to his knees and scrabbled his way under the car until his body was between the tracks, his face looking up at an underbelly of black steel that smelled of dead diesel. He heard the helicopter droning, using up its own reserves of fuel. He counted off the minutes of their search. The helicopter's buzz grew more distant.

Nothing to report. Must have been picked up by a knight in shining armour before we could get to him. I'll make another pass, but it's not looking likely. You'd be better off checking the connecting roads and paths in the immediate vicinity. Roger and out.

He thought of the things they had discussed, the two of them, in the restless shadows of the trees. A passing on of knowledge. A secret history. Before this betrayal. This farewell to arms.

How had it started, that final conversation?

– In 1980, Malcolm, my dear chap, I had my pancreas removed, an illegal operation conducted by a freelance surgeon, much like Doctor Losh, the objectionable sawbones in your employ. My pancreas was in perfect working order. As I fully expected it to be.

Why?

– Because I have perfection in me, Malcolm. I was born to it.

No, I mean, why did you have it removed?

– Oh, I see. Well, it meant that I no longer produced insulin. I became a diabetic. My blood would become sweeter.

You did it to make your blood sweeter?

– That's right, Malcolm. Yes, I wanted to improve my flavour. There is an interesting medical anecdote regarding diabetics. If you walk into a hospital ward and smell pear drops, it usually means, unless someone is actually eating those sweets, that someone is suffering – quite badly, I hasten to add – from diabetes. It's the ketones that are causing the smell. Basically, you need insulin to transport glucose from the blood to the muscles, where it can be burned as fuel. If you don't have enough insulin to do this, then the body converts fat into ketones to use as fuel instead. Too many ketones, for a diabetic, can spell danger.

You're at risk? You don't take insulin?

– I don't need it. I told you. I'm different. But you tell me. You smell that fruitiness on my breath? Like pear drops. Like nail varnish. It's heady. It's seductive.

Yes. I smell it.

– Well, you're not the only one.

Why are you telling me this? Why is this important?

– I'm telling you because I like you, Malcolm. You found me. You have sustained me, you've kept up certain levels that I've had to maintain, or I'd fritter away like froth, like flotsam in the wash of a powerboat. I'm still a player. I still matter. Things are going to happen in London that will turn your piss to ice, boy. I'm telling you. Get out while you can. While you still have the blood beating in your heart. Because believe me, anything alive in the capital when they, when they *relearn* the art of killing is going to be nothing more to them than a walking, no, a running, *no*, a *sprinting* snack.

They?

– I should say, we, really. A little offshoot of mankind, one of its vestigial limbs.

I don't understand.

– No, Malcolm, I know you don't. You're in this for the stumps. You have base desires, yet pedigree know-how. The thing is, your devotion to amputees is attractive to me, to us, for the reason that it signals a need in human beings for the unconventional. We know that when we reintegrate into society, we will be able to progress, to seamlessly knit ourselves into that pattern that so violently rejected us all those years ago.

– I'm putting it formally, I suppose. A different way of explaining our position would be that we intend to declare war on you fucks until there's nothing left but human chum. Four hundred years ago, we were chased out of this city *after being invited, begged to enter it in the first place.*

There's no need to shout at me, Gyorsi, I'm not –

– There's every need. Talking never achieved anything with your lot. Do you know how many people were killed during the Great Fire of London in 1666?

It wasn't many. I think it was six. Maybe eight?

– That's what the history books tell us. But they lie. If you believe it was started in Pudding Lane by a baker called Farriner – Jesus

Christ, who made that up? Mr Fiction of Story Street? – then you'll believe anything. Thousands died, Malcolm. Thousands of us.

And you want revenge?

– We want what's owed us. A piece of this city. Our own Palestine. And yes, we want you to feel the suffering we've known. We're hungry. We've been sucking on fresh air for centuries. We want some meat.

Why now? Why here? Wouldn't it be better to target a small village first? A sleepy seaside town? London is tough. It knows how to deal with terrorism.

– Not this kind, believe me. And the current crop of citizens . . . tough? Don't make me laugh. This city is so ripe you can almost smell it. You know the thing about plague? The weird thing? It comes when the environment is right. You look at the 1300s when agriculture failed and the country was ensnared in the Dark Ages. Poor climate. Famine. A population growing, outstripping the amount of produce that could feed it. War. Misery. When people are psychologically and physically prepared for plague, it comes, Malcolm. And it is coming again. The miasma. The people in this city are slow, fat, weak. They sit at their desks all day developing haemorrhoids and pilonidal sinuses. Fat accretes around their hearts. It creeps along their arteries. Infarctions and cancer hang around the population like hoodlums chewing matchsticks on street corners but they're being bullied out of things by the machines and the medicine. Age expectancy might be on the rise, but only because of the technology its health service can offer. Your senescence is unnatural, manufactured. We're here as Mother Nature's agents, to reimpose the balance.

– The fire was started to get rid of us, Malcolm. We were invited to rid the city of plague, and what thanks did we get? An almighty torch up our arses. How they must have patted themselves on the back when the fire was dead and both their blackbirds killed. Well, just as *yersinia pestis* lives on in its little hidey-holes around the world, so do we.

What do you want me to do?

– You've played your role, Malcolm. And you've played it well. You turned in an award-winning performance. It's time to take a bow and return to the wings. For your own safety, I recommend it.

But I can help you.

– No, you can't. I'm changing, Malcolm. I'm becoming something that will forget what it means to be human, in the way you know it to be. And when I've done so, I may lash out at anything in my way. One of the problems of our breed is a lack of control, or discipline. I'm hoping to rectify that.

But how can you do that? You're one of them.

– I'm not. Not yet. But I've been building to this moment all my life, ever since I realised I had their blood in my veins. My mother was not like your mother, Malcolm. My father was a human being. My mother loved him for a little while. And she was respectful of his remains; he's buried somewhere near Oxford. His bones have her little teeth marks all over them. She had pretty, childish teeth, my mother.

– These human traits of restraint and discipline, we need them if we are to abide. Once the firestorm of our making has been damped, and the Queen installed, I'll introduce level-headedness. I'll introduce the concept of moderation. Savages will not endure. I will make gentlemen of monkeys.

You? A moderate?

– Don't bait me, Malcolm. I won't rise to it. I did what I had to do to gain attention. They know who I am. They know of my dedication and my wish to subjugate myself to the new Egg-layer. I will be with my Queen and together we will oversee the coming of a new generation. London will be our spawning ground, and may the shit that survives know what it means to scrabble in the sewers for a living for centuries to come.

The new Queen. Where is she? Who is she?

– Oh, come, come, we both know the girl who is hosting her. I know you've taken a shine to her.

You mean it's growing inside her? Inside Cl–?

– Names mean nothing to me. She is who she is. We are who we are. Names are for dinner parties. She will be with me.

But . . .

– There are no more lines for you to recite. The final curtain is there for you to take. The audience is on its feet for you.

I don't want to leave.

– The Thames will run red, Malcolm. The infamy that is English litter will be replaced by scraps of rotting bodies. Skeletons will adorn the high street shops like Christmas decorations. It will be a festival for the carnivores. For our spurned people. We return. We rise again. And this time there will be no inferno, no scourge, to stop us.

They're like the plague *bacillus*, Malcolm. And there's irony for you. Hiding in old, unknowable places. If you disturb it, it will come again. You can't. You won't be a part of it.

I DON'T WANT TO LEAVE. I DON'T WANT TO LEAVE. I DON'T WANT TO LEAVE.

From: chewingman@yahoo.co.uk
To: saycheese@mac.com
Sent: Saturday, November 29, 2008 21:01
Subject: a wrnng 2 th wse

1 of us is cmng 4 u. b wtchfl

Part III

MIASMA

London my home is: though by hard fate sent
Into a long and irksome banishment;
Yet since call'd back; henceforward let me be,
O native country, repossess'd by thee!
For, rather than I'll to the west return,
I'll beg of thee first here to have mine urn.
Weak I am grown, and must in short time fall;
Give thou my sacred relics burial.

Robert Herrick, *His Returne to London*

19. THE ARCHIVE

A violet sky, the colour of which seemed to be leaking out of the corner of Bo's eyes, flapped and shivered like the mainsail of a ghost ship. The smell of fire, or its sour aftermath, clung to his nostrils. He felt he might be dying. Let that happen, please God, if this was the map taking hold, digging the colour of its roads into his veins and arteries. He couldn't settle on anything else. Even his obsession to find Vero was distracted by the map as it displayed its forgotten corners to him. It was like hunger. It drove away any other thought. He gave himself to the visions in the middle of thinking how he might combat them. He was swamped by the map's need to disburden itself to him of great reams of information. He couldn't receive it all, never mind process it. His nose began to bleed now as he was shown a place of staggering shadows, a place so vast that he could not quite see its ceiling. What he thought he saw when the light swelled enough to suggest glimpses of architecture made him wish for utter dark. He felt the concept of time dissolve around and into him. He became what he was looking for. He became the dust and sap that filtered down from that unholy roof. The map forced him to look.

Masons chisel the freestone freshly quarried, it being easier to work then, before the air hardens it. The stone responds well to the labourers' tools; freestone will not split into layers. The masons dress it into ashlar with scappling irons and carry the blocks countless miles to the site where stone and bone shall be melded. They built the sexapartite ribbed vault from the bones of bodies, the same people who had begged the ancient breed for help to fight the pestilence in their city and then spurned them. There are many men here at this secret cathedral. They catch oysters from the riverbanks and use the shells, along with splintered chunks from their victims, to pack the gaps between the ashlar skins as the walls rise. The men stand on withies, adding to the scaffold as the muscles of the cathedral are put in place. Nobody speaks. The air is too thick with dread. They want the job finished so they can go back to the quarry, where life is a known quantity, and there are no shadows cast where men do not walk, nor whispers where there are no mouths to bear them. The labourers have been sworn to secrecy at their task, and threatened with the removal of tongues if they should wag. The money is good. The masons keep quiet. But some of them cannot bear the strain of working under such conditions. The sound of bone splitting, of people tearing open under unspeakable pressures and stresses, gets to some of them. They whisper prayers into the putlocks ranged across the walls, as if the scaffolds that will plug into them might lock away their secrets and grant them reprieve from nightmares.

The sound of screaming men being bent and twisted into position high above the baying choir had been like angelsong to the ears of the breed ravaged by the Great Fire; it encouraged them to work faster, to hasten the day of their return, their revenge. And their work was lost under the weight of so much other industry. Churches were returning to London's skyline. This was just one more spire, one more reparation.

The roof was secured by great brackets that were joined to a series of cogs and wheels that were turned to take up the slack as the bodies spoiled and fragmented. The sound of moist bone grinding as the buttresses cosied up to it was satisfying to the breed. Now that the dead could no longer scream, they mimicked the sounds of their distress as they were bolted and strapped against the beams, their heads forced into gaps half their size, their spines wrenched out of their bodies as racks ratcheted them into tiny crevices: live wadding to seal any fissures. Others were trapped in giant vices and had their femurs removed: they were forced to watch, forced to stay awake, until the macerated network of veins and arteries around that large bone had flooded the area with life. The breed ran around beneath these human materials, mouths open to catch the red rain that pelted from their opened bodies. They fashioned a crude organ from the bones they harvested and danced and fucked to its dire melodies.

None of the replacement cathedrals and churches built in the capital after the ash had been swept away and the smoke had cleared were perfectly square or symmetrical; Londoners were desperate for services to continue and prayed while the walls were unfinished. So the new walls were built around the old, which were taken down later, making it impossible to provide direct measurements. Work always began in the east of the building because the choir was based there, and this was the part of the church used by the clergy. Their money made these areas things of rare beauty. The nave belonged to the townspeople and was left as it had been, or refitted at a much later date, and more modestly, if at all. Some places of worship do not even have a nave.

The Black Cathedral has no nave. It has no choir. No transept. It has a crypt, where its dead lie, and those who survived nestled against them to sleep. A train of wet, putrescent vertebrae provide hood moulds over the top of the windows. Unknown, unknowable ymagers have carved profane riots of physical depravity into the columns, padding through the church at bleak hours when all were sleeping, or struggling with dreams. Blood has been trodden into the floor for so long that it is the colour of mahogany.

Come aestivation, the cathedral was ready, its guardians in place. Having gorged, they dispersed like the clock seeds from dandelions opening in the capital where the cleansing fires had spawned rich, fertile ground. They slept, and the fury turned to mud in their veins. It would still be there when they wakened, centuries later.

20. THE MAP-EATER

The weather worsened. It became difficult to know when daylight began or ended because the skies were so close and grey, so loaded with rain, and lasted until true dark. Winter moved through the air like a dog in mist.

Bo listened to the cries outside the window and tried to immerse himself in a paperback, shivering as the cold penetrated the shop, his bones. He was wrapped in his own clothes, his biker jacket and the sleeping bag, but it didn't really help. It was as if the cold was emanating from within him. He felt sleepy, at times hollowed out, at times filled with sharp wires. The words swarmed like disgruntled insects on the page.

He wondered about Sammy, whether he was now dead. How pale he had been. Blood had settled in his foot, bloating it slightly, turning it the colour of ripe Victoria plums. His hair had turned the colour of snow. He imagined Sammy's heart turned to chalk in his chest. The lid had come off Sammy Dyer's little box of private terrors and he could find no way of slapping it back on. Since the appearance of Charles Bolton in Sammy's flat, there had been a steady diminishing in the man. No wonder, since he'd been forced to accept that a breathing corpse had been sharing what he believed was a bachelor pad for so many years.

The words he was trying to read shifted again, as though still in the process of being written. A sentence leaped out at him. He read: *He is here*, before it morphed into something far less threatening. Something about toast and honey and strawberry-coloured light on a porch.

There was the unmistakeable sound of the rotten wooden door being tested. He heard it moving against its makeshift barricade a couple of times and then splitting as whoever it was sought ingress. Bo put down his book and moved to the staircase. He slipped up to the first floor, checking out of the landing window on the way, but the yard was already empty. Now Bo felt his nerves come alive. Whoever it was knew what he wanted. He had purpose. This was not some random break-in.

He hoped it might be Laurier, come to save him and God knew who else, from himself. A police cell was an attractive proposition. It would be nice to go to bed at night and know that he wouldn't be able to do anything in his sleep beyond crack his head against the locked door. But Laurier would not come on his own. There would be police cars. It would be early in the morning. There would be an almighty racket when they slammed the doors down.

This someone was here to kill him.

He is here . . .

1 of us is cmng 4 u. b wtchfl.

He was not ready for this. He was barely able to look after himself in the day-to-day grind of staying alive, let alone defend himself. 'Be watchful'. He had been anything but. He thought that by closing the door he could close off any involvement, oblique or direct, with whatever was being marshalled in London's streets. Burying himself in fiction might mean that what was building out there wasn't real.

He heard footsteps gritting through the narrow corridor that connected the front of the shop with the rooms at the rear. He heard something grinding that reminded him of uneven layers of iron wound too quickly into a vice in his old metalwork classes at school. Pages fluttered. He imagined the figure feeling the residual heat of Bo's fingers on the jacket of the book he had been reading and knowing he was in the building. He was taking his time, aware that he had Bo cornered.

Eventually, footsteps came up the stairs. Bo readied himself. He understood, at a strange level, that the person approaching him was part of who Bo was becoming.

'London is a weak city,' came a voice, and it was nothing like Bo had imagined. It was muffled, wet, tortuous. He was put in mind of John Hurt's voice for John Merrick in *The Elephant Man*.

'It has endured for centuries,' the voice continued, 'but it's all husk, all wrapper and tinsel. The foundations of the place are as light and crumbly as old bone. This city is diseased, blind, burned. She's suffered pox, plague, cholera, leprosy. She's been bombed to fuck. She's made so many comebacks she doesn't know which way to face. She doesn't know when to call it a day.

'"When Trinovantum is on its knees, a new Queen shall come forward." This was to be our call to arms, the moment we could rise up and take our revenge on the city that betrayed us.'

The voice had become strong, cocky even, but Bo sensed an uncertainty behind the delivery. The other man was fearful of him, to some degree. Otherwise why wasn't he up here now, spilling blood?

'You know all this, deep within you. You feel it. You will take us into that promised land because you are the only one who can see where its borders begin. We shall follow you.'

He said the word 'follow' slowly, and Bo could almost see the sneer on his lips as he did so. They were thick, cruel lips, he decided, like those of various villains in the old James Bond novels he had read as a teenager. Grey, liverish, with gravestone teeth behind them.

'But I follow *nobody*,' the voice went on. And it was closer now. And Bo realised he had been mistaken. He had been tricking himself into thinking that he held some clout in this strange shadowline between worlds, that being in possession of the map gave him the kind of leverage that might stave off his death. But no such luck. This man, coming for him, was no more afraid of Bo than Bo was afraid of hot drinks. He was so certain of his superiority that he was comfortable about exposing his position. Stealth did not matter. He could, and would, do the job nakedly.

Bo's focus ranged around the room as he desperately sought a weapon or a way out. The window was double-glazed, and locked with an Allen key; it had not been left next to the lock for future residents. Then it must be downstairs, perhaps in a saucer in the kitchen, or in the cutlery drawer; the usual places where such paraphernalia ended up.

'There's no point in trying to run, *Messiah*. Even if you could outpace me, you give yourself away at every turn just because of who you are. It is now in your nature. You are as readable, as accessible, as that map you carry. I'm here to rip it from you, like an organ from its cradle of tissue. You are not deserving, and I do not acknowledge you.'

No weapons. Nothing to hide in or behind or under. No hatch into the attic. No secret door. Bo stole to the window and tried it. Locked. The Ninja was like some fabled green steed, nosing for the gate, achingly beyond reach.

A curtain rail offered the only possible weapon. He wrenched it from the wall and, as he did so, it dragged against the lintel, and what was resting upon it.

He heard the creak of the floorboard outside the door as he was working the Allen key into its special little hole. Bo slammed the heel of his hand into the frame and the window popped open. He was dangling from the ledge, preparing himself for the shock of the drop, but unable to let go until he had glimpsed the other man, fixed him in his thoughts.

The figure bested the black slab of the open door and swung his gaze towards Bo. A scarf was wrapped around his lower jaw. A pair of narrow oblong sunglasses obscured his eyes. He was lean, wolfish. His head was close cropped to the extent that Bo could see the beautiful shadows of its planes and angles, like something sculpted. His skin was as smooth and as flawless as China silk.

It was the symmetry of that face, rather than the iron in Bo's will, that sent him spinning off the ledge.

He landed hard, awkwardly, his left foot folding back under his leg as he spilled to the cracked concrete flagstones. He drew himself upright, gritting his teeth to the jags of pain that were trying to daub black grains behind his eyes, and fished in his pocket for the Ninja's keys.

'Where will you run to, *Messiah*? I'll stand here and admire the view, and I'll know. I'll always know.'

Bo kick-started the Kawasaki, almost fainting as his leg turned to fire. He slumped against the bike and, if it hadn't been for the cold slap of metal against his face, he thought he might have slipped off the bike and given himself to whatever the scarf-man wanted to do to him.

But the engine roared and, for the first time since he bought it, he was grateful for its insane acceleration. He snapped a look up to the window as he trundled the bike out into the alley. The strange figure was insouciantly waving him good-bye, leaning over the ledge like a neighbour having a chat.

Bo blew him a kiss and ramped up the throttle, left him behind in a cloud of angry black litter and dust.

21. CONTACT INHIBITION

Among all of the gale-assaulted, deracinated faces angling into the wind around the village, there was one that remained in Sarah's thoughts almost all the time. A great number of the Southwold populace were aged, relaxed into their bodies with the fragile grace of those having had years of practice, but this one, this tall man with a long, steel-grey ponytail and glittering eyes, seemed utterly out of context. He seemed simultaneously ill at ease with people and space. She often saw him walking unsteadily on the beach, or metronomically sipping from a pint glass of dark beer in one of the pubs, as if it were some new task that he had recently learned. She might have become used to him, assimilated him as part of the background like the fishermen, or the tankers on the horizon, were it not for his habit of becoming animated whenever she took Claire out for some fresh air. He always seemed to be at the edge of things. He always seemed to be watching. Sarah berated herself at first, blaming her hair trigger, suspecting a connection to Manser. But if Manser knew she were here, he'd be here too. Manser was not one for delicate probings, spies and reports back. He'd be here with his fists and his fury.

Still, it was creepy, the way this old man cropped up. He'd be in the aisle at the Co-op while Sarah did her shopping. He'd be on a table near to theirs when they stopped at the café for hot chocolate and shortbread. Sarah had taken Claire to the pub one night for hot toddies and the old man had been sitting in the corner shadows, wet gleams where his eyes should be. One windy day they'd been caught by the rain as they walked up to the pier. She'd hurried Claire beneath it, appalled by how thin and light she felt when she placed her hands upon her. They had sat in the sand and Sarah finger-combed Claire's hair dry. Claire, as she always had, leaned into her mother and Sarah had to stop herself from pushing her away at the feel of that large lump swelling her armpit and the area beneath her shoulder blade. Sarah had dabbed the lump with ointments and cold compresses, but it refused to settle. Her mind was filling with black futures. Chemotherapy. Surgery. Implacable faces over case notes bound for a file that read DECEASED. The old man came up from a groyne like the gradual lengthening of its own shadow. Sarah only realised there was somebody else there when he coughed into his fist. In his other hand he held a parcel of greaseproof paper, its base darkened by whatever was steaming inside. He stood there like an imbecile, nodding at them, bizarre jerks of the head, like a horse with its bit too tight in the mouth. Sarah ignored him, but Claire became more and more agitated. She fidgeted and mewled and ground herself into the sand as she were some kind of burrowing insect. The man half-offered the parcel, thought better of it, and moved away, looking back over his shoulder half a dozen times until the swell of the beach swallowed him. It seemed to Sarah that he was memorising their position, or more, fixing them in his mind, their aspects, their shape in the sand before him. Sarah had felt a sudden belt of fear. It wasn't that he was following them. That didn't bother her too much. She could cope with that known factor. What got to her was that he wasn't being subtle about it. There was no acceptance of any politesse, the rules of engagement in terms of stalking.

She stayed on that beach with her daughter far longer than she had planned, long after the rain had ceased and the fishermen with their tents began arriving on the shingle. Claire had relaxed again at the disappearance of the old man. They held each other and their hearts beat like those of trapped, confused birds. He was old. He looked very tired. He looked a man out of time. There was no meat on him.

No paunch, no dewlaps. But he had been anything but frail. His hands were large, the fingers slim and long. The fingernails had been like arrowheads. He moved like someone preserving their energy. It was cattish, stealthy, disarming. There was speed in him, and agility. He looked to have been bred for it.

'We might be leaving soon, Claire,' she said. 'It might be that we have to go.'

Her daughter did not nod, or shake her head. She did not ask why. Sarah was almost there with her, at that resigned state, allowing life to happen to her rather than being in some position to be able to shape it. She hugged her daughter more tightly and wished that whatever strength she had left, some of it might pass into her child, enough to see them through this.

He was on the beach again the following morning.

Sarah had already seen him, shortly after starting her shift at the junk shop. She had been trying to free up the routes around the shop – restacking plastic chairs, tidying piles of battered luggage, redesigning the flow of bookshelves – when she had been conscious of a face at the window, a figure watching her work. She could see, through the misted glass, the tight, gleaming shell of his hair, the deep shadows hollowing the area under his cheekbones. The banished tremors of dread on the beach stole back into her. This seemed to be her default feeling now. This was normality for her. He was gone as soon as she saw him, his head ducking down out of sight beneath the windowframe. She heard the muffled sound of footsteps scraping, hurrying away. The armful of magazines she had been shifting spilled from her grasp and slithered to the floor. She thought of sickness; she thought of guts. She had seen a pig opened by a slaughterman at an abattoir when she was ten. The pig had emptied as though everything inside it was untethered, sloshing around as random mess. Whenever she heard someone refer to butterflies in the stomach she balked at the lie. Not butterflies. Christ. She turned her mind to the task of clearing up, eager to rid her mind of the clinging, craven figure. She shifted a deck chair, its hinges rusted, its fabric worn to the point of disintegration. Behind it was yet another bookcase rammed with swollen paperbacks. She yanked the edge of it towards her. Dead termites and about half a pound of bone-dry sawdust tipped off the back of it on to the floor. The books were beyond rescue. Peeling the

covers apart to identify the authors only succeeded in tearing the face
off them.

What was he doing here? What does he want with us?

She swept the books into a black plastic bin sack and tied it off.
This she left with the deck chair in a growing pile of items destined
for recycling skips. She'd have to run them past Ray first, but he
surely couldn't sell this stuff. She paused a moment, listening. The
shadow at the window was long gone, but her disquiet was not so
eager to depart. She heard the grind of springs in the ancient sofa in
Ray's staff room as Claire shifted. She was trying to sleep, but the cyst
under her arm was making it difficult for her to relax.

His face whenever Claire was around. That soppy, doe-eyed look.
That yearning.

Sarah stared at the junk awaiting her attention. This was a building
with far too much stuff and not enough space. She could rearrange all
she liked, and get rid of the things that she'd be hard-pressed to give
away to the most needy, and still it wouldn't make much of a difference.
God, even her job was a mirror.

The snick of a lock. The creak of a hinge.

Sarah felt the slam of a door vibrate through her body, but when
she looked around, the entrance was still open. Must have been her
heart, then, she reasoned, as she hurried back to the counter and the
ante-room where she had left her daughter. The stifling threat came
at her like a swarm of wasps. It was all around; it didn't have a centre.
She couldn't understand her instinct to flee, but it was in her and she
could not ignore it.

Just an old man. Seeking comfort, seeking company.

She clattered through the counter, slamming the hinged partition
back with enough force to crack it. She saw that Claire was asleep, or
whatever passed for sleep in her lexicon these days, and the thin man
with the iron-grey ponytail and pale-green eyes was leaning over her
like a concerned grandparent. Claire's left arm was flung back over
her head; the lump tucked into the armpit radiated black lines of
decay through the muscles arranged around it. What wasn't that
colour of badness was an angry red. Sarah thought she could feel heat
driving out of her, even at a distance of six feet or so. The man was
cooing over it. A big butcher's knife hung from his fist.

Sarah slammed into him, piling her fingers into his hair and
dragging him backwards, her eyes fast on that flashing slice of metal

as it slit the air a foot away from her face. The smell of pear drops did nothing to soften his appearance. Claire was waking but was unable, it appeared, to invest any emotion in the scene playing out before her beyond a kind of vacuous amusement, as if it wasn't real, or was the dregs of a dream she had been having.

'Run, Claire!' Sarah screamed, as hard as she could, trying to pierce that infuriating bubble. The man was lying on top of her, but he wasn't struggling to get up. In the calmness he was displaying, Sarah believed she was dead. He seemed to know that he was going to disentangle himself, deal with this minor impediment, and continue his pursuit. He was calm, relaxed, sighing as though burdened by a particularly wearisome task. It wasn't helping that Claire was rising with the urgency of someone about to spend a lazy afternoon picnicking by the river.

She had to kill him, fast, and fuck any consequences.

She stretched out for the petty cash box at the same time that he was levering himself up on the hand holding the knife. She pushed herself off the floor and stamped down hard on it, trapping the weapon and his fingers against the concrete floor. In the same moment she swung the heavy metal box in a broad arc over her head, so hard that she was almost facing in the opposite direction, so she didn't see it connect with his left cheekbone with a crunch that reminded her of the sound celery made when you bit into it.

She whipped her head around to see him leaning against the wall, his face coming apart in his hands, expressionless, that same sigh whispering out of him. She came again, swinging the box in the opposite direction, a better aim now. She was going to take the back of his fucking head off. But he shifted at the last moment and propelled his right fist into the angle of her jaw, the petty cash box impacting harmlessly into the wall beside him. The world tilted violently away from her and she was almost amused to find that you actually did see stars when you were knocked senseless. She went down like something without bones, knowing what was coming to her but somehow unable to send the right signals to her muscles to get her out of trouble.

But it didn't land, that final sting, that switching off. She groaned and managed to turn her head enough to get a better view of the room. It was slanted, weird, a Dr Caligari room. The unusual perspective was giddying. A wedge of black was the underside of the sofa almost touching her forehead, the sofa where Claire had been sleeping. The room sprang up white and painful beyond it. The man was sitting by the doorway, regarding her daughter. His mouth was filled with blood; it ran down in parallel lines to his chin from each corner, turning him into a ghastly ventriloquist's dummy. His good eye was wide open, almost pained, almost beseeching. The eye she had damaged was a jellied, red thing sitting in its crackled orbit like some small, fatally shelled mollusc.

He tried to speak and the reason for the blood in his mouth fell out: a chunk of flesh, still dressed in a little patch of crimson denim. Sarah almost fainted when she realised it was a part of her own leg, the voice of its pain piping up as soon as the morsel had plopped free of his jaws, as if in recognition of itself. The man was shaking his head slightly now, and trying to say something, or saying something that she was failing to hear. Shadows played like black flames over his face.

Sarah struggled to her feet and the world turned the grey of cold porridge. She vomited a brown spray of partially digested croissants and coffee across the blankets on the sofa, crazily grateful that they were brown too and would help to reduce her embarrassment. The man didn't even register her any more. It seemed that his injury had caught up with him. He gazed beatifically at Claire as blood bubbled at his lips and his fist flopped around the handle of the knife as if it had become too slippery to hold.

She ushered Claire to her feet, dragging her by her cardigan and bullying her to the door. Claire moaned, flinched, as Sarah's hand connected with the swollen mass of tissue under her armpit. Sarah hesitated for a second, having to grit her teeth to the whiff of rot that breathed up from her daughter when she flailed, trying to break free of her mother's grasp. Fear was muddying her mind. What was wrong with her daughter? What had this swine done to her? She couldn't keep running. She couldn't maintain this level of anxiety without suffering. The moment she succumbed meant the end of things. Her daughter would be lost. As she left the room she saw the thin man turn his head to watch her leave. He was slithering in his own blood, trying to get up.

She took Claire out to the car and fastened her into it, then locked the door, knowing she could not leave without warning Ray about the monster in his shop. She felt squirts of piss lubricating her inner thighs. She yelled with shock as she saw a shadow grow on the shop porch.

Somehow she drove the six hundred yards to the pub without slamming the car into a shop front or a bus stop and parked as close as she could to the Lord Nelson. She was clambering out when she felt those black flames of shadow gather again behind her eyes. She clenched her fist against it, this mass of exhaustion and pain and panic as it tried to eclipse her, and fell from the car. A moment or two of grey, a solidifying in her mind of what was real. A second gone? Maybe more. A second too many. She pulled in a few breaths of cold sea air and made 'stay here' gestures with her hand, but Claire wasn't going anywhere. She had the thousand-yard stare. She was other places.

Sarah hurried away from Market Place towards the pub. She glanced back at the car before the edge of the buildings cut off her view of her daughter but the windscreen was a white bar of reflected light. Through the window of the pub she could see couples sitting together, sipping drinks, staring into the middle distance as if infected by Claire's malaise. The closer you get, the longer you spend, the less you share. She shivered as an image, unbidden, unfolded in her mind: her daughter withdrawing so far that any animation on her part would destroy her; opening her mouth to speak, her cheeks cracking and crumbling like casts of sand.

She burst through the door. The barman looked up, dishcloth fist inside a pint glass. The light in here, amber shot through with the acid primaries from the fruit machine, swirled in his spectacles. Claggy warmth enveloped her. She felt sweat blister her forehead.

'Do you fer?' he asked. She shook her head. Ray wasn't here. People picked up their glasses and set them down. They eyed her, happy for a diversion. An old man's teeth rattled in a slack mouth. Nausea hatched like a clutch of snake eggs in her guts. She pushed her way out of the pub and turned left, needing the space, the fresh slap of wind off the beach. A minute to gather her thoughts, to clear her head, then back to Claire and away. She'd have to write to Ray and apologise. She couldn't stay any longer. Something was gravitating. The pressure of it was like the coming of a summer storm. She was wilting, smothering. She scrambled for the door, and heads turned as the afternoon drinkers watched her go. Sarah didn't care. The keys to the car were in her hand and she couldn't remember digging in her pocket for them. The beach huts stretching off into the distance had never looked so scabrous and uninviting. Now she saw that there was some movement at the rear of the nearest; shadows lengthened and crumpled against the rise of the dunes abutting them. Sarah gazed back towards the car. The light had vanished; she could see Claire's head resting against the window. Cold salt air stung her lips where she had been chewing them. She dabbed a finger to her mouth: red.

She heard noises. Gasps. Grunting. Was somebody getting fucked behind there? She moved to see, despite the itch in her feet to be away. A figure was thrusting; pockets of wet air came from another positioned beneath it. Nothing good, she thought, and moved nearer. It was a weird feeling of exultation, exhilaration. Whatever was being done to this poor bastard couldn't be being done to Claire. Everything was pink and frilly in the world. Birds singing. Pour me a glass of bubbly.

But not shadow, after all, on those dunes. Every thrust of the fist from this hunched man brought a whoop of air and more blood splashing on to the sand. She could see from the limpness of the body that he was dead. Yet still the man stabbed and punched. How could he keep gasping if he was dead? The other man breathed evenly, if thickly. Then he moved enough for her to see how he was working the chest, the ribs imploded beneath his fists, the lungs massaged into animation by the blows even if their owner was long gone.

'Ray?' she said, although there could be no hope for an answer. His killer, though, turned to look at her with bleak, blurred eyes. He was focused only on the physicality of violence. His mind was miles away. He tried smiling at her, his face like something from a plastic surgeon's portfolio. His face seemed crumpled on one side, like a tin can with a hard-angled dent to it. There was a gleam, like remembered joy in his expression, the look of someone who has been transported back through time to a happier place at the scent of some evocative perfume. He turned further; the suck of his hands as they came free of Ray's chest made her legs fold beneath her. She put out her hand and then retracted it, afraid that he would reach out to steady her. She went down awkwardly on her knee; her shoe came off.

'Here,' he might have said, but his mouth was busy with something. She could think only of glistening red gloves as she hurried away, her shoe forgotten, only now registering how shockingly cold, how painfully bright the afternoon was. She ran hard along the main road, her teeth gritted against the way the world kept wanting to spin in a direction that threatened to spill her into the display windows of any number of shops. Sarah was crying by the time she reached the car. Claire was staring at her as if she were a complete stranger. She dropped her keys as she tried to unlock the door of the Alfa Romeo. She dropped them again and had to scrabble on the ground to pick them up.

'Come on!' she chastised herself. 'Come *on*!'

The door unlocked, the key stabbed in the fascia, Sarah checked in the direction of the beach and then her daughter in the rear-view mirror. Claire had the window down. Her face was upturned to the stream of air, her eyes closed. Her hand was tucked under her armpit. Her nails were worrying the fabric over the bump. Sarah turned on the radio loud to combat that awful skrit-skrit noise of her nails. The way he moved. The speed of the fucker.

Sarah backed the car out of its parking space with enough violence to bring people from the shops and on to the street to watch. She thought she saw Nick at the main entrance of the hotel, but before she could register his expression or whether he was trying to say something to her, she had turned and was roaring out of the village.

She didn't look at her daughter, or the rear-view mirror until she was back on the A14, speeding towards Ipswich. She had no idea where she might go. Away was good enough, for now. Her daughter's hair jerked in the blast of cold air coming through the window. Her eyes were still closed.

Claire said: *I want to suck his fingers*.

Sarah saw her daughter's nostrils flare: she was smelling the air for him.

22. HOW CAN IT NOT KNOW WHAT IT IS?

They sleep when he is awake. They are awake when he sleeps. A kind of sleeping. A kind of wakefulness.

They are like us and not like us. They have differences, difficult to see, but they are there. A bifid uvula. A silverish tongue. A perfection in the skin that abides no scars or blemishes. Their limbs regenerate. They have no gag reflex. The tips of their teeth are reinforced with zinc.

They hate him. They love him.

They are connected to him to the point where they feel his sadness, any pain that he sustains. They know of his lonely midnight erections, the way he masturbates over mental images of Keiko, the spike of orgasm. The tears and the yearning. They experience it all, but understand none of it.

Tiny flecks of magnetite in the thoracic cavity enable them to navigate: an organic compass.

They abhor and desire him. They fear him and dream of slitting his throat while he sleeps.

They like to kiss mouths, but not out of affection. It's a way of tasting what might become the next meal. They can secrete oil at will, enabling them to squeeze into places ordinary human beings cannot reach. They glow under ultraviolet light.

They have forgotten the art of murder.

Until –

Bo is dreaming. His eyes are open. It is raining hard outside. Inside too, in places. He is watching the water streaming down the walls. His dream occurs within the dry interstices.

He dreams he does not run from his hideaway on Bernard Street. He defends it doughtily, standing firm in the bookshop as the figure approaches, the scarf wrapped around the lower half of his face like bizarre armour. The man unhooks his blue-tinted sunglasses and places them in a pocket, patting it daintily as if about to sit down to a good book, or a cream tea. The man suddenly lurches for Bo and Bo sidesteps him easily, bringing his arm down hard on the back of his head. The man drops to the floor and Bo kneels on the small of his back, takes his chin between both hands and wrenches an awful, grinding crunch out of him. He flips the dead man on to his back and slides the scarf free. He sees a large, gaping mouth, the jaws unable to close properly because of the shocking array of weapons aligning the gums: broken glass, razor blades, nails, rusting bottle tops. Blood wells in the throat and spills over the brim of his lips.

He is dead, and he is not dead. The unseeing eyes lock with Bo's and are filled with amusement. *This is how you entertain yourself, Messiah?* they ask. *This is your wish fulfilment? Your dreamworld? We'll lock horns before long. And then we'll see who ends the game smiling.*

Bo rises, awake now, properly awake, and rubs his eyes, careful not to close them while facing a part of the building or a view from the window that might give his position away. He checks the barricade at the door is sound and returns to his task, stripping pages out of the old copy of *Razzle* he has found in the bottom drawer of a chest, the only piece of furniture in the room. These he applies to the panes of the two windows that look out over south Tottenham, piece by piece blocking out the light, the view, the outside world. The paper clings to the condensation on the glass, becoming translucent after a while, showing odd, superimposed images of women spreading themselves, or touching themselves. Like double negatives, like the duplicate worlds Bo inhabits when asleep. Before blotting out the last fragment of window, Bo chances a look outside. He keeps his eyes peeled wide, fighting the urge to blink. St Ann's Road moves off in two directions. He can see anybody approaching this derelict, partially burned block of flats from the front or behind, where a hole in the wall looks out on a grassy area filled with shopping trolleys, polythene bags filled with rubbish, spent fast-food containers and the carcass of a Vauxhall Chevette, home to two tramps who drink red biddy and fuck on the dented, guano-spattered bonnet.

This is not a busy pedestrian thoroughfare, although cars speed down it often. Across the road is an Indian restaurant and a grocer's shop. He watches a man stand in the doorway of the shop while he smokes a cigarette. In a window above the restaurant he can see another man talking to a woman while they wash dishes. He can hear the soft clash of cutlery as it is dropped into a drawer. He can smell the cigarette smoke. He can hear the smoulder of the paper as the man takes a drag. He can see the smoke thicken in the deflated balloons of his lungs. He can hear the clunk of a petrol hose being fed into a tank at the station fifty metres away to his right. At these super-sensitive moments, coming to him more and more now, he feels as though he is some kind of conduit for all sensations, a living filter for experience.

He sits in the centre of the room. The fire affected this flat only tangentially: blistered paint on the door, sooty fingers reaching halfway across the magnolia walls. The smell of charred things is still in the air, though the fire has been dead a full six months. Bo had to come out at 4 a.m. with Col, one of the staff writers, to photograph it. He watched a woman leap from one of the windows further along this floor and fudged the shot of her, capturing only the mad dance of her long black hair in the corner of the frame. She was fine, bar the odd cut and bruise. She sat on the kerb and watched her home burn while a neighbour put blankets around her and gave her hot sweet tea to drink. She had the look of someone who had missed a bus, or found the bottle of milk she bought from the supermarket to have soured. It troubled Bo that her hair was straight and calm. In the moment of falling, she had seemed alive. Now she appeared to have been switched off, as if she had realised that moment would be the pinnacle of what it meant to experience life. He did not see her again, and did not know where she went, but it felt good to be living in the same building as she had. Now the memory of her hair seems important for another reason, but he cannot jolt its significance from the tired mess of his mind.

He turns his attention to the interior, listening to the voice of the tower block. He doesn't think there are any other unofficial residents, but he never takes his time coming up the stairs, just in case. He doesn't want to see, or be seen.

Water is sluicing in and around the building as if trying to rinse away something bad. The chatter of wind in the bone-dry litter of rooms unopened for months. The patter of mice feet, and their echo in tiny, industrious hearts. What could be the wind see-sawing through the keyholes and cracks might also be breath in resting, still bodies. He turns himself off from what is beginning to unsettle him.

Now it is safe to close his eyes. In the instant he does so, he feels the answering flicker of thousands of eyelids, and a massed curiosity, a drinking in of detail that is limited to a few square feet of dusty, varnished pine, all he is allowing them. He feels the usual combination of filthy invadedness and heart-stopping excitement. And he sees their development.

He sees:

the woman carrying shopping bags from the Waitrose on Marylebone High Street. She looks up at a passenger jet making chalk marks in the winter blue. On Knox Street she is hit by icy blasts of wind and dips her head closer to her scarf. Tiny silver cats hang in her pierced ears. At Paddington Gardens she can hear children laughing in the attractive playground, but before she can draw level to see, shapes move out of nowhere: two men, suddenly there, as if they peeled themselves from the colour of the brickwork. She's shocked to indecision. She keeps her head down, her hands tight on her bags, and marches on. At the entrance to the Gardens, one of the men slips up behind her and grabs her wrist

LIKE THIS, MAP READER?

while the other sweeps a straight leg out and folds her over it

MAP READER, DO YOU APPROVE?

and they drag her into the shadows within earshot of those squealing children, jabbing her with their stings until she is still, her muscles seizing, her face warping with the pain and the toxins. They pull open her coat and blouse and with a horned, scalpel-sharp fingernail one of the men slits her open. They ransack her abdomen with a haste born of violent hunger. She's trying to scream but all that pours forth is a dense ruby froth. Steam from her unveiled body obscures his view

for a moment and then

a father and his son on Parliament Hill beneath a broad sky the colour of overripe apple flesh. They're kicking a ball back and to with the kind of easy skill that comes from long hours of practice. It's getting colder. All of the kite fliers have gone home. London sits in its basin away to the south beneath a caul of amber pollution.

Dad's asking him if he's serious about Jenny and he's shy from the questioning, he just wants to have a kick around. Two women walk out from the goal posts but he can see in the dad's eyes, and the son's eyes, that neither is certain that they were ever there on the other side of that thin barrier of wood.

'I don't fancy yours much,' says Dad, smiling at his boy. The smile masks his uncertainty. He doesn't like the way the women are staring at them. There's something too naked, too raw and bestial about it. They're dressed almost formally, their hair short and, he thinks, bookish; there's nothing lascivious about them, apart from the eyes, which he can tell from here are drinking them in, almost watering with the strain.

'C'mon, Jamie,' says Dad. 'Time to get home.'

THE SOLAR PLEXUS, MAP READER, FOR THE SWIFTEST PARALYSIS, YES?

They swoop after the man and boy and catch up with them before they reach the path that will take them to the park's exit. The Swiss Re tower catches a last ray of sunshine and turns it into a closing bracket; a car farts and belches along Savernake Road.

'Evening, ladies,' Dad says, and gives them his most winning smile. It's a smile that says, no trouble here. No trouble from me or my boy. We're good. We're on your side.

One of the women hits the boy so hard in the face with the heel of her hand that a rupture flashes red across the centre of his throat as his head snaps back.

TOO HARD, MAP READER. I THINK HE'S DEAD. SORRY.

Dad's shocked, gargled 'Hey' of protest doesn't make it past his lips. The other woman pulls him in close, bending him to his knees, peels back her skirt and sends the stinger at her groin powering into the hollow beneath his breastbone. He goes down like something shot. His eye is on that black, glossy ovipositor even as it snuggles back into its sheath, even as the breath catches in his frozen chest and his lips darken. They leave the boy. Dead meat is no good.

They drag the man to a hollowed tree and warehouse him, sealing him into the gap with mucus coaxed from their mouths. It looks, to him, as reality fades, that they are blowing him kisses.

Bo sees that opaque resin too, rising before his eyes. A blink and *five youths dressed in black leap from a window in Poland Street. They clatter into a drunk weaving along the pavement trying to strike a light from the wrong end of a match. Moments later, one of the boys spins away, laughing, raising a bright red lung in his glistening fist. Mouth open, he squeezes oxygen-rich blood into his throat as if he were playing in the bath with a waterlogged sponge*

and

at a school in Hammersmith, a loner pupil called Joe with alopaecia sits on his own in the corner of the canteen, picking at his sandwiches. The new girl comes to sit next to him. When the bell goes for the first double lesson of the afternoon, he doesn't get up. The shutters come down hard on the serving area. The girl reaches out a hand that he takes. She leads him to the gym. Inside, to the rear of the games teacher's office, is a storeroom filled with punctured footballs awaiting repair and old framed certificates telling of forgotten athletic achievements. She has trouble trying to sting him in the right place, and she cups his head in her hands so that she can look closely into his eyes.

WHERE AM I GOING WRONG, MAP READER?

She gently pushes him down to the floor and squats above him. With one hand she peels aside the gusset of her white underwear. She looks at herself with a detached fascination as she squeezes her buttocks together and makes the sting extrude, slowly, its tip weeping clear venom. She flicks it with her finger and it jounces and sways, making little involuntary thrusts at the air. She sees how its curve is causing her to slide ineffectually against him and repositions herself so that her hips are tilted at a higher angle than before. He lies beneath her breathing rapidly, his cheeks ashen, his shirt slashed, his chest and belly a red game of noughts and crosses. The breath tumbles out of him like someone stepping into an uncomfortably hot bath as she buries herself to the hilt into his groin.

She pulls open a false wall at the back of the storeroom and places the boy alongside the games teacher, who is bound in thick white ropes of hardened organic glue. His eyes move dolefully, his jaw is broken, more of the glue holding the mandibles tightly in place so that they can neither crush nor prematurely release the wad of eggs crammed behind his teeth.

The girl closes the partition and returns to the playground. There are fewer children, fewer teachers now. A police car is positioned by the headmaster's office. She turns her face to the sky and watches for the dark cloud.

Hundreds more incidents like that. Hundreds more requests for advice, for endorsement. It's not just a map that he carries, it's a blueprint for survival. He goes to the window and peels back a corner of a page devoted to the pros and cons of having sex in the workplace. He too looks for the dark cloud. The map has altered to accommodate it. Plenty of dark clouds. None that prick his interest.

The map is beginning to fascinate him. He wonders why it was that Rohan Vero was so eager to give it up. It folds around his thoughts when he is resting, like clingfilm around broccoli, settling itself into every niche of his mind as if it were custom-made for him. The grid is still there, pulsing away behind his perception. His hand does not bleed quite so much now, perhaps because he is under-standing the map's impulses to be read. Those impulses had made themselves known in the illusion of rotting hearts on his bedroom floor. You learned to get over that quickly. You recognised what was real and what turned out to be quirks of the map. The patterns on his hand shift as he moves through London searching for Vero. The map, as yet, is not helping him locate the man. It's an extraneous element; it has nothing to do with the real purpose, which he has come to recognise as the city subtly changes.

Lights are going out all over the capital. Roads that were long links between the hubs of what had once been isolated villages, long ago, are being truncated. Kentish Town Road is cut off before it is underway at Camden, where the overland railway bridge has been brought down on to the tarmac. Haverstock Hill is blocked at the junction with Prince of Wales Road. The Euston Road now ends at the Euston Underpass. A black melange of broken concrete and glass takes over from there, running all the way to St Pancras. There are no cars, no buses, running on this version of London's streets any more. They have been abandoned at the points where their journeys were curtailed by upheavals unlisted in the *A–Z*. Figures inhabit them, perhaps treating them as shelter from the cold, more likely using them as urban camouflage from which to launch attacks. Each night, the city sloughs off more and more of its logic and accrues the shadows and rot, verdigris and mould, lonely cold places where trouble can spawn. The city is slowly being cut off from the links that might take people away or bring help in. It is drawing its limbs into a shivering heart, like a flower thrown on to a fire. It is dying. It is waking up.

Bo's map delineates these new twists and turns to the roads before they materialise. In the darkness, he waits on the floor of the flat, hearing the groans and creaks as his town realigns itself into a place this breed can understand. The city is regressing; the city is becoming the disease that is spreading through Bo's body. He feels this when he's ventured out at night. He feels that he's the only solid part of the street, and that all else is liquid, unstable. He feels himself skimming through it, touching everything around him tangentially, like the tips of the feet of a waterboatman on a meniscus. Dribs of his surroundings sometimes catch on his hair, his clothing; he feels it tease away from the fabric of what appears to be real, a minute wrenching out of true, a needle drawn through a blob of paint: traces trail behind him for a span.

In the morning, the streets revert to their original status. They correspond to the orange and white lines of his street atlas. He feels safe going out during the day, but the roads he walks along feel faked, a mock-up on a Hollywood soundstage. The traffic is an animation. The people who cleave to the pavements are soulless marionettes shifting jerkily under an invisible puppet-master's strings. The lights that come on and go off are too measured, like a pre-programmed security system. Everything seems too precise, too controlled. For the first time he realises that thousands are relying on him; he is the finger that can slip the knot for them, allow the strands to come loose, to bring freedom to an oppressed race. He sees how he works outside any imposed realm. His world doesn't know, or care a fig, about the strictures of architecture or science or society.

And then Vero's haggard face rises out of the optimism and shows him the map's bonus features. His misery, his desperation, can he see any of that in his own face? He doesn't know because he hasn't looked in a mirror for weeks.

He retreats from the allure. He sees it for what it is. It's his own death sentence. It's London's own Holocaust. There's still enough of himself burning to be able to back away and fight.

He wonders where Keiko is now. Who she might be with. How she might be making love with that taut, supple loveliness of hers. She could make a kiss feel as though it were enveloping every part of your body when it was just your lips that were being touched. She could help him, he was sure of it. She could help him before it killed her.

He stares back at the floor as acid tears stream down his face. *Keep fooling yourself with that one*, he tells himself, *if it helps you any*.

'Vero!'

He regrets the outburst as soon as it's out. He shouted the name so hard that his throat is sore, and the silence around him carries a heavy, muffled tang, as if it were insulted. Dogs bark in the street. He hears a gang trilling and screaming as they run through the darkness. The map pulses behind his eyes, growing all the time, the number of people requiring assistance diminishing, the number of deaths and warehousings increasing.

Little corners of London are being turned into larders.

23. FOGBOUND

She kept her eyes dead ahead, concentrating on the beams from the headlights as they pushed through the light fog on the motorway. Nick had turned on the radio, some jazz station filled with noodling muted trumpets and shivering drums. She hated jazz, hated its lack of structure. It was lazy music, she thought, but it was somehow suitable now, a confused, rambling soundtrack to her life. In her mind, though, utter clarity, at least regarding one thing. London. She must get Claire down to London.

Nick had flashed her down on the country road out of Southwold. She had wanted to laugh out loud and scream hard enough to blister his face as he asked her where she was off to. *Are you okay?* he had asked. *Is everything tickety-boo?*

I just saw a man up to his arms in Ray. My daughter was almost taken from me. We could have died. Am I all right? Yeah, fair to middling. Mustn't grumble.

Acid-blue light was roiling around the deepening colour of the sky behind his head. She liked the image. The marriage of blues, his face. She liked his face very much, she decided, despite his dumb questions. She was happy to see him and happy too that he had offered to take her; there wasn't enough chivalry in her life. She was dead tired. The thought of driving any kind of distance made her feel sick.

'What about your car?' he asked her. She'd parked it in a lay-by. She shrugged. 'It doesn't matter. It's for the best that I get rid of it, actually. The people who want me, they know what kind of car I drive.'

'I'm just sorry you had to trade Italian pizzazz for this Swedish bucket.'

'Beige too,' she said. 'There ought to be a law against beige.'

'I think there is now. But there's a beige amnesty. If I hand this car in within thirty days they won't prosecute. To hell with it, though. I'd rather be a fugitive.'

'Claire –' she said.

'She's sleeping.'

She looked at him, at his soft, amiable features. He resembled a cat that has just eaten its fill and found the best spot by the fire.

'I might kiss you,' she said, her voice all wrong, the words filled with holes.

'I might let you.'

He was regarding the ugly bite in her jeans. Blood was coagulating around the torn edges like gleaming rubies.

'You've got a nasty gash,' he said.

'How would you know? You haven't seen it yet.'

That stung a laugh out of him, which suddenly turned to a grimace.

'What?'

'I just pulled something in my back,' he said.

'Christ, look at us both. A pair of infirms.'

'I'm very firm, thanks. Speak for yourself.'

The drone of the car cut through their banter. Shock caught up with her. She began to shiver so violently that her feet began to stamp into the footwell. Nick turned the heating up high and after ten minutes pulled into a lay-by in view of the level crossing at Darsham Station.

'You'll need a stitch or three in this beaut,' he said. 'Not to mention a tetanus shot. But this will do for now.' He reached behind the passenger seat and pulled out a first aid travel pack.

'Were you a Boy Scout?' she asked him, her teeth chattering against each other so violently it ruined the words.

'I'm not being forward or anything, but you'll have to pull those down.'

Together, with much hissing and groaning on Sarah's part, they eased her jeans down over her hips. The bite was surrounded by a bruise. Nick washed the bite with bottled water, then wiped it dry with some gauze and drew fresh cries from her with an antiseptic wipe. As best he could he closed the wound with four butterfly sticking plasters. He pressed a dressing on top of that and wound a bandage around her thigh.

'You look gorgeous,' he said. 'Anything else hurt?'

'No. You bastard.' The pain had stung tears from her, but she managed to smile at him.

They were quiet for a while, but the tension in the car became so great that she had to open the window. 'We need to go,' she said. She was staring at the rear-view mirror so hard it was as if she were willing the thin man to be there.

'Where?'

She couldn't answer.

'What happened?'

She told him and, as the details grew worse, her voice became more fluid, more relaxed. She wondered if danger was what she needed to make her feel anything like normal.

'Jesus, Sarah, we have to talk to the police. They have to –'

'No.' And then she said it again. And again. And suddenly she was screaming the word at him until her voice was cracking with the effort, her sight blurred with tears and confusion. She darted a look at Claire, appalled that she had forgotten her daughter, but she slept on, her thumb in her mouth.

Nick sat with his hands resting on the steering wheel, staring ahead at the level crossing. A large articulated lorry came thundering over it from the opposite direction, its cabin surrounded by high-powered lights. Sarah caught a glimpse of two large bare arms holding a steering wheel, a nameplate that said MACCREADLE. A Manchester City pennant. And then the lorry was slamming past them, rocking the car in its slipstream. She felt she should flag him down, implore him to turn back, stay away from the coast where danger awaited. But she knew that was no longer the case. The thin man would be coming. She could almost see the wraith that was his shadow presaging his arrival.

'Claire has . . . a condition. There's something seriously wrong.'

She could tell by the way he was looking at her that Nick was sceptical. But he didn't make any challenge. Instead, he reached for her hand. 'I'm sorry,' he said, flatly. 'I didn't know.'

'She has a lump. It's . . . I worry it might be cancer. But we need to get her to a surgeon. It needs to be removed.'

'Surely you should have done something about it before now.'

She felt a flare, but swallowed against her anger. 'I only just found out about it,' she said. 'It's been difficult for us,' she said. 'I thought maybe it would be all right, but Claire . . . she's been behaving oddly. I'm worried she might have some kind of attack. Epilepsy, catatonia. I'm scared that if I take her to hospital, and she needs to be kept in, I'll lose her. I've just felt that it was more important to get away. But you can run away for so long. After a while, it seems to turn into running towards. But now, this lump. It's out of my hands, almost.'

She saw uncertainty in his eyes. She guessed he might be ruing chasing after them, and wishing he was instead back in the hotel, polishing glasses.

Sarah said, 'You stop for too long and everything catches up with you. I don't know. That's how it seems to me. Anyway. I need to get it out of her. I need to find a specialist.'

'London, then?'

'Yes. Claire thinks so too. I wish it didn't have to be. But yes.'

He started the car and revved the engine, but this attempt to disguise his sigh – which fell from him like a collapse – failed. *Just get us to London*, she thought, her mind filled with glistening red. *Nothing else matters.*

The fog didn't look as though it were likely to lift. As they pushed on along the A12 it thickened around the car, gradually erasing the surroundings until only the headlights were picking out any detail, and that nothing more than the colour of the bitumen, the burnished grey snake of the crash barrier at the centre of the road.

She tried to sleep because it was late and she didn't want to be any more muddy-headed in the morning than she was no doubt going to be. Nick was unable to take the car much over forty miles per hour. At this rate it would take them another two or three hours to reach London's outskirts. Every jolt in the road knocked her awake. She kept expecting to see something clinging to the windshield, leering in at her with eyes that couldn't be focused on because of the busy, oily black hair tigering its face. Either that, or the car going into a violent roll down an embankment. She winced at the fresh memory of the fight with the thin man and pushed her thoughts elsewhere, but Claire was at the end of every trail. The car was suddenly too small for her. She needed to stretch her legs. She needed a drink and something to eat. She needed to behave like a normal human being for a little while.

'Nick,' she said, 'my leg's really hurting. You're right. We need to find somewhere to stay. We're not going to be able to do anything when we get to London. Not tonight.'

He nodded. Smiled. He switched off the jazz and took the Colchester exit off the dual carriageway. He found a Ramada hotel at the junction with the A120.

She wondered, as he parked the car, how many of the female staff and visitors to the Southwold hotel he'd whisked off here over the last few months. She allowed herself to be led through the entrance door where he signed them in as Mr and Mrs MacCreadle. The receptionist didn't try to hide her concern for Sarah's bloodied jeans and asked how she had done it.

'I trapped it in a restaurant door,' she said. 'Ten stitches.'

The receptionist sucked air through her teeth at the lie and slowly enunciated the word 'compensation', putting some emphasis on the final syllable. Sarah asked her if she had any painkillers. The receptionist took a box out of her own handbag and handed one of the blister packs over.

'Nice one,' Nick said as they caught the lift. 'She upgraded us to a bigger room. We should use that ploy again some time.'

Sarah hardly noticed the supposed opulence of the room once Nick closed the door behind them. She took a couple of pills, washing them down with a swig from the complimentary bottle of water. She lay down on the busy pattern of the counterpane and switched on the TV. Paying no attention to it, she kicked off her boots and carefully eased out of her jeans, jumper and T-shirt. She realised Nick was looking at her, and she supposed she oughtn't to be surprised. She was topless, wearing only a pair of black knickers. She was too tired to care about the scars on her arms, her stomach.

'I'll take that kiss now,' she said, as she dropped her head to the pillow. By the time he knelt down to offer it, she was already asleep.

24. IN

Gyorsi Salavaria entered the city on the evening of December 1st. It meant something to him that such an action should take place on the first day of the month. It was irrational, he knew, but such minor coincidences – which were not really coincidences at all – gave him the belief that he was operating on a clean canvas, with a fresh palette. It was a new day, a new month. A dawning.

He arrived in a car – a Cherokee Jeep – that he had stolen from one of the drives of the cottages near to the junk shop where he had courted Claire and her mother. To no avail. He had not driven for thirty years yet had not anticipated any trouble. Nevertheless, the alien dashboard, the automatic gears, the endless positions the seat could be adjusted to conspired to delay him to the point where he thought his theft might be over before it had really taken place. But by the time he got the car out of the country roads and on to the dual carriageway he had mastered its various peccadilloes. The Jeep was handy once he reached the city; four-wheel drive helped him over the bodies in the streets, the rubble strewn across the pavements and roads. Each judder and crunch sent a delicious, bracing pain through the bruises on his face.

The events of a few days previously had rocked him. He had believed his passage to the head of the colony would occur without obstruction. It had more or less been promised him, half a lifetime ago. He had paid his dues. He had kept his body clean. He had adapted it to make it more acceptable, in accordance with the colony's long, magnificent history. He had proved himself, his diligence and devastation, his fleet-footedness, his guile, on countless occasions. So what was happening? Why was he being overlooked? His prize had been snatched from him at the moment of his grasping it.

But he had to believe that he still had a part to play. After dispatching Ray he had returned to the junk shop and sat down at it's centre, his feet kicking out exhaustedly in front of him, the floor covered in black shards from old 78s, and closed his good eye, concentrated on reducing the boil of his anger to a manageable simmer, the rampancy of his heartbeat to something approaching normal.

It was important that things be done the right way. They had waited so long for this moment that nothing but the correct protocols and ceremonies was befitting of their reawakening.

He had drawn himself upright, the sun having disappeared from the sky a few hours earlier. He stood in the shadows and felt his confidence stream back. He had not been forsaken. He had had his wrist slapped. He was still involved and he would not allow himself to be bested like that again. There would be an endgame that depended heavily on his input, he was convinced of that.

And now here, in the city, the loud, looming lovely city. He could smell the madness in the air, that special miasma that London was blessed with, a perfume of carrion and cloaca, fast food, carbon monoxide, and sweat. The streets were empty and dark. His was the only car driving into the city along crippled, uneven Gower Street. He rode in past the cameras and speed traps, running red lights, driving on the pavement sometimes to avoid abandoned vehicles, sailing along a bus lane that, at any other time, would have landed him with a hefty fine. Already he felt like the king of the city. It was all laid open for him like a tart, or a dead girl's chocolate box of freshly exposed organs.

Take your pick, take the lot, help yourself.

It excited him in a way he had not experienced since his early days of killing. It was a lofty, buzzy excitement, highly addictive, definitely narcotic, the kind that initially fills you with euphoria before making you feel as though you've been flushed through with warm fluid, cleansed, turned into something that was only ever designed for relaxation. He always slept best after a murder, he found. It was a combination of factors that did it for him. The thrill of the expression was one, perhaps *the* one. It was the same for him in the way it is for some men who hunger for a view of women's breasts: they are essentially the same, but always different. He liked the segue from surprise to alarm to shock to outright fear. And yet fear, proper fear, was something that people did not often, if at all, know anything about. It was not the stock reaction to monsters and madmen in Hollywood films; it was something very different.

Fear manifested itself as a kindred spirit of humour. The people who were scared beyond reason had the look of people who were about to laugh out loud, he found. He supposed it must come from the same tap root of emotion. The person half frightened to death was the person who had been taken so far down the line that madness was the end of the line. Hysteria could take you in any number of directions, once its teeth were sunk into you. You laughed, you screamed, you died. It was a hell of an entertainment.

The first killing, back in 1973, had been that of a fifteen-year-old girl, Linda Meadows, a girl fresh out of school that he had shadowed for the best part of three weeks since seeing her emerge from a hairdresser's in Liverpool, where she worked as an assistant. He had gone in there once, having spent an hour drumming up the courage, and she had washed and conditioned his hair, shyly expressed surprise that a man should go to this trouble when they were more often than not in the barber's further along the street, having a dry cut and talking about football. He had spun her some story about how he was a junior minister up from the Houses of Parliament to visit relatives and he needed to have a professional haircut because he was appearing on a lunch-time television debate that very day. She'd asked for his autograph, which he gave her. He gave her a tip too, after the hairdresser had finished his short back and sides. He'd walked away, returning as it grew dark to watch through the misted windows as she brushed up all of the hair that had dropped that day. The thought of his hair mixed up in a refuse bag with other people's gave him a bizarre thrill.

He watched her leave the hairdresser's and walk to the bus stop, a hundred yards or so further along the street. A fish-and-chip shop was open behind it, and a couple of youths sitting on the doorstep tossed a few degrading remarks her way, which, he was impressed to see, she deflected with stoic good humour. She waited for a long time for the bus, and he admired the way she leaned against the wooden bus shelter, the natural poise and elegance of her long limbs that most other girls of a similar age and build might feel uncomfortable or gawky with. She was wearing a large grey coat with chunky wooden buttons. It seemed too large for her; maybe it was something she was borrowing from an older sister. She also wore blue jeans and white shoes. She fiddled with a thin gold necklace while she waited, her unmade face growing redder as the cold intensified. He remembered her smell in the hairdresser's – difficult to do with the pervasive odours of scorching hairdryers, shampoo and lacquer, but important to him, a part of the whole process and one that he could not do without. She was Charlie and peppermint creams, Daz and Imperial Leather. She wore lip salve. He liked the way she kept pressing her lips together after finishing a sentence, the slight gumminess there. He liked that she didn't ask him if he was going out tonight, if he had been on holiday. No doubt that would be drummed into her as her training increased. In that respect, he would be saving her from a lifetime of cliché and monotony.

He watched her get on the bus and followed in his Vauxhall Viva at a discreet distance. He didn't pay any heed to where the bus was heading. He just followed it, his eye on the soft brown hair in the window at the back of the lower deck. He guessed she was sitting here because the engine was underneath her; the bus was warmest there. But an irrational, excited voice in him said no, she was sitting there so that he could see her. Her special man from the House of Commons. The man she'd talk about to her family and friends when she got home. *You'll never guess whose hair I washed today. Look, I got him to sign my diary.*

He wondered if she had liked him, fancied him even. He could imagine walking out with a girl like that, taking her to bars and restaurants, showing her a good time. It was important that he be attracted to them. He knew this was a part of it, a part of what was required of him. They needed to know that in the deepest, darkest moments of his savagery, there was love; that his devastating attacks were motivated by love. Of them, of the victim. Love was all they asked for. It was the only thing that mattered.

And so she finally got off the bus somewhere in Old Swan, on her final night on Earth, and walked down four streets that diminished in size and illumination, until she was, Salavaria reasoned, close to where she needed to be. He parked the car and nimbly leaped out, just as she was shaking her door keys free of her cumbersome duffel coat.

'Have you ever considered a career in politics?' he asked her.

She turned around and smiled at him. He knew how he must look to her. One of his strengths was his ability to view himself in any given scenario. He had cinematic vision. He knew how the light and shade played with people. He understood the importance of drama, of impact.

Here he is, his back to the streetlamp, his collar turned up. Shadows must fill his eye sockets, and colour in the lines growing in the hollowed cheeks. His mouth, as all mouths do at night, in unnatural light, looks blue-grey. His hair, a long way off from becoming the silver tumble of its future, is black and shiny from the attention this girl lavished upon it. She is happy and sad at the same time. Something in her crumples, like spirit, like life itself. She gives herself to him as if this has always been a part of her design, the thing that defines her. It's as if it were written in pink ink in the pages of the diary she gave him to sign.

He holds out his hand and she shyly mirrors him. Without looking at him, she accepts his grip. He leads her off the road on to the recreation ground at the back of this terrace of tired grey houses.

'You are exquisite,' he says.

She says, 'Kiss me good-bye.'

He does so. It becomes a beautiful act, out there on the cold, faecal playing fields. In her bloody passing, she is sudden art, something to be framed and stared at by generations. Her death is a kind of life eternal. She will never be forgotten, she will always stay young. Her face will peer out from the pages of newspapers all around the world. Or this is how he sees it, applying a cosmetic from his own imagination to the bloody squirm of lips desperately trying to deliver a cry from behind his fingers. The fists with which she tries to box his head and balls become clenched hands of beseechment that the glory be delivered swiftly and painlessly. She swears at him, but he doesn't hear it. All he hears is her saying his name.

When the tragi-comic mask of her ending has been peeled from her skull, he unravels her on the dew-soaked grass and snaffles her thymus, her kidneys, her ovaries while they are still hot. He lowers himself on to and into the shallow hollowed bowl of her corpse and thanks her, sending every shred of goodwill he can muster into these gurgling remnants as they drain into the soil. Every twitch and flicker of his muscles is greeted by some tiny opposing suck of her own, as if she were trying to keep him here, to prolong the moment. But he peels himself away as the sky is turning ochre, the cold in his bones giving him an ache that will not relent until he has bathed for half an hour in hot water.

He staggers away. There is movement in the trees although the wind has long since died. He stands at the corner of the park watching the magical spill of dawn. Her face blazes across the synapses of his mind as if tattooed, branded there.

Ridding young people of life was such hard graft. They were strong. It clung to them, life, as tenaciously as a barnacle to a whale. Driving it out of them was exhausting; he understood, to some degree, how those who did it often were caught. You reached a threshold, a limit. Your body railed against the effort, physical and mental. You began to get sloppy. You made mistakes. You left clues. You began along the road where you entertained the idea of being caught. It was intoxicating to imagine the fuss that would be made of you. The attention. The infamy. Your place in the pantheon of serial killers. A kind of respect. A sort of life. You kidded yourself that you wanted that attention when all along it was because the misery of hard work was seeping through your bones like winter in a dying tree.

Not for him. The hard work was a stepping-stone to a different place. The hard work was a means, not the end. That was the mistake all of those other monsters had made. For them, the hard work was the result, its own reward. Such a reward can lose its flavour over time. Salavaria had known back then that his reward was a long way off. The hard work focused him on it. He knew he had to perfect his labours in order to put himself on the right track to reach that reward. He knew he would be closer to the grave than the cradle by the time it came his way. He also knew that nothing on Earth would stop him from claiming it, when the time was right.

Linda Meadows. Born January 15, 1958. Died March 1, 1973. Always in my thoughts. You tasted like burnt treacle. Thank you. Thank you.

*   *   *

Salavaria broke into the Monet Suite on the fifth floor of the Savoy hotel. He was invisible. He was wallpaper. Death had been dealt on the broad sweeping staircases; it had trickled down the marble and deep pile, puddled around his shoes. There was a cluster of severed heads on the concierge's desk, all bearing the same tired, nauseous expression of someone who has just stepped off a ferry in gale-force winds. Blood zigzagged along the corridors where bodies had been hauled off to be ransacked; red footprints marched into and out of trouble. Inedible organs had been discarded like the wrappers from children's sweets.

The clean were warehousing the dirty.

A conference suite was being used as a walk-in larder. Bodies were being stripped, laid out, shorn, disembowelled, marked with indelible pen: BEST BEFORE 3/1/09. Short, shocked screams were impacting against the walls and ceilings like sporadic gunfire. The atrium swimming pool was crimson, topped with pink foam and body parts that rolled this way and that in the delicate ebb and flow. A man in a dinner jacket, his bow tie loose, hanging at his collar, strolled along the corridor holding a human rib in each fist, blood splashed like a gunshot wound to his mouth.

Salavaria felt at home.

He moved through the suite, admiring the marble bathroom, the view over the Thames, the extravagant bed, and deep pile beneath his toes. In the full-length mirror on the wardrobe, he assessed his posture and shape, gritted his teeth to check how strong and white they were. While he was drawing a bath he heard the door breathe open. He moved across the tiles to peek through the gap; three men in long overcoats and short, dyed-red hair were moving languidly across the room, pausing to pick up and assess ornaments or check surfaces for dust. His attention dwelt upon the man at the rear, who drew shadow to him like the others, but nevertheless carried something, some lithe, sassy authority, that the others could never hope to shoulder. Violence steamed off him. When he turned and sat down, Salavaria found himself lifting a hand to his mouth in shock.

'I'm impressed,' he said, stepping from the bathroom. The two men accompanying this strange, compelling figure jumped, spinning to face Salavaria, struggling in their pockets for whatever weapons were concealed there. The third man kept his attention on the gew-gaw he had picked up from the table: a thick glass ashtray. His teeth tanged softly together.

'Doesn't that go through you?' Salavaria asked. 'I mean, Jesus, that would set my fillings off something terrible.'

The man ignored him. 'We go and get what we want,' he said. 'Obliterate the fuckers. Take over.'

'Well, yes,' Salavaria said. 'By the way, what's your name?'

'Names are for tombstones, baby.'

'Hmmm. I'm Gyorsi.'

'You can call me Graham Greene.'

'Graham Greene. Very well, Mr Greene. You're in my room. Would you mind fucking well not being?'

Now Salavaria was rewarded with a direct gaze. The other man's eyes were large and dark, even in this brightly lit space, as if they were congested with shadows created from within.

'I know why you're here,' Greene whispered.

'I'm ecstatic for you, really I am. But I have things to do. A long bath and a cocktail for a kickoff. I'd really rather you weren't around while I'm enjoying them.'

'We can take you to where you need to be.'

'I'm not a child. I can find my way around this stinkhole.'

Greene gave the approximation of a smile. His mouth seemed to collapse back under the bent fence of metal piled into his gums. Salavaria caught a coppery, carious whiff. A nasty-looking nail at the front of the lower jaw had dug itself a socket in the upper lip. It embedded itself there now, like a lock for his mouth. He seemed unfazed by the fresh blood leaking from the wound.

'I don't doubt it. I'm not offering you a bodyguard service. I know how dangerous you are. I'm just saying I can take you from A to B, without you detouring off to X, Y, and Z first.'

'Maybe I *want* to have a look around. It's been some time. I'd quite like to do a bit of sightseeing.'

Greene regarded him with a strange kind of patient disdain. Salavaria guessed that any expression on that face could never fall into a conventional bracket.

'I know why you're here,' Greene said, having to wipe and rewipe his mouth as it dribbled and frothed. 'And I know who you are. What you were. What you hope to become. We want to be a part of it. We want to be there at the start of this new order. Happy, of course, to doff our caps to the alpha male.' He lowered his eyes in mock tribute to the older man, and for the first time Salavaria found himself experiencing fear. He had to reach out and hold on to a chest of drawers to prevent himself from losing his balance. It was like receiving a blow. He realised now that his passage to the throne was not as clear as he had envisaged. Squirrelled away in the trees for decades, you developed a sense of yourself uncomplicated by anything as inconvenient as other people. Being alone became a habit; it was a difficult one to break. He was not used to such impudence, but the world had turned; it was only natural that youth should rise up against reputation. Perhaps Greene was unimpressed by Salavaria's history, but his henchmen, Cobain and Kubrick, were eyeing him with unalloyed reverence. He had them on his side for as long as it took for his ascension.

'We should warn you,' Greene said, 'there is an obstacle to our progress. A man called Mulvey. A reader of maps. A teacher.'

Salavaria couldn't tell if the way that last word was spoken was down to the ruin of Greene's mouth, or extreme sarcasm. He smiled. 'I'm on nodding terms with that concept,' he said. 'Each generation needs its hand holding, at least for a short while.'

'Yes, well,' Greene said, inspecting the crimson half-moons of his fingernails, 'the hand isn't so much doing any holding as breaking necks. Oh, he's put the hours in, but against his will. Now he's a conscious conscientious objector. And as much as it pains me to say this, he's dangerous.'

'Too dangerous for you?' Salavaria said, pursing his lips. 'I find that hard to stomach. Strapping chap like yourself. A fellow with . . . presence. With gravitas.'

Greene smirked. A fingernail found the edge of a torn piece of tin and played vile music against it.

'Kill this "teacher" for me,' Salavaria said. 'And I'll consider you for a nectaring.'

Greene's eyes flashed and Salavaria felt his pulse slow a little. It was in the bag. It was the reason he hadn't already been attacked. 'You know I have it in me, this essence, this dedication to the cause,' Salavaria said. 'I need a right-hand man. And I offer you immunity from the death hanging over your head. But we don't have much time. Bring me Mulvey's head, and we can iron out the details of how you'll become my prince.'

He heard a scream outside the door and a woman wearing a towel around her waist sprinted along the corridor, skin creamy with suds.

Salavaria saw claw marks in the prodigious meat of her breasts; the fear locked into her features ramped his heartbeat back up again. It was healthy, he thought, an experience not to be missed, knowing what it was to fear for your own life. The human face so often never wore that particular cast. It could inspire a rare beauty, he felt. The smell of her was wild, intoxicating. The fresh piss on her thighs was giving him a lusty headache.

'Now,' he said, moving towards the threshold, his salivary glands squirting painfully, 'we're all in agreement, I hope. So you'll excuse me while I sort myself out a spot of supper.'

25. THE MAP UNFOLDS

The Ninja pissed him off, in the main, but he couldn't argue that when he needed to be away fast, there was anything better. Especially now, in this city of abandoned or crashed cars, this city where the pavements and roads were smeared with human remains, like paté trodden into the floor. Buses were overturned and set alight; a thick pall of black, chemical smoke moved through the streets, shrouding one moment, revealing the next. He kept his head down and didn't study too much the shapes that the smog peeled away from or coagulated against. He opened the throttle when he could and relished the snarl of the four-stroke engine. He braked hard and late when he had to, accelerating away quick as he could when obstacles were rounded. He sensed the potential in the shadows of the trashed buildings; a coiling of kinetic energy. If he paused too long, they'd strike. His tenancy of the map meant that he had been granted some grace, but it would be a short honeymoon period. He could feel their movement, a rise and a sharing of knowledge. He could feel the map being scrutinised by eyes other than his own.

He pushed the bike hard again as he reached the bottom of the Strand. He leaned into the long turn around Trafalgar Square and tripped up through the gears so that by the time he passed through Admiralty Arch on to The Mall, the needle on the speedometer was hovering over sixty. He heard a scream and turned in time to see figures piling into the shadows of bushes by the Artillery Memorial at the eastern tip of St James's Park. The bike wobbled; he swore, on the verge of losing control. He managed to right the bike, and brought the speed down. He slowed to a stop at the gardens by the Queen Victoria Memorial. Bodies were draped all over the white marble. In such a short time they had grown more confident, rediscovered their threat. He looked up at the windows of Buckingham Palace. Some were shattered. He thought he saw something fleeing across the roof. Something that was not the Union Jack hung wetly on the flagpole.

He felt a bending in his mind. An unfolding. He felt the road beneath him shimmer and fade. He felt it grow uneven, tracks appearing out of the concrete like the muddied ridges of uncovered bones. He saw the map's history spreading out before him, its ancient reach, the stale breath of generations that had been born and lived and died as it accrued its wealth of knowledge, its cultural, spiritual content. The clatter of the wind on him was ice cold but he didn't feel it. He took the Ninja left into Birdcage Walk and forgot where he was headed or why he was even trying to go anywhere.

The map, giving up its glut of dirty secrets. It shows him a church. The walls will not remain still enough for him to absorb any detail. That recognisable shape is there, but it is a form made from smears and blur and suggestion. The smell of old fires, the cold reek of charcoal and burned meat creeps out of its history. His eyes slide off the walls. He is either prohibited from, or simply physically unable, through great fear, to see this place in full. And there's the suspicion, strong in him, that this is somebody else's vision, filtered down to him through the centuries. Another map-reader, perhaps the first. Dust and shadow now. Molecules in the earth. Lucky you.

Sky black with soot and grease. The smell of carrion and shit; animals lowing, sweating fear-tallow. Locked-in groans. A bell tolling far away, clapper cracked, dull, dead. Dread and panic in the air and bodies too weak to act. A sense of capitulation.

Drawing nearer, a feeling of resistance, as of walking against a fierce wind. The map showing him a gallery of the dead, men who perished in the creation of this twisted cathedral. Men who were not carried away, but found their resting place in among the stones they laid. The walls had taken on some of the physicality of the dead that adorned them. They writhed, muscular, torsional, lubricated with lymph. There was a skin covering everything. All light was absorbed by it, but not before the map showed him half-formed faces pushing out of the stone in a riot of pain and regret. He feels an affinity with this place he has never seen before. He understands intimately its measurements, its substance, the mass it possesses in space and time. Its thereness. He knows the bones of its flock are scattered in the grounds, knows their strange anatomy, the saddle in the pelvis which allows for poison sacs rather than sex glands, appurtenances the like of which should not be seen out of the bodies of serpents. Not men, but hunters. Predators. Not of this world. Not of this time.

There are ceremonies that were undertaken when they were stronger, not the vanquished breed creeping back from the margins in 2008. The map shows him feast days to commemorate the anniversary of this black cathedral's completion. Children brought up to the steps of the high Altar. A Reaper in vestments, garlands of roses on his head and bowls of incense urging smoke of many hues and fragrances into the heights. Children sent to be baked. Their heads fixed upon poles, borne before a wailing, slavering procession to a keeper at the door who blows the dead dust of these ground bodies towards the city. The horners that are around him answer in like manner. A curse upon the world. A line drawn in the sand.

The map shows him the way in which they have hidden from human eyes for generations. It shows him deep woods, a dense inter-twining of branches that has never known the touch of man. There is an impression of calm, of correctness; this is a place of peace. The trees form an impenetrable canopy and keep hold of the dark as if it were nourishment. Within that realm of shadow, a thousand glittering eyes turn to look down at him.

Bo recoiled, slamming back into real time, and saw that he had come to a standstill on Millbank. The engine was idling; he was sitting upright, his hands resting lightly on the tops of his thighs. The map stuttered and pulsed behind his eyelids, coming to life, disburdening itself of all its packets of information. There was nobody else on the road although he could hear shrieks coming from across the water. A maroon streak mimicked the white lines in the centre of the tarmac, stretching off in the direction of the Houses of Parliament.

He had seen something else at the moment of his snapping back to consciousness. He had seen, in the twisting dance of bad humours cloaking London, a face turn towards him, its mouth opening wide to reveal a skyline purged of danger. He saw the city hardening beneath that smiling mouth, and thought it might be a sign, disguised by the map, that the city would endure. But then he saw how he was wrong. The smile was nothing of the sort. It had been stretched wide in a posture of devourment.

26. SIX MILLION STRANGERS

Homemade signs were starting to go up on the streets. *Missing. Not seen since ... Can you help? Urgent. Desperate. Beloved. Please. Please.* Dozens of them fought for space on lamp posts, the windows of dead shops, fences, bus shelters, public phone booths.

Rita Maybury had taped up thirty copies of her own appeal before 8 a.m., swallowing hard against the conviction that it was already too late, that her husband's disappearance just over a week ago was the line drawn under their time together. She knew that Simon was gone, dead. Murdered. Yet she carried on with her task, because to not do it was to somehow negate who he was, and the link that she had to him. This, she supposed, as she trudged along Edgware Road looking for gaps among the other entreaties, was a way of letting go, of saying good-bye.

As the pages had been excruciatingly ejected into the feeder tray of her inkjet printer, she'd sipped her usual morning cup of camomile tea and tried to ease the knots of tension that were already hunching her shoulders, drawing a frown into the centre of her face. It was a tension that could not be relieved because it was present in anticipation of a familiar knock at the door, or a key in the lock that would never come. It was a tension that grew in her as she recognised a change in these streets she'd known all her life.

She didn't really believe in the effectiveness of this kind of aimless reaching out, and not just because it was like casting a hook into a river that had dried up in the hope of catching a fish. London was a cold city, she felt, even in the depths of summer. She had lived in the same flat in the same building on Homer Street, Marylebone, for the best part of fifteen years and still did not know her next-door neighbours' names. London was unfriendly, aloof. It was a city that seemed only interested in projecting its glimmer and glare, its shiny coat. It was a surface city. The people who moved through its streets, in the main, were tired of being charged ludicrous prices for houses, meals, ale. London was a vampire feeding on itself, she decided, only, unlike true vampires, this one didn't need inviting over the threshold first. It sat, corpulent and drowsy, in an armchair in every house within those eight hundred square miles, beckoning its inhabitants over every now and then for another drag at their weak, irritated veins.

It didn't help that it made you feel like you were dying on your feet, most of the time. She had been shocked to see her reflection in one of the windows, as she reached up to fix another poster to the glass. It had been her mother she saw, in the tired cross-hatching of wrinkles across the soft skin beneath her eyes, the wide, slightly froggy mouth, the beginnings of dewlaps and crows' feet. Age found you so quickly in this city; it gathered subtly, like the mantling of snow on a ledge, without you noticing. Without Simon, she was alone and lonely, and the city just loved that. It collected loners like it did pollution and violence. She had another thirty, forty years in her, foraging in London's relationship bins, if she was unlucky. Simon, at least, would always be young in her memory. He had that.

Finding the right photograph was a most distressing job. She wanted to put up the picture that showed him in his best light: happy, well groomed, handsome, something from the days when she had fallen in love, when he was striking, funny, the reason for the stitch in her chest. But nobody would recognise that man now. You had to be true to the present, if you wanted a chance to find the person who was lost. So she had pulled out his passport photograph, which he had renewed only the previous month. He was old, she saw now, like her. Old, tired, resentful. It was a knife in her stomach to think that she might also appear that way to him, or that she was why he wore that look. It shocked her to see him as a stranger already. She was studying him properly for the first time since they had married, two decades before. His hair seemed greyer, his eyes underlined with bluish skin, pouches of fatigue. His mouth was turned down at the corners where she had once believed it did little more than laugh all the time. Staring at him, at this new image, was like reciting a name you knew well; after a while it lost its meaning, its sense. Everything became alien the longer you studied it. The things we take for granted are usually the most remarkable. Ears had always given her pause. Ears and elephants. You didn't get weirder, for her money.

She giggled a little, at the way she could mull over trifles such as these when the city was sucking its people into black holes from Hammersmith to Homerton. What were the police doing? Screaming around in their cars like blue-arsed flies, sirens going, lights flashing, and little else as far as she could tell. It was the same those days after 7/7. She'd seen a car with the word BLOOD on the side of it. She'd seen men wearing bulletproof vests running with walkie-talkies. There had been figures on the roofs of tall buildings with binoculars. It didn't make you feel any safer. Quite the reverse.

She took the last few of her sheets down the ramp outside the Odeon Marble Arch, into the labyrinth that was the subway network feeding Oxford Street, Hyde Park, Park Lane, and Bayswater Road. The colour grey had been discovered in these alleys, she suspected. The tiles, the people, the smell, all of it was grey. There used to be music, at least, to improve the squalor, played by apt guitarists and violinists and saxophonists looking to make a few coins out of the day, but even that was absent now as she taped her husband, her man, this two-dimensional representation she no longer recognised or understood, to the drab walls that used to tremble under the weight of all the traffic that surged above and below.

She moved deeper into the tunnels, flinching, as she always did, to find a crumpled figure under a mess of cardboard and old blankets, about forty metres further along this stretch, which led to an open section where the public toilets were located, before leading to the ramps that rose to the walkways surrounding Hyde Park. He was doing his best to squirm away from the cold into a tight mass of ill-fitting clothes and blankets. His head was partially buried in the hood of a sleeping bag; it twitched and jerked like something independent of the rest of him. An odd, muffled popping noise accompanied each tic. A crumpled cardboard sign in front of him read: *No food. Hungry. Please help.*

She dug in her pocket for some loose change but dropped it before she had a chance to place it in his white plastic cup.

'Simon?' she said, her voice startling her as it bounced back, hollow and cold, in the dampening tunnel. But how could it be? Her husband was tall and fair; this man, although lying down, was undoubtedly shorter, and in possession of long dark curls. Her husband wore jackets and black jeans; this man was wrapped in a tatty grey fleece and tracksuit bottoms. Then why was he wearing Simon's necklace? She knew it was his. It was a unique thing, something that had grown over the years they spent together, a black thong that was threaded with mementoes of holidays to Hawaii, Bali, Mexico. The twist of polished lava chinked against the blue-green glass bead and the steel ingot.

It was his. It was her Simon's necklace.

'Why have you got that?' she said. 'That necklace. Where did you get it?'

The pale man shifted on his blanket. He stopped trying to burrow his head into the sleeping bag. The muffled popping noise ended. He withdrew slowly, and she was horrified to see a brown, crusty ring of what could only be dried blood flake away from the open throat of his shirt. Tiny white fragments, like chalk, clung to the corners of his mouth, which was further decorated with gummy black deposits. She caught a whiff of something that reminded her of childhood, something mealy that she forever linked with kitchens and dogs. Marrow, that was it. The dogs gnawing at the ends of bone, trying to get at the jelly within. The dull cracks and pops of their teeth as they tried to gain purchase.

He murmured something incoherent and she wondered if he was high; his pupils contained a blissed-out dilation, a sense of somebody being somewhere else. His hand moved free of the sleeping bag and she saw, before a lip of worn fabric flopped over and concealed it, something that looked like the bare curve of a collarbone. She was shocked to stone, but more by his beauty than anything else. His face carried an unholy symmetry; she found herself mesmerised by his perfectly level eyes, and the deep sweep of his cheekbones. Under all the grime and gristle, here was an angel, she felt.

'Simon,' she whispered. 'Do you know where he is?'

The pale man was trying to stand up, but his foot was caught inside a coil of blanket. The sleeping bag gaped again and this time something else slithered free. A large black eye socket gazed up at her, a grinning white bar of teeth punctuated by a single gold crown. *Simon has one in exactly the same place*, she thought. And then, as the insane danger of the situation slammed into her, *at least I won't have to carry on with these stupid posters.*

She hiccupped laughter and vomit into a cupped hand, a gesture that managed to retain the feminine elegance that Simon used to tease her about. *You could make unblocking a drain look attractive*, he had once said to her. She stepped away, conscious that if she fainted now, she was dead, and unable to back up that compulsion with any hard evidence. It was just a man on his uppers, eating something . . . exotic. Something he'd found in a restaurant skip, or a fast-food binliner. Or on a hospital gurney.

Something he'd hunted and slaughtered with his own hands.

She turned and fled, feeling the handful of hot black bile slide from her skin as easily as her grip on reality seemed to be doing. She clattered around the corner and almost immediately saw his shadow jag after her, rising and rippling into the apex of the tunnel's curve like a Halloween trick made from torchlight and inventive fingers. She was on the ramp now, in view of open air. She started screaming for the police, for help, for God. She looked back and the figure had stopped, was pacing back and forth in the shadow just beyond the threshold like a panther in a cage. She reached the top of the ramp and Edgware Road stretched away ahead of her. A strange silence fell and she became aware that everyone on the pavement had stopped walking and was looking at her. Nobody made any motion of assistance. They stared at her in the vacuous yet flinty way that the pale man had done. Suddenly, the spaces of London yawning around her were too small, too restrictive. Everywhere she looked was a dead end, a trap, despite the expansiveness. She suffered a clear, crisp hit of pure panic, a weird mix of claustrophobia and agoraphobia, a conviction that she was being pulled inside out, and then she was running, hysterical, eyes wide, mouth agape, making as much noise as she could.

She veered this way and that, like an eland on the veldt, surrounded by lions. The people around her moved slowly in, closing off any escape route. She tipped out into the road and a car clipped her left leg, lifting her, propelling her and twisting her body over.

Her forehead hit the kerb and snapped her neck like a handful of kindling. But she was dead before she landed, her heart having arrested. They moved in quickly as her throat filled with blood, cooing at the beautiful blue bruise that it created.

Although what happened directly after the collision was anything but, Rita Maybury's demise was one of only a handful of deaths in the city that day that could be described as something approaching natural.

27. WELCOME TO THE JUNGLE

'Did you see that?'
'No. What was it?'
'I think there's been an accident. A crowd of people. We should go and look.'

Nick looked at her as if she had suddenly expressed a desire to grow a beard. 'There's what looks like an accident on every street corner. The place is a fucking nightmare. Smashed cars all over the place. Something's seriously fucked here. We, at least, need to relax a little bit. No more dramas for a while, yes?'

'My daughter is ill, Nick. *You* relax. I'm going to get her well again.'

'Well, you'll have a better chance if you try not to get involved with every incident that occurs.'

Nick sighed and concentrated on the road. Sarah found that her blood was up; she could do with a fight. She had an impulse to start screaming and not stop until she had forced all of the panic and fear out of her body. The gaggle of rubbernecking bodies on Edgware Road began to disperse, even as they guided the car in the direction of Oxford Street. She thought she saw someone with too many limbs duck into the subway, but she reasoned that it must have been a bag, or the stray arm of a coat that had not yet been slipped on.

'We need Harley Street,' she said.

'Later. I have a friend who lives on Percy Street, a little one-bedroom flat on the top floor. Nice place. She'll be happy to put us up for a day or two. You need a base of operations. We need somewhere we can come back to. Shelter.'

'You know lots of places to stay,' Sarah said. 'Must be useful to have a bed in every town.'

'It's hardly *every* town,' he said, and gave her another look. She knew that look. She had seen it before on previous male friends she had considered becoming intimate with. They didn't know how to take her, in general. Didn't know if she was being serious or introducing a barb in her comments, to test them. She sparred too much, she knew, but she couldn't help it. After Andrew's death (murder, Sarah, it was murder, don't forget it), she had been loath to entertain even the thought of intimacy, let alone the men themselves. And being with Claire, looking after her, looking out for her, was pretty much a full-time job, so the most contact she ever enjoyed with men was occasional flirting. She didn't have the hours in the day, nor the privacy, nor the energy, for anything more interesting.

Hard tears surprised her now, overwhelmed her, and she bawled into her hands, grieving for her daughter and for herself, the life that had been put on hold for such an inordinate stretch that it could no longer lay claim to the noun. She had been shocked that she did not feel worse about her daughter's condition. She tried to trick herself into believing that it was because she was young and strong and healthy, too beautiful to succumb to anything as invidious as cancer, and that she herself was so tired it was impossible for any other feelings to make themselves known. But the fact – the harsh, despicable truth of the situation – was that she was *relieved*. The development, the ripening of that strange black fruit in her armpit, had given her a weirdly euphoric feeling, because if Claire died, she would be free. The guilt that replaced this was almost a physical crushing, and she determined to save her daughter as much to keep her safe as to try to atone for the dreadful, unforgivable happiness that her deterioration had provoked.

She regretted her spikiness with Nick, and apologised quietly. He simply shook his head: it wasn't an issue. She closed her eyes against tears that reminded her of childhood, so eager and hot were they. She felt a sharp ache in her throat from the pain of her sorrow. The people she most relied on were the people she most abused; it had been the song of her life, and she didn't like it any more.

They turned off the main drag and took back roads to Percy Street. Nick parked the car and fed coins into a meter. He pushed a button on a plain door. A wine bar spilled music on to the street a couple of doors further along. She could see people inside sitting around a table. Sarah found herself craving that sort of simple enjoyment: a bowl of chips and mayonnaise, somebody laughing at her jokes. A drink too many and not having to worry about losing a little control. Her life had been taken over by a constant low-level panic that had fended off any ability to enjoy herself. All of her laughter had been black and fearful, infected with insanity. She couldn't remember the last time she had given herself to a moment – a kiss, an orgasm, any moment of warmth or affection – that took her out of herself in the same way that recent bouts of deep anxiety did. She was on call, like a busy nurse, a slave to her emotions, all of which seemed to be ragged and bruised. She felt old and unloved. She felt like something peeled out of reality, a dark decal destined to be stuck to a recently completed model that would never be picked up or looked at again.

'Maybe her intercom's shafted,' he said, pressing more buttons on the entrance panel. 'Are you both warm enough?' Sarah shook her head. He handed her his coat and she draped it around Claire's shoulders as a resident buzzed them in, identities unchallenged.

They climbed three flights of stairs, all bleached with the light from naked 100-watt bulbs. At the top, Nick held up a finger and whispered. 'Take it easy with this woman,' he said. 'She's damaged goods.'

Before Sarah could ask him what he meant, he tapped a knuckle against the door. Something moved inside the flat, a sliding sound, of coats hanging up on a hook being moved to one side. A shadow flickered across the peephole.

'Are you there, Tina?' Nick called.

'Nick?' A voice that, to Sarah's ears, sounded right on the edge of what was normal, shivered behind the solid wood. She imagined a woman clinging to the handle harder than was necessary, and she felt a thrill of fear. She had always hated top-floor flats, she felt they were fire disasters waiting to happen. Half a dozen locks and bolts were shot. The door cracked open an inch. A bright-blue eye surrounded by damp red blazed from the gap.

'Nick.' The name was spoken half in relief, half in accusation.

'Hello, Tina.'

'What are you doing here?' And, before he could draw breath to answer: 'Who are they?'

'This is Sarah and her daughter Claire. They're friends. Claire's in need of some help.'

'*She's* in need of some help?' Tina yanked at the door at this unexplained indignation, forgetting that the security chain was attached. The door closed, then reopened. 'Get inside, the lot of you,' she said. 'Quick.'

They moved past her into the gloomy flat. All of the blinds were drawn. Nick appeared as concerned as she did. He stood in the centre of her living room gently clapping his hands together, a dark look on his face.

'So again,' Tina said, entering the room. She was carrying an eight-inch filleting knife loosely in her hand. 'Who are these people?'

'My name is Sarah Hickman,' Sarah said, brightly, extending a hand that was not accepted. 'I met Nick in Southwold. He drove me here.'

'Why?'

Nick said, 'Why are you holding a knife, Tina? What –'

'*I'm asking the questions. This is my flat.*'

'My daughter's unwell,' Sarah continued. 'She needs to see a specialist.'

'You going to find one of those in my place?' Tina watched as Claire folded herself into the sofa. She took a step back as if fearful of some contagion.

'No, Tina,' Nick said, as gently as he could, 'but we need somewhere to lay our heads.'

'Why would you come to London?' she asked.

Nick turned to Sarah with a pleading look in his eyes. He was lost. He was scared. It was an innocuous question, a question that surprised Sarah, but it seemed to have completely floored him.

'Why wouldn't anyone come here, Tina?' he asked. 'This is London. Everyone comes to London. What's frightening you?'

Tina regarded Sarah with a mixture of contempt and curiosity. Sarah couldn't work out how old the woman was. She could have been any age between 25 and 50. Her hair was long and blonde, streaked with black dye. It reflected the light in broad blades as if it were metal. She wore a tight black T-shirt and distressed blue jeans. A scuffed leather jacket and Puma trainers. She looked ready to go out, but the flat was in the kind of state that suggested nobody had left it for days, maybe even weeks. Stale air stirred awkwardly around them like fog in a forest.

Tina's eyes were watery and emotional. She'd been through some kind of punishing mangle recently. She was staring into the abyss. A vein of hard iron ran through her, though. Sarah could see it in the relaxed but determined way she handled the weapon, in the aggressive posture she was assuming. *I'd have her on my side in a fight,* Sarah thought.

'Have you been driving with your eyes closed?' she asked now. 'Are you telling me you haven't seen anything strange, something *not fucking right?*'

'Tina,' Nick said, his hands spread, his voice conciliatory, 'this is London. You're always going to see odd things.'

But Sarah was thinking: *It was an arm. It was a fucking arm.*

'Go down there. Go on. Have a drink. Take a walk around the block. Come back in twenty minutes and tell me this city isn't up to its throat in deep shit.'

'All right, Tina,' Nick said, and Sarah could see how he was itching to be away, that he had made a mistake in coming here, that a new decision had been reached.

'Come with us,' Sarah said, as he moved past her towards the door.

'You must be fucking joking,' she replied, her fist tightening on the knife's handle, as if she had just been challenged. 'I'm here for the long run.'

'What did you see?' Sarah asked.

She saw Tina snap her lips shut. It couldn't have been more final a gesture had she used a zip, or sewn them together. Those wet eyes of hers watched them leave, through the closing door, until, bizarrely, they were back where they had started: jittery, unsure, on a cold landing.

'Come on,' Nick said, his decisiveness returned.

'But Claire –'

'Claire will be better off here,' Tina said. 'Trust me.'

Sarah couldn't, but knew she had no choice. She followed Nick out of the door. The rhythm of the locks followed them down the stairs.

'Where are we going?'

'I've got friends in Reading we –'

'*Reading?* We're not going to Reading.'

'We can't stay here. Did you see her? I mean, I know you don't know her, but believe me when I say that she's not normally like that.'

Sarah closed her eyes against yet another moment that seemed to be drifting free of her controllable orbit.

'Just hang on, Nick, please.' She held up her hand and licked her lips. 'She's spooked by something, obviously. Paranoid. And I know how quickly that can get on top of you. But let's just do what she suggested. Let's have a beer and talk about it and later we can come back and set about trying to calm her down.'

'But –'

'I am not leaving. You go, if you want. Thanks for everything, but I'm coming back here in twenty minutes. With or without you. I'm sorry.'

'I'm with you,' Nick said, softly, making his own conciliatory gesture again. 'I'm with you.'

The Jack Horner on Tottenham Court Road was about as good as any pub on a hugely busy main road in the centre of a big city could expect to be. It was thick with chattering people, and noisy music filled in any gaps. Sarah strode up to the bar and ordered two whiskies, determined to snuff out Nick's wavering with a little decisiveness of her own. She took the drinks to a large table by the window already taken by a couple conspiring over their pints but who were happy to let half of it go. Sarah took a stiff swig of her scotch and Nick followed suit, although his brief grimace told her that whiskey was not his drink of choice.

'Never mind,' she said. 'It will wake you up.'

'It's you who looks tired,' he said.

'I am tired. This is what it looks like to fear for your life. This is what it's been like for the past eighteen months. Claire in her condition hardly makes a difference, in a terrible way. Was she ever really there? That's what I keep asking myself.'

'I didn't mean anything by that. I just . . . you look as if you could do with a rest.'

'There'll be time for that,' she said. She had finished her drink, almost without realising it. She wanted another. She turned to look at the bar and something funny struck her. She turned back to Nick and swallowed hard. 'I think Tina has a point.'

'About what?'

'I don't want to be here any more.'

'Why not? It was your idea.'

'I know.' Her voice had turned to shapes of breath. 'Nick.'

He was frowning, but now he looked beyond her at the pub. And she saw in his face that he had caught it too. She turned her attention to the oily tears slowly sliding down the side of her glass and tried to unpick the scene that had met her when she turned around.

She had seen a pub filled with people. They were standing at the bar, they were sitting on chairs and at tables. They were talking. But something wasn't right. She edged a little nearer to the couple sitting on the other half of her table, but the din of the music was too great for her to be able to pick out any words they were sharing.

Sarah said: 'Nobody's drinking.'

Nick let out a little yapped laugh of incredulity. Drinks were arranged on the counters and tabletops, but nobody was lifting them to swig or sip.

'They're like actors at a dress rehearsal,' she whispered. A cold claw scuttled up her back; sweat turned her forehead to bubble wrap. It was fascinating to watch, despite her discomfort. The more they observed, the more they saw how the actions of the people in the pub were slightly awkward, processed, like the received movements of animals taught to behave in a certain way.

'What's going on?' she asked Nick. 'It feels as if we've stumbled on to a film set. You ever notice, in films, how characters sit down to dinner and then never eat anything? It's just scenery and props, background for what they're saying to each other. This is like that.'

'But what are they saying?' Nick asked. 'I can't hear any words. Something's off.'

He was right, she could see, and she was grateful that he was picking up on something she'd perceived. It was the rhythm of their speech. It was all wrong. There were none of the false starts, dead spaces or collisions that occurred during a normal conversation.

Individuals spoke and stopped and their partners took up the baton. There was no laughter, no raised voices, no coughing. Sarah couldn't understand how she had missed it when they first walked in.

'What's going on?' she said again.

Nick said, 'They're looking at us.'

'No they're . . .' But she couldn't finish the sentence. Nick was right. They were looking at them, she knew that to be true, but confirming it was like trying to nail jelly to a wall. She could feel eyes on her, despite the way the pub's inhabitants seemed to be engrossed in each other. Every time she turned to challenge somebody's gaze, the stares slid away like leftovers from a plate.

'This is what Tina was talking about, wasn't it?'

'I think so,' she replied. 'A part of it, because I don't really understand. It's not as if they're a threat. It's not something that would make me lock myself in my flat and get tooled up with the kitchen equipment. This is the centre of London. A fight breaking out in this pub? There'd be riot police all over the place in minutes.'

'Nevertheless,' Nick said, 'it's spooking me. I think we should go.'

He drained his glass and placed it on the table. He stood up. The conversations around them died. The music snapped off.

He looked down at her. The little-boy-lost look was back. She reached out slowly and touched his hand. 'Let's go back to Tina's,' she said. She rose slowly and the couple at the end of their table now turned and watched them nakedly, their heads moving in little saccadic jerks as Sarah and Nick made their way towards the door.

Someone was moving from another table, a woman with short black hair and a beige trouser suit, and Sarah knew by the way she was studiously avoiding looking at her and Nick that she intended to block their exit.

'Come on,' she said, firmly. She grabbed Nick by the wrist and yanked him towards the door. The smartly dressed woman was trying to pull something out of her pocket but it was snagged on the lining, or it was too snug a fit to be cleanly pulled free; either way, it was giving them a chance.

Others were moving now, but Sarah couldn't understand their reticence. They moved as a unit, getting up from their seats at the same time. It was like watching a lazy swarm of bees. If they wanted to attack, they could do so with ease, but something was holding them back. It was warring with whatever had impelled them to show such hostility to a pair of strangers. As they rushed past the black-haired woman, who was wearing a perfume so overpowering that it caused Sarah's eyes to water, she thought she recognised what was holding their reins. But then they were in the street, and Nick was sprinting back towards Tina's flat.

'No,' Sarah cried. 'Not yet. This way.'

She led him quickly north along Tottenham Court Road, casting nervous glances back towards the pub, but nobody had followed them outside. Plasma displays in electronics shops poured garish colours across the hard, cold pavements. Sarah imagined her blood joining them and ground her teeth hard against each other. Just a weird pub full of weird fuckers, she thought. Just London, doing what it did best.

The absence of traffic unnerved her, as did the lack of pedestrians. There were one or two people around, and they paused to watch Sarah and Nick as they hurried by, but nowhere near as many as she had encountered on her trips to the city in the past. It was as if it were Christmas morning, or the day of a state funeral. There weren't even any buses. In the windows of burger bars and kebab shops she saw staff in aprons standing behind counters preparing nothing for customers who stood silently and politely in a queue waiting for it. She saw news sellers in a booth at Goodge Street station without newspapers to sell. It was a replica city, a toy, with real-life players. Everything seemed stylised, posed.

'This way,' she hissed, turning sharp left. She led Nick along Tottenham Street. More shops and restaurants. More pubs with people playing a role. What at first she had thought was the reflection of streetlamps in windows she now saw were faces pressed against glass, looking down at them as they passed by. These were haunted, cadaverous faces, partially obliterated by the ground-in filth on the panes, and the oily light, like something from a painting by Bacon or Munch. She was worried that some of the windows were smeared with more than the usual city detritus, but the light was too poor for her to tell.

They turned left again into Charlotte Street and moved up past the hotel, where diners sat around tables wiping clean mouths with clean napkins and nodding over empty place settings. Tina was over-reacting, Sarah thought. It was just the festive coma that hit the city every year, come a little bit early, that was all. Too many office parties and free booze. Late nights and last-minute business to attend to. Plus the usual jaded look of the urbanite. She wasn't a Londoner, no wonder she should be so stunned by the blank faces and alien gestures. Tina was suffering from cabin fever and paranoia. She had been stuck indoors too long by herself, with only the violent news to reinforce her prejudices against the city and its inhabitants.

You keep fooling yourself like that, Sarah, if it makes you feel better.

It was only when they were nearing Tina's building from the other end of Percy Street that she saw something to persuade her that Tina had made the right decision and, short of being a thousand miles away, was in the safest place of all.

A man was sitting on what seemed to be a small, misshapen sofa discarded in a back alley. He was aimlessly picking large chunks of stuffing from the split in the fabric, tearing them free, and then studying them under the lamplight before either discarding them or bringing them up to his face to be sniffed. Sarah couldn't be sure, but the sudden thump in her chest suggested that her hunch – that the sofa wasn't actually a sofa but a human body – was closer to the truth than she wanted to acknowledge. She hustled Nick through the main entrance and up the stairs. Tina opened the door, perhaps surprised they had been so tardy in returning, perhaps that they had returned at all.

'You saw something,' she said, a look of triumph on her face. 'The locks. Fasten them.' And then: 'Our world is changing.'

I work in the media. Press and publicity for a TV channel based in Victoria. I sweet-talk journalists into doing features on programmes or people in programmes that we produce. It's an interesting job, an involving job, and I'm pretty busy most of the week. It's a good press office. I've made good friends there, had a few lovers, gone to some blinding parties. I know my work and my people. I'm aware of change. And change has happened.

It was just over a week ago. I got to work and nipped down to the canteen to get my breakfast muffin – honey and oats – as always, and a grande latte. I flirted with Kenny on the till – he's this extremely friendly, extremely camp Irish guy, whippet lean, very chatty with everyone – and I was in good spirits as I walked back past the reception desk to the lifts. As usual, I call a lift and a little huddle of colleagues unknown to me gathers behind. There are a lot of offices, a lot of employees. I smile at the occasional face that's familiar to me. Smiling. I used to smile a lot. I didn't always look like this. Nick will vouch for me.

In the lift, it's so lazy really, I'm based just a couple of floors up and the stairs are quicker most of the time. But I've got my coffee and my muffin and a heavy shoulder bag and so I get in the lift and I'm pressed up against the glass wall and I can look into the street – it's one of those trendy Richard Rogers buildings, all open, glass and steel – and we're swooping up and I can see people in the street and something's changed. People aren't moving the way I remember they moved. I don't recognise the scene spreading out in front of me. It's the same view I've taken in pretty much every day of my time there, six years and counting, but this particular morning, bam, I don't get it. It's like one of those child's games, spot the difference, two pictures of the same thing next to each other, but there have been some changes made to one of them, and you stare at it for a while until they make themselves known to you. This was just like that.

I stay in the lift even though it opens on my floor. I stay in it long after the others have got out, and I've descended to the ground floor again. I must go up and down ten times in that lift, trying to pinpoint what's wrong with the picture. My coffee goes cold.

I finally get out of the lift convinced that the main road is narrower and, somehow, the sky is . . . closer than it used to be. It must be something as weird as that to account for so many people moving in such a strangely fluid manner. It's as if they don't have bones. They glide along. And they look from side to side with big eyes and oiled movement . . . until somebody walks by them and their heads follow the path of the other in these horrible, horrible jerky motions.

(Yes, yes, that's right, that's what we saw too, isn't it, Nick?)

It's like somebody pretending to be a spider, or one of those awful fucking preying mantises. It's camouflage. You see a stick insect on a branch and you think, clever, but now I can see it, it's a stick insect. It's something pretending to be something else. It doesn't fool you any more. And now I've seen these people, these strange people, I won't be knocked off kilter again. They're the image in those stereograms when it finally swims out of the background mess. You can't not see it any more.

In the office I was pretty shaken up. I was trying to process what I'd seen. One of the bods in the stills department, new guy, starting that morning, came and introduced himself. I didn't hear him. I was just watching his lips move, and trying not to declare my revulsion at seeing his little red hole of a mouth, ringed with teeth that were too white, and the horrible noise coming out of it. He seemed too clean all of a sudden. Too polished. I knew that was a part of the strangeness. He looked like the 'after' picture in those dental adverts for tooth whitening. There wasn't a hair out of place. His breath had no odour, good or bad. His skin was so perfect it was almost translucent. It was firm on his face. I felt as though, if I could close my eyes and touch it, it would be like caressing a baby's cheek. I remember sitting there thinking, he won't have a penis, it's too awkward, too ugly. He'll be smooth down there, like an Action Man doll.

A guy, Keith, I work with leaned over and offered him a muffin. The new guy took it and ate it quickly, and everything about what he was doing was wrong. He didn't say anything else; he just ate. It was like watching a bad actor doing a passable job on a role. Something you couldn't describe was getting in the way of your acceptance.

He went away, and Keith pulled a face, which reassured me that I wasn't just being paranoid. I got up and followed him part of the way to his little booth. I watched him regurgitate the muffin into a plastic bag, which he tied off and stuck in the bin. Then he sat in front of his monitor and placed his hands on the keyboard and he didn't do anything. He didn't fucking move. If he had an OFF switch, someone had flicked it.

I wanted to grab my bag then and leave. I was so scared I was in danger of blacking out. I was so scared I peed myself a little bit. It just shocked out of me. I went back to my desk and pretended to be busy. I picked up the phone and started doodling on a pad. Everyone in the office was sitting at their workstations making the right motions but not doing any work. You've seen extras in films set in the office, or in adverts about finance. You see them talking into their headsets and you know all they're saying is any old nonsense that comes into their heads. The odd smile. The occasional nod. It's all rhubarb. I was sitting in the middle of a hoax, and I wondered, who is this all for? Is it me? And I couldn't believe that there weren't more like me. People who weren't, well, glass.

Glass that had somehow learned to move.

I took my bag, and got hold of my letter opener in my other hand, and – this is the hardest thing I've ever done – moved off through the office, feeling the office change behind me. I knew they were all turning to watch me go. I could hear the skin of their necks shushing against their shirt collars. I had this awful feeling that I wasn't going to get out. I would be thrown into an office and turned to glass myself. But nothing happened. I wanted to tell Keith to get out, but I didn't know if he was like them, and whether if I said something he'd sound the alarm.

I walked the corridor that bridges the open reception area beneath me. I saw a security guard leaning over the face of one of the receptionists, his back convulsing. When she moved back into view, she was wiping her mouth with the back of her hand. I saw a commissioning editor in his private office closing the blinds as he reached into his top drawer for what looked like a wax model of a baby. I was having trouble breathing by the time I got to the other wing of the building, and hid in a cubicle in the toilets, took some Ventolin. Someone came in and sat in the cubicle next to me. I heard awful sounds. It sounded like someone tearing great fistfuls of hair out of a head.

I ran out of that building. I nearly took the revolving doors with me. I didn't get a cab, or a bus, or the tube. I ran and stumbled and ran home in my dainty little shoes, an hour and a half. Too scared to stop because there was always some other blank face coming out of the houses and shops, looking like it had been made over. Everywhere I looked there was something that might not be what it seemed to be. Even in the distance there was ambiguity. I saw a figure bending over another figure in the peace park in Tavistock Square. They might have both been naked, but the figure on his knees might also have been wearing a shiny red top. I hope. I fucking hope. A bus went past and the windows in the top deck had been vandalised, someone had covered them in red paint. I saw the shape of a hand in it, and I don't know if it was a print, or a real hand, pressing against it, trying to get out. I saw a man through a pair of billowing curtains in a posh hotel in Bloomsbury, just before the breeze died and he was hidden again, with his face buried in the stomach of a black cat.

I got home and I stood in the centre of my living room and I was so tense, all that lactic acid built up in my arms and legs, I was afraid to sit down in case I shattered. I tried calling Keith but there was no answer.

I was so hungry I went to the fridge and I ate a tub of vanilla ice cream and a box of Tuc biscuits. It's like seeing people eat dinner *through the window of a restaurant. You can't help feeling peckish yourself. I realised that all I'd seen all morning was hungry people. People eating.*

Three days ago, around four in the morning, someone tried to get into my flat. I heard them at the door messing with the lock. I screamed my head off. I switched the stereo on and played U2 at full blast for twenty minutes. They went away pretty fast: I only got a glimpse of a shadow running down the stairs, but I didn't hear a door slam. I didn't see anyone legging it down Charlotte Street. Nobody came to see what the fuss was. Nobody complained about the noise.

I won't leave this flat again. I'll die of hunger, maybe in a month or so, but I'm not leaving. No fucking way. There are other people in this block trying to get to me. They're sitting in their rooms, looking up at the ceiling, wondering how to break in. There are people in this block who want to fucking eat me.

'That's a bit melodramatic, Tina, don't you think?'

'No, I don't,' she said, giving Nick such a stare that he had to look away. 'I hear them at night, in the flat underneath this one, scrabbling at the ceiling with their claws –'

'Claws? You've got dogs for neighbours now?'

She ignored him. '– and then they'll come up that stairwell and test the door, wait on the landing until morning. This has been going on for days. London is overrun. It's like woodworm. Everything's getting eaten from the inside out. Pretty soon, this whole city is going to be one empty shell.'

Nick said, 'They go back inside when it's light? How civilised.'

Tina turned her attention to Sarah. 'So what did you see out there?'

Sarah nodded, as if doing so would give Tina the alliance she needed without having to describe their experiences. She reluctantly told her about the pub, and her sense of something out of kilter, and how, once she'd noticed the lack of drinking or smoking or ordered speech, she couldn't understand why she'd not locked on to it the moment they had walked through the door. She could see that Tina was pleased that elements of their stories chimed with each other. Sarah told her about the sofa, or what she had hoped was a sofa, what her brain had not allowed to view in its stark truth. Tina's hand on the filleting knife tightened and relaxed, tightened and relaxed.

'It's being in a city that doesn't help,' she said. 'Everything's magnified. But even then, you live here long enough and you see things so weird you barely even blink. You never look twice. If what went on in London happened in a sleepy seaside town, the military would have been mobilised by now. You'd have tanks rolling down the high street. But London is built on weirdness. It celebrates it. It's stained into its history. People move to the city so they can be peculiar and feel comfortable about it. Nobody cares. Every fetish and kink and perversion is catered for in its secret rooms and back alleys. You can blend in no matter what your needs are. You can disappear. Men and monsters, rubbing shoulders in the street. It doesn't help that on the surface of things, it doesn't look too mad a situation. There's no martial law because everything's happening quietly. It's like rot. Like cancer. By the time the cavalry come trotting in here, the guts will have fallen out of everything. There'll be nothing left to rescue.'

Nick got to his feet, ran the back of his hand over his mouth. Despite his returning cockiness, he continued to be nervous, Sarah could tell, even though she was still learning about him. He snatched the phone up, put it to his ear, asked the question even though his expression was already answering it.

'I tried calling friends, relatives,' Tina said. 'Do you think I'm stupid? The phones are down.'

'What about your mobile?'

'No signal.'

Nick shook his head and slipped his own phone out of his pocket. He flipped it open and stared at the display. 'Fuck's sake,' he said. And then: 'Sarah. What about yours?'

'It's probably fine, but it's in Southwold, on the junk-shop counter.'

'Fuck!'

'I'm sorry. I'm really sorry. But I was in kind of a rush, remember?'

He sighed and tried his phone anyway. He looked as if he might hurl it at the wall when it did not respond, but he reined in his anger and pocketed it instead. 'Might just be a busy zone here. Probably work later.'

Sarah went to him, stroked his arm. 'We have to believe there are others out there like us, looking for people like us. The city hasn't just turned into a freak arena overnight, you know.'

'It's not overnight. This has been going on for days, maybe even w–'

Sarah shot her a look and for a moment, Tina's face darkened before she nodded gently and averted her gaze. Sarah sensed a change in the balance of power. The other woman was clearly a loaded gun on a hair trigger. She could go off at any moment, and probably often did. She didn't like her authority, such as it was, being challenged. She was alone, and used to taking orders from herself, nobody else. You could see it in those cold blue eyes. Sarah turned back to Nick to see if he had anything to add. His face was the colour of whey. He shifted, as if about to make some kind of defiant gesticulation, but then he suddenly appeared too weak to do anything.

'Aren't we jumping the gun a bit?' he said. 'I mean, what are you actually claiming? That London is being overrun by monsters who . . . what? Pretend to do the things we do?' He laughed a little, nervously, almost over before it had begun. There was incredulity and desperation mixed in his eyes. You could see him wishing for Southwold's lack of complication, where the only drama was in the weather.

'Sounds about right to me,' Tina said, avoiding Sarah's gaze and any rebuke waiting for her there.

'But why? Why would anyone go to that trouble?'

'I don't know,' she admitted, but her triumphant expression had not left her face. 'Why does the insect pretend to be a leaf?'

'To prevent itself from being seen,' Nick said.

'Exactly.' Bolstered by her train of thought, she met Sarah's gaze head on. 'They don't want to be seen. It's too early for them to announce themselves. They have some reason for biding their time. They're waiting for something.'

Nick said, 'You're fucking mad.'

'Well, you'd know, I suppose.'

Sarah saw how Nick's temperament was just as fragile as Tina's, but in a different way. Whereas she was looking for an opportunity to let off steam with an argument or a slanging match, Nick was forever wrestling with the phobias and paranoias queuing up at a door he could never quite manage to close. He was brave, she knew that, but he was as vulnerable as a sandcastle at the edge of the tide. She suddenly realised what an achievement it had been for him to make it this far without some serious failure in his deportment. The cracks were beginning to show now, though.

Tina put down her knife, perhaps encouraged by her uninvited guests, and headed for the kitchen. 'Can I get anybody anything?

Tea? Coffee? I've only got powdered creamer; the fresh milk went off days ago.'

'I'll nip out and get you some,' Nick said brightly, although his face retained its cheesy hue. Every shred of his being said that he didn't want to go back outside, despite his stated scepticism.

'There's a brave lad,' Tina said. 'But I wouldn't push your luck. Some of them, as Sarah saw for herself, have already caused harm –'

'I didn't see that,' Nick said. 'I didn't see any of that.'

'– so it's probably safe to assume the rest are capable of the same behaviour, if not right at the moment.'

Sarah watched Tina as she clucked about her kitchen, and admired her attempt to retain some sense of normality in the teeth of insanity, or violence, whatever it was that was testing this little garrison she'd created. The neatly folded tea towels, the lack of washing-up in the sink, the militarily precise stacks of crockery in the cupboards contrasted sharply with the barbed wire and staves of wood nailed across the windows, the battery of knives spread neatly on a table-cloth like a surgeon's arsenal. Despite her assurances that she would never leave the flat, there was an emergency rucksack parked by the door, open to reveal a torch, a flask, a first aid kit and spare clothing.

'This must have something to do with Claire,' Sarah said.

'Your daughter?' Tina called, her voice tinny and hollow in the little kitchen. 'How?'

'It can't be the case that two separate incidents of madness can go on in two separate places and not be interlinked. I don't think I could cope if there wasn't some connecting thread.'

Tina returned to the room holding a teaspoon between her fingers. Behind her, steam from a kettle swarmed across the ceiling. It must have been cold in there because the steam was dense, folding and roiling like bad weather. The moisture in the air caused the metal of the spoon to gleam; Tina's eyes too. It sustained the feeling that Sarah was in the middle of a long, strange dream; at any moment she would waken with Claire by her side, asking if she fancied going to see a film, or sharing a portion of fish and chips, as she had been wont to do. Thinking of her like that was more dangerous than talking about her as just another problem, in a room shared by other people trying to deal with other problems. She felt tears rise.

'I have to find help for her,' she said. 'But you get here, you get to this big place and . . . I don't know where to begin. Or how.'

'I'm sorry to seem callous, chick, but I really don't care. I don't know you. Ergo, I don't take risks for you.'

'I wasn't expecting you to,' Sarah said, unable to keep the frostiness from her voice. 'I'm just looking for a way in, that's all. I'm happy on my own.'

'Not that I'm sending any mixed messages, but *on your own* equals *dead*.'

'What do you expect me to do?' Sarah spat.

'Die,' Tina said. 'Some of the day you can feel fairly safe out there. Daytime mostly. Night? Forget it. Fucking mayhem. And it's getting worse.'

'How do you mean?'

'What you saw tonight? How you felt? I'm guessing your blood was up. I'm guessing you didn't feel too hale and hearty. Running legs you had on, I'm guessing. One wrong move and fucking bye-bye.'

'You could describe it like that,' Sarah said.

'Well, a week, ten days ago, that's all, I look out the window there and all I see are people inching along the pavement with their eyes buggy as fuck. Like old men with thyroid problems. Fast learners, though. Believe me. Fast. Last night I saw a pack of three young guys rush along there like they'd had their heels greased. They smashed into a woman so hard I think I could hear her neck break even from up here.'

'What about the police?' Nick asked. 'Aren't there any patrols? Any sirens?'

'You can forget the police,' Tina said. 'I saw a kid out there sucking what looked like a red lollipop – I wish I could say it *was* a fucking lollipop – and he was wearing a policeman's helmet. No patrols. No riot shields. No turtle formation. The police are dead. Or in on it. Whatever.'

Nick snatched up the phone again and frantically dialled numbers until Tina stood over him with a steaming mug. On it was the legend: *Instant male. Just add beer.*

'Have a think about it, if you can detach yourself from your own problems for a minute. You came here in the car. You see any police on the motorway? Think about how much traffic you saw on the roads.'

Nick spread his hands and looked into the space between them. Sarah nodded. 'You're right. No police. I've been looking out for them. And traffic . . . well, let's just say that we had no jams on the way in.'

There were other things now, tickling at her memory. Peripherals. Things that she barely registered, like the music from the stereo or the pain, dulled by Solpadeine, that was throbbing in her thigh. Figures in dun fields that she had taken to be scarecrows and a suggestion of movement in them, beyond what the wind was inspiring. She had turned to see what she thought was heather clumped under a tree, but her mind was now insisting it was a body opened from throat to groin, its innards frozen into grey-lilac foam. Cloud shadow racing over the countryside. But the skies had been clear. She had slept a little in the car. Uncomfortable, claggy sleep. A dream of hunting. Of pursuance.

'Hot tea, my dear, lots of sugar,' Tina said to Nick, for the first time her voice carrying a trace of tenderness. Sarah wondered how much more had existed between them in the past, and found her comparing herself with the other woman, wondering how they made love (if they ever had); how easy, or hard, it had been for her to achieve orgasm with him. Whether Nick would prefer her or invite Tina into his thoughts at the crucial moment.

She felt another stab of guilt at mulling over such crap when her daughter was suffering agonies. Could she be excused for being an animal, like all human beings? Didn't others experience the same moments of farce in the face of tragedy? Weren't there always going to be nose-pickers at the graveside, thoughts of *Playboy* models while the wife bore down in the delivery room? If that was the case, then the animals outside were off the hook too. She felt her craw fill with bile to think of how quickly death could be at your shoulder. How easily it could fill your spaces, overwhelm you. The world would turn whether she or her daughter were a part of it. She oughtn't hold anything against Tina for wanting to look after number one. She was a woman who understood the fragility and value of life too, that was all.

She breathed deeply and sipped her tea. It was good, reviving. Her mother had always given sweet tea to her when she felt ill, or sad. But she doubted it would work with Claire. The way she was lying on that sofa, all angles and pallor, it seemed that nothing would revive her, or bring her back from where she was drifting.

'I'm going to try to find a doctor,' she said. 'I'm sure I'll find one happy to wield his scalpel among all the nippers and tuckers on Harley Street.'

'It's a bit late for that,' Tina said. 'You think surgeons don't have homes to go to? You don't think that some of them might have caught wind of what's up and buggered off to their country retreat to hide?'

'The hospitals then,' Sarah said. 'I can't believe the patients there will have been abandoned.'

'I wouldn't bet on it.'

'Then I'll find a knife and operate on her myself.' Seeing Nick's scepticism etched on his face decided her. 'I have to start somewhere,' she said. 'Do you have any better ideas?'

She could see he wanted to urge her to stay put. It didn't bother her that he was losing any courage he might have had or she suspected him of owning. She couldn't judge people as being lesser than her just because she was brave enough to go outside. There was nothing at stake here for him. She had to question herself. Would she have gone to the trouble Nick had if the roles were reversed?

'You don't have to come with me,' she said.

He was shaking his head. 'I'll come,' he told her. 'When?'

Sarah turned to Tina. 'When's this window of opportunity you were talking about?' she asked.

'I'll give you the all clear when it looks good,' said Tina. 'But don't ask me to come with you. Don't dare.'

'How are we supposed to believe that you're like us?' Sarah asked, suddenly, almost regretting the words even as they piled out of her. But she had to know. 'How do we know you won't pull the knives out after we go to sleep and start slicing bits off us?'

'You don't,' she said. 'But here we all are. I know as much about you as you do about me. I'm happy here. I'm safe. If you don't like it, if you think you might be at risk here, then leave. Find another little stronghold.'

Sarah shook her head. 'I'm happy,' she said, finally. 'But I don't trust you.'

Tina smiled. 'Welcome to London,' she said.

28. BAD BOKEH

Humanities One, the British Library. It was a pale form of shelter, he supposed, but it was working so far. He wanted to approach the other people sitting at the long desks ranged around the grand open space and ask them how they could be so calm when the centre of where they lived was fragmenting so horribly. They turned pages, they made notes. They were blissfully unaware. Bo wondered if he would prefer to be like that or in his current state, knowing the danger, the horror, if not the impulses behind it. At least he felt tooled up with some kind of information, no matter how patchy. These poor people had it coming to them. But what to say by way of warning? There's a man out there with a face full of sharp litter, hoping to eat you? Look in the quiet rooms of unassuming houses. Look for misted glass and bloodshed. Look for yourselves.

He couldn't do it. At best he would be laughed down, at worst he would be told to hand in his card and shown the exit and that would be another refuge closed to him. He wondered briefly if that was what his internal motors were pushing for, flushing him out into the open for the inevitable epiphanies and confrontations to take place, but although he understood the logic and the relief to be found in such an outcome, he shied from it, from the raw self-destructiveness of an act that was so unlike him.

He rubbed his arms – it was always a touch on the chilly side in here and he always forgot to compensate for it in his choice of clothes – and turned his attention to the large entry doors as another reader came through, flashing her ID card to the security guards at their desk. He kept hoping to see someone he recognised, someone to encourage him that he was not alone; in truth he was hoping Keiko might arrive, but no friendly face had shown itself as yet. At least to balance that out there was no obvious hostile presence either. No staring, either blatant or peripheral, no sense of danger encroaching, no seeds on that strange eyelid grid of his, exhorting him to help. No pain or wetness in his hand. It was as if he were sealed in lead here, impervious to anything looking for him on the outside. Why was that? How could it be? He had seen them everywhere else. On the forecourts of petrol stations, on boats on the Thames, in the park, in windows of houses both run-down and luxurious. All of his hideaways became known to them and invaded by them before too long; they were like cockroaches.

Maybe now, as he thought this, they were forming an orderly queue at the admissions office, applying for their ID cards, explaining their need to do some research.

A woman working steadily through a great stack of political biographies looked sharply up at him as he tried to contain his laughter. He gripped the edges of the book he was holding and forced himself to relax. He had been trying to shave an hour or two off his sleep patterns and was down to maybe four or five hours a night now, although his behaviour during his waking hours was becoming increasingly erratic. They could tell something was not right and had been pleading with him to rest, to close his eyes so they might properly blossom.

It's part of what being the map-reader means, one reminded him. *You should give yourself to us, to your task*, another said. *You asked for the map, you must shoulder your responsibilities.*

And another, darkly, added: *If you do not do your job, the map will be taken from you. Do not expect to survive this process.*

He was reaching a crossroads, clearly. He would need to step out in one determined direction before long or face being pulled apart by competing forces. Something inside him that was being eroded by this new element in his life, that was compelling him to help the development of this strange breed, was eager to complete the transition, but he was not so far gone that he did not balk at what that induction demanded. He feared for his sanity and his strength, appalled that the breaking down of his defences might include a sudden appetite for human flesh. As long as he was in command of his own thoughts, he would fight that. Which meant that he was inviting his destruction at the hands of those relying on him to forge a path for them in the city. Already some splinter faction, headed by the grotesque in his scarf and red, shorn hair, were intent on killing him no matter where his loyalties lay. Hiding was the coward's way, but it was the only way, as far as Bo could see.

His fingers fumbled with the edges of the photographic volume he had meant to peruse as a form of solace, but the images were too violent, too close to what he was experiencing to offer any sort of comfort. Even from a purely technical point of view, he was unable to admire the work collected in front of him. Increasingly, photography was redundant in his life, despite his insistence on carrying the Ixus around in his pocket. Documenting the savageries of the world could only work if you distanced yourself from what you were framing through the viewfinder. As the target for so much of that threat, it was something he could not claim. The images he saw on these glossy pages were not the world-class achievements of unique visionaries, as he might once have decided, but the shameless invasions of opportunists. He persevered, though, if only to keep his brain occupied and distracted from fears of attack, or thoughts of sleep.

Another hour passed. He felt his eyes grow heavy, but could not allow himself to sleep, not yet. Sleeping gave the green light to the others. He had to find an irregular pattern so that they were disoriented. He wanted their behaviour to lack any fluidity, at least until he had found Vero and forced him to take the map back. Then they could do whatever the fuck they wanted; he would be gone. The burned rubber and exhaust fumes the only clue as to how. He would scoop up Keiko and take her away from the danger, smother her with kisses and apologies, beg for forgiveness. *I never abandoned you*, he would tell her. *I abandoned myself. You weren't safe, nobody was safe, the way I was.*

She'd castigate him for his behaviour, for his lack of faith in the strength of their relationship; she would be ice cold with him for days, maybe even weeks, but he knew she would come around eventually. He had to believe that. Especially if he could make her see what he was dealing with. The scars on his hand would persuade her. The drop in weight. He could show her how he drooled when blood was nearby. He could get her to follow him as he picked up the scent of a fresh corpse and watch as he dug it up for others to devour while he fought the craving to do the same, like a recovering junky locked in a room with a hill of cocaine.

Coffee, he thought. *I need coffee.*

He pulled on his jacket and walked past the security staff, who were deep in conversation, worried looks on their faces, too involved with each other's problems to notice him leave, and headed down to the café on the floor below. Industrious students were hunched over laptops plugged into the wall. Couples shared muffins and lattes. A large screen highlighted current exhibitions. Cool gusts from the air-conditioning sifted down from the vents.

Bo bought a cappuccino, avoiding the inspection of the staff, and took it to a table at one end of the seating area, his back to the wall so that he could see everyone as they entered or exited. Driven by an embarrassment that had always attended him when he sat on his own in public with a drink or a meal, he reached in his back pocket for his notebook; he'd almost forgotten it since this whole episode began, but there it was, filled with the notes from his job at *The Urbanite*; names of those he had photographed, the meetings he had attended, appointments he had kept. Business cards were tucked into a cardboard wallet at the back of the book. He flipped through them, wondering if this plumber was now something crazed by the smell of dead things; if this taxi driver had dismembered anybody in the back of his cab; if this Detective Inspector . . .

Laurier. Bo got up immediately, answering an urge to call him. He had to give himself up. There might be a cell in it for him. Counselling. Treatment. Maybe, if he explained his plight, the map could be forcibly removed with radiotherapy, chemicals, surgery. He could prove that he was the graverobber that the tabloids were foaming about. He would show them the desecrated graves that had yet to be reported.

He almost ran to the public phone booth situated by the locker room. He fed coins into the slot and dialled the police number. It rang two dozen times before Bo realised it was not going to be picked up.

He rubbed the card with his fingers and felt an odd depression on the surface. Turning it over he noticed a mobile phone number had been written in Biro on the other side. He tried it. It rang for so long he thought the network provider's answering service was about to kick in when the dialling tone vanished, replaced by thin, tortuous breathing.

'Joseph Laurier, please,' Bo said. High heels clattered across the hall behind him. He could hear water in the fountain, the tearing of a receipt from the register for a customer in the bookshop. He heard people transferring their belongings into clear plastic bags used in the reading rooms. He closed his eyes. Nobody was answering although there was clearly someone there.

'Detective Inspector Laurier? Is that you? This is Bo Mulvey. You remember? You know, Richard Dreyfuss.'

'Mmf.' Tired. Frail.

'Sorry? Look, I'm ringing about the graverobber. I need to speak to you. I have something to confess.'

Something approximating a moan floated down the line to him. It sounded tired, pathologically tired. Bo could imagine it belonging to a much older man, not to someone as lithe and lucid as the snide, hawkish copper, someone who had struck him as enjoying his job perhaps too much. A lifer. A pro. He could tell from the sound that Laurier was in trouble, that he might even be dying.

Bo didn't know how to fill the silence that pooled between them. It struck him that of every person he knew who could offer him help and strength, Laurier had always been his best bet, if only he'd been able to shrug off the feeling that the policeman was too dismissive of him, or, conversely, too suspicious. That he suddenly sounded like an invalid was a shock that broadsided him.

'Where are you?' he asked.

'Aah,' Laurier managed. 'Aah.' And then the link was dead.

Aah. Bo bit his lip. It had to be. There was nothing else it could be; nothing else he could think of.

Yard.

London was a different city now, in early December. Bo was hit by the immensity of the place, or rather, the loneliness of it. Hardly anybody walked its streets; those that did were as owl-eyed as himself. He told some of them to leave, to get in the car and go, but they either looked at him as if he were mad, ignored him or told him to go himself, without any of Bo's firm politeness. There were no cars, no buses. He wondered what the state of the country beyond the metropolis must be like for there not to be helicopters in the sky, men in khaki driving jeeps, troops dressed for biological warfare, rifles at the ready, reporters from all corners coming to find out why London was going to sleep.

He took the Ninja south through Holborn, along Kingsway to the Victoria Embankment where three men in suits hailed him and pursued him east, parallel to the river until he reached the Houses of Parliament. He swung around Parliament Square into Victoria Street. Outside the glass front of the Department of Trade and Industry, a woman with red, shorn hair threw a blazing carrier bag at him. It missed him by inches, landing on the road where it burst, sending a long arm of fire across the tarmac; the smell of petrol followed him, as did her mostly unintelligible stream of invective.

He turned on to Broadway and stowed the bike out of sight behind the Italian restaurant in front of New Scotland Yard. His blood was up, his legs jittery from the unprovoked attack. He scanned the street for other threats. There was no uniformed constable at the door to greet him. The eternal flame was doused. A figure slouched in the doorway of the Post Office across the road, reluctant to step out from the shadows. A man in a hooded top was too intent on what he was scooping into his mouth from a greasy cardboard box on the steps outside St James's Park tube station to notice Bo cautiously approach the entrance to the police headquarters.

There was nobody at the reception desk. Potted plants were strewn across the floor, their pots shattered. Soil was scattered around, imprinted with frantic footprints. An arc of dried blood was a ghastly rainbow painted upon one wall. A lift door was opening and closing on a motionless leg poking out into the corridor. Bo stood for a moment, listening to the building make itself known around him. The lack of traffic, of phones ringing, of the general hubbub of people milling around, meant that the steel and concrete and glass moaned and sighed with the infinitesimal strains of realignment, or in sadness at some of the things they must have witnessed over the years, or over the last few days. Perhaps even hours.

Bo couldn't understand why Laurier was still in the building, with the stink of death coming off it in hot, hard pulses. Maybe when he had said, had tried to say, 'Yard', he had meant some other place bearing the same name, or perhaps Bo had simply misheard him. But he doubted it. Laurier would have come here once the trouble started, to co-ordinate responses in the incident room, or whatever it was called here in the real world. Any involvement he had had with the police had generally come from TV. He imagined plain-clothes officers, dour experience burned into tired eyes, smoking over plastic cups of coffee while 'Guv' told them to get out there, knock on some doors, do some legwork. It would be good to find such a room to find out if they had any more clue than he as to what they were up against, and what measures had been taken by way of a response. He guessed, then, that some kind of planning suite was what he needed to look for. First, though, it made sense to seek out Laurier's office.

In a visitors' book behind reception he found several entries by people coming to fulfil appointments with the Detective Inspector. Most of them referred to an office on the sixth floor, according to a building plan taped to the rear of the reception desk. Bo slipped along the corridor to the lift. He stepped inside and, gritting his teeth at the churned pulp of the dead man's face, dragged his legs inside, allowing the lift doors to close. He punched the relevant button and the lift ascended. They were passing floor four when the dead man sat up. He was spitting blood and air from a vague hole in his face.

'That Bernard? That Bernard?' he was saying, or trying to say. His head was like a garishly decorated cake whose centre was under-cooked.

Bo crouched and put a hand on the man's back to support him. It was incredibly hot and slicked with blood. He pressed his fingers into the man's neck to search for a pulse but they kept slipping free. Some of the man's own fingers were gone, snapped off like green twigs from a branch. Through the blood on his leg Bo saw that most of his left calf had been stripped away from the bone. He couldn't see from the damage how much of his face remained. Death was all over him; he just didn't seem ready to acknowledge it yet.

'What happened?' Bo asked.

'Hundreds,' the other man said, suddenly becalmed as if all he had been waiting for was the sound of somebody else's voice. He heaved air through that puncture with an intensity that belied his condition. Bo could feel the strength ebbing from him. He smelled the sudden, sour smell of waste as the man emptied his bowels. Everything was abandoning this sinking ship, but he clung on. 'I ran. This way. Because I didn't –' and here he actually laughed, an awful, ragged, sucking wheeze that Bo flinched from '– want my. Death. To be. Captured. On CCTV.'

'Do you know Joseph Laurier? Where I can find him?'

'I don't know if. Anybody. Survived.'

'But I talked to him on the phone, not too long ago.'

The man slumped a little in Bo's arms; a red eyeball swivelled towards him.

'They were. Fast. But clumsy. Like kids, really. They were like kids let loose. In a toy shop. They held me. Down. They ate. My leg. My fuh– my fucking. Leg. While I watched. They left. Everyone for. Dead. They didn't. Finish. Anybody off. No mercy killing. Terrible injuries. Pain. The pain so. Bad. But I don't feel. It. Any more.'

'Laurier,' Bo said.

'Kill me,' he said.

'I'll get you an ambulance.'

Another snort of laughter. A choking fit. He felt, beneath Bo's hands, like something bad liberated from an abattoir skip and shovelled into a thin bag.

'There are no. Ambu. Ambu.'

He lay there, saying 'Ambu' until the life drizzled out of him. The lift had stopped at the sixth floor, had opened and closed its doors for him and was now waiting for further instructions. In a moment of claustrophobia, Bo lurched for the button to open them again, spilling him into a corridor filled with more crazed red daubings. He felt insanity reach out like a boy in a childhood game of tag. He flinched from it. Concentrated on breathing. Concentrated on one foot in front of the other. Getting through, because there was no alternative. It was this, or the black hole.

Bodies were strewn about like garden furniture after a hurricane. Some of them were still breathing, but so terribly injured that the rise and fall of their chests was as much as they could manage. Bo ignored them and moved deeper into the maze of offices. He proceeded slowly, conscious that the violence was long over, but aware too that all of its perpetrators might not have vacated the building. The hum of strip lighting was all he could hear.

And then, gradually, the temperature increased. Bo hesitated, wondering if a fire had broken out somewhere up ahead. But he could smell no smoke, nor hear the kind of subdued roar that a house fire creates. Sweat stippled his skin, prickled beneath his clothes. The blood of the man in the lift was turning to gum on his biker jacket. He edged forwards, wishing he had a weapon, and closed his eyes for a few seconds. It was enough to have a swarm of warnings pop behind his eyes. He was being begged, cajoled, and demanded out of the building. The tiny grid opened into a furious network of bright activity. There were fizzing seeds all along it now, where previously it had hosted the occasional blip. Something had been activated. Something that he was not meant to know about.

He felt a convulsing inside him, a great shock. Perhaps his task as the map-reader, as this superficially alien city's translator, had come to its end. Perhaps now he was disposable. They knew this place as well as he did, no doubt more so. Its old patterns had come shining through the modernism. The shape of many of its streets were really no different to the way they had been five hundred years ago. London was still a warren. It jealously retained its shambles and alleys, the veins of darkness feeding that tired, determined heart. The force of their alarm and anger knocked him; he put out a hand to steady himself and it slid across the wall, as if it itself were sweating.

He inspected his fingers and found a thin mucus coating them. Here and there it threatened to thicken, became tuberous, like the dense funnel webs of spiders he had searched for as a teenager on tropical holidays. Further along the corridor, as it twisted and turned, these rudimentary 'webs' became more structured, substantial. They began to interlink, providing awkward obstacles for him to climb over. The lights here had been switched off, or had failed in the bizarre humidity. Bodies began to appear, bound within these snowy pockets, ostensibly unharmed, but grey-skinned, drugged into lethargy. He recognised Laurier as one of them.

His mobile phone was on the floor by his side. Most of his body had been concealed behind a thick weave of matter. His jaw was bruised badly. Some kind of thick parcel tape was wrapped around his chin and traversed the top of his head. He looked like an old cartoon of someone in a dentist's waiting room, bandaged up with toothache. The depth of the lines in his face were accentuated by the gloom. Bo found it touching to see his tie remained impeccably knotted. One tiny red dot of blood in the centre of his chest spoke of the only discernible wound to his body. Bo couldn't understand the sudden delineation, a border between carnage and preservation. It was almost as if they were being saved for later. In the coming of the thought was the conviction that he had hit the nail on the head. They would be back, then. Or others would, to raid this drop-in larder.

'Mr Laurier?' he said, and his voice fell flat among the webbing as if it had absorbed any hope it might possess.

There was a slight twitching in the cheek. A shivering of eyeballs behind lids thin as tissue paper.

Bo reached out and touched his arm. Laurier's eyes snapped open, glassy with shock or pain or the trauma of recent memory. His lips parted slightly. He managed to say something that might have been *graves* or *Dreyfuss*. The tape was preventing his mouth from properly forming the words.

'Let me help you,' Bo said, checking behind him in case this was some form of trap. The corridor was empty. He reached out and picked at the leading edge of tape. Pulling it away produced a strangled sob so he let go and went back to one of the desks, where he found a letter opener. He used it to slice the tape at the gulley to one side of Laurier's throat and the detective's jaw popped open, shockingly wide, like that of a snake's in the moment of its unhinging. Laurier might have yelled, or screamed, but Bo didn't hear it because he himself was screaming. He scuttled back as dozens of tiny, translucent eggs poured from between Laurier's lips. Laurier was coughing and choking and groaning with pain; Bo saw now how his jaw had been dislocated to prevent him from chewing the eggs to death. The eggs shivered on the floor and it struck Bo that they were trying to right themselves before crawling back to Laurier's warmth.

Laurier was staring down at them, wide-eyed, his jaw quivering, hanging off his face, creating a terrible, crocodilian gape. Bo began stamping the eggs into the thin, worn carpet tiles and didn't stop even after he had finished them all off. He was seeing them everywhere. But gradually he wound in his panic, helped by Laurier making soothing noises. If he could manage that through the level of pain he must have been experiencing, then Bo could grant him some reasonable behaviour.

He began slicing at the rubbery mesh that shackled Laurier, but it took a long time to free him as the knife kept getting trapped in its warp and weft. Laurier was shaking his head. Either at Bo's cack-handedness or the unacceptable scenario in which he found himself immersed, Bo couldn't be sure. It wasn't a great time to ask him.

'I'm getting you out of here,' Bo said. When he was able to use his hands on the loose edges of the web, the plasma came away more readily, stripping free of the wall. He helped Laurier step clear of his prison, but had to hold the older man upright because all of his strength was gone. His limbs had turned to rubber. He saw movement under the shirt, and more eggs spilling free of the folds in his clothing. He picked Laurier up, bracing himself against the trickle of any of them into his hair or against his skin, and forged his way towards the office bearing Laurier's name. Next to it was an incident room. Inside there were three woman wrapped in cocoons, all with tiny red dots on their chests, their jaws strapped up. Their eyes swivelled beseechingly towards him. Torn, ragged documents and files were scattered on the floor and the desks. Maps on the wall had been shredded. Some of the polystyrene tiles in the ceiling were gone, revealing wiring and pipes; broken bits of the stuff lay around like snow.

'I'm sorry,' he whispered, backing away. 'I'm so sorry.'

He retraced his steps to the lift and stepped out into the war zone of the ground floor. He managed to get Laurier to hold on to him while he kicked the bike into action, then they sprinted out of Broadway just as a tide of figures came howling up Petty France brandishing bricks and bottles and pieces of timber.

Bo said: 'Where do we go?'

If he smiled, his imprecise reflection in the dull steel reminded him of himself, almost.

For as long as he carried the map, he would be known to them, in every kind of way. They only had to wait for him to close his eyes and they would have their own chart leading them to where he slept. If they no longer needed him, he was perhaps more desirable dead than alive, especially as he had resisted conforming to their ideals. What worried him was the sadness, the grief, he had felt as he mashed the life from those grubs into the stained carpet of New Scotland Yard. It spoke of some tough spine of loyalty to this strange people who had invaded his life and wrenched it out of true to a point where he doubted he would be able to reshape it into anything resembling what had gone before. But it was a loyalty forced upon him. He was being coerced. He wanted no part of it. He wanted his old life back, or a facsimile of it; even that would be welcome. As long as Keiko was still involved, nothing mattered.

Laurier was asleep behind him on a deep sofa. Bo was trawling the airwaves on a radio he had found in the kitchen but all of the stations were down. On the short-wave band he had chased a weak signal for twenty minutes, some male voice chattering at a hysterical rate, a pirate transmission he hoped, but it always broke apart into static at the moment he thought he might make sense of it.

They had forced their way into an abandoned house in a well-to-do street in Pimlico where Bo had drawn a hot bath, stripped Laurier and scraped the last of the eggs from his armpits and groin into the toilet. He had bathed the older man like a baby, keeping a hand behind his head so that he would not slip under the water. What Bo had expected to be a tiny scratch on his chest turned out to be an ugly hole, the size of a match-head, which had become infected. The flesh around it was puffy and sickeningly soft, like the skin that has formed on a loose custard. It was coloured black, with arresting green and purple iridescent flashes, reminding him of ham on the turn. He had cleaned it as rigorously as Laurier could stand and applied whatever appropriate creams and sprays he could find in the first aid kit in the bathroom.

Laurier had faded in and out of unconsciousness, and any attempts to speak had been stymied by Bo's tight bandaging of his ruined jaw. He had attempted to force liquid food through his lips before Laurier drifted off into deep sleep. Soup, milk, honey; he had managed to stomach only a little, but he looked significantly better than when Bo had stumbled upon him back in SW1. Bo considered, briefly, trying some of that simple nourishment on himself, but still his body was not ready for it. However many days he had existed without food was already too many. By rights he should be dead. He had massaged the hard prominence of his ribcage, the hollows creeping into his face. He was a cadaver with vast reservoirs of energy. He was dead on legs that refused to accept it. Maybe when (if) the spell was broken, he would drop into death with uncanny, tasteless speed. Sustaining himself on things found in no conventional recipe book was a taboo he was not prepared to think about. He could not believe that he would take such a route, even in extremis. His appearance suggested he was on some extended fast; that was eminently preferable.

Now Laurier's shallow breathing provided a strange comfort to Bo, whose short span of lonely nights had nevertheless got to him, depressing him more than he could understand. He had happily spent a large portion of his youth a single man, yet here he was, suffering loneliness for the first time in his life. Context was all, he supposed. He pushed himself away from the radio and perused the bookshelves of this invisible family whose house they had invaded. There were books here that he had read, or at least owned. He saw that kindredness as a tacit green light to the breaking and entering of which he was guilty.

He wondered where the family that once lived here had escaped to, if they had escaped at all. The thought of them still in the house somewhere, in the cellar perhaps, or wadded in the musty corners of the garden shed, bound and gagged, home to thousands of hungry white worms, was too much to deal with; he could not bring himself to confirm it, despite the angelic countenance of the children in the framed photographs on the mantelpiece, the apparent love that streamed between the parents.

He had been the catalyst for all of this. He had incited this city-wide riot. Eight hundred square miles, maybe more beyond the city's confines, had turned into a morass of missing people and ravaged bodies. If he hadn't been so stupid, so desperate to inject a little excitement into his life, this would not have happened. There was no fast track to success, only to misery. Or maybe all of this would have happened anyway, just starting with some other poor bastard accepting the map. Bo's feeble attempts to hunt Vero down now seemed to be even more pointless. Even if he found him and forced him to take back what he had been so quick, so grateful to offload, he didn't see any quick fix to the ruins that faced him when he looked at what his life had become. He had turned his back on Keiko, no matter how altruistic he believed that act to be, his job was gone, his health was fucked. He had nothing but a bike and a head full of horror.

He had killers on his trail.

He returned to the kitchen and sat down on the stool. The radio spat at him softly. He snapped it off and Laurier's rasping breath filled the space. Saving the Detective Inspector was a pointless exercise, a token reaction to the badness piling in on Bo's life, yet he could not have left him there, despite all the other innocent bodies chosen as live incubators. He should have torched the building; death must have been a better option than what they awaited.

His hand twitched and burned. The blood had dried and run across the skin so often that it looked like something from the props department of a horror film. The skin was stained mahogany. It jumped and crawled with black code. It seemed to be more than what he was. He had visions of it growing, feeding off the rest of his body until he was a withered attachment being dragged around. He stared into the complex weave of welts and scratches, as if some route might make itself clear, but all he could see was damage. Blood traced the delicate diamonds of his epidermis. It dimpled every follicle and pore. Veins pulsed wetly, as if psyching themselves for a push into the open. Blood was all his hand had become. It was senseless. Separate. It was so alien to the shape and manner of his right hand that it might have been grafted on to him, taken from something better left unseen.

Laurier's breathing grew irregular. Bo did not move to be by his side. Laurier was beyond comfort. Bo watched the other man digging at the bandages around his jaw; they loosened. Laurier's eyes grew fixed and his mouth gaped. Bo saluted him. 'Help, police,' he said.

Bo smiled into the burnished steel again. The mangled reflection suggested that a grimace was all he could muster, that humour was now eradicated from his life. *You should have stayed alive for this,* he thought, and brought the cleaver up and down on to his left wrist in one swift, fluid motion.

Part IV

APPETITIVE BEHAVIOUR

Someone once said that all behaviourism in nature could be referred to hunger. This saying has been repeated thousands of times yet it is false. Hunger itself is pain – the most severe pain in its later stages that the body knows except thirst, which is even worse. Love may be regarded as a hunger, but it is not pain.

Eugène Marais, *The Soul of the White Ant*

29. MERCY MISSION

Sarah stood by the window to see if the moon was visible tonight. The moon had been a comfort to her as a child. Her own mother used to tell her that the face she could see up there was the face of her father, who had died when she was very young.

'He had been staring up at the moon, when his illness became too much for him,' her mother had told her. 'And when he died, the moon stayed in his eyes, you know, as though his eyes were a camera that had taken a picture. Trapped it for ever. Your father's face was captured by the moon at the very same moment.'

'They swapped faces,' Sarah had said, decisively, she remembered, as if she would believe it even if her mother had said otherwise.

'That face in the moon, that's your dad, keeping an eye on you. Keeping you safe.'

She often looked out for the moon now when she felt lost or alone or afraid. It was nonsense, of course, but because her mother had said it, and it had helped her, it wasn't really nonsense at all. It was as true as God or Santa Claus or insane men screaming towards her from dark corners of the world to try to destroy her. It was true if she wanted it to be.

There was too much cloud cover to see the moon now, but it was up there, a milky heart in the grey. Even that diffuse light was of some comfort.

'It's time to go.'

Nick leaped as if stuck with a needle. 'Now? Can't we wait till daylight, for Christ's sake?'

'You know me well enough to realise that isn't going to happen. I need to find a doctor. I need to get help.'

'But you were out there earlier. You saw what happened. You saw what's going on out there.'

'Yes I did, but I can see what's going on in here too.' She looked at Claire under a blanket, saw her quaking, saw the sweat on her face, the dark rings around her eyes. The blanket was up to her throat. By morning she might need to move it six inches north.

Nick put his hands to his face. 'I can't do this. I can't go outside again.'

'I'm not asking you to,' Sarah said, soothingly. But she felt her confidence leak quickly out of her. She was aware that she shouldn't rely on a man she barely knew to put himself in situations he didn't deserve to be in, but she had blithely assumed he would back her up, especially after what had happened on the beach back in Southwold. Here was a man who had seen too much already. It was unfair to expect him to prolong his exposure to risk; it had gone beyond trying to impress her to get inside her knickers. Deaths were occurring. He didn't want to join the statistics. There was nothing left on his meter. He was spent. Fair enough.

She turned to Tina. 'I'll knock on the door when I get back. One-two. One-two. Okay? So you know it's me. Let me in quickly, won't you?' Tina nodded, and handed her a knife. She was moving her mouth as if trying to say something, but Sarah didn't want to hear platitudes or rousing speeches of derring-do, especially from a woman who couldn't back them up with actions of her own. She took the knife that Tina proffered and left abruptly. No good-byes. No last-minute efforts to muster support. She forced her legs to take her down the stairs and into the street before she could persuade herself that this was suicide, that her bravery was an illusion brought on by too little food and not enough sleep and that she should get under that blanket with her daughter upstairs, where it was safe.

Things outside had changed. She had never been in a city where the light was as subdued as this. Some spots of light remained, but too many huge pools of blackness stretched out between them. Nothing moved in those oases, but it wasn't them she was worried about. The darkness seemed congealed, filled up. It settled against her skin like soot. *Keep moving*, she thought. *Shift yourself.*

It was quiet now, but she didn't feel that was of particular significance because she couldn't remember if it had been quiet earlier too, when they had set out to confirm Tina's concerns about her city. It was a city's size crowbarred into a town or a village's sensibilities. It was unnerving. Places such as London were rendered pathetic by such anomalies. It had always been a big come-on of a city, used to thundering thoroughfares and clogged pavements. Seeing it weakened like this made her vulnerability more acute. If London couldn't roll with the punches, how could she be expected to?

She spotted movement on the corner of Charlotte Street and sank back into the deep shadow of awnings near Tina's entry door, fighting the urge to call out, to confirm to herself that these were normal people in a normal place living normal lives.

She was grateful for her instincts. *Keep following those*, she told herself. *Say how you feel and act on it. No questions. No arguments.*

Twenty feet away, two men in charcoal suits drifted along Percy Street like sharks cruising the shallows. One of them was wearing the skin of a woman's upper torso like a stole. Her boned head hung down over his shoulder, flapping with each step, measuring out the distance they were travelling with her empty black eye sockets. He twisted and twiddled one of her nipples distractedly as he chatted to the other man who toyed with a rosary of teeth and chewed on something too large for his mouth, now and then spitting dark juice into the gutter.

Sarah checked her breathing and moved off once the two men had crossed the road in the direction of Bedford Square. She moved north, quickly, flitting between the pools of shade and never lingering too long, never positioning herself with acres of black space at her shoulder. She couldn't believe she had given up Southwold for this. Not for the first time, she mulled over the possibility that madness was eating away her brain. These things weren't real. They couldn't be real. Which meant that she was deranged. Fine. Everyone was mental these days.

She wedged herself in a doorway to view the road ahead and then made a spiderish dash to the next little sanctuary a few metres further along. In this way she covered the distance between Percy Street and

University College Hospital in half an hour. It was frustrating to be able to see her goal throughout the journey, but she knew that to break her cover and run was to invite failure. There was too much riding on this. If she died, Claire was finished. That was all she had to know; then it was easy.

No figures moved that she could see in the windows of the National Health Service building. She edged along Grafton Way, keen on scouting the area around the hospital first before she attempted to enter it. There was no point in being cautious up to a point and then abandoning that for a gung-ho approach once her destination was reached.

There was a makeshift car park on the south side of the street; an excavated pit that sank below the level of the road, guarded by a booth and a barrier. Several cars were positioned around the uneven ground. Shadows shifted within them. Other figures loitered by the old UCH building. Badness radiated from all corners.

There was the muffled sound of a heavy iron gate and the jolt and shudder of a mechanism. More metallic squeals and thuds. A yellow skip was wheeled into the street from a side door. Almost instantly, a crowd gathered around the large bin, jostling for position. A whispered roar. She could practically feel the heat of their need. Sarah saw it as a good diversion and was readying herself for a sprint past them so that she could approach the hospital from the junction of Gordon Street and Euston Road, when she heard footsteps, lots of them, in the direction she had arrived from. Her distraction was such that she almost lost balance and fell from the kerb into the road. She recovered and stood trembling by the wall, her hands flat against it, growing colder against the cement while she waited for something to develop.

A hundred or so figures turned into the road and she saw she would have to approach the crowd at the skip or risk walking against this gang as they marched towards her. She began to inch her way towards the skip, wondering if she could pass herself off as one of them. She pulled the knife from her pocket. The handle felt alien to her grip, suddenly too slippery. She felt her mouth become stripped of fluid, her tongue turning within it like a loose pebble in the drum of a washing machine. As she gained ground on the rabble, she saw that the skip bore red letters that she couldn't quite read. She saw an S and an A. She saw the word CAUTION. She saw the interlinked circles of a biohazard sign. A woman broke clear of the pack and staggered to one side, her hands wet, holding her face. Holding something *to* her face. Eating.

The gang behind her were almost upon her. Sarah knew she stuck out, was too timid, too undecided. She'd be unmasked within seconds. She launched herself away from the wall and ran towards the skip. She began yelling, as the others were, and jutted out her hands, being careful to conceal the knife in her palm. The jag of adrenaline helped her overcome the stifling fear of attack; being able to scream when the last half hour had been a suffocatingly quiet odyssey was relief of a kind too. She rammed herself into the thick of it, finding liberation in being able to muscle up against the monsters instead of shying away from them. Her confidence escalated, despite the squirm of their bodies against hers. A man appeared over the lip of the skip and handed out fistfuls of sealed yellow bags and small yellow buckets. These were received joyously, and cracked and torn open with the zeal of children being handed a tub of sweets. One of them was slapped into Sarah's hand with enough force to make her cry out. She dropped it when she saw what the rest of the words on the side of the skip said: MEDICAL SHARPS – DISPOSE OF PROPERLY.

People around her were ramming spent syringes into their mouths and sucking whatever juices they could from them. Others gnawed dried blood from broken glass vials and test tubes. Sarah backed away, checking her hand to see that the skin had not suffered a needle-stick injury.

Then she heard someone say: 'She's not with us.'

Sarah abruptly turned and walked away, knowing that she had been discovered. She felt her skin tighten under the heat of dozens of eyes. Quiet descended. She knew she was being assessed. She knew that to look back at them was to give herself away. They weren't sure about her. They were waiting for her to run, or throw a nervous glance. She forced herself to walk steadily. A man hurried out from behind a plastic curtain in the delivery bay at the back of the hospital. He had his lips clamped to a slashed blood bag and was trying to guzzle the contents before whoever was behind him caught up. More bags were clutched in his other hand; they shook and sloshed like strange octopoid creatures. Cries rang out from around the skip. Here was a feast. The scraps were discarded; leather hit tarmac at pace.

Sarah put her head down and ran as three men crashed out from the delivery bay in pursuit of the bloodsucker. She risked assessing the scene behind her as she reached the corner of the street; she had been forgotten in favour of the dense red booty now being wrestled from its owner, who was sitting on the floor, his eyes wide and glazed, like a sated drunk.

No more distractions, she thought. No more ifs and maybes. Be certain. Focus. Stay alive.

She stole along Euston Road like something borne on the breeze. She could hear terrible sounds – snapping, splintering, liquid half-cries – coming up from the underpass but made no detour to explore further. The great road was dead in either direction, off towards the Westway or back towards King's Cross. Snatches of wild sound volleyed into the desertion. She heard mad laughter and screams in the direction of Hampstead Road.

There were no security guards on the doors, no nurses or porters or patients hurrying or strolling around the substantial entrance hall. Windows were cracked and smashed. A computer terminal was so much plastic rain across the floor. A wheelchair lay buckled on its side, one wheel turning slowly. A piece of gauze with a cloudy red centre hung from a piece of timber that had smashed through a wall. On the reception desk a partially eaten boy had been discarded; even the tongue lolling from his mouth had a chunk bitten out of it.

Okay, Sarah thought. You became inured to it after a while. After a while it was just a part of the scenery. You took it in, you processed it, you moved on.

She walked corridors that didn't seem to have an end, past doors bearing signs she didn't understand. The high, clinical reek of hospitals bleached her nostrils. Every turn she made was another into the unknown; she did not know what she was going to come up against. She poked her head into a staff room with a nurse sitting primly on a sofa with a pen and a book of wordsearch puzzles. The mug next to her still had steam curling off it. The nurse was in some kind of catatonic state, her face grey, fixed upon the puzzle grids as if she were determined not to allow what she was witnessing around her spoil her tea break. Sarah could not rouse her. She was stone.

She found toilets that she could not fully open the doors to. She pushed a piece of broken mirror in through the narrow gap she had managed to create and saw a mountain of bodies piled up just behind it. None were moving. She had to swallow hard against a deranged conviction that Claire was at the bottom of that heap, even though she knew her daughter was snoozing fitfully on the sofa back at Tina's flat. It was the curse of being a parent: visions of hell, even while your children were sitting happily nearby. You trim a hedge with shears and imagine a playful hand slip between the blades at the moment they hack shut; you reverse the car out of the drive and feel the sludge of a tiny body trapped beneath the wheels. All of it fantasy, all of it fuelled by worry. She supposed it was a good thing, this panic button always being on. It meant you were always on the look-out for potential hazards, but it made for an exhausting life. Those bodies had horrified her, but there was no choice but to go on. She had to do something.

It was the start of a long night. A night of a dozen hospitals. The doctors, the surgeons, the cleaners and receptionists were all gone or all dead. It became attritional. She would not be beaten by what was obvious. She would not return to Tina's flat, to her daughter, without her knight in shining armour. Nor would she accept that she was reluctant to return to the responsibility she bore, that she was looking for an end to her life tonight. No, that wasn't it. No.

She travelled on foot and by the end of it, as the weak sun turned the roofs liquid white, she found herself close to collapse. She was in the car park of the Chelsea and Westminster hospital on the Fulham Road, with no knowledge of how she had arrived. She had seen so much depravity that it had her questioning her motives. If this was normality, then what was she doing? Accept it and assimilate. Death was on the cards anyway; it just meant that living this way would bring it along a bit quicker. She was about to head back to the city centre when she decided to have one last look around. It would be just her luck to throw in the towel now while a convention of the best lump surgeons in the world were having tea and biscuits inside.

More of the same. It was wallpaper. It was background. She looked through the sprays of red and the jagged ends of bone. She had learned early on not to hurry along the corridors lest she slip in some slick of serous fluid or another. As with all the other hospitals, she found more people the deeper she proceeded. Some were dead. Some of them were doctors, the knowledge she craved trapped for ever inside their cold heads. There were further signs that the devastation had occurred recently. And there were fresh atrocities. She stumbled upon a ward of twelve lifeless in-patients that had been feasted on while they drowsed, splayed ribs in their opened chests like some unspeakable attempt at culinary presentation. Each had been stabbed violently in the arms and legs first, the blood that had flowed from the lesions showing that the victims were alive at that time, before any fatal wound was inflicted. These poor people had been attacked in their beds by things that wanted them to suffer in extreme agony before they were killed. Who would do that? Why would they do that?

A shadow moved. 'It's because their hearts will taste sweeter.'

Sarah screamed.

'Violent death,' he said, tipping his head in the direction of the corpses. 'The liver releases a great whack of sugar to help the fight for life. The liver doesn't know it's inside a sick body lying in a hospital bed pissing through a catheter. It's thinking fight or flight. It's thinking, "I don't want to die, here . . . have some jungle juice and let's get the fuck away". But if the victim dies quickly, the sugar stays inside the stopped heart. Bingo. Supper time.'

'Are you a doctor?'

'No.'

'Then stay away from me.'

'You won't live.'

'I think I'll have at least a say in the matter,' she said. 'Just fuck off. I'm doing fine. I've got a knife.'

'I'll get you a fork and you can eat yourself before any of the nutjobs in here do it for you. I can help. Really, I can.'

Sarah maintained the distance between them as the shadow moved deeper into the room. She could hear the rasp of its breathing. He was not in good shape. 'You don't sound in a fit enough state to help yourself, never mind anybody else.'

'Appearances can be deceiving,' he said.

'Tell me about it. You might have a belly full of these poor bastards for all I know.'

'I've resisted that,' he said, forcefully. She believed him. She couldn't understand why, having not even seen his face so far, but she believed him nonetheless. 'I am like them, but I'm not like them. I helped them. Unwittingly, unwillingly. Occasionally it felt as though I was on their side. But I'm not. I know I'm not.'

'What's your name?'

'Bo. Bo Mulvey.'

'Why are you here?'

He moved towards her and again she stepped back. Footsteps outside the ward. Hard and fast. Many.

'I'm here because I did a silly thing,' he said. He showed her his heavily bandaged hand. The dressing was streaked with oil and blood and grime. But then so was the rest of him. His hair was lank, greasy. His skin was grey and tired, loose on his obvious bones, and painfully thin. Sarah thought that if she touched him, her finger might poke through. 'I've been searching the city for painkillers. The heavy-duty stuff. But there's not a lot of it left.'

'You did that to yourself?'

He nodded. 'I did it to stop myself . . . turning. I'm not sure it's worked.' He turned his head away from her. The footsteps were joined by hollers and whoops, the sound of bottles smashing and, shockingly, the sound of gunfire.

'I'm leaving,' he said. 'You can come with me if you want to. But make up your mind quick. I don't want to die here.'

'I can't leave. I'm trying to find a doctor.'

He laughed.

'Fuck you,' she spat, and jabbed the knife in his direction.

'Okay,' he said. 'Good luck.'

He moved past her and she smelled how ripe he was, how death was trying to bring him down if only it could get a grip on him. Without thinking she reached out a hand and grabbed his jacket. She said, 'Help me.'

'We have to leave,' he said. 'Now.'

'Help me find someone. A paramedic. A surgeon. A fucking ambulance driver. Do that and I'll put the knife away. I'll trust you.'

'What makes you think I need your trust?'

'You're crying,' she said.

He raised his hands and batted at his cheeks, shocked by the tears.

'You fighting against this. It's a lonely job, yes? I'm right?'

Bo couldn't speak. He wanted to run. He wanted to get outside and keep running until his lungs combusted. But the gutsy blonde with the knife and the attitude had rattled him. And he liked it. It gave him the nudge he needed, the hand on the back of the head forcing him to look in a direction he had been ignoring for too long. She seemed to understand him, without him needing to open his mouth. He had missed that in a person. There was a way out of this that did not involve the extreme measures he was drifting towards.

'There are no doctors,' he said. 'They were targeted. When you're trying to wipe out a race, you don't want anybody around who's useful at patching people up again.' He took a risk and grabbed her elbow, steered her into the corridor away from the approaching rabble. She allowed him to lead her, folding the knife into her pocket.

'I think I realised that hours ago,' she said.

'Then why are you here?'

'My daughter needs help. What do I do? Give up? You don't have kids, do you?'

'No.'

'Well, take it from me. You don't give up. Hospitals were the only place I could go.'

Bo made a noise that might have been laughter or bafflement but came out like a cough from a sick man. 'This isn't a hospital any more,' he said. 'This is a fast-food restaurant.'

'I have to try.'

'If there's anybody here who can help you, they're dead. Understand that. We need to get moving.'

She pulled clear of him. 'Let's get one thing clear, bucko,' she said. 'I don't take orders.'

'You do now,' he hissed, clamping his good hand over her mouth and pulling her through a set of swing doors into the stairwell. A doctor was sprawled over the edge of the upper landing. Her head had been chiselled open for the goodies inside. It was a neat operation; the body's white coat was spotless, the brain scooped out with minimum fuss, like a scrupulous breakfaster at a lightly boiled egg.

Bo frowned hard at Sarah when she began trying to bite his fingers. He put a foot to the door to prevent it closing completely, and through the half-inch gap that remained she watched as a jumble of shadow moved stealthily into view. She slackened against him as the shadows resolved themselves into three figures. Their heads were shaved, dyed red.

'What?' she mouthed against his skin.

He pulled her back. The door closed, but not before they noticed the lead figure halt and swing his head their way, his mouth dropping open like a badly packed tool bag.

'Who was that?' she whispered as Bo led her down the stone steps, her voice breathy as if they had just seen a cinema legend nonchalantly strolling along.

'Someone I wish I didn't know,' he said. 'Someone you certainly don't want to know. Someone who wants me dead, and I'm not sure why. He's going to have to get in a queue for that before long.'

'Did he see us?'

'I doubt it. He had his mouth open, though. He might have heard us. He might have smelled us.'

He paused at the landing and listened. Nothing.

'I think we might be all right. Come on.'

'Where are we going?'

'Basement. We can get out at one of the refuse collection points.'

'But that's where they congregate. I saw them. It looks to me as if they're after easy food.'

'Everywhere is easy food now,' he said. 'We don't have any good options available to us. Some of those things, they're clever, adaptable, mean enough to get their meat wherever they want it. They'll bring it down in the street if they can. Others are weaker and stupid. They'll grub about in bins. They're like us. That's the problem, really.'

'Who are they?'

'We can talk about that later.'

To the left, at the foot of the steps was a large locked door with a glass window. Through it Bo could see banks of switches and fuse boxes. To the right, the corridor led to a locked partition accessible by key card. The red light in the security housing glared at them. They stood looking at it for so long that Sarah believed it must change colour because of their interest in it.

'Wait here,' Bo said at last.

He was not gone for long but Sarah didn't like the feeling his absence inspired. Before meeting him she had been alone. Now he was gone, she felt lonely. It bothered her that she should feel so different in such a short time. It was needling that she should be so fickle, when she had never dreamed she was that way inclined. Nick had helped, but his help was of the puppy-dog variety, there was always the feeling that he was waiting for his reward. This guy was driven, and that made her feel safer.

He returned with a big smile – which helped the parlous state of his face, but not much – and a key card.

'Where did you find that?' Sarah asked.

'On the doctor with the open mind,' he said, and swiped the plastic across the housing. Even after the light had turned green and a soft, pneumatic *thunk* heralded the release of the door, Sarah was convinced the red light was still showing, it burned in her memory so brightly, no longer a no entry indication but now more of a warning. They passed through the pharmacy, Bo smashing cabinets and stuffing his pockets with drugs – 'There's got to be something here that can do me right, no?' – and on through another linking corridor to the mortuary.

'Great,' Sarah said.

Bo indicated to her to be quiet and used the card again on this second security mechanism. The door released itself. Refrigerated air flowed past him and tightened her arms. They moved through an admission and removal area into body reception. Beyond were stacked the storage fridges. Everything was covered in red handprints.

'Oh my God,' Sarah said, when she saw the bodies.

'It's okay, they're dead.'

Sarah tugged at his leather jacket. 'I'm sold on what you said about getting moving,' she said. 'Let's go.'

But Bo was moving deeper into the room. His boots sloshed through shit and chemicals; the drainage gullies were blocked with body parts, hanks of hair, torn clothing. A woman was lying across a laminar flow table, her lower half gone, a grey spaghetti remaining. There was a partially sucked Polo mint in her gaping mouth. Three more bodies were drunkenly slouched against the wall, the eyes that remained in their faces opaque with death, or shock.

'What are we doing here?' Sarah asked. 'You looking for a date?'

'Weapons,' Bo said. 'Knives. I don't know. Drills? Meathooks?'

'Okay,' Sarah said, happy for a task. She started on the drawers and immediately found a cleaver. 'Some butcher's shop this is.'

'Bag it,' Bo said. He put a cartilage knife and a couple of bone rongeurs and Austin chisels in his pocket along with a packet of circle-curved suture needles. 'Bag it and take whatever else you can lay your hands on.'

They'd done a circuit of the mortuary and were heading for the door when the first heavy blow rang along the corridor.

'Fuck,' said Bo.

'This was a trap,' Sarah said. 'You tricked me.' She checked behind her but there was no exit. The windows were either as small as letterboxes or secured by bolted steel bars. Another blow. The sound of glass cracking, of metal gritting, squealing as it was wrenched free.

Bo craned his neck. 'There's a dozen of them. Maybe more. They haven't necessarily seen us.'

'Fucking great,' Sarah said. She felt close to tears. She felt hungry. 'I haven't necessarily shat my pants, but all these things . . . they're on the cards, aren't they?'

'We hide,' Bo said.

'What? Where?'

'The refrigerators.'

'They'll find us.'

'If they're looking for us.'

'What else would they be doing?'

'Same as they're all doing,' he said, bustling her towards the rear of the mortuary where nine great vacuum-locked doors stood. 'Looking for food, scraps, whatever they can get.'

One of the bodies on the floor rolled over, spitting crimson sputum from his grey-blue lips. Bo tipped him back over on to his chest and jumped down hard on the nape of his neck. Sarah turned away when she saw his intent, but could not block out the deep, dense sound of bones crunching.

'Come on,' he gentled. 'Come on.'

He threw open the first of the doors, indicating she should do the same. There were four drawers in each refrigerator; all of them were occupied. Something wasn't right, but her mind was so fogged with fear she couldn't pin it down.

'Get in,' Bo urged. He was clambering into a drawer that contained a child, a boy in his early teens who was so white he was almost indistinguishable from the hard plastic that contained him. More blows rained down on the security doors. She heard the door groaning as it came away from its hinges. She slid into the drawer, shutting her eyes to the figure that was already in there. She smelled of germicidal soap. She could almost believe she was lying in the dark with Claire, and that everything was all right. She closed her eyes and dragged the drawer back into its sheath, scrabbling with the door, pulling it behind her as the security entrance crashed free and the world was filled with footsteps and screams. The threat of imminent death was so great that she found it inside herself to reach out and hold the inflexible creature lying beside her. Who then shifted in the dark and said: 'Do not scream.'

30. RECOVERY

Manser moved at night. He moved slowly. He avoided main roads back into the heart of the city. It was difficult to find a time when quiet dominated, but after 3 a.m., most of London seemed to be tucked away indoors. He knew there were likely to be more people about the closer he got to the river, but for now the anonymity, the desertion helped. A few hours at a time was all he could manage anyway. When the thickness of the night became loosened, the sun still a good two hours away from putting in an appearance, he melted from the street. He found an unalarmed scaffold in Walm Lane; a loose corner of tarp covering a skip in Sherriff Road; a child's tent in an Abbey Road garden. He slept fitfully, if at all. Pain held his hand like a concerned parent throughout, never letting him out of its sight.

He grew to appreciate the pain as it ate through what remained of his face. He crunched on painkillers almost continuously, relishing the bitter taste on his tongue, the slightest distraction from the monumental suffering that threatened to take him out of himself to the point where he might decide to climb a pylon or jump from a tower block or hurl himself in front of a train. The pain he knew he must best if he was ever to entertain the thought of loving his stumps again in the future. How could he be tender to the dying if he thought for a second that they were too engrossed with their own private agonies to be able to enjoy his passion? He had to cling to that belief that there was a future. It was all he had.

But that wasn't strictly true. There was Salavaria. He was a good reason, a great reason to stay alive. Manser realised he, himself, might be a bad man, in the classic, villainous sense of the word, but at least he was honourable. He loved his friends. He was loyal. He couldn't abide, couldn't understand, the betrayals that occurred so frequently within the underworld he inhabited. If that was naive, then guilty as charged. He believed in honour and trust. He was solid, dependable. He was The Ton. Mister 100 per cent. And what had it brought him?

He gingerly touched his face, wincing at the crisp/sodden mess of it. It worried him that he could not feel certain parts despite his fingers sinking into a spongy mass that ought to have had his flesh singing. Dead nerve endings. Dead. The thought that it was in him, death, even in this limited way, traumatised him to the point where, if his tear ducts weren't melted shut, he might have cried himself into a coma. And yet it was other things too: emboldening, chastening. He understood a little bit more about the enormous forces needed, both physically and psychologically, to introduce death to a living thing. The body was fragile: there were many ways you could kill, many ways to die, but the body was also strong, ferociously strong. It did not receive death easily, and once it was in the vicinity, the body fought like fury to repel it.

Sunlight. He had been so enraptured by his fantasies of how he might ruin Gyorsi Salavaria that he had forgotten the cramp in his legs and the grief lacing his chest, neck and head. White fire lanced his eyeballs, despite it being only the palest cream of pre-dawn. He had to retire from the day, before it became blinding, before his body rebelled and put him into a state from which he would not recover. He'd have put on his beloved sunglasses if his ears hadn't been burned away.

Patience was all. At the end of the road, Salavaria would be there. The cunt would be taught some regal lessons. It didn't matter how far the road was, or how long it took for him to travel it. It was unimportant what state he was in when he got there. He would get there.

'Jez, you dumb bastard,' he muttered to himself. 'You traitor. You fair-weather friend. I thought you were loyal. I thought we were mates. Jesus.'

Things were changing as he snaked towards St John's Wood. The houses seemed to be hunched in towards each other, as if in a conspiratorial huddle or quaking before some unimaginable fate. Every window seemed to have been punched in or blown out; glass teeth were bared at him as he trudged further south. He sought shelter in a car showroom just before the main road turned into an ugly collision of shops, fast-food joints and piddling side roads. He searched for sleep in the back seat of a Mercedes, his face turned in to the soft leather upholstery. He could hear nothing. London was a grave waiting to be filled.

Sleep, or an approximation of it – a troubled, fevered greying of consciousness – greeted him with fantasies of soil. He was grabbing fists of earth and ramming them into Gyorsi Salavaria's mouth, which was as wide open as it could be without splitting from the strain. Staples were punched into that rigid O of his lips, attached to chains snapped tight against the confines of his dream. Salavaria's teeth were sharp and vulpine, stained plum from the decades of blood he had supped upon. His eyes were wide with terror. It was almost too much to take and he shied from the face, confused by his feelings. It didn't seem right that a man such as Salavaria, a monster, a strong man in every sense, could be reduced like this, brought down to the point where he was a snivelling, abject wreck, even in the context of a dream, a fantasy.

I fear him, he thought, and the soil in the packed throat trickled out as the lips somehow managed to curl into a smile. The staples bit deeper and blood traversed the shining rim of his mouth. Salavaria was the ultimate survivor. Would Manser, had he been in the same situation, have been able to put his head down, banish himself from society, hide in a hole for thirty years? Thirty *years*. His patience was utter. His devotion to his beliefs unshakeable. How could he hope to knock him off course? He didn't have a shred of that drive, that hunger.

He woke sweating, shaking with cold. Salavaria was climbing out the hole of his dream, the staples straining against his lips, tearing through them, turning his mouth to a pulp of blood and mud.

'He works alone, Jez,' he said, shakily. 'You never stood a chance.'

Manser moaned and struggled upright, his legs squeaking against the plush interior of the car, and the sound was enough to banish the dream completely. He slid out of the back seat and walked shakily across the road to a petrol station. The small shop annexed to it had been raided, its windows shattered, produce looted. Most of the shelves were bare, but he found a loaf of bread that was relatively free of mould and a partially consumed pack of dried fruit. He sucked gingerly at the bread, the apricots, wincing as his face came alive with reminders of what had happened to it, until he had a paste he could swallow. He sipped at a bottle of dandelion and burdock. The food brought him back. He found his mind clearing, his confidence returning. It prodded and played with Salavaria again, diminishing him, breaking him down into what, essentially, he was: old. Yesterday's man. Come on, Manser. You're The Ton, not him. He's ready for his slippers. He's ready for his liquid meals and free bus pass. You were his crutch, his meal ticket. He's rusty. He's been talking to trees for a generation.

It was late afternoon. The sunlight was a dim, dusky red falling on the south-facing rooftops and Manser imagined them as fading reflections of the atrocities he would stumble upon within the next few hours. That colour was all he could think of as he traipsed the final few miles along past Lord's cricket ground, into Lisson Grove and the heart of Marylebone. There were fewer people around than he had expected, although he reasoned that he was now the kind of person people went out of their way to avoid. He walked into an empty pub on Harcourt Road and poured himself a lager from the tap, sipped it through the cracked blisters of his lips while staring at the pale Swedish church across the way. He drew a little peace, a little strength from that simple building. He rested. Music played from a CD unit behind the bar. Louis Armstrong on permanent loop. *What a Wonderful World. Nobody Knows the Trouble I've Seen. Baby, It's Cold Outside. Mack the Knife.*

When the shark bites, with his teeth, dear, scarlet billows start to spread . . .

He managed to eat some peanuts and climbed the stairs at the back of the pub to the catering quarters. A dumb waiter was stuffed full of corpses to the extent that he couldn't tell how many bodies were inside, or whose limbs belonged to which abject expression.

A counter looked out on a tiny beer garden inhabited by blood-drenched picnic tables and parasols. Beyond that, a block of flats rose four storeys, white-painted brickwork tigered here and there with deep scarlet. A man was sitting on his balcony looking north towards Regent's Park with a pair of binoculars, his long hair prancing about in the stiff wind. Against his chair rested some kind of decorative sword. A few balconies along, a woman was tying a rope ladder to the railings. Shouts were coming from somewhere, alternately reasoning and incomprehensible, furious. Manser filled his pockets with short, sharp steak knives. He moved across the landing to the bathroom where he found a small tub of painkillers. He popped two in his mouth and crunched them and moved towards the front of the living quarters. A TV was on, spilling white noise across a carpet rioting with beige paisley. A woman was on her knees, collapsed into the sofa, her back peeled open along the spine. A younger woman, perhaps her daughter, lay with a pair of headphones on, staring up at the ceiling, her face blue. There was no obvious damage to her body. He leaned over her and was mildly shocked to see her eyes following him. He reached out and tweaked the skin of her collarbone. No reaction. Breath very shallow, hardly there at all. She had been left for dead.

He found more rushed murders as he walked down to Baker Street, more bodies put through the agonies of death without actually meeting it. A traffic warden was sitting back against the large window of a charity shop, making slack, whale-like noises, his head jerking and twisting as if on the end of an inebriated puppet-master's strings. He had vomited down his luminescent yellow singlet. His face was bruised and swollen where someone had beaten him; Manser was able to discern cleat marks from the sole of a boot in the scuffed, torn skin of his forehead. Some effort had been made to cut part of him away – the heavy serge material on his arm had been scissored open, the exposed flesh gouged – but it was a rushed job. It was as if whatever had attacked him didn't have the time to finish it off. Manser felt his gorge rise at the thought of being left brain-damaged, alone. He, at least, had some idea of who he was and what he had to do. His mind had not been switched off, although, at the height of the pain, he wished that were an option.

He waded through bodies in the chemist's for a handful of energy tablets and more hardcore analgesics. He suffered a bolt of pain as he reached the junction of Baker Street and had to wrench himself back out of sight; a swarm of people, perhaps as many as two dozen, were striding up Paddington Street, their hands full of bats and hammers. He was certain one of them had hold of a chef's blowtorch. He could do without any more of that.

They would surely see him if he didn't get out of the way immediately; he could hear their footfalls. They were so close he thought he could hear the ticking of watches on their wrists. He flattened himself against the doors of the cinema, the Screen on Baker Street. One of them swung back; there was nobody in the booth. He hurried down the stairs, the loose flesh on his face screaming at him as it struggled to part itself at the red juncture with those hard, carbonised remains; and looked back up to the street, where shadows were already coalescing, shapes smearing up against the glass door, which had only just settled back into position. He saw the top of the head of the last man in the crowd turn his way, perhaps alerted by the tiny shiver of the door as it came to rest.

Manser sank further. The bar at the bottom of the stairs was deserted. Glasses were smashed and a popcorn machine had overflowed; the stink of burning sugar came at him from all angles. A fug of tan smoke riffled around the ceiling. Postcards were scattered all across the floor. He received a brief, almost nostalgic twang of excitement at the sight of a female cinema attendant whose foot had been separated from her ankle. She had died in an awkward position, half-kneeling, half-lying on a box of carpet cleaner in a staff room she was presumably trying to get into to hide at the critical moment. Whoever had taken her foot had discarded it almost immediately.

A change in the air pressure. A corner of a newspaper on the counter lifted and sank. Manser panthered across the bar to the swing doors of the screen room. He eased them open, tensing himself against the creak of oil-shy hinges, a noisy breath of stale, inner air, but it never came. He moved inside and helped the doors close, his eye on the landing as a shadow grew into the wall and a hand landed on the banister's curve where it swept into the last section of stairwell.

Manser allowed the door to seal itself and turned to the auditorium. Heavy velvet curtains obscured the screen. Every seat was occupied, every head angled forwards to catch a performance that would not be delivered. Manser shot a look at the projectionist's booth; the window was smeared. He moved down the central aisle, the hairs on his skin rising as he felt the empty gaze of dead people drilling into his back.

He heard the jolt of a hand on the door and he jinked left, dragging a young boy from his chair and ramming him into the foot well, taking his place as a parallelogram of light raced across the walls and two bobbing shadows moved into the theatre. Impossibly large, they bled across the acoustic panelling and on to the velvet before the door closed and ushered them into the gloom. Manser kept his eyes riveted to the curtains and began to see patterns squirming there. Pain was beginning to filter through the screen he had erected with those painkillers; he wished he had necked a few more before this eminently avoidable situation had transpired. All he had to do was play dead, and he was halfway there anyway. He could feel baubles of sweat begin to decorate his face.

The velvet twitched. In his periphery he saw a figure step into line with him and stop. A mealy smell assaulted him, of raw meat, of offal. He felt something squirm across his thigh but could not look down without giving away his position. The boy under his feet bucked twice, as if trying to get up. Fear took up the sport of his blood, ripping through his veins with something that was so hot or so cold there was no difference in it. The thing on his thigh dug in, as if testing the plumpness of his muscle. It felt like a crab had gripped him. He wanted to cry out, to brush it away. The figure to his right proceeded with his leisurely pursuit, sweeping his gaze this way and that along the sallow ranks. His mate was just behind him, the thin waterproof material of his coat shushing and hissing, sheened with plaques of dried blood. Like the man ahead of him, he stopped level with Manser and placed a finger against the blackened wasteland of his temples. What felt like an electric bolt flashed down the side of Manser's head.

'No fresh here,' the man said. 'No fresh.'

They stood at the foot of the theatre and looked back at the audience, then trawled slowly back towards the exit door. Manser was fighting black, lazy slaps of unconsciousness now, his face so slicked with sweat he thought it must surely be his undoing. He risked a look at the man at his side. He was sitting bolt upright, his neck cricked violently to one side. His eyelids and lips were gone, his cheeks scraped from his face like the flesh of a mango from its skin. He might have been viewing a film after all, a comedy, or a high-octane thriller. Here comes the car chase. Here's fun. I can't bear to watch.

He dug his fingernails deeper into Manser's thigh. He was trying to breathe but could manage little more than a series of short, thin gasps through the dried-out tablets of his clenched teeth. Manser slapped his hand away and risked a look back up the aisle. The two men were at the door, conversing. The boy continued to buck under Manser's feet. He had to close his eyes to the thought that he was convulsing, suffering a heart attack, maybe. Dying.

The men finally finished their discussion and returned to the bar. Once the doors were closed again, Manser levered himself out of the chair and helped the boy back to his seat. It was too late. It was too late for any of them. He looked around at the ravaged faces, some in suffocated agony like the man seated next to him, some in grey, silent fugues where the fluttering of eyelids was the only indication of life continuing. Others were trying to get away, squirming on the floor ineffectually. Manser tried to imagine what had happened here. A mighty attack had taken place, a smothering of some kind. The occupants of the cinema seemed brain-damaged, starved of oxygen to the point of death and then let off the hook. Inexpert murder, or the behaviour of sick ghouls. It was hideous. It was monstrous. And it reminded him of himself.

Nauseated, he moved back up the aisle, listening carefully at the doors before easing them open a crack. Seven figures were in the bar now. One of them was gnawing at the foot of the dead staff member.

Manser returned to the screen, intending to find an alternative way up to the street via the fire escape. He missed the lean athleticism that he had once had, now robbed from him with the shriek of nerve endings whenever he so much as tried to blink. He reasoned that the pain must mean that he had not suffered any infection. He remembered relatives cooing over the cuts and scrapes on his knees and elbows when he was a boy, telling him that a sting when ointment was applied was a good thing. Pain was a friend to us.

'Oh yes,' he whispered. 'My best fucking mate, pain.'

It had become so acute that at times he felt it had formed its own rendering of him: a vague Manser shape, an homunculus, that was connected to the corporeal version like a shadow. It had its own blood supply, its own organs. He felt as though he could turn around and touch it, it was so vibratingly real, a sensation somehow beyond normal experience, beyond emotion. Once, he had cried when he was hurt. Now it was as if tears were too flimsy a reaction for what he was feeling. Death was too flimsy for this.

He paused regularly on his climb back up the stairs, giving half a mind to torching the cinema to put the poor bastards out of their misery. But fire was not something he felt able to be near any more.

Baker Street was deserted again, the baying pack having moved on, perhaps to the nearby Hilton Metropole or the Landmark, hotels where there were doubtless potential victims holed up in their rooms, plenty of 'fresh' for them to be getting on with. He thought he could see little oases in the upper floors of the banks at this busy junction, and further along Paddington Street, in the office blocks and high-rise residential flats; coy movement at skyscraping windows. But it could just have been the shift of clouds in the glass, or the mopping up of survivors by those monsters perspicacious enough to realise that there was more going on in the streets of London than merely at ground level.

Salavaria's stink was all over this.

The mistake he had made, he realised now, was to listen so much to Salavaria over all that time he had visited him in the forest, but never take anything in. All this froth about suitability to his people, of the flavour of blood, of destiny and promise; he had thought it the controlled ravings of a man thirty years lost to society. He had taken his eye off the ball. London was his wake-up call, in more ways than one.

He had to stop and lean against the railings of a park. At its far end, a children's playground sat forlorn and empty, its gate wailing as it swung on its hinges. The reflection of the polished slide was not a colour he felt comfortable with. He was violently sick, from the little touches of unpleasantness revealing themselves to him or the visions of Salavaria, he wasn't sure. He watched his brown vomit collect pathetically around his shoes. Peanuts and beer. He needed to get some proper sustenance inside him, if there was a fight to be had at some point.

He staggered the two hundred metres to Marylebone High Street and walked south along it, until he found the road he needed, a little avenue off the main street. He did not know if he would find the address turned into a pastiche of an abattoir. He was steeled for some measure of red; it was in his blood, one could say.

He thought he saw the man in the window of the flat but by this time he was failing fast. He wasn't sure what he was seeing any more. The light was slicing into his eyes; he had spent more hours than ever before on his feet, plodding that last leg into London proper. A rest was on the cards, but it was touch and go as to whether it would involve soft pillows or a mouthful of cold hard kerb.

He rang the buzzer. A shape appeared through the frosted glass of the door, might have said something, shouted something in shock. Manser might have spoken in return. And then he was falling hard against the man, who smelled right, even if he could not make out any features. That smell. Kind of chemical. Kind of biological. Kind of fucked. He was home. He was safe.

31. FLIGHT TO THE SOUTH BANK

Tina said again, 'Who the fuck are they?'

Tea wasn't going to work this time. She handed a bottle of vodka and a shot glass to Sarah. Sarah took the bottle and swigged from it. She sat on the sofa next to Claire, who had found sleep. She cuddled her daughter, paying no heed to the lump. It was a piece of her. It was warm. A strange part of Sarah was able to love it because of this. Eddie and Lamb were standing by the wall. They leaned against each other. Their faces were guarded, filled with hoods and shadows and circles.

'They were hiding at the hospital,' Sarah said. 'We couldn't just leave them there.'

'Oh, you could you know, if you tried,' Tina said. 'We don't know they're clean. Why did you have to bring them back here?'

'*Because they were being chased.*' Sarah's face was as open and as daring as a cellar door. Her eyes bulged, her lips thinned out before gritted teeth. She felt dangerous, on the edge of things. They stared at each other for what seemed like an age before Tina's attention flickered.

'What about her anyway?' she asked, indicating Claire as she stirred on the sofa. 'The state of her. She could be contagious for all you know. What is it convinces you she's clean?'

'She isn't clean,' Bo said, staring at the stained, swollen portion of her T-shirt. 'But she isn't contagious.'

Sarah watched him. He kept closing his eyes, as if the sight of Claire had overwhelmed him, as if she were someone famous, and he a starstruck fan.

'While we're playing this game, lover,' Tina said, 'who the fuck are you?'

'I can help,' Bo said. 'I'm involved in this. But we don't have much time. We have to get her out of here.'

'Be my guest. There's the door. Pardon me for pointing it out, but you could have just missed out the middleman and fucked off straight away.'

'We're not leaving without you. Nobody stays behind.'

'I don't need a knight on a steed, petal,' Tina said. 'I'm not going anywhere.'

'You might,' Bo said, standing and pushing by her to get to the kitchen, 'if you'd seen what I've seen over the past few weeks.'

'We can stand here arguing the toss all you like, hotpants,' Tina said, watching his progress across her flat, her knife held out in front of her as if it were some kind of tracking device, 'but I'm staying here precisely *because* of what *I've* seen. And we can all get our dicks out and play whose is biggest if you like, but it isn't going to change a thing. I stay. Help yourself to a big slice of fuck off on your way out.'

Sarah was tired of the bickering. She blocked the other woman out and concentrated on her daughter. She gently stroked her temples, as she had done when Claire was a baby; the motion had often carried her swiftly off to sleep. Sleep. Now there was a thing she wouldn't mind a little of, but she doubted she'd sleep again after this day. She wondered if it would take a lifetime to forget the species of cold she had discovered in that refrigerator. She still did not understand how they had survived. A few times during the unconscionable minutes they had to wait, she thought she might cry out, but the cold, and the girl's hand over her mouth, always kept the impulse at bay. She could hear awful things happening behind the door. Squabbling. Feeding, like the troughing of pigs. At one point she thought she could hear a bone being dislocated at a point where the ball met its socket. How did she know it wasn't Bo being jointed, or Bo joining in with the feast? She realised she was hungry herself; her stomach rumbled and she was sickened by her reactions. The flat truth was that Lamb had saved her life in that freezing coffin. Tina couldn't know that. Tina didn't matter.

'You made your first mistake,' Tina was saying now. 'You got boxed in. Always have a second exit. Always.'

Eddie and Lamb were watching the violent exchanges with dark, worried eyes. They appeared not to have slept in weeks.

'This is Eddie and his daughter, Lamb.'

'Lamb? Oh that's just beautiful,' Tina said. 'Insert your own slaughter gag here, here, and here.'

'It's her nickname,' Eddie said. 'Her real name is Rachel.'

Bo strode over to the man and the girl, who both shrank back as if trying to become absorbed by the wallpaper. He shot the sash window open as wide as it would go and got down on his haunches in front of them. The girl was perhaps thirteen, her body beginning to blossom beneath the vestiges of infancy: a toffee-coloured Stussy T-shirt, trousers like white noise, a denim jacket studded with badges of Robbie Williams, McFly, Tracy Beaker. Her legs were long and gawky, wrapped around each other like thin, knotted branches. She was pretty, but it was also a hard face. Bo wondered maybe if the shutters had come down during what she had experienced recently. Where was her mother? The answer to that question might just be staring back at him with gritty grey eyes.

'Hold out your hands,' he said.

Eddie said, 'You're just as much under suspicion, in my book.'

'Then let me ease your worries,' Bo said. He ripped off the bandage on his wrist, ignoring Sarah's protestations, and showed them the stump. Three fingers so far, tiny and malformed, were regenerating through the ugly, raw wound. He wriggled them. Lamb turned away, her face draining of colour.

'Suspicion justified,' Bo said.

'Leave her alone,' Eddie said.

'You asked for it,' Bo replied. 'Now give me your hands.'

He checked their skin and eyes. He told them to open their mouths.

'What are you looking for?' Nick asked.

'Signs,' Bo said. 'There are ways to tell them apart. In the colour of the tongue. In the shape of their throats. The quality of the teeth.'

He looked up at Nick. 'They do not abide scars of any kind, nor marks. No freckles. No moles. It's a kink in their gene pool. It's called perfection. Skin deep, that is. In many other areas, such as killing, they're God-awful.'

Eddie said, 'Do you believe that we're drawn together by ancient catastrophe, that history has a design for us? Especially the tragedies? Only the tragedies?'

She got to her feet and moved to the door.

'Beware your history,' Eddie said. 'Fear the actions of your forebears. That is what this is all about.'

Bo moved back. 'They're clean,' he said. 'By which I mean they're dirty. Like us . . . Like you.'

'And what about you?' Nick said, unable to keep the barbs from his voice. 'How long before you ship us to the others, use us as a tasty dip for your Doritos?'

'I'm not going that way. I swear.'

'Oh, that's all right then. Only just met you, don't know a fucking thing about you, but it's all right because, hey, you gave me your word.'

'You have to trust me.'

'Bollocks.'

It was getting warm in the overcrowded room. Bo couldn't keep his eyes off the nightmarish distension in Claire's armpit. It looked as if a head were trying to push its way out. He thought he could see movement beneath the skin. He tore his gaze away, shaken. 'We have to decide on a plan of action,' Bo said.

Sarah, to her credit, cut off the hisses of breath that Tina and Nick were inhaling, ready for another tennis match of *fuck you*, by saying: 'He's right. Let's stop butting heads. We have to stick together. Stay alive. I probably wouldn't have made it back without him. I'm with Bo. I go where he goes.'

Nick seemed crestfallen although she had not intended it as a rebuke; Tina wore an expression she suspected was fuelled by what she perceived as Sarah's fickleness. Tina seemed to be ready to offer her opinion, but her features softened, she reined it in. Instead, she asked Sarah about her quest to find a doctor.

'There were none. We have to be careful. A bad injury now and there's nobody around to kiss it better.'

'How does that work?' Nick asked. 'I mean, no doctors? It was hardly an exhaustive search.'

Sarah was suddenly irritated by him, by his constant stream of questions and his inability to provide any answers. 'It felt pretty bloody exhaustive to me,' she said. 'I put in some miles last night. I pounded some corridors. No doctors. No nurses. Couldn't even find a porter.'

'We must keep trying,' Bo said. 'Claire is in danger. We have to keep moving.'

'Where?'

He seemed caught out by the question. He shrugged, rubbed his jaw. 'The river. We find a boat. We get out that way. Cross the channel. Find somewhere safe. I don't know.'

'And you're just going to lasso us all into this little quest of yours?' Nick asked.

'It's not just about Claire,' said Bo. 'We have to leave. If we stay here we will be overrun. They are getting stronger. The roads are blocked and the train tracks out of the city destroyed. They are cleansing the streets of resistance.'

'Cleansing?'

Bo nodded. 'They're preparing their nest.'

'What's that noise?'

'It could be my guts,' Sarah whispered. 'I haven't eaten in what feels like weeks.'

'Me neither,' Bo said. He went to the window. Claire was leaning against it in her bra and shorts. It was hard both to look at and look away from the creamy lump that was crammed into the junction of her armpit. Claire was red-faced, feverish, visibly shaking as she tried to keep her temperature down, ever since Bo had suggested the thing inside her desired heat. She was murmuring something over and over; Bo placed a hand on the back of her neck and leaned in close, said a few words of his own. Outside, movement was everywhere; shadows flickered, like flames on chemical fuel. He saw gangs chasing down hopelessly slow people trying to make a break with suitcases or buggies, or children in tow. Death was unfolding before him in any and all permutations. There were flensings and decapitations; heads being wrenched; the necklacings of stripped captives; nooses lowered from balconies. Sudden flame leaped from office-block windows. Bodies fell great distances, perhaps still alive before they impacted, perhaps the last act of a desperate bid to get away. He saw the muscles of a bare-chested man strain to the point of rupture in his desperation to detach something from someone screaming to be killed first. He saw cars tearing along Tottenham Court Road, colliding, ploughing through shop fronts and receptions. The screaming was such a constant it became easy to tune it out, like muzak. A woman stabbed a man so hard, so many times, there couldn't have been much left of him to absorb the blows. A man strangled a woman with spiritual concentration, before tenderly moulding her into positions where he could shear away at her soft, vulnerable areas with his teeth.

This is London. This is us.

When he came back to where Sarah was lying on the floor, scanning first the rest of the room to check the others were still asleep, she moved over to make more space for him. He sat down and took the plastic water bottle she offered him. He tried to drink without spilling any, but his good hand was shaking so hard that it was impossible. He saw Sarah tip a glance at the windows, but she didn't go to check on what he had witnessed. He could tell she had already seen enough.

'It was stupid of me to go to the hospitals,' Sarah said.

'You don't have to keep saying that.'

'I know. But part of it wasn't just about finding help for my daughter. I had to get out. I was suffocating in here. I don't know why they want to stay. Don't they feel trapped?'

'They would feel trapped no matter where they were. But don't be too harsh. They don't have quite as much of an investment in all of this.'

'I'm glad I went.'

'Sorry?'

'To the hospital, no matter what I keep saying. I'm glad I went. You were there, eventually.'

Bo smiled. It felt good in his face, but a little painful, as if he had called upon muscles to lift and carry that hadn't been used for a long time. 'That might not necessarily be a good thing. Nice of you to say, but it could turn out to be premature.'

'I don't think so. You've come this far. You did so much. You won't let it happen now.'

'It might be out of my hands.'

'Then *I* won't let it happen.'

Bo turned his head slightly. She studied the shape of his face, the longish nose and heavily lidded eyes. It was an angular face, although there was a softness in it too. It was hawkish, yet kind. He had strong hands – well, hand – and a deep chest, although he had clearly lost a lot of weight.

'Claire,' she said softly, so that her daughter would not hear.

Bo returned his attention to her. 'Hm?'

'The way you were looking at her.'

Bo shook his head, then seemed to come to some sort of decision. He said, 'The lump. It's not cancer. It's no cyst. It's one of these creatures. Well, not just one of them. It's the reason all of this is happening.'

'I don't follow,' Sarah said, through a mouth that seemed to be irising closed, drying out, turning frozen.

'It's the Queen.'

Sarah tried to laugh, but the sound escaping her lips was a collapse of air. 'The Queen?'

Bo closed his eyes. He saw a dark wet sea of emerald green. He smelled the trapped fusty air beneath canopies; felt it settling like hoar-frost against his skin. He saw the reflected glitter of thousands of retinas as they drank in her shape, smelled the musk of her sex. The reek of butyric acid; the signal to noise. He felt a change in air pressure as they unfolded from their perches. Something huge blundered through the undergrowth. Blind. Mind addled by desire. The fresh scent of seed powering off it. Female screams deadened by the proximity of flesh.

'Your daughter was raped.'

'Oliver?' Sarah gasped.

Bo frowned. He shook his head. 'This was no human being.'

And now Sarah was gabbling about how she ought never to have let Claire out of her sight. Thinking they were safe, thinking they could get back to a normal life: boyfriends, jobs, college, a future. She told him about the boy, Edgar, in Liverpool. She could see in him now what she had seen in the thin man in Southwold. That unhinged look. That desire. Her daughter was the pooch in heat that all the scummy dogs in the neighbourhood were drooling and howling over.

'I noticed something about them,' she said, once she'd calmed down and enough quiet had filled the flat for her to imagine the conversation had not even taken place. 'They seemed to be confused, blank. Like an old man raised on typewriters being given a laptop and expected to carry on without any help.'

'That was happening while I was awake. They've moved beyond that now. They're in charge, you might say.'

'Who are they? What is it we're in the middle of?'

He told her about Rohan Vero, who seemed to have been a part of his life that was so old now that he imagined him in sepia tones. He told her about the map, and his hand, and the strange organic grid that rippled behind his eyelids. He told her about the horrors of the graves, of Liverpool Road and Eton Avenue, of his life as a resurrectionist, deliverer of meals on wheels, unwitting trainer in the art of murder. He explained what he had learned by the osmosis that had come from living within a hair's breadth of something at the polar extreme of what he believed himself to be. That they were ageless and sad, but not for pitying. That they had a genuine grievance against the city. That despite their slumber, they were already infiltrating every crevice and crack in London's tired old body and were close to overrunning its heart.

'But this happened so long ago,' Sarah said. 'They're belly-aching to the wrong crowd.'

'Eddie was right when he talked about forebears. It's about bloodlines,' he argued. 'And, well, it's about blood too. It's as simple as that. You wake up, you're hungry. They're breakfasting like kings at the moment.'

'On us.'

'Yes. They've always had quite a taste for our kind of meat.'

She grimaced. 'But they *are* us. They're cannibals.'

'No. They've evolved to look like us. A tiger walks down the high street and everyone fucks off. But you can get close to someone, close as you need to be, when you look like them.'

'You look like us,' Nick said, startling them both.

'I'm not rising to it, Nick,' Bo replied. 'I've already told you. I'm in between. I'm dangerous. But I'm your best bet, too. I haven't given in to the temptation and I don't intend to.'

'That's what you say. But I'm warning you. You come near me and I won't hesitate to stab this –' he brandished a screwdriver '– right through your dirty little heart.'

'Or maybe you could just shake my hand, depending on how all this turns out.'

'We're all going to die. That's how this is going to turn out,' Eddie said in a low voice, his attention on his daughter, who was sleeping against his arm.

'That might well be the case,' Bo said. 'But it's all about how you do it, isn't it? I'm not going to die sitting on my arse in this room, pissing myself, puking, crying, begging them to take my daughter, not me.'

'You don't know if that's how it will go,' Eddie said, his head jerking up to meet Bo's gaze full-on.

'But you know it might,' Bo said. 'Give your daughter some hope, even if you don't have any. Be a fucking father.'

Eddie looked as if he might take it further, but Lamb moved in her sleep, put her arm across his leg. He visibly slumped, the tension seeping out of him, and he placed his hand on her head, stroked her gently.

Bo looked at them all closely, each in turn. He was trying to see something that would trip them up, hinder them, weaken them. He saw it in all of them and none of them. Sarah's weakness was the desperation of her search to free her child. It could conceivably compromise their aims, but then, that unshakeable drive was also her strength. He knew, from the moment he met her, that he was grateful she was on his side. Her single-mindedness would be a boon if she could channel it correctly at the critical moment. Of the others, only Claire seemed capable of seriously hampering their progress. Her weakness was obvious in the firm cluster of metallic blue that was visible in the yoke of her arm. She was staring back at him with a kind of baffled determination, as if she were unable to reconcile her condition with the bizarre grouping in which she found herself. Nick and Tina stood close together and Bo didn't know which of them was the more scared. Tina plumped cushions on her sofa as if she were preparing for a marathon session in front of the TV rather than a suicidal dash across central London. Nick kept looking around, perhaps for a weapon, perhaps to keep himself busy so that his trembling would not be so apparent. There was also his barely disguised contempt for Bo and his jealousy at having been nudged out of some position of prominence, perhaps where Sarah was concerned. Bo wanted to disabuse him of the notion; that kind of thing was as far away from his mind as his hand was from his wrist. But they had no time to waste on cautious discussions, reassurances, promises. Bo felt sorry for them, but he had no choice but to force them through this hoop. To leave them here was to let them die.

Eddie and Lamb – she had woken up now – held on to each other and batted whispered reassurances to and fro. There was a slowness running through the group. They were lame backmarkers in a stampede of wildebeest. They were going to be taken down. But what else could they do but try?

'Why can't we just stay here?' Tina was asking, again. 'I mean, I stockpiled all this food. I mean, why did I go to all that trouble if we're just going to run for it? And where are we going? Why is where we're going any better than here? I mean, this is *my* flat. I should be making the dec–'

'That noise again,' Bo said, and Sarah heard it too, a faint rhythmic sound, like that of a spoon violently scraping the bottom of a pot. Bo stood up abruptly, causing the legs of the chair to skid on the floorboards. The sound stopped, but after a few seconds it began again, more urgently.

'That's not good,' Bo said.

'What isn't?' This was from Nick. Sarah thought that the faint hysteria in his voice made everything he said seem like some garbled code for *I wish to fuck that I hadn't clapped eyes on you.*

'That noise. I don't like it.'

'It sounds like something being scratched.'

'Gouged, more like. It sounds like someone hacking through the wall with a chisel.' As Bo cocked his head, he saw Sarah shift her position on the blankets she had been sleeping on. She made to rest her head on the elbow that she placed on the floor. Almost immediately she sat up and stared down at the bare wood.

'Get up,' he said to her. 'Get up. *Now.*'

'I felt this weird vibration,' she said to him, pushing herself to her knees. 'Coming right up through the –'

There was a deep snapping sound; the floorboard that she was levering herself up on burst apart, spraying splinters and blood in a sudden, shocking spume. Something white moved up through the breach until it was flush with the surface. Sarah's jaw dropped and she scooted back on her arse, knocking over mugs of tea and knives, and cracking her head against the corner of a coffee table.

Teeth. Grinding up through the floor. She stared at them while blood leaked out of the wound in the side of her head, wondering why she couldn't feel any pain, wondering, crazily, how she had discovered a wonderful new way to anaesthetise people: shock the living shit out of them. The teeth were bared, slicked with blood from their own beribboned lips. They thrashed and tore at the edges of the hole and were replaced by a hand with horribly long fingers, horribly long nails. At the same time a weight crashed against the front door of the flat, popping one of the locks clean off its housing.

'Jesus fuck,' Nick said.

Eddie said, 'They're coming through the door. The door! How do we get out?'

Bo turned to Tina and spread his hands. 'Well?'

She was staring at the hissing, chomping mouth as it tried to gnaw off another chunk of wood. The hand reappeared, lashing around as if it could exercise an effective attack if only it could find something to grab hold of.

'Tina. Now.'

'There's a hatch, just by the door. A hatch to the attic.'

'Christ,' Nick breathed. He was hopping from one foot to the other as if he were in desperate need of the toilet. 'What was it you said about exits?'

'We have no choice,' Bo said, already moving. Sarah was at his heels. The others scrambled to their feet and dithered in the area between the front door and the ruined boards.

'Is there a ladder?' Bo asked.

'You have to pull it down,' Tina explained. 'It's folded into the hatch.'

The door bulged as more weight flew against it. Another lock sprang free. One of the bolts bent. A large split appeared down the centre.

'What is it they've got, do you think?' Lamb asked, her head against her father's chest. Sarah thought that she looked as if she might try to burrow into his jacket at any moment. 'An axe? A sledgehammer?'

'Hunger,' Bo said evenly. 'And determination.' He flipped the catch on the attic seal and a fold-up aluminium ladder concertina-ed into the hallway.

'Come on,' he said, clapping his hands. 'Let's go.'

'You go first,' Nick said.

'Oh for fuck's sake, Nick,' Sarah said, and started up the ladder. She saw his nervous little look behind him and bet he had rued his challenge as soon as it was uttered. She had to believe it was safe up here. If it wasn't, if they were as crazed as the attack made her believe, then they would be coming in through the ceiling, through the windows as well.

It was hellishly dark in the loft. She pulled herself up, then twisted around to duck her head back through the hatch, just as Nick was about to follow her through.

'Tina, do you have a torch in your bag of tricks?'

She saw the other woman shrug off her rucksack, and then Nick was barrelling past her and she reached out her arms for Lamb, who was next. Then Eddie, then Tina, brandishing a large Maglite, then Bo.

'I'm guessing we can't lock the hatch from this side,' he said.

'No,' Tina said.

'At least we can pull this ladder up. That should stall them for a minute or two. Any luck with a route out of here?'

The beam from the torch picked out a surprisingly uncluttered, relatively dust-free space. A water tank, a few picture frames and a small box of cheap white crockery were the only stored items. There was an unpleasant stuffiness, a smell of mice and damp. The attic was walled in at each end of Tina's flat space. There were no windows.

'Shit,' Bo said. 'I was hoping this might be a communal attic, that it would run the whole length of the block.'

'We're fucked,' Nick said.

Bo reached out and grabbed him by his shirt collars. Tina's grip on the torch slipped as she recoiled from his violent reaction. Clownish light jounced around the ceiling boards. Some of them were rotten and cracked; she could see the silvery sarking beneath, the insulating barrier against the roof tiles.

'Say that again and I'll make sure you are,' Bo said. 'Let's do this as a unit. We have to work together.'

'Do *what* as a unit?' Nick asked, but the aggression had fled his voice. There was an incredulity there now, born of the fatalist's logic. 'Die?'

Tina's hand steadied in time for Sarah to see Bo push Nick away and move into the centre of the attic, where he was able to stand erect. From beneath them, the sounds of rending wood deepened and quickened. Another clatter as the third or fourth lock burst. They would be inside within a minute. Sarah imagined her blood on this attic floor. She didn't want her body to be left here; this was no place to die. She didn't want mice running over her. She didn't want to be a fixture with a few tatty frames and chipped cups.

She reached up and tore away some of the fibrous insulation.

'Cover your mouths,' she said, and lifted her jersey to mask the sudden dense rain of dust and filaments.

'Here,' Bo said. 'This one's loose.'

'This one too,' Sarah cried.

'Punch it out if you can. Use the butt of the torch. Use anything.'

Tina pushed through and cracked the rubber casing of the torch against the tile. It flew out of its position, causing a small landslide of slate. 'If I'd known about this, I'd have had the managing agents in,' she said. 'Do you know how much my service charge is each year?'

'We'll never fit through that,' Nick said. 'There's too much timber in the way.'

'Much of it is rotten, Nick,' Bo replied. 'Come on, give us a hand. And watch out for nails.'

They all hit out at the slates and the battens they were positioned upon. Some of them gave way easily; other sections were more resistant. Sarah didn't like how slowly they were progressing. At the moment they had a hole that Lamb would barely be able to fit through, let alone the larger members of the group. An almighty crash heralded the invasion. It wouldn't take long before they realised what had happened. The thought that very soon she might be dead – or worse – turned her bowels to soup.

And then a large section of the ceiling simply gave up the ghost and slithered into the gap they had created. The noise was immense; if the creatures in Tina's flat had been unsure of where they had vanished to, they knew now.

Bo was up through the fracture in no time, reaching back through it to help the others on to the roof. The cold slashed through Sarah's thin woollens and she wished she'd slung on a coat before leaving. Underfoot, the tiles were slippery and steeper than they had appeared from the inside. Her legs wobbled a little when she realised how far up they were; there was nothing in the way of balconies or trees or soft earth to offer a barrier if she should trip and fall, just fifty feet in which to get used to the idea of soft meets very hard.

It didn't help that the darkness was so complete up here. There were no streetlamps working, no ambient light of any kind. She could see a fire, though, on the roof of the Centre Point building; another on the summit of the BT Tower. Standing on that unstable roof, wondering if she should kick off her shoes so that she could gain a better grip with her toes, she thought about Christmas and the lack of decorations anywhere. She felt briefly panicked about what to buy Claire, whether she would appreciate some clothes, maybe some amber jewellery – she reckoned it would suit her eyes, her skin colour – and almost laughed out loud at the peculiar way the mind worked, at the impossibility of her situation.

Eddie came up last. Bo and Nick had him by the arms when he pulled a face. 'My belt,' he said. 'It's caught on something. Wait. *Wait*.' The last word came out as a strangled runt of a sound. Bo could see enough of him to know he wasn't wearing a belt. Something had hold of him.

'Eddie,' he said.

Eddie's head snapped back. His grip on Bo's hand suddenly went into spasm; Bo felt nails sinking into his flesh. Then the grip slackened just as swiftly. Eddie opened his mouth to say something, shook his head once and fell back through the hole, almost pulling Nick with him. They saw his mouth welling with blood, and then a horrible swarming as he was buried beneath dozens of bodies.

'Run,' Bo said.

They slipped and skidded along the apex, heading west, as far as Percy Street went. At the last section of roof before they met Rathbone Place, Bo paused to look out into the road to check their positioning. Sarah glanced at Nick, who was watching Bo, and she felt a strong belief that he might nip over to where Bo was crouching and push him off the edge. His body actually swayed towards Bo, and she couldn't persuade herself that it was just his compensation in the teeth of a stiff winter wind. She moved quickly, positioning herself between the two men, looking back at Nick, whose expression was as flat as any of the slates they were standing upon.

'Inside,' Bo said, jerking his thumb at a rooftop window beneath them.

'Where's Dad?' Lamb asked.

'He's dead,' Bo said to her, grabbing her arm with his hand and forcing her to look at his face. 'We go on. You come with us or you die too. We have no time to discuss this. No time to grieve.'

'Where?' she asked, trying, and failing, to maintain the shape of her mouth.

'South Bank. Come on.' He knelt down by the window and tried to lever it open with his fingernails. It was locked. 'Christ. What is it with Londoners? "Here comes the apocalypse. Hang on, let me switch off the iron and make sure everywhere's secure. Have you got your keys? Have you got your wallet?"'

He tore off a roof tile and started ramming it into the centre of the glass, pausing now and then to cast nervous glances back into the darkness above Tina's flat. Limbs were flailing at the hole; they were slowing each other down, trying to be first on to the roof.

'We'll find a boat at the South Bank?' Lamb asked, tiny inside her father's jacket, her face huddled against her chest.

'Yes,' Bo said, shifting to accommodate Sarah, who joined him in trying to break the window. He shot a look at Claire. She did not look as though she would make it to the south of Rathbone Street, let alone the South Bank. Her skin was so tight with cold that it was raised into pimples visible from six feet away. She was the colour of cream on the turn. She was no longer shivering, which either meant she had become so used to the cold that she didn't feel it, or she was moving into the primary stages of hypothermia. She didn't hear her mother say her name or, if she did, she neglected to respond.

'Why is she even here?' Tina asked. 'She's death on legs. She's no fucking use.'

'She's more fucking use than you,' Bo snapped. 'Can we have less whining and more working together, please, people? Otherwise we will *all die.*'

Another blow, perhaps fuelled by this outburst, fractured the glass. Sarah saw a hundred tiny reflections of her face where a moment before there had been one. She could no longer see Bo in there. It was as if his own blow had banished him from reality. She had to look up from the window to confirm his presence beside her.

Bo hit the glass again. His hand went through to his elbow. He turned to her. 'Ouch,' he said. 'That smarts.'

They kicked out the glass attached to the frame and Sarah shone the torch inside. It appeared to be a loft conversion, an office or study. Bo lowered himself into the room clumsily, his moist stump flailing on the roof like a strange severed serpent as he slid inside. The others followed quickly, Sarah bringing up the rear. She dropped into the arms of Nick, who lowered her gently to the floor, his hand lingering too long on her backside, his eyes trying to send her messages that she had neither the time nor the inclination to acknowledge.

'Try the light switch,' somebody said. The voices were so close as to have all cadence muffled. The dark sprang back and everyone winced. Blinking furiously, they looked around as the room took shape. Bookshelves were rammed with paperbacks. A glass-topped desk played host to a laptop and a pair of round-rimmed spectacles. A poster of the pop group Sparks was Blu-Tacked to one wall alongside photographs of children pulling faces for the camera. Old Manchester bus timetables were stacked on a frail wooden chair. A naked dressmaker's dummy possessed enough latent threat to guarantee a wide space around it.

'A den,' Nick said.

'Writer,' Bo said, pointing at the rows of paperbacks bearing the same author's name and title.

'He's got some fucking story now,' Nick said. 'Wherever he is.'

'Let's get out of here, please?' Sarah urged, moving for the door. Bo held up his hand.

'Go slow, okay? We don't want to go storming into a wall of teeth.'

The door gave on to a tiny landing shared only by a toilet and a washbasin. They filed silently down the narrow staircase to the next floor, where a plastic wash basket was filled with children's clothes. A muddy football kit. A leotard. Socks on the floor that had been badly aimed or poorly thrown.

There were bookshelves containing a selection of modern novels and 19th-century classics. There were vases containing powdery flowers. A cardboard box contained unsorted newspapers, comics and magazines. There were more books crammed into an alcove on the next landing down, which was widening as they descended, allowing them to travel two abreast. Blood was smeared – a failed child's handprint – on the cream-painted wall here. Lamb's breath was coming in wild stitches. Bo glanced back at her and saw that she was staring up at the ceiling. He followed her gaze and stopped abruptly. Sarah said, 'My God.'

Two small bodies were hanging in the high corner above the stairs. They were misshapen, bent into unnatural postures by the force of the glue that had been bound around them, coating them with a syrupy white residue. Halfway up one of the 'ropes' that was suspending them was a confusion of hair and flesh. An arm was caught up in that knot, along with what looked like a jawbone. The bodies turned on their bindings, and into the silence created by the group's shock, they heard the creak of tensions being released. They moved on. In the living room on the ground floor they found the parents sitting naked against the wall, sealed together with more of that strange resin, their heads bowed, arms resting against their knees. But for the holes in their heads, the teeth marks and tears in their abdomens, they looked as if they were meditating.

In the kitchen, shinbones were stacked like so much firewood. There was a human head on top of the fridge, a note to buy more matches pinned to its desiccated cheek. Sarah moved slowly through the dead centre of the room anxious not to touch anything. Her breath felt extremely cold in her lungs. She saw a painting of a marigold on the wall; a photograph of a man in the driver's seat of a sports car, laughing.

Nick's voice was so dry with fright that for a moment, Bo didn't recognise it. 'What is that stuff?' he asked, reaching out a hand to touch the glue that bound the dead to each other and the wall.

'It's to keep the bodies fresh,' Bo said. 'Ideally they want to keep them alive. They'll paralyse them –'

'Paralyse them?' Nick said, rediscovering his punch and truculence. 'How?'

'With a stinger.'

'A *stinger*? What the fuck *are* these people?'

'They're not people.'

'They look like people. A fucking *stinger*.'

'The stinger is designed to keep them alive, but to put them out of action.'

'Why?'

'So that they can lay eggs in the body.'

Lamb was whimpering. Tina turned to Bo. 'Do you have to talk about this now? Isn't it all bad enough without you giving us a biology lesson? I mean, what does it matter that we know? What the hell does it matter?'

'It matters to me,' Sarah said. 'I want to know what we're up against.'

'We're going to die,' Nick hissed, then shut his eyes as Lamb began to cry. 'I'm sorry,' he said. 'I'm sorry.'

Sarah said, 'So they keep the body alive, as food for the eggs when they hatch?'

'That's right.'

'So what's the story with Claire? How come she's mobile?'

Everybody turned her way. Her skin contained a blue tinge. Dark shadows clung to her face like horror paint. She bore their appraisal stoically, staring back at them as if addressing a challenge. She made to speak, but didn't seem to have the strength to carry a sentence to its end.

Bo said, 'She's not like the others. She's the vanguard for the second wave. She's carrying a Queen in her. They wanted her to be able to get back to where she came from. To a place with lots of people.'

'Lots of food,' Sarah said.

'Then we have to kill her,' Nick said. His voice was matter-of-fact, like that of a child who has just worked out a problem for himself.

'That's not going to happen,' Bo said. 'She can help us. With her, we might be able to clean up this mess. As soon as she begins to warm up, she'll be detectable. The place will be swarming.' His words faltered. Suddenly he went down on one knee and blurted a black gruel of vomit and blood. Sarah rushed to his side and held him at the point when it seemed he must keel over. She was shocked by how light he was, how thin and hot. Although only having met him recently, she felt as wounded by his apparent weakness as if she were his sister. This was a dying man. If anything, the metamorphosis he was fearing, and battling against, was what was keeping him alive.

She helped him to his feet and assisted him to a chair. He sat down with a sigh that rattled out of him. Lamb had switched on a TV. The signal was deteriorating, but through it they could make out shaky pictures of people fleeing and screaming. Then white noise as the cameraman dropped his equipment, presumably to allow him to run faster.

'They're everywhere,' Lamb said.

'A fucking stinger,' Nick said. 'What about Bo? Has he got a stinger?'

'No,' Bo said. 'I'm the navigator. I've been laying down routes for them to follow. Unconsciously, I should add. I'm still learning about my place in all this. I'm trying to make things right.'

'We should go,' Lamb said. Her voice was the only solid thing about her. She looked as if she might disintegrate. She looked like something created from a thousand butterflies. 'This place, it looks like a larder to me. They might decide to return to feed.'

They moved to the front door where Nick checked the street. The pub opposite seemed busy. Shadows moved in the ochre windows. The light was soft, welcoming, innocent.

'We have to believe they are everywhere,' Bo said. 'Nowhere is safe now.'

They filed along Rathbone Place to Oxford Street, which they crossed as swiftly as they were able. Despite the great buildings on the north and south sides of the street, Sarah felt painfully exposed, more so even than when she had been on the beach at Southwold. Off to Centre Point to her left and Oxford Circus to her right, the street was deserted. There were no faces in the shop windows, no sounds of traffic or music from the Soho pubs and clubs where there was usually a beery, bawdy cacophony.

They passed into Soho Square, staying on the path, until they reached the small mock Tudor house at its centre. Tina and Lamb brought up the rear.

'Keep going,' Bo said. 'We don't stop. We stop, we die.'

'Let's run,' Nick said. 'I'd be happier if we were fucking running. All this creeping about . . . Christ.'

Claire was trying to say something but Bo put out a hand to quiet her. 'Just relax,' he said. 'Don't get excited. We can't run because that would raise your body temperature. But try to breathe normally.'

'Breathe normally, he says,' Nick sneered. '*You* try breathing normally with half your clothes off and your heart beating like –'

'SHUT UP, SHUT UP, SHUT UP, SHUT UP!' Sarah was shocked to find herself reacting in this way, especially as she felt so serene inside. She was with her daughter, they were still alive. She realised she was making a big mistake when she felt Lamb's hand on her arm and saw a glimmer of panic sweep across Bo's features.

Nick was still reeling, aghast at her attack. His expression changed too, though, when he heard the squeals and yells, strangely muted and muffled, as if the people releasing them were doing so while swaddled within thick scarves or balaclavas. There was the occasional metallic impact, as if a large hammer or pickaxe were being swung into brickwork.

'Where are they coming from?' Nick asked, twisting around as if trying to keep his eye on an irritating insect. 'I can't tell.'

'Underground,' Bo said, turning his attention to the house. 'This must be some kind of vent for the tube. Feel.'

He was right. The fabric of the house was warm to the touch, and vibrated with the movement of motorised exhausts. He put his ear against the wall and the screams seemed perilously close, as if they were centimetres away from him, on the other side.

'They heard me,' Sarah said. 'I'm sorry. I lost it. I didn't mean to do that.'

'We need to leave,' Bo said.

They headed south along Frith Street, taking the path of least resistance, despite Bo's wish that they should make as many jinks and kinks as possible in order to put any pursuers off. Nick was right to argue that they travel in as straight a line as possible. It would minimise the possibility of coming across danger. Which was not to say it didn't happen. Crossing Shaftesbury Avenue and heading down to Seven Dials along an Earlham Street turned into an obstacle course by a series of upturned market stalls, they were attacked by four women wielding cleavers turned black with dried blood. One of them clipped Tina's shoulder but didn't do much more than help open the seam of her jacket.

'This way,' Bo yelled, dragging Tina with him. Her face was bone china.

Sarah shepherded Claire and Lamb ahead of her, and became so conscious of the lack of shelter at her back that her skin and scalp tightened, waiting for the fatal blow. They were perhaps ten yards away, close enough to hear the measured pattern of the women's breath. Behind all that blood, the shreds of muscle and fat, Sarah could see they were beautiful. You could fall in love even as you were being ingested.

'We're not going to make it,' Nick said. His eyes were egg-large. Snot was smeared across his upper lip. He was running just ahead of the girls, whipping his head around to look over Sarah's shoulder every few seconds. Just as she was sure she could feel the hot sweet breath on her skin, the ghost of swiping fingers millimetres from purchase, someone wailed sorrowfully off to their right. Everyone turned to look. An old couple were stumbling through the shattered remains of James Smith & Sons holding, between them, the hands of a boy who could have been no older than five years. Umbrellas and walking canes were ranged around their feet. The woman had stumbled into a stand and spilled them. She was on the ground, broken jags of glass sticking out of her knees. The man was pleading with her, trying to get her upright. The little boy stood between them, crying uncontrollably.

Sarah sensed a difference. The threat was off her, as swiftly as a sudden change in temperature when standing beneath a shower. 'Oh, no,' she said. But there was another voice, coming from a black, foetid mouth in the ancient, lizard part of her brain, that was whispering, *good, good, them, not us.*

Bo had heard it too, and was acting on it. 'Keep going,' he said. 'Don't look. Don't fucking look.'

But she did look and, as they followed the curve of Shaftesbury Avenue right before heading left up Endell Street, she knew she would not forget the look of terror on the little boy's face as the women changed course and opted for easier prey. The cleaver rose and fell, rose and fell. At the sound, Sarah was thrown back twenty-five years to an image of her dad digging for potatoes in their garden, the spade hitting chunks of brick in the soil.

'Survival of the fittest,' Nick said, offering her a little smile. 'If it hadn't been them, it would have been us. Would have been your daughter.'

She couldn't bring herself to say that she thought it might be better that way.

By now they were some way east of where they had planned to be. It was getting late. The streets were becoming more crowded with things needing nourishment and not that many people left to offer it. Bo led them up the steps of a sports centre and through swing doors into a reception area. When they were inside, Bo shut the doors and shot the locks. They bolted through the turnstiles and into the female changing rooms. Abandoned clothes hung from coat hooks, but there was no blood here. No bodies. They moved on, through the showers and on to the cool, tiled edge of a swimming pool that had been drained of water. Their footsteps made weird, edgy echoes that shot around the cavernous space and ricocheted off Sarah's nerves. A single hand lay palely by the pool edge, like a peeled crab.

'The clever ones, the survivors, will all be inside now,' Nick said to Bo, as if trying to persuade him that he had made the right decision. 'I say we stay here till morning.'

'We might not have till morning,' Bo said, jerking his head Claire's way. She had stepped into the drained swimming pool and was hunched up in a corner, hugging her knees to her chin. A container of brightly coloured swimming aids – floats, noodles, armbands – only served to highlight the horrible porridge-coloured mess of her skin. The egg was a horrid cobalt protuberance. Even at a distance of around thirty feet, the others could see it beginning to move in the groove of her armpit. Sarah was fascinated and appalled at the same time. How did you cope with that sensation in your own body? Could you even try? Was Claire already sloping through internal territories of insanity? Black jungles that kept her busy, kept her from thinking too much about what lay ahead for her? She was getting to know the lay of a land that would be home for the rest of her life.

'You're right, though, we're pushing our luck out there. But we need to find Claire somewhere cooler to sit.' As Bo spoke a suspicion about what was happening, or an answer to it all, danced just out of reach. He couldn't follow the thought back to its root; it got cut off by his own skewed loyalty to the monsters and his increasing fallibility. He felt close to vomiting again but managed to hold it back.

'Of course,' Nick said, and the little smile he had given Sarah had not yet vanished, 'it might be that they didn't attack us because they recognised you. I mean, when you're trying to find your way around, you don't stick one to the navigator, do you?'

'Believe what you want,' Bo said, his voice a tired rush. 'Those who want to come with me will come with me. You go your own way if it makes you happier.'

Now the smile did falter, as Nick looked around the group, and Sarah saw that he had no confidence in offering anybody the option of a splinter group led by him. He might be suspicious, but he was a coward. 'I'll check the windows,' he said. 'See how secure this place is. I don't want to run into a mouthful of cleaver again, not unless I'm packing something that will give me the chance of a fair fight.'

Bo's nausea undermined him. He felt his weakness come through; it was a fragile, etiolated feeling, like hot glass teased thin and long. Lift his shirt and there'd be cracks showing in his skin, he was sure of it. He left the pool's environs and entered one of the staff offices behind the reception area. It was an uninviting room, coldly decorated in stark, unimaginative grey tones, but anywhere away from the others was good enough for him at that moment. Sarah followed, keeping her distance, unsure of what was happening to him, other than it not being good. She watched as he dragged a wheelchair out from behind a desk and began to unfold it. He seemed to be diminishing by the second. She was sure that the first time she had seen him – admittedly skinny, but also purposeful, determined – at the hospital, there was more to him than what she saw now. He was a jumble of badly arranged bones beneath that hulking biker jacket and flapping jeans. His appearance reminded her of childhood, sneaking into her mother's room to try on blouses and skirts and dresses that were many, many sizes too big for her. He fell into the office chair. It was like someone finding their own off switch. He was still. He looked like someone who might never get back up again.

Sarah returned to the pool and asked Lamb to stay with Claire. She parried the inevitable protests and questions, promising she and Nick would be back soon. Nick seemed to perk up, the admonished dog given a tickle behind the ears, and bounded after her.

'Windows, then,' she said to him as they ascended a tiled stairway to the first floor. 'There's probably a fire escape too. We need to make sure the doors are blocked.' She shuddered. 'And that there aren't any of those bastards already in here, waiting for the dark.'

'We should look for weapons too,' Nick said.

In a public swimming baths? Good luck, she felt like saying, but she didn't. Nick had been knocked back a little too much lately, she thought. He was trying. But then she remembered how he had suggested Claire ought to be killed back at Tina's flat, and she didn't let herself get too sympathetic.

They found a storeroom containing cabinets that revealed nothing more deadly than row upon row of hanging files. A fire extinguisher was rejected for being too heavy and too cumbersome. The windows were old, etched with a defunct company logo, but solid and barred.

Nick found a box of polythene-wrapped black sweaters and tossed one to Sarah. 'I noticed you were shivering,' he said. She tore it open. The legend STAFF was outlined in large white letters across the back. She wriggled into it. It was thick and instantly warming. She took a couple more for the girls.

'Thanks, Nick,' she said. 'I feel better already.'

'What happened with us?' he asked her, trying to appear casual as he poked and prodded around more boxes and chests. 'Where did everything go pear-shaped? I thought you and me. I thought, you know . . .'

'You thought there might be a fuck in it, at least.'

'You think I came with you all this way just to dip my wick? I admit, after the other night, when you undressed in front of me. When you asked me to kiss you. I thought something might develop, yes – but I was thinking of more than just sex.'

Their search of the storeroom complete, they moved back into the corridor. Up on the left were the doors to the public toilets. She followed him into the gents.

'Love. Marriage. Kids. Old age,' she said, her voice echoing against the tiles as the door closed behind them. Two cubicles. Two urinals. A mop in a bucket. As weapons went, it was not promising. The windows in here were all locked and barred too. You came for a swim here, there was no escape.

'Maybe. Maybe, yes,' he said. 'After what we went through in Southwold. After that connection.'

'Love is dead, Nick,' she said. 'Look around you. I doubt we'd find a registrar able or willing to splice us together. We might find one that wants to slit our necks. And five will give you ten that old age is something we'll never experience. I'm not even sure about the next ten minutes. I've enough love for my daughter, that's all.'

He stepped towards her and placed a hand on her breast. She didn't move away. She stood her ground. 'What are you doing?' she asked.

'Seducing you. Trying to make things right.'

She closed her eyes. 'Nick. We are in the middle of the end of the world. People are dying. People are dying *right now*. I don't think Bo is going to make it through till morning. And he's our best chance of surviving.'

'I disagree,' Nick said. He was stroking her breast now, palpating it through the thick cotton of the sweater he had given her, allowing his thumb to snag the soft bulb of her nipple as he moved his hand around its curve.

She was enjoying it, that was the galling thing. The last six months had been a lonely, cold time spent watching the shadows through the window or waiting for the phone to ring, keeping tabs on her daughter, driving through the dark, driving through rain. Running away. Running away. She had had no down time. No time for tenderness or reflection. She had once been the kind of woman who enjoyed long baths, glasses of red wine, music, books. She was now the kind of woman who had no time for any of that. All of her sensuousness had been driven out of her by the relentless pursuit of sanctuary.

'Ah, Jesus. What the hell,' she sighed, and, lifting her sweatshirt, she guided his hand to her bare flesh. They gasped together at the sudden new sensation – the chill of his hand, the heat of her tit, the softness, the tenderness – an intimacy that had felt as though it had been deleted from humanity over the course of the previous few weeks.

He drew her against him and pressed his hungry open mouth against hers. She felt his groin grind into her own and she met it full-on. His fingers reached for her buttons and as he popped them open, one by one, she pressed him back into a cubicle. She kicked the door shut and flipped the lid of the toilet down. She pushed him back so that he was sitting and quickly removed her jeans. Her thighs slithered deliciously against each other. She was wet. He could have been anyone. That was what made this suddenly okay. Let him believe what he wanted. Let him think she was The One. He was a moment of pleasure for her and she would take it. That was all.

The door of the cubicle swung shut, but not before she saw a shadow lengthen on the polished, faux-marble floor tiles. It could have been the outer door slowly swinging closed on its ageing pneumatic hinge. It could have been Lamb or Claire coming to find her, or maybe even Bo coming for a piss. She couldn't stop the laughter in her throat. Nick moved back to look at her face, ever the victim, a silent question in his own eyes: *are you laughing at me?* Her need was so great that it blinded her to the poverty of her surroundings.

She tugged at his belt, fumbled at his zip until he was freed; cold but thickening in her hand. She didn't notice the wayward splashes of piss on the floor or the toilet seat, or the unholy fug its stench provided. She didn't care that the toilet bowl was brimming with waste or that there were depictions of vulvas drawn in indelible marker on the door. She didn't notice the glory hole in the dividing wall or the wad of toilet paper that filled it. By now all she was aware of was the burn in her cunt and how she might douse it.

Nick positioned her against the wall and lifted her right thigh. With his other hand he thumbed aside her gusset. She directed him into her and almost bit her lip as he slammed himself home. Almost immediately, despite the frenzy of his rhythm and the anxious breath in her ear, she heard slow footsteps. A shadow fell across the thin rectangle at the base of the door. She clearly saw the shadow broaden as it turned, presumably to face the door. She heard a settling sound, as if whoever it was had leaned against the thin melanine barrier, perhaps to listen to what was happening inside. Despite this distraction, and the feeling that it was one of their party – she had to cling to that idea, the alternative was too harrowing to consider – she was losing herself to the pleasure that Nick was sawing into her. She could feel herself zeroing on a climax, at the same time both the most recognisable sensation she knew and the most foreign. Even when the door began to bulge inwards, she didn't quite get it, not at first. She thought it was the approaching orgasm bending her mind. Although she was so close to the release she wanted, she pushed Nick away. He too seemed on the brink; he surfaced from its narcosis like a sleeper rudely awakened.

'What?' he gasped. His penis bobbed violently with the beat of his heart, like something nosing the air, trying to get back to where it needed to be. She pointed at the door as she stuffed herself back into her clothes. Now she pointed at the gap above the partitions dividing the two cubicles. She mimed going over; any movement of theirs would be screened by the extra few inches on top of the doors. Nick was shaking his head, *no, no*. But she couldn't understand what he was objecting to. He still had not dressed himself properly. He was dwindling before her in every possible way. She left him there. She was up and over the partition in a few seconds, as the door split and collapsed inwards. She offered Nick her hand, but his attention was on what was coming in to take Sarah's place.

She dropped to the floor and tried to open the door, but it was jammed in the frame, perhaps by the destruction of its neighbour. She worked at it, trying not to make any noise while trying to understand why Nick was making no noise. Wondering if he was dead yet, wondering if he was winning the fight. She would help him if only she could get this open. And then she heard an awful wet splintering noise, so deep as to make itself felt within her chest. Blood appeared, fanning swiftly under the partition. Horrified, fascinated, she noticed she could see the violence being visited upon her erstwhile lover in its deep red reflection. The paper wadding in the glory hole tipped out and through it she could see Nick's eye, dead, imprinted forever with the unspeakable acts that had sucked the life from him.

More splitting, crunching sounds. Whatever was working on him had enormous strength. She used that sickening noise as cover to wrench the door clear. But as she was gathering herself to make a dash for the exit, she heard the killer barge free of the cubicle.

She quickly pushed the stall door closed. There was a brief rush of running water – was it washing its hands? – and the roar of the hand-dryer. She was convinced then that it knew she was there and that the noise would drown out her screams, her cries for help. There was an unbearable wait. She imagined the door slamming open and being invited into some vibrating blood-flecked maw a dozen times over before the hand-dryer ceased and silence rushed in.

It was bluffing. It was waiting for her. Nick's blood, pints of it, pooled around her feet and she felt her gorge rise as she imagined much of it thrumming in the head of the penis that had been inside her only minutes before.

She could not bring herself to check how safe things were. Her hand remained pressed against the door, obscuring the puerile graffiti, until it seemed that it too was a part of the profane decor. Seconds, or hours, passed. She thought that if she tried to move, the blood would have coagulated, gluing her to the floor. The light in the bathroom seemed to be fading, yet she could not buck her paralysis. It was too risky; it might be the move that would signal her death.

She listened hard, hoping for some indication that the monster had left. And then reason began to speak to her.

If it thought you were in here, it would come for you. Look at what it did to Nick. What fear could it have of you? You would be finished by now, if there were any shred of suspicion. Your blood would be mixing with lover-boy's.

She pulled the door open, her heart too large, too noisy for her frail body. Bo was standing there, his jaws slathered with blood, Nick's liver in his fist. He said, around his mouthful of food, 'Are you all right?'

But no. Reject that. Filthy mind; Judas mind. Reject it.

She was alone.

He woke up from a dream in which he was freezing to death. His throat hurt. Under his fingers, the pages of thousands of books felt as smooth as porcelain. He was in the busy reading room, Humanities One, at the British Library. Every desk was occupied. He was sitting at desk number 2375, his favourite because it meant he could watch the people as they came and went. No matter how much he drew the edges of his cardigan around him, the cold would not retreat. His skin rasped whenever it met itself. The pick-up counter, usually so busy with readers collecting or returning books ordered, was unattended. The occasional trill of a Windows-operated laptop or the fanfare of a Mac was missing. There were no sneezes or snuffles. No coughs.

Everybody was naked. Everybody was dead. He was naked too, his skin as thin and blue as eggshells.

He came to in a dark room, breathing musty air that smelled of chalk dust and chlorine. He shifted and knocked over a brush, a pile of photocopied leaflets advertising New Year swimming-pool discounts. Someone was calling his name.

He got shakily to his feet and pulled open the door of the storeroom. He listened for the voice. It didn't repeat itself. He strode across to the swimming-pool entrance. Lamb, Tina and Claire were sitting in the same corner of the empty swimming pool, their voices incomprehensible yet constant, rolling and humming around the great marble arena. He cut through the hubbub with a question.

'We haven't seen them since they went off to check the windows and look for weapons.'

'Weapons?' Bo said. 'This isn't a fucking barracks.'

'Don't tell us,' Tina said. 'You know what they're like. There's no reasoning.'

'Did you hear someone calling my name? It sounded like Sarah.'

'Maybe in your dreams,' Tina said, a little smile showing through the strain.

'Maybe,' Bo agreed, recoiling from her grim expression. Humour failed like something dead on a cake when all you wanted to do was survive. Her smile looked unnatural, ill fitting, as if she had somehow stolen the mouth of another person in an extreme attempt to make herself appear normal. 'I'll be back in a moment,' he said.

He thought he heard something being knocked over, above his head. He trotted up the stairs and saw Sarah at the other end of the corridor, a wastepaper basket rolling away from her feet. She looked dazed, lost, until she saw him approaching. Then she stopped, her eyes alert, fastening on him like something on the hunt for prey.

'Where's Nick?' he asked.

'He's back there,' she said. 'In the . . . in the loo.'

'He's all right? I mean, what, he's taking a piss?'

She was staring at him. He began to feel uncomfortable. It was as if she were trying to read him. He looked down at his hands and heard her take a little gasp.

'No,' she said. 'No, you washed your hands afterwards. Your manners are impeccable.'

'Sarah.'

'Don't come near me,' she said.

He explored himself. He rubbed his tongue across his palate, searching for the flavour that would damn him. 'Sarah, where is Nick?'

'You tell me. You tell me, Bo, you fucker. I saw –'

'You saw what? You saw me?'

She didn't say anything. He had to cling to that. 'You didn't see me, did you? Please say you didn't see me.'

'He's dead,' she said. 'Jesus, he's deader than dead. What you did to him . . . I –'

'Please, Sarah. You didn't see me.'

'That doesn't mean it wasn't you.'

'I was asleep.'

'All the more reason to suspect you. You told me yourself, you don't know what being asleep, what being awake, what any of it means any more.'

'I know,' he said. 'But I promise you I'm fighting this. I'm not giving in to it. I won't give in.'

'So you say. But you don't know who you are, Bo. The graves you opened. You don't remember doing any of that.'

'I'm coming back from it, Sarah. I'm in charge of myself.'

'You don't know that. You say it, but you don't know for sure.'

She was right. His tongue was running across his teeth now, checking for any terrible shreds. The action reminded him of his own face reflected in the photographs from Abney Park cemetery. He thought of his hands scrabbling at the seals of soil-encrusted coffins. He thought of the dirt and the decay packed under his fingernails. Tossing gobbets of spoilt flesh to the weak, their eyes upturned, like thin dogs impatient for a titbit.

'You have to trust me,' he said, and hated the puling slant to his voice.

'I can't do that,' she said. 'I don't trust anybody any more. It's me and my daughter and everyone else might as well be dead. We'll go with you, but we'll be watching you every step. And I swear I'll kill you if you fuck us over.'

'Okay. That's okay.'

He looked as if he were going to say more, but he simply nodded shyly and turned around, tucking his damaged hand into the folds of his jacket.

'Bo?' Sarah watched him go, unsure of what was happening. She knew he was innocent. She could not quite bring herself to believe he would commit such a terrible assault on Nick. He was confident in his innocence, and that must be good enough for her.

But that also meant that there was something else in the building with violence on its mind.

She hurried after him. So caught up with what might be hurrying after *her*, she failed to see how the dynamic within their group had shifted until she saw Bo standing as if preparing for a dive, at the lip of the swimming pool. Something wasn't right, but there was nothing in the way these people were reacting, or failing to react, with each other that talked of discord. Beyond a general malaise, a reluctance to be marshalled or led, they were a bunch of people trying to survive. They were afraid, hungry, cold. Should it bother her that Lamb was no longer crying about her father's horrible death? She tried to remember what she had been like after Andrew had died and she supposed it had been the same for her. Shock, numbness. You didn't cry much if you couldn't feel anything.

'It's going to be light in a couple of hours,' Bo said. 'And it seems we have an unwanted guest here. We need to move on.'

'Where's Nick?' Tina asked, staring at the bloody footprints Sarah was bringing towards her.

'Nick's dead,' Sarah said. Everybody looked at her, except for Bo. She hated herself for looking down at Bo's feet, but there were no bloodstains, nothing on him.

'Where's your jacket, Tina?' she asked, her voice trembling. 'You were wearing a large jacket when we got here. Why did you take it off? It's not exactly tropical in here, is it?'

Now Tina turned her dark eyes on her, her brows gathering like miniature stormclouds. 'What are you saying?'

'I'm saying everybody is under suspicion.'

'Then ask yourself some questions,' she said. 'You're the one traipsing blood all over the place.'

Sarah had to stop herself from attacking the other woman. Her fists were clenched so tightly that she thought her fingers might break. But why shouldn't she be pointed at? She was the last person to be with Nick. Maybe she had killed him. Maybe she was infected with this abhorrent hunger. Maybe they were all cleaved to this breed, their minds so destroyed by the fever for meat that they couldn't settle upon the truth.

'Knock it off,' Bo said. 'Let's just simmer down. We can't sit here playing judge and jury. If Nick's killer isn't one of us, then it might still be in the building. We're still exposed. We're vulnerable. I say we go now.'

'Wouldn't it be better to wait until daylight?' Tina asked. 'Wouldn't it be safer, travelling like that? I mean, don't we have a better chance in here against one than out there against . . .'

Her voice trailed off; Sarah could see she didn't want to attempt an estimate.

'We need sleep,' Tina now said, instead. 'We could take it in turns keeping watch.'

Lamb said, 'I'm all for killing it,' but her eyes didn't possess any of the steel in her words.

'We're safer awake,' Bo said. 'All of us. It's when I'm sleeping that you need to watch out.'

Tina was agog. 'You mean you control their level of consciousness, depending on whether you're asleep?'

'Something like that. They've been absorbing behaviour from me, a kind of osmosis. They've needed to relearn how to do it. Walking, talking . . .'

Sarah said, 'Ripping off heads.'

'It was taken from me, this knowledge,' Bo said. 'I never offered it.'

'And all because you asked to see a map?' Tina asked.

'My life was in the litter tray,' Bo explained. 'I thought it might spice things up for me, my work.'

'You were right.'

'If it hadn't been me,' he countered, 'it would have been someone else.'

Tina said, 'So you're saying we should be grateful to you?'

'Not at all,' Bo said. 'But you might cut me a little slack. I didn't ask for *this*. I'm trying to help. I'm trying to make things better.'

Claire stood up. Lamb went to her as if there had been some secret signal between the two of them. Sarah didn't know whether she felt jealous or reassured. 'Did you find anything we might use?' Lamb asked. 'Before . . . before Nick . . .'

'Folders. Files. Plastic wallets,' Sarah said. 'That's about as dangerous as it gets. We should have spent the night in an abattoir. But we have some stuff from the hospital.'

'It will have to do for now,' Tina said. 'So. I'm getting jittery hanging around here. Nick's body is getting cold upstairs. There's something in here with us. I say it's time to leave, before it gets peckish.'

They were gathering themselves, congregating in the entrance hall, when Sarah hung back and was violently sick. Bo noticed, but did not offer any assistance. Their eyes met. He smiled briefly, grimly, and nodded. She nodded back. Shock and fear had stolen any colour that had remained in her face. She was soapstone. Hurrying after them as they filed out into the grey dawn, scrubbing at her raw lips with the back of her hand, she tried to clear her mind for whatever might ensue, knowing things were far from an end, knowing it was all likely to get far worse but incapable of framing anything in her thoughts that didn't involve Nick . . . and the thunder of his body as it was systematically dismantled.

She moved through the group until she was at Bo's shoulder. She didn't look back at the public baths, too afraid that she might see the architect of their misery in a window. She didn't know what was worse, the possibility that an attacker was stalking them, picking them off one by one; or that it was walking alongside them. *Keep your friends close, your enemies closer.* Bo was close enough to touch, if she so wanted.

'Why Bo?' she asked.

'Sorry?'

'Bo. What's it short for? Is it like Beau? You know, like Beau Bridges?'

'Nothing so pretty as that,' he said. 'My name isn't really Bo. It's Joe. But I couldn't say that when I was a baby. It always came out *Bo*. And it stuck.'

They emerged on Long Acre. Clothes shops, in the main, punctuated by the occasional pub or sandwich joint. A car was overturned, its innards burned out, molten tyres hanging off the rims. Six feet away, the carbonised remains of its driver were dead on the ground, in a pose that suggested he had been trying to drag himself clear of the wreckage.

'My God,' Sarah said, and tried to shield her daughter from the shocking tableau.

'Forget it,' Tina said. 'Keep going.'

Bo said, 'The plague hit this part of London hard. It was rife here in 1665.' He was standing in the middle of the road, looking around him as if he were a tourist in an unfamiliar city. 'There were pockets where it spread like wildfire. The black parts of a colour-coded map. We might have made a mistake coming this way.'

'What do you mean? It was your idea to go in this direction.'

'He lured us,' Lamb said.

'They will have congregated in the places where food was most abundant,' Bo continued, ignoring her. 'They will have filled their bellies here in the past. You don't wander too far away from the water-hole.'

'Can we go?' Sarah asked. 'We should at least keep moving.'

'There was a plague pit not too far away from here,' Bo said, with the kind of relish a *bon viveur* might afford a bistro within sniffing distance. He was looking around as if its location might become known to him; Sarah thought he might suggest they go and admire it. She heard his belly rumbling.

'Fuck this,' she said. 'I'm off.' She gathered Claire under her arm and marched hard against the scream of the warning sirens in her mind. The others hurried to catch her up.

'Which way, Claire?' Sarah asked. 'What do you think?'

Claire seemed to be coming out of the stupefaction of her situation. She was rallying in a way that Sarah could barely comprehend. If Sarah had been in a similar situation, she believed she would have opened a vein by now. But that was the beauty of human nature; there was always someone else stronger than you. Sarah was glad of that. Lamb too seemed to be recovering from her own problems; the pinch and the pallor of her face were receding and she was displaying a nice line in sarcasm and bite. Let Bo fawn over the city's bleak history, let his juices flow.

They negotiated the warren of side streets running south off Long Acre, the high-class fashion boutiques and accessory shops, the overpriced burger-and-noodle restaurants, the tiny pubs, and members-only clubs. Sarah learned quickly to stop flinching whenever they walked past a display in a window containing a mannequin. She forced her attention on what was directly ahead and what might be coming at them from behind. In this way, they made progress, emerging from the tight knit of alleyways on Southampton Street that fed them into the Strand. Like the other arterial roads they had crossed, this too was devoid of human life. There were plenty of cars and buses, abandoned, parked in the skew-whiff attitude that suggested hasty abandonment, but no hint of what had happened to their occupants.

'We have to cross the river,' Claire said, her voice slurring badly.

'Why don't we take one of these cars?' Tina asked. 'I mean, wouldn't it be safer?'

'Maybe,' Sarah said, 'but it would be slower too. You could drive to the next barricade of vehicles and swap to a new one, I suppose. Keep doing that until we got to where we needed to be. Or died of old age first.'

'I'm just trying to help. There's no need to be snippy.'

'There's every need to be snippy. Nick is dead. Maybe if we were a little more on top of what we're doing and what needs to be done, he would still be with us.'

'You were with him when he died,' Tina ripped back at her. 'What did *you* do to help?'

Sarah opened and closed her mouth. She felt like a bee whose sting had been deployed; close to unravelling, close to losing her belly all over these cold paving stones.

'Let's deal with what's happening now,' Bo said, catching up. 'We can argue about right and wrong later, when we're safe.'

They moved along the Strand until it diverged, turning into the loop of Aldwych to the north and Lancaster Place to the south, which would deliver them on to Waterloo Bridge. As they hurried on to the bridge proper they heard a high-pitched whining sound, underpinned by a seething, insectile rasp. Bo ushered the others onwards, appalled by how exposed the bridge had left them. He had once kissed Keiko on this bridge, late evening in June, a buttery sun turning what seemed like every window in the world into a square of gold. He had imagined that kiss reflected in all of those pieces of glass and believed that they would remain there, strange ghosts trapped for ever, imprinted on London and subliminally appreciated by any office worker who spent a few idle minutes looking out at the scenery.

A swarm rose from the Strand Underpass. He took in the scene for as long as it took to understand that he was looking at hundreds, not dozens, and they were all carrying either weapons or limbs or heads. They spotted Bo and their song found a new intensity. They arrowed towards him.

'Run!' Bo screamed, as much to himself as to the others. Already the horde had cut the distance between them by at least a third; Sarah was the only one of their group who was athletic enough to be able to cover the bridge's span without being caught, but she was hanging back, encouraging Claire and Tina, who had no chance, she was carrying too much weight. Lamb was crying and screaming. Their last chance at remaining on the north bank of the river had gone; their pursuers had drawn level with the walkway down to the terrace at Somerset House. Very quickly Bo realised what they were going to have to do.

There was no discussion to be had; he simply had to show them what was required. He sprinted until he overtook Lamb, who, despite her hysteria, was still a few metres ahead of the others. Light-headed with the sudden bolt of activity, and the insanity of what he was about to do, he stopped and turned to regard his companions. Wordlessly he climbed the three white bars on the guardrail alongside the pavement. He ignored Sarah's pleas. He looked back at them and beckoned with his finger. Then he leaped.

It is difficult to survive the river. Despite a sometimes placid surface, the currents within can run at well over three knots, a speed almost impossible to swim against. The water is a mix of fresh and salt, which reduces buoyancy. Bo Mulvey dropped nine metres before he hit the Thames, which was just two degrees above freezing, and was dragged under by the weight of his clothes and the current. Within a few seconds he had travelled the length of Victoria Embankment and resurfaced by Blackfriars Millennium Pier.

He knew that if he did not get out of the water soon, within another thirty seconds he would be dead.

He thrashed around wildly, trying to see if the others had followed him into the water, and saw a figure falling from the bridge at the same time that the great mass of the chasing pack reached the point where he himself had jumped in. And then the water grasped him again and he was pulled down into its green-grey heart. His lungs were burning by the time he was belched back out, a little closer to shore, and coming up fast on a small boat anchored between Blackfriars Bridge and the Millennium Bridge. He managed to throw out his good hand and snag a float, the rope biting into his freezing skin, which already looked like the hand of a dead man: blue, claw-like, yielding to the processes of rigor mortis.

He clung on with every shred of strength that he had and wrapped a leg around the tip of the float. He was then able to use his other hand, or the stubby fingers sprouting from it, to try to gain purchase on the side of the boat. He slipped a few times, gashing his head on the wood and almost spilling back into the water, but eventually he slithered on to a deck swilling with blood and skin and bones. A man with a bloody grin painted around his mouth, making him resemble some hellish clown, came at him with a gaff. Bo heaved himself to his left, his damaged hand slipping in the grim detritus and causing him to go down hard on the side of his head. It was awkward and ugly, but it saved his life; the curved hook of the gaff sank into the meat of his thigh, rather than his chest. Almost in defiance of the cold, his leg filled with fire as his assailant used the gaff to drag him closer. A priest appeared in his other hand in readiness for the *coup de grâce*. Teeth jumped and rattled across the deck like dice as the wash from another boat slapped against the hull. The tension in Bo's leg receded a little as his attacker compensated for the swing in balance. Bo kicked his leg into the other man's knee, crying out as pain bolted along the length of his femur and replaced his pelvis with a cradle of molten bone. The gaff came out of his leg with a nauseating suck. He dragged himself further up the boat, still shooting glances at Waterloo Bridge but unable to see anybody at the railings any more.

What Bo thought at first was the man's penis lolled over the waistband of his baggy purple tracksuit bottoms, but this organ bore a sharp black barb and receded, like a lipstick, into a sheath where a navel might have been expected. As he leaned in again to swing the gaff, the stinger protruded once more. Bo kicked out at it, trying to avoid the gaff's delivery. He rolled over and tried to stand but the deck was too slippery, his leg too painful. His hand buckled beneath him as the deck forced his weight on to an impossible fulcrum; he went down and saw the shadow bloat around him. He closed his eyes, hoping that the hook, when it met the back of his head, would kill him swiftly. But the blow never fell. The chop of water suddenly shifted direction, sending him jerking away from the spot where the gaff now landed, embedding itself in the deck.

Bo turned over quickly, raising a hand in defence, but the attacker was busy trying to pull the weapon free.

The map burned in his brain, trying to turn him from what he was about to do, but he had already seen the hanging oil lamp in the wheelhouse. He grabbed it and smashed it down on the other man's head. Fire streaked along his entire length but the man didn't seem to notice, so preoccupied with the gaff was he, to the point where Bo thought he might have to abandon the boat and take his chance with the Thames again. But then his attacker seemed to realise what was happening and let go of the wooden handle, tottered to the side of the boat and folded over it, silently, into the river.

Bo skidded back, clamping a hand over the pumping wound in his thigh, and managed to get to his feet. Inside the boat he found a tea-towel miraculously free of the blood that was otherwise splashed all around the cabin. An arm was hooked almost casually over a work surface in the galley. Bloodied clothes were piled in a corner of the deck like souvenirs. He tore the towel into lengths and bound them around his injury.

The engine of the boat started without any trouble. He directed it back towards the bridge where he had abandoned his colleagues, in the vain hope that he might find them bobbing merrily in the water, waiting to be picked up. He couldn't see any of them. Either way, they were all dead. Just being able to see the ribboning water from a safe position, the current knifing through it, was enough to make him feel faint about how close he had come. He had beaten high odds to get out of that. The only thing he could think of – the crumb of comfort – was that drowning was an infinitely more acceptable death than what that chasing pack had intended.

He felt his stomach spasm involuntarily; he loosed another great glut of treacly vomit over the side of the boat. Fish gathered instantly, jostling for titbits. Was that blood, making it turn that colour? He gritted his teeth against a sudden throb of neuralgia that skated around the contours of his face, as if he had been touched by an electrical charge. Not good. Not good. He saw the sky changing colour, from a wintry morning blue to pale grey, and wondered if this was how death began for people. Brain cells popping off like lights on a satellite image of the world as night's leading edge swept across it. Everything shutting down, withdrawing, turning in on itself.

But what was helping to kill him was also keeping him awake; the pain in his leg hammered nails through his groin every time he moved. He steered the boat west, towards the buildings of the South Bank. He could see no figures at all now; he felt like the last man alive on the planet. No other boats moved on the river. He caught a glimpse of black sweater on the bank and his heart leaped. He powered the boat over to the silt and ditched it. The boat grounded itself, tipping over as he made his way on to the deck, propeller roaring, black exhaust fumes belching into the sky. Bo lowered himself gingerly to the shale.

'Sarah?'

She was blue in the face, her skin elsewhere leached white like old bone. Grit and weed were stuck to her lips, her hair. Bo touched Sarah's neck. He found a pulse, weak, arrhythmic, but a pulse nonetheless. He felt a bitter pang of guilt about his relief that, of all of them, it had been Sarah who had survived. He cast around him for evidence to the contrary, but there were no bodies. He doubted he'd find them so close by; chances were, they'd be washed up far away, if at all.

He slid his arms under Sarah's body and tried to lift her. Somehow he managed. Hobbling badly, he carried her up the stone steps and over the gate beneath Waterloo Bridge. The National Film Theatre was a desolate witness, their crumpled bodies reflected in the large, dark windows. The second-hand book tables riffled in the breeze, many of them dislodged from their regimented stacking by some recent flurry of violent activity. At least there were no bodies here. He needed a break from that. It was so quiet. No jets nosing along the river's trajectory on course for Heathrow; no skateboards; no chatter about Chaplin or Tarkovsky or Hitchcock at the tables outside the NFT café. The thrum of traffic on the bridge above, a constant at any time he had spent down here in the past, was absent. London seemed poised. A point had been reached where resolution was the next step. The city seemed to teeter on invisible brinks. He closed his eyes and the map showed him the carcasses of offices and blocks of flats. He saw this unholy breed feeding and warehousing and securing, then pushing on, pushing out, creating a cordon of horror. At this border, fierce fighting with a perilously thin line of troops. Infiltrators in uniform turned their assault carbines on their fellow men. An endless swarm of attackers scuttled across the urban battle lines, strong now, focused, suicidal in their intent to keep the nest clear of invaders. Beyond, the map showed him smoking cities snaking north: Birmingham, Manchester, Liverpool, Newcastle, Edinburgh, Glasgow. Sacked, sucked-clean zones of high population, trembling in a vacuum, waiting for the next stage of their annihilation. Bodies wadded in bedsit corners, heads locked by a froth of capture adhesive knitted from flagelliform glands; the victims forced to watch as the things that would kill them hatched from chrysalids.

Bo came back, gasping, his eyes stinging as he opened them to the bleached greys of the South Bank.

'I don't know where to go,' Bo whispered to Sarah. 'I don't know what's next. I need some kind of guide. I always have.' He closed his eyes again and now the grainy little grid that spilled across his inner vision was faint, fragmenting. The map was dying. He had done his job; he was expendable.

He rubbed Sarah's face and hands. He knew he must either get her indoors or into fresh clothes soon before her body temperature hit a low that it could not return from. He half-carried, half-dragged her through the sliding doors of the NFT and laid her on the floor. A dead man sat on a stool, his upper body propped against a table furnished with an untouched slice of chocolate cake and a cold latte. Bo stole his jacket and jeans, grinding his teeth against the man's stiffness, hating the assault on the corpse's dignity but knowing that the victim would probably have consented to his extreme actions, had he been able. That's all right then. That's all right. Okay. All's fair in love and –

'SARAH!'

She came out of it, a little. Her body flinching from his shriek. He pulled off her wet clothes and massaged her rigid flesh. He beat and slapped at her until her skin filled with colour. The regenerating fingers of his damaged hand weren't yet developed enough for him to comfortably button and zip her up in her new clothes but at least now she was dry. He dragged her into the booth where the coffees and scones were served and switched on one of the toasting grills. He positioned her beneath it. The heat was glorious; Bo had forgotten what warmth meant. He began to cry.

'I'm dying,' he said, as he tried to coax the stiffness from her face, her arms, her legs. 'I'm dying, and for what? What have I done in my life?'

'Have you loved?' Sarah asked, her eyes closed, her voice so soft as to make him doubt he heard it. He pressed a finger to her lips and her eyes flickered open.

'Yes,' he said. 'I've loved.'

'Then you've done something valuable. And anyway –' she rolled on to her side with arthritic slowness '– you saved my life. That has to count.'

He fetched her a bottle of water, which she waved away. 'I don't want any more of that shit. I've probably got a few litres of Thames inside me. We ought to get vaccinated.'

'We will,' he said. 'But first we have to find the nest.'

'And then what?'

He shrugged. 'Destroy it. Make sure we isolate them. Make sure the Queen cannot be born.'

'But we lost Claire,' Sarah said. 'She was incubating it.'

'She jumped?'

Sarah shook her head. 'I held her hand. We were about to leap. But she pulled free. She was waving to them as I stepped off. As if they were old friends of hers.' She covered her mouth with her hands. She couldn't stomach her wish that her daughter was dead. Death was the best way out now. She was actually hoping her daughter would die. A week earlier she'd have killed herself before thinking that. How did you get from that to this? How did you lose all hope so quickly? She thought of them hunched over her, performing some sick birthing ceremony upon her. 'How do we find this place, this nest, without her?'

'We'll find it,' he said. 'I found the house of flies. I can find the nest.'

'The house of flies?'

'Charnel house. Dead zone. Home to all the map-readers, if they want it. The map was first unfolded there by the man who discovered them, brought them into the city.'

'We get to the nest and we burn it . . . then Claire will be free?'

'I don't know. I hope so.' He couldn't stomach the lie, but trading truths was not going to have them back on the road soon. He couldn't tell her that the Queen was within a human host because it meant ready food after the hatching. And that, destroyed nest or no, the egg was going to crack open anyway.

'The others,' Sarah said.

They went outside. Bo hurried to the railing to scan the choppy river again. They walked a little way west along Queen's Walk, stopping occasionally for Bo to hoist himself up to look down on to the banks, but nobody could have survived this long in those conditions.

'Dead,' Bo said. 'Or if not, then as good as.' His face hardened. His voice too. 'I wouldn't know where to begin looking for them. It's too dangerous and we don't have time.'

He led Sarah along the concourse between the Royal Festival Hall and the Hayward Gallery to Belvedere Road, which runs parallel to the river, servicing the South Bank. Scaffolding concealed the true skin of the buildings along here, which were receiving a face-lift. Cranes and pile-drivers dominated the surrounding airspace, some bearing Christmas lights and decorations.

'I'd forgotten how close we were to Christmas,' Bo said.

'What day is it?'

'I don't know,' he said, with a little nervous laughter.

Some of the brick netting had come free of the scaffold ties and was flapping violently in the wind. Bo saw the sole of a boot poking free of one of the walkways. A construction worker in a yellow helmet had either committed suicide or been hanged from one of the scaffold's transoms.

'So much work going on here,' Sarah said, shivering despite the heavy clothes she was wearing. She had not asked him where they had come from, but he knew she must have a good idea. She hugged them to her, looking pathetic and frail within the large-shouldered jacket. 'I'm lost. I don't know where to begin.'

Suddenly, belying her brush with death, and the bruised, pale taint of her skin, she screamed her daughter's name.

'Hey,' Bo said, grabbing hold of the jacket sleeve and turning her gently to face him. 'We've come this far. Keep on top of things.'

'You too,' she said, trying to smile but succeeding only in forcing the tears from her eyes. 'I don't like it here,' she said, turning away from him. 'This architecture. It's so cold. So angular. They should leave the scaffolding on. It's doing it some big favours.'

She was moving away towards Concert Hall Approach, and he watched her go. A rare shaft of sunlight picked out the great curve of the London Eye; it warmed his face a little. Sarah turned back to look at him and raised a hand to shield her eyes from the glare. A simple gesture, a human moment, but it pierced him deeply.

Part V

FIFTH INSTAR

To each its mess.

JH Fabre

32. HIVEMINDS

'This way,' he said, increasing his pace.

Sarah was finding it difficult to keep up. He was leading her deeper into a part of London that seemed permanently dark. The brick guards, bright-orange debris netting and duckboards conspired to shut out the light; the criss-crossing galvanised steel tubes were fingers laced across a reticent face. She thought she could hear music struggling through the complex system of couplers, uprights, ledgers and braces, or maybe that configuration of steel was creating its own tune, as the wind fluted across its open ends.

He stopped on occasion, moving his head fractionally, as a mantis will alter the line of regard it affords potential prey. He would frown, or swear, press the heels of his hands into his sunken eye sockets as if digging for inspiration. Then he was off again, skipping through the metalwork like something born to it, like an ape to the jungle. At the foot of a polypropylene debris chute, he paused and listened. Then he opened his eyes and turned to her.

'We're close,' he said.

She no longer knew where they were. They seemed to have been running for hours. At a guess, they were in the white spaces of the

A–Z, a waterfront wilderness somewhere well east of Docklands, a forgotten reach of land that was yet to be reclaimed and turned into millionaires' counting houses, and might never be. It was a desert of failed factories and machinery frozen by time and bad air. All that she could see around her was the paraphernalia of abortive repair. Decaying brickwork had been abandoned before it could be healed, leaning walls forsaken in the act of being braced and corrected. The workforce still in evidence were few and dead. One man was hanging by his foot from the cabin of a crane, some forty metres above the construction site. Another peeked over the edge of a duckboard, a frozen javelin of blood hanging from his throat. She never got used to the shock of so much death around her, but she was unable to shy away from it. She searched each face hungrily, needing the truth to be rammed home, needing a constant reminder that this was the end of things.

She followed Bo through the clutter, stumbling on the half-bricks, timber and abandoned tools lying on the floor outside the building. It seemed like a film set, something that looked realistic from a distance but did not stand up to close scrutiny. She noticed, as they got closer, that the scaffolding was scorched, the debris netting melted in places. Some of the bodies here smouldered. Heat ghosted into the air but there was no obvious source. For the first time, she faltered in her determination and hung back, even as Bo was moving towards the ladder that would take him into the scaffold proper, his boots crunching into plaster dust and pebbles of broken glass. When she glanced over her shoulder, the landmarks of the capital were nowhere to be seen. They were in a rotting urban hinterland. An in-between place that was cold and scarred; a dead zone that would never be improved, no matter how much money was thrown at it. There were some places that people just did not want to go to; some places that were barren for ever. Die here and you would not be discovered for months.

They pushed through rotting wooden fences bound with rusting wire. A large edifice, shaped vaguely like a church, was sheathed in buckles and chains and pipes and tarpaulin. Boards covered its windows. The brickwork seemed swollen, bruised. The steeple was like a crooked stovepipe hat, latticed with iron supports. Bo's hands rested against the patterns of the bricks, traced their black pointing.

'You can wait, if you want to,' he said, noticing her unease. 'But I have to go in.'

'There's no door,' she said, as if that were reason enough for a retreat.

'I know,' he said. 'But then, this place isn't a building. It's a shell. It's camouflage.'

'I'm scared,' she said. On another day she might have been pleased to have her suspicions of this site confirmed, but the knowledge that they were on the doorstep of hell was threatening to blow all her circuits at once. 'I'm scared,' she said again, needing to have it aired. Needing someone else to know.

'I know,' he said gently. 'So am I.'

As he stood on the ladder, looking back at her, she had never seen anybody look so tired, or old, or frail. He needed her as much as, perhaps more than, she needed him. How could she let him go on without her? She went to him and followed him up the ladder to the top level of scaffolding. The wind was stronger up here; it blew smartly through the corridors, the concussions of the plastic sheeting deafening. The brick shell that Bo had referred to felt hot to the touch whenever she put out a steadying hand as she moved along the duckboards. All of the windows she had thought she could see from the ground were false, cleverly painted *trompe l'oeils* to deflect closer inspection. She was about to ask him how he expected to get inside when a figure stepped out on to the end of the scaffold. She recognised him as the strangely dressed character from the hospital. His mouth was a riot of blood, metal, and infected tissue. She could smell him from here, a carious mixture of sour rot and rust.

He was trying to speak through that swollen car-crash of a mouth but all she could make out was a lot of aggressive noise. She saw him twitch his shoulders and clench his hands as he marched towards Bo, his physicality in stark contrast to the other man's. His feet were certain on the planks; it did not seem to concern him that they were many metres off the ground. From here, at last, she could see the familiar London architecture, far in the distance, but it offered no succour.

'Hello,' he managed to enunciate. 'You made it, then. No more kiss-chase around those shitty streets, hey? My name is Greene, by the way. Graham Greene.' Greene doffed an imaginary cap and bowed low. 'Say hello to my companions. Stanley Kubrick and Kurt Cobain.'

She heard the skip of feet up rungs she had just vacated. Two men with a similar look to Bo's attacker hefted themselves on to the platforms, sandwiching them. She looked around for a weapon, but all of the tools that might have passed for one were down on the ground. The men held claw hammers and cold chisels. One bite from this Graham Greene would be worse, she felt, than a bludgeoning.

'Your daughter, our host, is with us now. The girl is about to become the mother. You've done a grand job, but now it's time to forget her.' Greene turned his attention to Bo. 'And you, sir. You should have retired days ago. I can help you with that.'

Bo suddenly launched himself at the man. Greene was on his back foot and his expression, such as could be read in that riot of metal and pus, was one of surprise. He parried Bo's kicks and punches and laid him out flat with a head butt to Bo's nose. Sarah heard bone crunching and Bo's hands became ribboned with blood as he tried to staunch the flow.

She slammed her heel against one of the couplings that conjoined the cross sections of scaffolding tube. It sprang clear and dropped to the planks. She wrestled the tube free and turned to face the pair inching towards her from behind. Their weapons were raised now, but they spent more time keeping tabs on what was happening at the other end of the walkway than in their own task. She was determined that this lack of respect for her should be their undoing. She waited until their attention wavered again and attacked. She skipped a couple of feet forwards, bringing them within sudden range of the steel tube, which she swung in a low arc from the left, cracking it into Kurt Cobain's left hand, forcing him to drop the chisel. As Stanley Kubrick swept around his partner, bringing the hammer down in a slashing movement across his body, she ducked hard to her right, scraping her face hard against the hot bricks, and felt skin come burning off the side of her face. She blinked and spat away the grit, fighting to close her mind to a sheet of pain as it tried to tuck itself around her head.

Kubrick was off balance now, the weight of the hammer having missed its intended strike bringing his arm down to his right-hand side. He was between Sarah and Cobain, whose left hand was clamped under his right armpit as he struggled to recover from the shock of a hand of bones being turned into so much calcium dust. Sarah kicked out at Kubrick's left knee and, as it folded, tipping him back towards her, she shifted her grip on the tube to its middle and swung again, this time in a tighter, swifter arc, punching it up into the jawbone. Kubrick's head snapped back and he fell, lashing out his arm to prevent him from toppling over the edge of the scaffolding. Grunting with the effort of moving so quickly with such an unwieldy weapon, Sarah thrust it at his head, at a point just behind and below his left ear. The tube ground into his scalp, removing a great curl of flesh. Her momentum forced Kubrick's elbow to bend against his will and he folded over the horizontal brace, tipping, without a sound, into the void.

She flashed a look back at Bo and saw it was not good; Greene was kneeling above him, trying to throttle Bo, who was wriggling ineffectively beneath the bigger man. She turned back to Cobain as he was trying to shape a grip on the chisel with his other hand. His damaged fingers were already cartoonishly swollen, filling with blood that seemed to have come directly from his face. She stepped back, preparing herself, her breath coming hard and hot through clenched teeth. She felt alive. She felt more alive than ever before, and she knew he could see it. He was uncertain about her. His face twitched with more than just pain.

The fire in her belly. The murder in her eyes. She was ready for him.

'Come on, you cunt. You fucking freak cunt,' she said.

He moved towards her and his face hardened. His mouth twisted, showing large, brilliant-white ursine teeth. The slitting of his eyes. He charged her. She was slow to respond this time, her arm growing tired of the tube's weight. She managed to parry his first thrust with the chisel, but it was weak. The tool drew blood to an eight-inch strip of her forearm. She grunted and stepped back, tried to bring the tube around in front of her to ward off the chisel a second time, but she forgot about his other hand, which came up under her guard and punched her hard in the throat. Her teeth bit her lip and she felt an instant patina of hot blood spread across her tongue. She spat in his face and in the instant he blinked it away she brought the end of the tube down hard on the toes of his left foot. Blood turned the eyelets of his shoe bronze. His posture changed; she flashed the tube to her other hand and swept it behind his weight-bearing right leg. She kicked out at him and, although she didn't connect well, it was enough to unbalance him. He dropped the chisel and fell. She kicked at his face repeatedly, gasping as the toe of her shoe sank into the meat of an eye. He made no sound. She rolled him off the edge of the duckboards and swiped a hand over her own face, shifting sweaty blades of hair out of her eyes, smearing what felt like a pint of blood across her swollen jaw.

She turned and saw Greene looking up at her, his hands around Bo's neck, his mouth wide open in shock or triumph, she couldn't be sure. The red security lights gleamed in the cheap jewellery of his gums. Bo was arching beneath him. Slowly, almost tenderly, Greene closed his mouth and lowered his forehead until it was resting on that of his prey. She saw his muscles grow beneath his jacket as he went for the kill.

She screamed and it was the sound of more than who she was. She believed, in the seconds before she drove the end of the pole into the bullseye of Greene's head, that her daughter's voice was somehow caught up in the cacophony, emboldening her. Greene's head snapped back and to his right. She saw his left eye turn red, an expression of astonishment – perhaps at her gall, perhaps at the intensity of the pain – but no, it was down to a loss of sensation, for he was unable to move his left leg, his left arm. He slithered off Bo, who rolled away, coughing and choking, spitting up long strings of bright-red phlegm. Greene was trying to drag himself upright, his right arm curled around one of the oblique support spars, but she could tell by his abject expression that he knew the game was up.

'What are you going to do?' he asked. 'Kill your daughter? Because that's what it will take. Do you think you can do that?'

His voice was just noise now, a noise that she couldn't stand. It caught on her teeth, like tin foil. She launched herself at him; he closed his eyes and tilted his head back. She hit him so hard that he was dead before he hit the floor, the flesh of his neck filling with black.

The build-up of unused fuel in her limbs made her begin to shiver. Death had been moments away; it seemed it had been at her elbow since the day she gave birth to her daughter. She imagined herself with some sort of mark of Cain, singled out as a target that Death was drawing an ever more accurate bead on. There was no euphoria at having survived the onslaught. There were too many next times to have to worry about.

She edged towards Bo, needing to know if her guardian, her saviour, her friend was still alive. Lights were popping off all over the buildings on the Victoria Embankment and beyond. London's muscular architecture: Swiss Re, Tower 42, Centre Point, St Paul's, all of it had been subsumed by the darkness, and didn't she know just how that felt.

'Bo,' she said. 'Hey, guess what? I do trust you. I really do.'

She levered Greene away and watched him roll silently off the edge of the planks into the night. Bo looked heart-breakingly small beneath her, like a young boy who needed his mother. She threw away the tube and knelt by him. Blood had caked heavily on his face, spoiling his angular beauty. His nose was horribly broken and she wondered if its splintering had killed him. But now she saw how she had underestimated his desperation. Black bubbles skittered across his mouth.

Haltingly, he said: 'Imagine the hell his parents went through when he was teething.'

The scaffold completely surrounded the building. Bo was getting increasingly frustrated by the apparent lack of an entrance, kicking out at the tubes, stamping his feet against the duckboards and making them rock alarmingly. Sarah was about to suggest they descend to the ground and start again, that they must have missed something, when he collapsed. She ran to him, grabbing his jacket as it seemed he was about to roll off the edge of the walkway. He was barely able to hold himself up with his arms, so spindly and weak were they; they shook as a steady black stream of vomit poured from his lips. It seemed he was too weak even to retch.

'Don't give up,' she said to him. 'Not here. Not when we're so close. Don't die on their doorstep. Don't give them the pleasure.'

But then it was over, the torrent becoming a trickle, becoming drips that he spat and rubbed away from his mouth. He was coughing – jarring, squealing hacks – that sounded as if they must be coming from lungs made from twisted metal and broken glass.

The wind was becoming lustier. Soon it would be impossible to walk upright on this scaffold. Already she could feel the braces and ties tensing as the construct was tested by the gusts spanking in from the east. She could hear the overture of the storm that was thickening further out over the Thames estuary. She saw a deepening in the darkness, as if something solid were being pushed through the air, *into* the air, increasing the pressure around them. The warning light at the tip of the tower at Canary Wharf was slowly snuffed out.

Claws of lightning raked at the city and she had to turn away, in fear of what those sudden flashes might illuminate.

Bonfires were being lit along the riverbank, and further afield, dotted around the city's northern borders as far away as Ruislip, Stanmore, Enfield and Dagenham. Occasional screams twisted out of the confused dark. There was gunfire too, and a crisscross stab of torches. She could see orange points of light shimmering on the water and smell wood smoke. She wondered how many of those fires had been started by people, real people, like her. And how many were improvised barbecues knocked up by diabolical chefs. It was heartening to think that there might be little pockets of resistance still surviving in the torrid streets. She wished she could connect with them in some way, but how could you know for sure who was genuine and who was all too ready to split you open like ripe fruit? A jangling sound drew her attention away, back to the furnace-like heat of the wall. In places it had blackened, as if at any moment flames might spill out from the weakened pointing.

She said, 'Do you hear that?'

Bo was sitting on the planks, all the fight gone from him. He looked like a child who has played to the point of exhaustion, ready to teeter over into sleep in a second. He nodded. He was looking up at the thin plastic sheeting that was slung over the uppermost points of the scaffold. He drew himself shakily to his feet and made to climb on to one of the beams.

'No,' she said. 'Let me.'

She hoisted herself up to the makeshift roof and yanked at a portion of it until the ties loosened and she could raise her head through the gap. She sucked cold air through her teeth as the roof of the building stretched away, seamlessly merging with the featureless night beyond it, suddenly giving her the impression that she was not on the doorstep of one of the most populated cities on earth, but in a limbo where nothing but this edifice existed. The wall itself was nothing more than a skin to conceal what she now saw inside. An Escher-like series of stone stairwells traversed the black windowless fist of profane architecture that lay, steaming, before her. It looked less a building and more a hard knot of muscle, like a heart defying the crematorium's flame. The odd adjunct of narrow steps resembled veins lacing its chambers.

She felt Bo nudge up beside her. The sight of this vast necropolis gave him a boost from some deep source of energy that his body had not appeared to possess any more. His posture improved; the glimmer of a smile touched his face.

'I knew this was here,' he said, 'waiting to be found. But even seeing it, I still can't believe it's real. It's just . . . it's beautiful.'

Sarah clenched her teeth, jabbing herself with the reminder of what he was, or might still become. Despite his help, his willingness to put himself in jeopardy for her and readiness to attack the creatures he was so much a brother to, there were moments, as now, when he became his own warning. *How far gone was he?* she wondered, as she divided her attention between the gnarled surface of the nest and Bo's rapt profile. *Is there a way back for him?* She reminded herself that she had cleaved herself to him, assured him of her faith in him. She must not allow herself to give in to suspicion. If he had been going to swap allegiance, she would be dead by now.

She supposed the building *was* beautiful, in that it was something she had never seen before. The truly alien possessed its own charm and fascination. It was like being a child again; that capacity for awe restored in full. But she shook herself away from it, knowing how close fear had been to those experiences.

'Claire is in there,' she said.

He cried out as he swung his injured leg over the edge of the brickwork and shakily lowering himself on to the first of what looked like a million thin steps down to the skin of the nest. She followed, wishing there was a rope to hold on to. If she slipped, that was it. The depth of the drop seemed crazily plumbless, much greater than that on the other side of the wall. She drew the jacket more tightly around her, found gloves in the pockets that she pulled on, silently thanking the dead man in the NFT. A piece of paper too, with a shopping list on it: *milk, eggs, nappies, cereal.*

Other lives. Other tragedies.

As she descended, her eyes intent on the poor stone steps, her hand lightly touching Bo's shoulder, she thought about how many other families had been shattered by what had come to London, and – who knew? – maybe other parts of the country as well. How many mothers were hauling themselves through the rubble to search for lost children? The notion, although repugnant, also served to fuel her. She was not alone, no matter how wretched conditions became.

Her blood sugar was so low she felt she might faint at any moment. The exertion of her fight on the scaffold sat thickly in her limbs, stiffening her. But eating seemed utterly inappropriate, especially when she considered that Claire was unlikely to be eating, whether through fear, or inability, or by her kidnappers' design.

The steps zigzagged down to a floor that was littered with dung and the bones of small mammals and birds. There were fresh footprints in the scum; discards of bondage lying around: rusted cuffs, broken chains, buckled leg-spreaders. Fat misshapen candles bled orange light and a carrion stink. The air was damp. It nestled in the lungs like catarrh; a smell of waste that was so redolent of ammonia it burned Sarah's throat as she breathed.

They were close enough to see that the skin of the nest was exactly that. It was huge, composed of human tissue, turned by centuries of pressure into grotesque knots and swirls. Here and there a face could be discerned, crushed and curved into aspects of agony. The hide was a patchwork of colours, all of them variations of mahogany, and it was awash with some kind of heavy oil that kept it moist. She glimpsed slight movements as portions of jowl or chin or brow realigned themselves microscopically within the great crucible of flesh. Mites and worms burrowed into or out of the leathery mass. She saw fingers with wooden rings, wrists with bronze bangles. She saw hanks of hair that were braided into fashions forgotten by history. She kept wanting to see lips trying to form words, to articulate the complex misery that she needed a voice for. But nothing lived here. She could hear the grind of wet bone as the building shifted on its poor foundations. Greenstick fractures in anonymous limbs created weird U-turns and loops that anatomy never intended.

She wanted to hold Bo's hand but he was still guarded about his repairing fingers. He held them close to his body, as if he had a fistful of jewels he didn't want to share. She consoled herself with thoughts of Claire; it was as if, like Bo, she possessed her own uncanny radar. Claire was alive within its range; the restless seed on a display, the answering blip to the sonar's call.

A horribly sexual aperture appeared in the surface of the nest.

She thought of her child's face at the moment she was born. Andrew had been listening intently to the radio that was playing in the background – he had wanted to make a note of whatever recording was being broadcast so that they could buy a copy and listen to it to remind them of the moment – but Claire had arrived at exactly one o'clock, to the strains of a news jingle. She had held her for so long in those first few hours that her fingers had sunk slightly into the unformed bone of her skull.

The slit parted, gummily.

She thought of the sacred smell of her baby's head. How her heart had missed a beat at the moment Claire latched on for her first meal at the breast. She thought of Claire's hair, so blonde as to be almost luminous. It hung around her head in defiance of gravity, light as air. She remembered trying to brush it and only succeeding in making it more flyaway.

Claire was alive for as long as she gave her mother strength.

'Bo?' she said.

Bo stood before the opening, his eyes restless upon it, as if he were expecting it to speak, or attack. Finally, he shot a resolute glance back at her.

'We go in,' he said.

Sarah's first impression, on appraising the density of darkness's approach through that irreligious doorway, was that she would not be able to see anything, that its colour was so impenetrable as to be solid. Yet there was movement too, the blackness ribboning like the currents she had earlier escaped, threatening to spill out: thousands of flies, millions of them; the kind of lazy, corpulent flies that meandered drunkenly through the air at the tail-end of summer.

Bo showed no hesitation in driving a path through this droning barrier. Sarah followed, disgusted, batting the tiny bodies away, clenching her teeth as they became caught in her hair or landed on her face. She smelled a wave of rot that was so intense as to be an assault. Spitting, shaking her head, she emerged on the other side of the curtain into another kind of darkness.

Eventually, she noticed streaks of detail seeping out of it, like the strange oily rainbows that film the meniscus of a puddle. Highlights, if that was the right word, in cobalt, coral, teal. Haematoma colours that picked out the unspeakable hammerbeam roof.

Her feet moved tackily across the floor. In places, they made small pleshing sounds. She couldn't yet see what was causing the wet, and wasn't sure she wanted to. She wanted to call Claire's name, but something held her back. Not the possibility of stirring something best left avoided, but because to speak her daughter's name would be, somehow, to sully it in here. This place was not deserving of a name that meant light.

She realised she had lost sight of Bo and almost whimpered with childlike panic. But he was just a little way in front; she could make out the shape of his head as he swung it this way and that, searching for some sign of what was happening here or what dangers might be revealed. He seemed comfortable enough, perhaps because his eyes were better prepared for this kind of darkness. She felt a frisson as she realised what this signified. She was on her own, species-wise, despite Bo's promises and efforts, but all of her fears dissipated when she came upon the first of the bodies.

The light was improving enough for her to be able to see the extent of the wounds that had done for it.

The body was lying face upwards, but closer inspection revealed the torso to be arched to such an extent that no portion of it touched the floor. The cerebellum and the sacrum were the two ends of this bridge. The stomach had sunk into the corpse like a deflated balloon. Blisters and lesions skipped across the flesh. The mouth was wide open, the legs spread. It was as if whatever passed for life inside for these creatures had fled at such speed as to have ripped the body apart. And yet a look of peace and satisfaction hung around the features. She looked as though she had died after a particularly enjoyable meal, or in the midst of a fine dream.

A little further on she found another body, similarly positioned. A few feet away there were two more. More lardy candles pushed back the dark, providing pockets of half-light the colour of tanned leather. She lifted her head and saw Bo frozen before what appeared to be a mountainous shape that would not resolve itself. Her eyes slowly grew accustomed to the murk, allowing her to recognise the tumbled mass ahead of her as an avalanche of cadavers. Her heart was beating so hard it was hurting her eardrums and she didn't know why. She simultaneously felt herself to be at the end, and at the beginning, of things. But there was also the nagging suspicion that her daughter might be lying at the bottom of that scrum, despite her earlier confidence. Just the rank humours and the lack of light, she thought. Just the depression of maintaining hope. Nothing was harder than being an optimist.

Bo was now standing some way off from the main gathering. He was inspecting another body that was different from the rest; Sarah could tell that even from this distance, even in this poor light. It was thin, mummified almost, as if it had been dead for centuries and preserved in the frigid, arid conditions of this sepulchre. Bo fussed around it with a tenderness that both touched and concerned her. He was still acting too flakily to convince her that she was truly safe with him, but retained enough of what she supposed it meant to be human to stoke her encouragement.

Bo said, 'They're all dead.'

'But that's a good thing, yes?'

'Bees in winter,' he said.

'What?' Sarah asked.

'I'm not sure about this,' he said. He appeared worried, thoughtful.

'Who fucking cares? It's voodoo. It's juju. It's *War of the* fucking *Worlds*. Switch on your targeting hologram thingy,' she said. 'Zero in on *so what*. It's over. We just have to find Claire.' Now she felt some muscle come back to her. She called out but there was nothing to bounce her daughter's name back to her; the syllable fell, as leaden as any of the bodies surrounding her. She might as well have been speaking in a vacuum.

'It's not all we have to do,' he said. 'The bees in winter. They die when their work is finished. The hive is complete. It's primed.'

She was losing her patience with him. If Claire wasn't here, then she wanted to leave; she would be somewhere else and somewhere else was where Sarah needed to be. 'What are you talking about? They're dead. Something's finished them off. Common cold. Food poisoning. Boredom. Let's rejoice. Let's set off some fireworks. But let's find Claire first. Please?'

Bo didn't say anything; he was distracted, still hunkered down, staring at the bodies as if they might suddenly reveal their mysteries to him. 'Everything that went before this was about preparation,' he said. 'The city has been cleansed. It's like . . . like insects. A first wave doing reconaissance on a new site for the colony. They mop up. They scorch the earth. Get rid of any threats. When the coast is clear, when the conditions are right, their usefulness is over.'

'And they die.'

'Yes.' Slowly, he stood up. 'They'll collapse in the street. The city will be reclaimed. And then they'll return. A second wave, a stronger breed, will hatch. They'll get everybody. Nobody will escape them.'

He looked like a man on the brink. He was looking around him as if he could see this new dawn trembling into view.

Sarah turned towards him. Pale-red light from the fires along the bank underscored his features, picked out some form of triumph there. She asked, 'Are they still chasing us?'

He shook his head. 'She was carrying the Queen. While you were looking after her, they knew she would be protected. What could be a better guardian than a mother? They let us get this far. As soon as we lost her to them at the river, we became useless. We are nothing now.' The redness flashed over his eyes as if they were filled with blood. 'But while she's alive we might have time to end this. There might be a chance for the city yet. And your daughter. They're foolish to turn their backs on us.'

Sarah thought she saw bitterness in him at this rejection. Their stain was in him yet. 'Where is she?' she asked.

'She's near,' Bo said. 'She's so close I can taste her.'

33. THE SEVEN CHIMNEYS

Salavaria felt the impact of failure burn through him like electricity twisting out of a malfunctioning wire. He was aggrieved that he had even given Graham Greene the time of day, yet he had allowed himself to be persuaded, perhaps after seeing his own body reflected in the cruel bathroom mirror at the hotel. A lifetime spent away from the accoutrements of vanity did wonders for self-confidence. But thrust back into a modern city where image was all, well, it didn't take long for the doubts to begin. He looked old. Despite eating frugally and healthily, despite putting himself through a regime of exercise every day that would have shamed an athlete, he could not stave off the damage that years visited upon the flesh. His reflection had shown him a weak man, fading fast into senescence. Although he was still physically strong, he had lost the ability to diminish people merely by regarding them. Aging men did not carry the swagger, no matter how hard they tried. And now that the sliver was in him, it was doing its best to worm its way deeper, to unstitch him completely.

He had not possessed the guts to stand up to that freak of nature with the mouth of an ironmonger's dustbin. That Greene was out of the frame was of no solace to him. It only served to highlight his impotence. Mulvey was a slippier fish than he had given him credit for. The hope that Greene and Mulvey might cancel each other out had been misplaced. But he had to believe that thirty years of belief, of training, of mental preparation, meant more to his destiny than the seat-of-the-pants heroics of a reluctant navigator.

His time was still now, he had to believe it. The Queen was about to be born; the first wave's shoring up of the city's boundaries was ample proof of that. Some places, such as the tiny alleys – Lumly Court, Bull Inn Court and Exchange Court – that linked Maiden Lane to the Strand, were so rammed with grinning dead that he would have needed to climb over them to get through. Bodies lay dotted around as far as he could see. He found an articulated Scania lorry on Whitehall, its windshield smashed in. The keys were still in the ignition. He kicked out the remaining glass from inside the cabin, and dumped the driver on the pavement. He started the engine and floored the accelerator. By the time he hit Westminster Bridge he was doing sixty miles an hour, shunting vans and cars out of the way, grinding bodies through the wheels and axles like some mobile mincing machine. He almost lost the lorry at St George's Circus, turning hard left into Blackfriars Road, but although the wheels bumped and juddered, threatening to jacknife the HGV into the obelisk, he was able to correct the steering and roared on towards Bermondsey, his heart in his mouth, the excitement of decades peeling him clean, giving him the illusion of childhood again. The road became pearlescent under a sudden slice of moonlight. It was as much of a sign as he needed. The air seemed to crystallise, as if he were in the rarefied atmospheres of the far north. He felt as though he were being purified, prepared; some secret, forgotten gene was fizzing into life with an ancient set of pre-programmed commands. He drove on auto-pilot, barely registering the street names and buildings that flashed by. For the last mile of his journey he might as well have been driving with his eyes shut, his destination so bright it burned a hole through his thoughts.

His foot came off the accelerator without his knowing it. Close. Close. Some monumental heat radiating out of that urban snake of decayed buildings, spent factories, fossilised machinery. He felt a portion of his mind closing down, the part of his brain that had helped him endure the decades of stagnation, that had stood by him as his bearing on the world dwindled, and whispered that he still mattered, that he still had his part to play in this formative drama of the 21st century. At the same time, another, alien chunk was stuttering into life. It was the confirmation, if any were needed, that he was a synergy of worlds, he was the man best designed to take the reawakened breed into the next thousand years. It didn't matter to him how it had happened, whether his male ancestor from way back had been in love, or forced at stingpoint to inseminate his freakish mother. What mattered was that he was at the leading edge of that bloodline, the conscious spearhead, the man of the moment. Happy birthday.

He muttered that song tunelessly to himself for a while, blinking at the unfolding within his thoughts, coming to terms with the manifold skills being revealed to him. Without his realising it, the lorry had stopped, coming to a standstill on the shattered forecourt of a building project that had never been completed. He sat there for what might have been ten minutes or ten hours, staring at the bedraggled chain-link fences and padlocks, the faded security warnings, a line of spit spiralling from his slack mouth as the images of race memory rioted through his mind. He saw through the eyes of his true father – how ever many hundred generations separated them didn't matter – the man who dislodged the pebble that caused the dam to collapse. Centuries folded like paper, allowing their distant surfaces to meet. He suddenly knew the man as intimately as he knew the shape of his own hands.

He was aware of the arthritic pains he suffered in the ankles of both legs, his halitosis, the poor state of his teeth, the milkiness of his sight as a cataract thickened in his left eye. He saw him walking through the narrow streets of the city befouled by corpses in the road. Outside every sixth timber-framed house a fire burned, in an attempt to drive away the humours of the Black Death. Salavaria could taste the shit and decay hanging in the air. He heard moans and pleas rising up from behind sealed doors marked with red crosses or painted appeals to the Lord for mercy, petitions that went unheeded by the watchmen standing guard. He saw a man with a bludgeon chasing a thin dog into a corner where he hacked at it until it was silent. There were no children playing in the toxic streets, just meringues of filth, drifts of blowflies, the frequent sight of a body hastily wrapped in a sheet and tossed on to a cart, destined for a plague pit saturated with quicklime.

Voices, raised voices, discordant with hysteria, seethed around churches stuffed with people desperate for divine intervention.

He visited the pest houses constructed north of Old Street and Tothill Fields – the Seven Chimneys – a verminous social club for the dying where membership involved skin devastated by buboes and stains and you were never allowed to leave. There he talked to one of the infamous nurse-keepers, a woman so desperate for financial reward that she was willing to risk infection if it meant she could fill her pockets with booty from the patients she hurried towards death. For five shillings, she showed him what hell contained. He saw their bodies in coffins waiting for collection; men trying to walk with sticks, their faces nothing but gritted bars of teeth as the ulcers in their legs bled and wept. A child in bed, too weak to cry any more, holding on to his dead brother for comfort. A sea of vomit. The fevered jabbering of people mere heartbeats away from death, their last dozen breaths carrying garbled rumours of a saviour waiting out in the deep rural thicket north of the city.

The journey. The houses diminishing, the encroaching countryside of Stoke Newington, the plague pits being excavated there. Showing his permit to the patrols at the edge of the city. The deep, rural clean. Days of wandering. Getting lost. Losing his walking cane. The descent of calm, or madness. The endless, bullying green. A panic that the same ground had been covered; a belief that death was wandering here too, picking up his trail, charging through the trees with the flavour of his shadow in its craw.

Great hunger, deep thirst. A sense of no longer knowing who he was or why he had come here. The permit turned to pulp in his tunic by a sweat that seemed to come direct from his organs, a hot offal reek as he felt himself being devoured from within. The sense that the trees were becoming denser, the grasses so long that they prickled against his throat. The strange illusion that meant he could see the stars shining down through what ought to have been an impenetrable summer canopy.

Realisation. As the stars blinked. And began to move. Dropping from the trees in their thousands. Needle fangs bared. His entreaties. His fear and relief. His invitation to return with him and rid the capital of its filth.

Salavaria whooped in a great lungful of cold air, his head beating as he was rammed back into the reality of Brompton Road. He didn't know how long he had gone without breathing, but the redness in his eyes and the battering of his heart spoke of minutes. Tears filmed his cheeks. He ached for the man who had tried to save his city and was then repaid by being banished. The Great Fire of 1666 had been down to an arsonist's intent, not the accidental negligence of a Pudding Lane farriner. What had the pompous mayor expected? That the hordes streaming into his city would somehow separate the plague from its hosts and suck it down like Thames oysters? That they went on to consume the clean living was a minor problem. It was expendable collateral; many more thousands would have perished had there not been this crucial intervention. They ought to have thought of it as a reward. Medals should have been pinned on their chests; instead they had been chased by the fire from the streets they enthusiastically purged.

Something caught his eye; moments of heat in this cold wasteland. He jerked his head to the left and saw footprints as though written in phosphorescence, fading on the lime-whitened sliproad. Someone was here. He felt a sudden grip of panic as he considered that his prize might be stolen from him at the last. He elbowed the driver's door open and leaped down. At the crippled gates he paused for a while, his feet covering the footprints that were dying into the cold of the ground. He placed a hand on the fence and pushed his way inside.

34. COLOSTRUM

The cathedral seemed to have no end. The dark waxed like a film of oil on water. It adhered; it fretted at the nostrils and lungs like black asbestos. Occasionally a wall would bow inwards, as if victim to a massive failing in the foundations, and a face would stretch and quiver into view, features so maimed as to suggest something beyond human. Bo wondered where the black throats behind all those silent screams might lead to.

'A bit heavy on the old numinous,' he muttered.

'What?' asked Sarah.

'Never mind.'

They were sinking. There were no steps, but both felt the strain on their calves as they negotiated the incline, and had to lean back so as not to slip. Sarah did not want to touch any part of this place.

Bo said, 'I liked to go to the library, you know, the British Library. Sit in a corner, watch the people come and go, flip through the pages of the great photographers as well as the photographers that deserved to be called great but never got the recognition. I loved that library. Go for a cup of coffee, maybe lunch. They always had an interesting exhibition on, and a great shop where you could buy books, gifts, pencils. I loved their pencils.'

He reached out and touched her hand. She laced her fingers into his and squeezed. She could feel his pulse in his wrist, so forceful that it might break out of the papery skin. She realised she was not breathing. He was whispering; it was hard to hear him above the clamour of her own heart.

'But it was always a bit chilly there. In the little handbook they give you if your application to become a reader is successful, it says that they have to regulate the temperature, keep it on the cool side, on the dry side, to protect their books. And that you should dress accordingly, so I had a pullover of some sort with me whenever I went, even in high summer. In Humanities One, where I always did my work, there'd be this racket as the air-conditioning switched on to balance the temperature and humidity. It could really throw you out of what you were doing.

'I was there recently. Hiding from these fuckers. Trying to get my head around it. Trying to get my head straight. Knowing that outside there were things happening in the street. Horrible things. Bodies being dragged into the shadows of St Pancras. Things happening. But inside, I never saw one of them. They never came near the place. Because it was too cold for them. Not a great place to hatch your offspring. Which is why it's so hot in here.'

It was getting hotter. Sweat created a barrier between her skin and her clothes. There was a terrible smell of things gone beyond the animal rankness of decay and now broken down to constituent chemicals. There were notes in the air that Sarah could not identify because she had never smelled them before. They were so offensive that she had to breathe through her mouth. Deeper still, and she was convinced they were underground, a suspicion confirmed when she heard muffled echoes, shouts and screams, perhaps from some tube tunnel close by. They stopped talking to each other, and simply kept walking through the softness, here and there slithering, here and there tripping over some mushy obstacle, hands entwined, waiting to find whatever there was left to be found.

After what seemed like miles, like hours, Sarah thought she detected a change in the darkness. It became more granular, less intense. She couldn't perceive shapes, beyond Bo's hunched, intent posture, but she was grateful for that. Eventually, the path began to constrict around them and the heat intensified. She couldn't shake the thought of guts, imagined herself unable to return, being peristaltically fed into some large chamber where she and Bo would slowly be digested. After a nasty few minutes when the walls of the corridor began to brush stickily against her face and she was almost bent double with the cramped conditions and her burgeoning claustrophobia, the corridors quickly spread wide again, and began to honeycomb.

'Shit,' Bo said. His voice came at her as though through layers of hot cotton. 'Now what?'

But there was no hesitation on her part. A sweet warm smell, a smell that meant life itself, was streaming along the farthest right channel. She moved to it immediately.

'Sarah, wait.' Bo hurried after her, and clasped the hand she had shaken free. 'What is it?' he asked. 'How do you know?'

'Mother's milk,' she said. And dragged him after her. It didn't take long. Soon they were in a chamber scattered with clothed limbs that had been wrapped in preservative matter. She stared at a fist clenching a pair of spectacles. The walls took on a corrugated aspect here; behind the largest of the folds, something mewled.

Bo turned to regard Sarah. His eyes were filled with tears that wouldn't come. He nodded towards the crease. 'Claire is in there,' he said.

Her own tears beat him to it, squirting out of her as if released by a hidden switch that had just been thrown. Bo was saying something to her, something about guardians, but she couldn't properly hear him. It didn't matter. She had decided she could hear the measured pattern of her daughter's breathing. She could smell the apple goodness of her hair, feel the babyfine perfection of her skin.

She stepped forwards and three things happened at once: the fold in the wall quivered apart, allowing a woman she had never seen before to emerge; Bo's hand gripped her arm; and something jealously guarded by the darkness moved into the chamber behind them.

Before she could say anything, Bo said, 'I have to go and speak to her. I'll be back in a minute. Wait here.'

The pressure behind his voice told her that this tiny, slim girl with long black hair and Japanese features, a bottle-green sweater clinging to her delicate curves, must be precious to him. She was studying Sarah intently, but without any hostility. Sarah was so taken by Bo's obvious tenderness towards her, the way he approached and reached out his hand to touch the girl's face; so filled with the urge to run to her daughter, that she forgot all about the shadow behind them until Bo had led the woman to one side and Sarah was alone, the soft sounds of the cathedral's constant fluxing and realignment whispering to her like the incremental growth of trees in a wood.

How could Bo expect her to wait? He didn't have children of his own. He didn't understand. She strode quickly to the crease and, grinding down against her revulsion, peeled it open. She was greeted by gummy walls that pulsed and moaned. Strange blues and purples streaked with violet. Membranous colours. Placenta colours. The heat was moister here, it hung in the air like steam. She didn't like the way occasional tendrils framed her to the point that she seemed to be bleeding into the damp air, as if she were losing herself to something equally insubstantial. She felt the centre of herself crumble and imagined herself silently imploding, sucked into the vacuum where her heart used to beat. Detail began to ooze out of the fug. She saw a figure coiled on a bench. Sweat gathered. She rubbed the itching cuts on her arms, irritated by the heat and humidity.

She sat down at the end of the bench and waited. She didn't feel able to reach out and touch the figure because she didn't know if it was Claire and if it was dead.

She closed her eyes and the shadow that had been creeping behind them turned to blood that ran and ran, filling the entire subterranean complex. She didn't care who it was. The more the merrier, she decided. Things would end, one way or another, here. She opened her eyes and the figure on the bench, lying naked with her back to the room, turned slowly towards her. Her eyes were black discs, her mouth a collapsing black bar.

The mist intensified. Sarah saw, before the whiteness eclipsed it, a grubby vest, smeared with blood. A hole in the armpit.

'Claire?' Sarah said.

The figure on the bench turned her head. 'Mum?'

Sarah gasped and hot air flooded her chest. Her daughter was inching her way around, albeit haltingly, perhaps because the wound was so debilitating. Sarah rose and reached out to help her when she realised that it wasn't the wound causing her to hesitate, but the thing that was clamped to her breast, champing and drooling at her nipple like a blind hairless mole. Claire wore the drowsy expression of someone mollified by drugs, although Sarah was convinced it was down to the suckling effect of the creature pawing at her chest. She felt conflicting emotions rock through her. She had never been able to get her daughter to drink the milk she had made. Sarah had suffered badly with mastitis after the birth, and her cracked bleeding nipples had not been the best enticement to Claire to latch on. Her jealousy at seeing her daughter effortlessly nourish this beast on her belly was tempered by a pride that made her heart swell, at the same time as sickening her, filleting her of all sensations, opening her up to the realisation that her daughter was no child, that all innocence was lost.

Memories of Claire's hand reaching out to touch her face, the wonder of her daughter's eyes upon hers. The toy, a cheap plastic fish, that she would not let go of on pain of tears. The first instance of joined-up laughter, the giddy lack of control of it, at something as everyday as water poured from a tap. She felt a pang for all of that. She felt knifed that it was gone for ever.

She did not possess the strength to drag that thing from Claire's nipple and rip the life from it – with her teeth if need be. She wished she had the steel to give herself up for the betterment of everyone else, but she was too weak, too selfish. Not while Claire was breathing.

She backed away, stepped out beyond the fold in the wall. Cooler air swept into the thin gaps between her clothes and her skin. She would fetch Bo. He would know what to do. He could read the situation better than she could.

A sudden smell of pear drops.

The thin man who filled the doorframe was larger, somehow, than the dwindling creature she had seen picking his way around Southwold. He smiled. The bite mark in her thigh jumped with recognition.

'Stay away from her,' she managed, glancing around her for a weapon. There was nothing. But it didn't matter; she doubted anything she could lay her hands on would be substantial enough to harm this man who seemed so driven.

His pupils had swelled to a point where it seemed they must take over his entire eye. She saw his nostrils flaring. The dented, bruised knot on his jaw where she had struck him with the cash register glistened as wounds reopened under the clenching of his teeth. He wasn't even acknowledging Sarah's presence any more. He began to take off his clothes, moving into the room as he did so, dominating it with his bulk, causing Sarah to back away until the writhing faces in the wall were pressed up hard against her.

'Leave her alone!' she yelled, and lashed out with her fist, catching him above the left eye. He blinked the blow away, scowling slightly as if he couldn't understand what had assaulted him.

She was about to go for his face again with her nails, perhaps try to pull him down by the hair, when her daughter's voice called to her. It was lower than she remembered it, thick with what she suspected was desire, but she hoped was the deadening effect of the steam and her fatigue.

'It's all right, mother,' she said. 'Let him come to me.'

She froze at that order, utterly bereft, unable to coax any kind of decisive movement from her limbs. She felt her flesh puckering at the way Salavaria sauntered towards her daughter, his prick thickening with each step. But there was nothing she could do. She could not bring him down. She could not go against what her daughter demanded, even though she did not seem enough herself to be making such decisions. Sarah dropped to her knees. She had not eaten for such a long time; she felt faint, imperceptible, so pale as to not be there. She could almost believe that the thin man had been unable to see her. She was water. She was air.

She moved back outside the fold in the hope that Bo was there. She listened for his voice but could not hear anything. She called out: 'Bo?'

Bo had been unable to speak at first. He was slaughtered by her simple beauty; glad that she was here, but unable to figure out why. The map had shown him so much, but not those who were betrayers of his trust. He loved her so much that the word did not do his feelings justice. She had moved slowly towards him and folded herself, in that way she had, on to a hard wooden bench with such grace that it looked as though it must be the most comfortable seat in the world. She pressed her hands together, her lovely almond-shaped nails catching his eye before she buried them between her thighs and dropped her head. She always adopted this pose, a religious posture almost, when she was expecting an apology from him. But not this time.

'Keiko,' he said, the name suddenly alien to his tongue. He could say no more.

Keiko was wearing her favourite jeans, snug-fitting and riding low on her hips. When she wore them, he said, she could be as mean as she liked to him and he wouldn't mind. He would let her grate him like cheddar cheese as long as she was wearing those jeans. The smooth slope of her throat beneath her jumper was maddening. Her skin was like a narcotic coating, a habit that he could not kick. He wanted to reach out and stroke her throat now. To kiss her, inhale the maddening scents that her flesh breathed out.

'I'm sorry,' she said. 'I sold you.'

Bo stared at her. He shook his head, but minutely, as if he would not yet allow himself to completely deny her. He did it again. He tried to absorb what she was saying, but he could tell from her posture and the misery pulling her face down that this was going to be anything but a reconciliation.

'You sold me,' he said.

She nodded. Now she tilted her head and gazed up at him through her fringe. The freckles across her nose. The chocolate of her irises. She was the same woman he had taken to see *Eyes Wide Shut*, who had gripped his hand in the cinema when Dr Bill Harford is ordered to take off his mask. She was the same woman who had knelt on his back, as light as wax, to knead his shoulders with massage oil. She liked to make love while Harold Budd played on her stereo. She got hungry after sex and wanted cocoa and bacon sandwiches, no matter the hour. He knew her to the point of knowing her out of existence.

'I arranged for Rohan Vero to be at the Princess Louise when you were there. He was weak. He was not the man to take us into this new age. We needed someone young and powerful and . . . creative. Someone with a vision, an eye for how the world is framed, is viewed.'

'So give Rankin a call,' Bo said. 'Fuck's sake, Keiko. I love you. And you shove my head in all this shit? You bring me to the point of death?'

'We needed someone with passion. Someone who was hungry, who needed to fulfil his potential.'

'You needed a failure, you mean. And I fit the bill. Couldn't hack it as a photographer so –'

'I love your photographs,' she protested. 'But I made the right choice. You were all over Vero when he dangled that carrot. You wanted a challenge. This was tailor-made for you. It was what you were born to.'

'Turning me into a monster? Making me hungry for . . . for . . . making me dig up *graves*? I was born to that?'

She did not flinch from his sudden rage. She took it all until his attack became more personal. He accused her of self-absorption, insensitivity, lacking patience.

'Patience?' she snapped back. 'Patience? You don't know the meaning of the word. What is it to sit in a waiting room to see a doctor about an ache? A splash in the pond of time that doesn't even make a ripple. We know what it is to wait. To wait for food. I know some who waited for the taste of blood across a span from the Great Fire to Waterloo.'

The fight was gone from him. He said, 'Tell me you're not with them.'

'I am with them,' she said.

He moved to her and reached down to her throat. There was a tiny constellation of freckles there that he had often observed with an astronomer's doggedness. He loved the contrast of it against her skin. Now he saw them for what they were; a part of the illusion, a way to keep him sweet. He picked one of them off with his fingernails and flicked it away.

'How often did you have to reapply those?' he asked. 'You'd have made a great continuity artist.'

She was rising to leave. He didn't know if he was strong enough to stop her, or whether he should even try. The genie was out of the bottle. Killing Keiko wasn't going to make things better. It would only add another layer to his misery.

'This is your life, then. Protecting this cradle of filth. Keeping watch. What a lonely job. What an existence.'

She was not rising to his bait. He thought she might say what she usually said when he was digging his fingers into the parts of her that might hurt. *You don't understand.* And that was right. He didn't. He didn't want to.

There was a scream, a man's scream. Bo wondered if it was a warning, but agony had fuelled this. He knew about screams now. He was an authority. He followed Keiko back to the fold and Sarah was standing there, her face grey with shock.

'What is it?' he snapped.

'Claire,' she said. 'My baby.'

He pushed past her and into the frills of the wall. Sarah was behind him, but he stopped her from looking in at what was happening. After a few seconds, he had to stop too. Blood crept towards him along the tiles like a slow tide. He stepped back and closed the door before it could reach him. Sarah was becoming hysterical, screaming at him to stop the thin man, whatever he was doing. Screaming at him to save her daughter.

Bo said, 'It isn't your daughter who needs help.' He thought of Claire, how willowy she was, how tiny her hands, and what those hands had done in order to get at Gyorsi Salavaria's innards.

35. CROSSFIRE

The horribly burned man came in fast, faster than his condition should have allowed, but Sarah could see his eyes were drug-glassy and wild, and the saliva was creaming from his lips. The skin of his face was charred, and deep red cracks were seated within it; the blistered fat beneath pushed against the faultlines like the melted cheese of a pizza. He was fighting his obvious pain with long, cathartic shrieks. His hands were treacle-black, misshapen; he held guns in both and was shooting randomly. Another man, in a stained butcher's apron slathered with blood, capered in his wake, the scalpels that jutted from his fists glittering in the gunfire.

A hole punched through the Japanese girl's cheek. She turned her head as if startled by something. Blood slipped from her mouth in a perfect vertical. There was too much noise for Sarah to hear Bo's scream, but the tendons in his neck told her he was giving it all he was worth. She watched him break her fall. She watched him trying to plug her bleeding wounds with his fingers.

Claire was sitting on the floor watching the action unfold. Sarah stumbled towards her and gathered her in her arms, trying to shield her. The thing her daughter clasped to her chest kept appearing in little slashes and teasers of colour, its tiny eyes and teeth flashing with acid-white movements. Its wraithlike cheeks and chin were oily with blood. Sarah heard, she felt, something scratching within the layers of Claire's clothing. Madness, no doubt, pawing at her mind, looking for a way in. A bullet caught Claire in the shin, shredding the flesh back to the bone. She turned her attention to it and began howling, bucking on the floor as if she had been holed in the throat. 'Claire,' Sarah whispered, trying to establish whether any major blood vessels had been hit. 'It's okay. It's all right.'

The shooting had stopped. The burned man strode up to Bo, who stood up and attacked, utterly silent, intent. There was a long, grunting struggle. Sarah felt faint when she saw Bo's fingers in the cracks of the man's burned face, trying to prise it off like an implacable lid. The burned man was keening, trying to get his arms free. She saw the danger before Bo did. She was sucking in breath to warn him when the burned man whipped one of the gun butts across Bo's temple. Bo staggered to the side, his hand to the wound, blood welling between his fingers. The burned man waded in and, studiedly, repeated the assault, this time to the back of Bo's head. A wet impact; Bo collapsed. The burned man turned to his companion, who was smoking a cigarette, the end of which was patterned with bloody prints from his fingers. A comma of blood could be mistaken for a kiss-curl on his forehead. 'Get the fucking girl,' he rasped.

'Manser,' Sarah said. 'Oh my God.'

'I know, I know,' Manser said. 'Crazy, isn't it? A brand new look. Everyone wants it.'

He held his gun out straight, although she could see it wobbling as he drew a bead on her. He was scared. Or in pain from his wounds. Maybe both. You didn't come back from a burn like that, she decided, especially if he hadn't had it treated. He was dying. You could see it in the rot eating him inside out. You could see it in his grey lips and grey tongue. In the deep shadow scoring the flesh that hadn't been ravaged by flames.

'Where's Salavaria?' he asked, and then: 'Aw, shit.' He could see, protruding from the scalloped wall, what remained of his erstwhile partner, his old friend, his nemesis. Manser seemed to diminish, as if he had been defeated. Salavaria was little more than a head with its spine still attached; he was like an oversized snake that has forgotten how to propel itself. Manser shot him twice in the face. The thing on

Claire's breast whiffled as it was shocked awake, and burrowed deep into her blouse. Sarah shuddered, held her daughter close. That scratching again. More intense. And not just from Claire's clothing. Something beyond. Something trembling through the floor.

'I want you to just stand back,' he said. 'I'm taking the girl.'

'Fuck you,' Sarah said. Manser swivelled the gun in her direction again. He pulled the trigger. The dry click was somehow louder than the detonations that had preceded it. He tried the other gun. Again, the hammer fell on an empty chamber.

'Jesus wept,' said Manser. 'It's an AK-47 for me this Christmas.'

Sarah leaped at Losh as he bent to separate her from her child but a stiff arm across her chest knocked her back against the wall, winding her. Losh dragged Claire upright by the hair. He magicked one of his blades against the shadow beneath her jawline as Sarah made to retaliate, then replaced it with a blood-stained cloth which he positioned over her mouth and nose; Claire turned limp in his arms.

Manser was nodding his head. 'Tops, Loshy. You can have jelly for afters tonight. Give her here.' To Sarah he said: 'Give her up.'

As he turned to leave, the chamber began to flood. At first Sarah thought the walls were collapsing and that the scraps raining upon Losh and Manser were the tortured faces shearing clear of their housings. But then she saw the likeness between them and the thing that Claire had been giving suck to. She felt leathery skins scrape against her as they cascaded into the chamber. They left her alone, and she knew it was because they could smell Claire on her, in her. How many had she set free? Losh was brought down not by the enormous weight of them as they lighted in his hair and dragged themselves up to his shoulders, but by a dozen of them targeting the weak spot where his foot joined his leg, slashing into him with teeth and claws, stripping him to the bone in seconds. Sarah heard the *thwock-thwock* of his stump as he doddered on, his shod foot left behind. The chamber had constricted; he was trapped between the walls. He might have been screaming but then so were they. Blood was up: Losh's and theirs. A frenzy of movement and distress. She felt something hot and salty spray across her cheek; the mist in the chamber had turned red. Losh had stopped screaming.

On the floor lay the Queen, badly injured by one of Manser's random bullets: the reason for Claire's histrionics, not fear for her own mother, nor her own flesh wound. She swallowed the jealousy and called her daughter's name until all feeling left her throat. But all she could see was the back of Manser batting away the shadows, his determination alone, it seemed, hastening him from the slaughter-house. The Queen began to screech, a sound of many nails on a chalkboard. *Kill it*, thought Sarah. *Put it out of its misery. And ours.* But the sound was too regular to be one of pain. It was a warning siren. It was a call to arms.

Slumped on the floor, Sarah tried to blink a trickle of blood from her eyes. Through the fluid, she thought she could see the mouths in the walls moving in concert, assuming the shape of her pain. But her grief was too large, too intense, even for this ancient sprawling site of immense suffering. Nothing could contain it. What did the word 'daughter' mean, after this? What bond existed between a tired woman who had given everything and a young girl with black, hungry eyes who was able to pull a man apart as if he were no more a challenge than a Sunday roast? She could not think of her as Claire any more. You give the child the name you hope they'll grow into. Sarah hadn't the words to describe what it was that her daughter had become. When do you give up? When do you let go of your children?

She slithered across to Bo and pulled him from the girl. His birdlike weight, his angles and edges, his cold, were all wrong, but she hugged him fiercely, protectively. He was all she had.

But no, that wasn't the case after all.

36. AKA

Manser parked at midnight on South Wharf Road, by the junction with Praed Street. This was the last of about a dozen cars he had used to get back, having to swap every half mile or so when the build-up of abandoned vehicles became impenetrable. He was exhausted. He didn't have much time left. The agonies that had flared across his face, chest and arms over the past hours were gone, substituted by a creeping numbness. He could not understand how he had managed to drag the girl up that interminable stairway and down the treacherous scaffolding. More than once he'd thought, fuck it, let her fall. Let it all fall. But he had come this far. He didn't know how he was going to do this. But in death, he was going to have one last stab at life. Salavaria had been taken from him, but by God, the Hickman bitch would not get away.

Instead of going directly to the dilapidated pub on the corner he forced his aching legs to take him to the canal where he listened to the song of the Marylebone Flyover, hoping for calm, strength. The sounds emanating from that elevated sweep of road were anything but soothing. The mechanical chunter of caterpillar tracks and diesel, military vehicles that reminded him only of the way those fucking mouths had split open, jaws unhinging like snakes ready to swallow him whole. The hiss of tyres on rain-soaked tarmac put him in mind of nothing but the wet air that had sped from Losh's chest when they burrowed into him. Farther afield, concussions and stitches of gunfire. London was fighting a war that was already lost.

By the time he returned, he saw in the pub a low-wattage bulb turning the glass of an upstairs window milky. He went to the door and tapped on it with a coin in a pre-arranged code. Then he went back to the car and opened the boot. He wrestled with Claire and managed to clamp a hand over her mouth, which she bit, hard. Swearing, he dragged a handkerchief from his pocket and stuffed it in her mouth, punching her twice to get her still. It was a good thing he could no longer feel anything in these limbs. She had teeth like razors. Flaps of skin hung off his roasted palm; he was bleeding badly. Queasy at the sight of the wound, he staggered with Claire to the door, which was now open. He went through it and kicked it shut. Upstairs, Harrison, the landlord, was sitting in a chair containing more holes than stuffing.

'This was a good boozer before it was closed down,' Manser said, his excitement unfolding deep within him.

'Was,' Harrison said, keeping his eyes on him. His eyes couldn't have been wider, more terror-filled, had he stapled them open. 'Everything changes.'

'You don't,' Manser said. 'Christ. Don't you ever wash?'

'What's the point? The smell confuses them. They don't come near me. They don't even know I'm here.'

'Nobody comes near you, save me. And only because I have to.'

Harrison smiled. 'Didn't anybody ever warn you not to piss off the people you need help from?'

Manser swallowed his distaste of the smaller man. 'Can't we get on?' he spat.

Harrison stood up and stretched. 'Where's your partner in grime?' he said, luxuriously.

Manser pulled a wad from his jacket. 'There's six hundred there. Privacy please.'

'Let's call it eight hundred.'

A pause. Manser said, 'I don't have it with me. I can get it tomorrow.'

Harrison said, 'Looks of you there'll be no tomorrow.' But he got up to leave anyway.

As he opened the door, Manser said, 'Nip outside for some fresh air. See if you can't get yourself eaten.'

Harrison flipped him the Vs, said, 'Nice tan,' and left.

The first incision. Blood squirted up the front of his shirt, much brighter than the stains already painted upon it. A coppery smell filled the room. The pockets of the pool table upon which Claire was spread were filled with beer towels. Losh was there in his mind, talking him through it, keeping him focused.

'Soft tissue?' Losh said now.

Manser's voice was dry. He needed a drink. His cock was as hard as a house brick. 'As much off as possible, I'd say.'

'She won't last long,' Losh said.

Manser licked his lips. 'She'll last long enough. Longer than me.'

Manser reached for a Samsonite suitcase. He opened it and pulled out a hacksaw. Its teeth entertained the light and flung it in every direction. At least Losh kept his tools clean.

An hour later: 'Is she okay?' Manser asked. He heard Losh's laughter in reply; an infectious sound. Soon he was laughing too, despite the pain it ratcheted around his face. As he unbuckled his trousers, a movement brought his head snapping up.

Manser said, 'Who opened the window?'

But Losh had deserted him.

Nobody had opened the window; the movement of the lace curtains was being caused by the glass as it bulged into the room. Manser tore them back at the moment the glass shattered in his face. He screamed and fell backwards, tripping on the bucket of offcuts and sprawling to the floor.

His face was burning again. He was blinking furiously, but he couldn't see anything out of his left eye, only feel the sound of glass splinters grinding in there. What he could see through his right made him wish for total blindness. It seemed that strips of the night were pouring in through the broken window. They fastened themselves to Manser's face and neck and munched through the flesh like cater- pillars at a leaf. His screams were low and already being disguised by blood as his throat filled. He began to choke but managed one last hearty shriek as a major blood vessel parted, spraying colour all around the room with the abandon of an unmanned hosepipe.

He saw Sarah stepping towards him, her face screwed up with anger and grief, a cleaver in her hand. She began hacking at his neck but he could hardly feel it. So much blood had drained from him that the edges of what he thought were real were fraying, turning grey, flitting away like burned paper.

'For Andrew,' she was saying, 'for me. For Claire. For Claire. For Claire.' The blows rained down on him. It was almost comforting. He wanted to say something to her. He had always wanted to talk about their names, Hickman and Manser. He wanted to tell her, *where you end, I begin*. He thought it would be amusing, romantic even. But what remained of his sight filled with red and he could understand no more.

37. HARDWIRED

B o drifted along streets he barely recognised. He felt as light as a polythene bag, and sometimes imagined he was moving as swiftly as one snatched up by the wind. In one hand he carried a five-litre plastic container sloshing with petrol. Sometimes he thought he could hear her ghost as she followed him, a heel scuffing against the kerb, the vicious *swit* of her belt as she tied her mackintosh more tightly around her.

A long narrow band of pale yellow and green on the horizon marked the beginning of the new day. By the time he reached the cathedral and climbed the scaffold, that colour had deepened and pushed a hefty wedge into the dark. He piled the bodies into the nave and placed Keiko on top. He poured every drop of petrol on to the cairn of bodies and stepped back, blinking, the fumes blinding him for a second.

He said to her, 'You sent me those emails.'

'Yes,' she said, and her voice was as he remembered it: clean, clipped, alluring. 'I was trying to help you. I didn't want to see you get hurt.'

'You didn't want to see me dead before I'd finished my job, more like,' he said.

'However you want it, Bo,' she said. 'You were always like this, chipping away at supportive things I said, suspicious of everything.'

'Well, it stood me in good stead, didn't it?' He pulled a box of matches from his pocket. Most of them were damp, but he struck them anyway, enjoying the theatre, enjoying the panic he imagined would be in her eyes.

'What's the matter?' he asked. 'The gig's finished. All the punters have jumped in their cars and are on their way home. There's no point in hanging around. This lot have done all the encores they're ever likely to do.'

'We will come again,' she said.

'Not if I have anything to do with it,' he said.

'You won't be able to stop yourself,' she said. 'It's in your blood. It's part of your code. It's who you are.'

Bo stopped striking matches. Outside he could hear the *thrum* of attack helicopters as they swooped low over the city. Under that was the sporadic sound of gunfire, precise, military bursts. A voice rasped like an insect through an amplifier in authoritative tones. He imagined tanks rolling down The Mall, troops in combat gear, picking over the remnants of the city.

'There's timing for you,' he said, but his voice had lost any of its cockiness.

He imagined her smiling at him now, in that way she used when she wanted to get something from him. He remembered how she used that smile when she emerged from a steamy bathroom, her robe barely on, to ask him for a massage.

Of course, he'd said. *You can brain me with a rake and drown me in porridge as long as you smile like that while you're doing it.*

He looked down at his ruined hand, at the way the fingers were slowly lengthening through the riot of muscle and ligament that was trying to make a fist of itself. That was the reminder, if he needed one, of what he was, who he had become. Surely they could not rally after this. The Queen was dead. Claire was dead, or as good as. There were no more hosts. Surely?

'We can be together again,' she said, reaching out a hand.

'I loved you,' he said. 'I wanted to marry you.'

'We can talk about it,' she whispered. 'Come with me.'

The next match he struck flared wildly. 'Praise the Lord and pass the ammunition,' he said.

He stared at the flame and curled his injured hand around it to protect it from a sudden breath that rose in the lungs of the foetid edifice. He sensed the cathedral shifting around him, the faces loosening, turning his way, moaning in what might have been approval or objection. He closed his eyes and saw the map. It was reassembling itself, reformatting itself. *Not on my fucking watch.*

He tossed the match on to the pyre and reflexively stepped back as the petrol ignited and a sheet of flame rose into the heights. She might have been reaching for him. Her thin, delicate fingers.

'We'll be together,' he said. 'For ever.'

He caught hold of Keiko's hand and allowed her to drag him screaming into the blaze.

EPILOGUE

S he had been back home for a day. She couldn't understand how she had got here. She remembered the maelstrom of leathery limbs and needle teeth, remembered being born from the warmth of her companions and standing up to find Manser little more than a pink froth filling his suit.

She saw the bloody, tiny mound of towels on the pool table. She saw the bucket; the dishcloth had shifted, revealing enough to tell her the game. Two toes was enough. She didn't need to be drawn a picture.

And then somehow she found herself outside. And then on Edgware Road where a pretty young woman with dark hair and a woven shoulder bag gave her a couple of pounds so that she could get the tube to Euston. And then a man smelling of milk and boot polish she fucked in a shop doorway for her fare north. And then Preston, freezing around her in the early morning as if it were formed from winter itself. She had half expected Andrew to poke his head around the corner of their living room to say hello, the tea's on, go and sit by the fire and I'll bring some to you.

But the living room was cold and bare. She found sleep at the time she needed it most, just as her thoughts were about to coalesce

'Incendiary stuff . . . A writer of rare – if warped – imagination.'
John O'Connell, *Time Out*

'Conrad Williams does desperate depraved characters like they've just been invented, in authentic London locations that ooze evil and despair. His prose is muscular and beautiful, his narrative drive locked in fifth gear. Weird fiction just got weirder. Squeamish? Forget it.'
Nicholas Royle

'Conrad Williams is one of the unsung heroes of fantastic fiction. Williams has the unnerving ability of depicting the most appalling human atrocities in achingly lyrical prose, which has the effect of making them more disturbing still.'
Mark Morris

'Williams may be in the process of developing a new genre.'
M John Harrison

'I loved it. His portraits of everyday loneliness are brilliant. Altogether I thought it one of the finest and most haunting modern spectral novels I've read.'
Ramsey Campbell on *Head Injuries*

'. . . beautiful prose in this brooding and mysterious tale . . . A first class novel.'
Peter Crowther, *Interzone* on *Head Injuries*

'Lean, compelling prose marks this out as a thriller of real distinction.'
Crime Time on *Head Injuries*

'Conrad Williams' debut novel casts an irresistible spell.'
Andrew Hedgecock, *Time Out Net Books* on *Head Injuries*

'An impressive tour de force that ranges from grimy magic realism to outright horror.'
David Langford, *SFX* on *London Revenant*

'Williams creates existentialist horror with hallucinatory imagery and prose that is as muscular as it is tender, and laced at times with quite extraordinary beauty.'
Nicholas Royle, *City Life* (Book of the Week) on *London Revenant*

'The book moves from moments of lyricism to moments of utter disgust with little clashing of gears.'
Roz Kaveney, *Time Out* on *London Revenant*

'*Use Once, Then Destroy* is one of the most solid collections of disturbing but engaging work you're likely to find on the shelves today.'
Tom Piccirilli

'Williams is without doubt one of the finest fantasists writing today.'
Tim Lebbon